THE ROAD
TO
Redemption

A FINDING GRACE Novel

Book 1

D.M. DAVIS

The Road to Redemption
Finding Grace series by D.M. Davis

ISBN13: 978-0-9997176-7-7
ISBN10:
Published by D.M. Davis

www.dmckdavis.com
Cover Design by D.M. Davis
Cover Photo by Shutterstock
Metallic Logo by Carrie Loves Design
Editing by Tamara Mataya
Proofreading by Mountains Wanted Publishing & Indie
Author Services

This is a work of fiction. Names, places, characters and
incidents are the product of the author's imagination and are
fictitious. Any resemblance to actual persons, living or dead, events
or establishments is solely coincidental.

This story contains mature themes, strong language, and
sexual situations. It is intended for adult readers. Some scenes may
contain triggers.

Playlist

1. *Rescue* by Lauren Daigle
2. *Thinking out Loud* by Ed Sheeran
3. *Stay with Me* by Sam Smith
4. *Kiss Me* by Ed Sheeran
5. *Beam Me Up* by Pink
6. *Home* by Philip Philips
7. *Make You Feel My Love* by Adele
8. *Your Body Is A Wonderland* by John Mayer
9. *Hallelujah* by The Canadian Tenors
10. *Stay* by Rihanna
11. *Wake Me Up* by Ed Sheeran
12. *You Say* by Lauren Daigle

Additional Novels

BY D.M. DAVIS

UNTIL YOU SERIES
Book 1 - Until You Set Me Free
Book 2 - Until You Are Mine
Book 3 - Until You Say I Do

FINDING GRACE SERIES
Book 1 - The Road to Redemption
Book 2 - The Price of Atonement
Book 3 - A New Beginning
Book 4 - Finding Where I Belong

STANDALONES
Warm Me Softly

Dedication

This book is for me and all the women who feel they aren't quite good enough. Not pretty enough. Not skinny enough. Not smart enough. Not worthy—enough.

This is not my story, but it is my struggle—my search to find grace within myself. To come to love the woman I am, not who I wish I was, who I would be if I ate less and moved more, if I was bolder, prettier, sexier, funnier, taller.

It's about learning to bloom where you are planted, finding the joy from within, but most of all know that I—and you—are worthy of all life has to offer. We just have to believe, have faith, and open our hands—palms up—ready to receive.

This is Lauren's story of finding the grace to love herself.

THIS IS WHERE IT BEGINS.

Note to The Reader

Don't let the FINDING GRACE series name fool you. This is not a religious book. Though there are religious undertones, above all else, this is a steamy romance with hints of paranormal. The paranormal aspect grows as the series progresses, but at its heart this is a love story with all the wonderful gooey details of what happens between a man and a woman when they fall in love, and all the magical moments thereafter.

Bad things happen every day, in *large* and *Small* ways.

Small things shouldn't change who you are or the course of your life.

But sometimes, those small ripples can change you greatly—the person you are or desire to be—or change your direction in life. That small ripple then becomes a large ripple because of the impact you allow it to have on you—to have on your life.

At other times, *large* things can happen that should completely change

you—the course of your life—and yet, they don't. Instead of changing you, that large ripple makes you more of who you already are. Instead of changing the course of your life, it makes your course truer, allowing you to fiercely follow your intended path.

Bad things happen every day, in *large* and *Small* ways.

It is how you *Respond* to these ripples *That Truly Matters*.

DM DAVIS

TABLE OF CONTENTS

Playlist iii

Additional Novels BY D.M. DAVIS iv

Dedication v

Note to The Reader vi

Ripples vii

Prologue JULY 4

PART ONE: **The Beginning** JANUARY **11**

  Chapter 1 12

  Chapter 2 27

  Chapter 3 35

  Chapter 4 FEBRUARY 51

  Chapter 5 61

  Chapter 6 71

PART TWO: **After Effects** **86**

  Chapter 7 87

  Chapter 8 97

  Chapter 9 108

  Chapter 10 118

  Chapter 11 133

  Chapter 12 141

PART THREE: **Letting Go** **149**

  Chapter 13 150

  Chapter 14 163

Chapter 15...172

Chapter 16...181

Chapter 17...187

PART FOUR: The Road to Redemption **198**

Chapter 18...199

Chapter 19...217

Chapter 20...226

Chapter 21...238

Chapter 22...250

Chapter 23...263

Chapter 24...279

Chapter 25...289

PART FIVE: Hibernation **297**

Chapter 26...298

Chapter 27...313

Chapter 28...320

Chapter 29...335

PART SIX: The Light Returns **346**

Chapter 30...347

Chapter 31...358

Chapter 32...370

Chapter 33...385

Chapter 34...397

Did You Enjoy This Novel?......................................**416**

About the Author **417**

Acknowledgments 418

Additional Novels BY D.M. DAVIS 420

Stalk Me! 421

Prologue

JULY

I CAN BARELY SEE PIERCE ON center stage from our shitty seats at the bar, but well enough to know he's staring daggers of lust at my best friend Holly. He's playing his guitar like a rock god, reeling in the audience—

the women—with every strum of his six string, yet after every verse his eyes return to her.

He's got it bad.

She's oblivious.

We've been friends for years, all of us, since freshman year at Texas Tech when Holly and Pierce first began doing their *I want you, but I'm not ready to have you* dance, never moving beyond the friend zone.

He flirts.

She thinks he flirts with everyone.

He doesn't. He only looks at her with eyes that burn straight to her soul.

If she'd only see it. Believe it.

Feeling the beat, I want to get lost in the lyrics I know by heart and dance with abandon to the music that does something to me. Something deep, sensual, and relaxing. If only I had my own soul-searing rock god to dance with.

I grab Holly. "Come on."

Reluctantly, she lets me pull her to the dance floor. It doesn't take long for her to relax and enjoy herself.

She's liked Pierce for…well, I can't even remember a time she didn't like him.

Holly's a good girl. I mean, a *really* good girl.

Pierce is a good guy hiding behind a bad boy rocker persona.

Maybe tonight one of them will get up the nerve to take it to the next level.

I'm gonna try my darndest to help her out. Not that I'm an expert on men. Far from it, but it's different when it's not me. I've had a man. He may not have been a rock star, and he may not have rocked my world. I'm not sure *rocking my world* is even a real thing. I'm starting to believe it's only a fairytale.

A dream.

A fantasy.

A fantasy I'm all too good at dreaming up. A fantasy of a man who wants me like no other, who sees me like no one ever has, and loves me as I am. Deeply. Madly. Endlessly.

Yeah, it's a fantasy. That kind of love doesn't exist. At least not for me.

"I need a drink." After working up a sweat to four songs, Holly motions to the bar, looking back to be sure I'm following.

She may not be good with guys, but she's a great friend. Protective. She's only five months older than me, but you'd think she was my older sister, that she spent her whole life looking out for me instead of only the past eight years. We're nearly inseparable. If she were a guy, I'd totally marry her. She's my standing *plus one*.

"A Silk Panty Martini and a Diet Coke," she hollers to the bartender.

With a nod and a wink, he gets to work.

We dab the perspiration from our faces with cocktail napkins and sip our drinks.

"No wonder we're such good friends; you're as bad as I am with men." It's not breaking news, but it bears repeating. I give her a light shove on her shoulder. "Go talk to him.

They're going on break. If you don't talk to him, what was the point of coming? To be groupies?" Actually, groupies would be hanging out with them, which we aren't even doing. We're less than groupies at the moment. A *groupie* would be an upgrade.

"Lauren," she pouts.

"Nuh-uh. Don't *Lauren* me. Go say *hi*."

With a little liquid courage, she makes her way over to Pierce, who's hanging out with the band in a circular booth, ignoring the groupies trying to get their piece of him. I keep tabs on her from our spot at the bar. My heart soars when his face lights up at the sight of her walking toward him. He stands up and motions for her to slide in next to him.

"Go get him, Holly. He's all yours," I whisper to myself.

A nudge from behind has me turning to a familiar face with a broad smile and gray eyes.

"Hey, Kyle."

"Hey, Lauren. You having a good time?"

"Yeah. You?"

"Yeah, I'm diggin' the music. Pierce and the guys have come a long way from their garage band days." Kyle and Pierce grew up together, neighbors, and are still friends after all this time.

I nod, remembering the first time I heard them play in college, in Pierce's parents' garage. They were rough, barely even a band, but you could tell they had something. Pierce had something. You could see it in his eyes. You could hear it in his songs. You could feel it in the way he spoke about music. Now, here they are making a living at the thing they love. Very cool.

Kyle motions across the room. "You know those guys?"

"Who?" I try to follow his eyes.

"Those two assholes holding up the wall, looking like they don't belong."

I spot the guys he's talking about. One blond guy and the other dark-haired. "No. Never seen 'em before."

"Huh. They've sure been watching you and Holly. Keep an eye out, and I'll do the same."

His concern is appreciated, yet a little alarming. "I will." I glance again at where they were a moment ago, but they're gone. I scan the room. "I don't see them."

Kyle looks around. "I guess they left. Good."

I visit with him and his girlfriend, dance with them, by myself, and with Holly when the band is playing again. She's beaming. So happy.

We call it a night around eleven. We both have work in the morning, and unlike Pierce, we can't sleep till noon.

She's giddy on the walk back to the parking garage only a few blocks from the club. They made plans to get together. "He's gonna call. He swears."

"He will. He's into you. Don't doubt that."

She shrieks way too close to my ear and grabs my arm. "Do you really think so?"

I laugh. "I know so."

"Thank you for coming. I never would have come, much less talked to him, if you weren't here."

"You're welcome. I'm glad I came. I had fun." I suck at

acting my age—going to bars, dancing, drinking—having a good time with friends. Though this old soul has never felt all that young, it's nice to remember that I am.

She shrieks again, shaking her hands and her head. "Okay, calm down. It's not that big a deal." She talks herself down from her jittery excitement.

"Actually, I think it's a pretty big deal. You've liked him for so long. It's great to see you both taking the next step. You never know, he may be the one."

"Do you think?" She glances at me with tender, hopeful eyes.

"I do."

I cover my ears, preparing for the shriek that never comes as we step off the elevator and onto the garage level where her car is parked.

A shudder runs up my spine, causing the hairs on my neck to stand at attention. The feeling of being watched puts me on high alert. I turn, latching on to Holly's arm, the need to get out of here pulsing in my veins. That's when I see him, the dark-haired guy, coming around the corner.

"Holly, run!" I push her away, flinging myself at him, but I'm jerked back, grabbed from behind.

"No!" Rage screams through me as I claw at the arms banded around my waist, breaking ribs and squeezing the air out of my body.

"Run, Holly! Run!" I gasp.

Screams fill my ears as I watch in slow motion as the dark-haired guy lunges for Holly.

No. No. No!

Let us then approach the throne of grace with confidence, so that we may receive mercy and find grace to help us in our time of need.

Hebrews 4:16 NIV

PART ONE:

The Beginning

JANUARY

Chapter 1

LAUREN GRACE FRASIER

ON MY WAY TO THE OFFICE, I stop to get Silvy a coffee. She's always doing small things like that for me. I owe her more than just a few specialty drinks. Though, I'm not even sure you can call what she drinks coffee—in my uneducated opinion, it more closely resembles dessert. I don't drink the stuff. I'm more of a Diet Coke girl.

The shop is booming with Monday morning patrons in the throes of caffeine withdrawal. There's a lot of grumbling and heads buried in their cell phones. There are no smiling, happy faces, except those working the counter, and with how fast they're talking and moving, I'd say they've already exceeded their caffeine quota for the day.

I'm not in caffeine withdrawal, and I left my phone in the car, so I might be the only customer who's actually happy and looking around people-watching. We've got two lines going. I'm fourth from the front in mine. Glancing over to the other one, my eyes land on a smoldering, handsome man in a suit and overcoat. I say smoldering because he's hot as hell and seems pissed off all at the same time.

He's facing forward, hands clasped—not on his phone. Bonus for him. His short brown hair is tousled with hints of curl that make him look playful, whimsical even. His strong profile etched with chiseled features, sharp nose, furrowed brow, and clean-shaven jaw erase my whimsical musings from a moment ago. Everything about him is hard and cool except for his lips—which are full and sensuous, a stark contrast to the don't-fuck-with-me aura he's giving off.

Sadly, the young woman behind him is trying in vain to get his attention. She bumps into him and apologizes with a hopeful smile, but he simply nods and turns back around. She sways from foot to foot. I imagine she's trying to think of another tactic.

Bravely, she taps him on the shoulder, and when he

turns, his scowling face doesn't soften. I can't hear what she says, but he simply shakes his head. I can feel her dismissal from here. He's not open for business, and she's blind to his "closed" sign.

I feel sorry for the girl, but also find the whole situation amusing. She's trying so hard to be seen, and he is trying so hard to be left the fuck alone.

As he turns around, his eyes catch mine and stop—locking in like a missile heading for its doomed target. My breath hitches. The intensity of his stare sends tingles in places I've ignored for far too long. I hide my reaction behind a smirk that grows into a full-fledged smile and a chuckle. His eyebrow rises, and the corners of his succulent mouth curl into a barely-there smile.

Be still my heart. *Seriously, get a grip.*

I bite my bottom lip and turn away, focusing on the menu above our heads, but really, I'm steadying my treacherous heart that's trying to jump ship and climb aboard his.

Is it hot in here?

Our eyes only connected for seconds, but it was enough to see a flash of warmth in those chocolate, almond-shaped eyes. I thought he was hot in profile, but the full-on frontal is defcon delicious and dangerously panty-dropping-worthy.

Actually, I think my panties might have incinerated.

I make it to the front of the line and place my order. After paying, I move to the middle, waiting for Silvy's coffee.

A flush of heat radiates from my right, and I realize Mr. Dark and Dreamy is standing beside me, close enough for his arm to graze mine.

Oh god, he smells good. Like fresh shower with a hint of spicy cologne and pure male. I want to rub all over him, breathe him in, and lick places I'm sure I shouldn't.

I close my eyes and take a moment to breathe his scent and feel his presence.

"What was the smile about?" His deep timbre close to my ear sends a tremor down my body. *Holy hell. He has a British accent.*

I look up, and I mean up. He has to be six-three, at least. My eyes connect with his, and the warmth from before is still there. "I'm sorry?" I manage, even though my heart is racing again.

"Back there." He motions behind him. "You were watching and smiling. Why?"

"Oh, well..." Honest or lie? "You have quite a don't-fuck-with-me look going on." Honest it is, then.

He seems stunned by my bluntness, but before he can respond, my name is called. I grab my coffee and plan my escape route before forcing myself to face his deadly, heart-wrenching beauty. No one should be this handsome. There's no way this man isn't hit on every day, all day. It has to take tremendous effort to remain so stoic and closed off. "Good luck with that."

Yeah, his indifference is really a siren song to women, and probably men, to meet his challenge and climb his icy Mount Everest.

His hand shoots out to stop me, his head shaking in disbelief that I'm running off.

Yeah, I hear your siren song, but my climbing legs are broken.

He must read something in my eyes, or on my face, or my own neon sign above my head that says "out of order" as he lowers his hand and graces me with what I think is a rare, full-on smile. He nods, his eyes gleaming with warmth and sadness. "Goodbye, Lauren. It was a pleasure."

I arrive at the office on time, wishing I'd picked up a Diet Coke for myself along with Silvy's coffee…errr…dessert. But then I'd be late, and it's already going to be a busy day. There's print work to finalize for our in-flight magazine. I've got one more layout change I need to finish, approve, and then it's off to the printer. Water is my usual drink, at least until the afternoon, but today I need a little more. The run-in with Mr. Dark and Dreamy has left me shaken. But not stirred. Definitely *not* stirred.

"Lauren," Silvy calls as I turn the corner to my office.

Glancing over my shoulder, I motion with my head for her to join me and continue to my desk. I plunk down her coffee and pull out my laptop as she walks through my door.

"Good morning, sunshine." Her perkiness brings a curve to my lips.

Why does she even need coffee?

"Mornin'." I hold out her drink. "For you."

"Oh my god, you didn't?"

"I did."

She replaces the cup in my hand with a larger Styrofoam version. "I did, too."

She brought me a Sonic Diet Coke. "I was wishing I'd gotten one on my way in."

"Great minds think alike." She plops in a chair, beaming, and takes a sip of her morning sugar fix. "Oh my God! This is so good."

Chuckling, I imagine the sugar racing through her body making every cell vibrate with excitement. "I don't know about great minds, but we definitely have each other's backs when it comes to feeding our addictions."

"Yes, great minds," she reiterates with an exaggerated eye roll.

"Thank you." I sigh in relief, some of the stress leaving my body as I take a long draw.

It's only a Diet Coke, Lauren. It's not like she took away all your work and sent you on vacation. Still, it's the small things that matter sometimes.

"Lauren?"

"Yeah." I meet her apprehensive gaze.

"Have you thought any more about that class?" She

places her hands on my desk, leaning forward. "I know you're not crazy about trying it, especially not alone. I was thinking I could take the class with you. You know, for moral support. Plus, it wouldn't hurt to learn a thing or two." She sits back and shrugs. "Who knows, we may meet some cute guys."

Her look of hope is hard to deny, but I'm not ready.

Will I ever be?

"Can I think on it?" I know I said that last time. "A week. Give me a week."

"Sure." She's disappointed.

"I promise, I'll give it serious consideration." I think I've said that before too, darnit.

Avoidance much?

"Okay, no problem."

I catch her before she disappears through my office door. "Thanks again for the drink."

"Yeah. Thanks for the coffee." Her smile doesn't quite reach her eyes.

I hate disappointing her. I'm not sure what a week will do to make me ready to take her up on her offer, but I breathe a sigh of relief knowing I have seven days to think it over before she brings it up again.

As I wait for my laptop to boot up, my thoughts return to the coffee shop and the overwhelming need I felt to go back inside as soon as I stepped foot out the door. It was as if I was losing the ability to breathe the farther I got away from *him*. I stopped on the sidewalk a few feet from the entrance, clutching my chest and *breathing* to be sure I still could. Nearly as fast as the episode hit me, it was gone.

Mr. Dark and Dreamy delivers a powerful punch. It's a good thing I escaped as quickly as I did—relatively unscathed.

THEODORE THOMAS KELLEN WADE

Bloody. Fucking. Hell. What was that?

She completely blindsided me. For a man who speaks for a living, I lost the ability to do so when my eyes locked on her smiling face. Quite a remarkable face at that. I don't think I've seen blue eyes such as hers. It wasn't only the colour. It was the intensity behind them, the need, the desire, the recognition—a feeling of coming home—that was a punch to the gut.

Her comment about me giving off a *don't fuck with me vibe* is spot on. It's a persona I've perfected over the years.

Yet she was completely unaffected by it. She found it humourous, whereas I was flustered by her all-too-seeing eyes.

I managed to pull myself together long enough to spit out two phrases, but I was foolish enough to let her leave without anything more than her first name and a lingering ache in my chest.

Coffee in hand, I rushed to the door hoping to spot her on the street and remedy that misstep. Unfortunately, the vision from a moment ago was nowhere to be seen. Air missing from my lungs, blood pounding in my ears, and a hunger I have never felt before had me struggling to get to my car so I could sit before I fell over.

Never has a woman affected me like this. Never.

The trek to work is mindless as I replay the morning's encounter over and over. I'm a bloody fool for letting her get away. That connection—damn that connection—was a living entity, a live wire. My fingers burn to touch her. My lips tingle to join with hers. And yet, for all the sexual attraction, it's deeper than the physical. It's as if the universe opened up and offered my soulmate on a coffee-laden platter, and now that she's gone, the awakening induced is painful, remorseful, like I left half of me behind.

Which is ridiculous, considering my heart's on lockdown. My ex stole my soul, and even the philosopher in me doesn't believe in soulmates, much less the romantic that died over four years ago.

I bury the fanciful notion, snuff out the light lit by the

blue-eyed vision, and get on with my day of educating privileged, overindulged, hormone-riddled new adults who believe the world revolves around them, and that I'm merely here to serve them knowledge in meaningful thought-inducing chunks, earning them a place on the Dean's List and love from their parents.

My morning coffee exchange has me off-kilter. It's exam day, and I'm restless. I have assignments to grade, but I need to maintain the appearance of watching their studious faces as they work their way through the test, ensuring no one cheats. Thankfully, this class meets in the lecture hall where there are more seats than students, allowing room to spread out.

Only twenty minutes remain, then I'm done for the day. I'm usually more attentive, but exam days bore me, and *LaurenGate* isn't helping. I prefer interacting with my students, keeping them engaged. Lately, though, the distraction carries over to non-exam days too.

I need to work on that.

"Professor Wade?" Speaking of privileged, overindulged, hormone-riddled new adults, the shrill voice rings in my ears like a storm siren.

I look up, not because I want to see her face or acknowledge her presence, but if she knew I recognize her voice, she would take extreme pleasure in that knowledge and believe it means something it does not.

"Ms. James?" I arch a meaningful brow and deaden my eyes. She'll find no life or hope in my gaze.

She tongues her pen, sucking on the tip coyly as her

fingers run up and down her cleavage.

My cock shrivels, urging my eyes to look away. My stomach revolts and wants to show the class what I had for breakfast. I clench my jaw, not willing to give up my LaurenGate coffee—the only good thing this day holds thus far.

"For question six…"

I swear she said *sex*, not *six*.

My favourite student's head whips up so fast I fear she may have whiplash and glares at Susan James, confirming what I heard was accurate. Sam, Samantha Cavanaugh, is an exception to my harsh opinion of most of my students. She's hardworking, highly intelligent, and doesn't attempt to use her feminine wiles to leverage higher grades. She is also deeply in love with one of this town's hottest bachelors, Joseph McIntyre. Ms. Cavanaugh's interest in me is professional—educational—and for that she has my esteem and full support in a purely platonic, appropriate manner.

"—are you wanting our essay to be expository or persuasive?" Ms. James drones on.

"Read the instructions," Ms. Cavanaugh responds with a level of annoyance she can get away with.

A few other students murmur similar responses, no less irritated. I want to high-five them all.

I motion to the class as Susan James glares at Sam before returning her hungry gaze to me—lucky me. "Listen to your peers, Ms. James. All the information you need is provided on the papers in front of you." *If you gave your schoolwork the same attention you give me, you'd be passing with flying colours.*

I give Sam Cavanaugh a thankful nod and assess the class as they settle back into their test, dismissing the unnecessary interruption.

Students like Ms. James make me doubt my chosen profession.

I'm keen on investments and writing. Perhaps I should seriously consider a change of vocation. I long to shed the curmudgeonly charade before it's no longer an act.

"This is your ten-minute warning."

Come on clock, can't you tick any faster?

I check my phone hoping for a distraction. I'm happy to see a text from Reese.

Reese: *Wanna meet for a beer?*

Me: *Yes. What time? Where?*

Reese: *5. Usual place.*

Me: *Aces.*

Perfect. I could use a pint or two, and it gives me time to run my errand before meeting him.

"Five minutes. As you finish, place your exam on the corner of my desk, then you're dismissed." That is my final warning. I'm sure many won't finish. I'm an arsehole *and* tough.

I eat up the last few minutes responding to emails.

When my alarm chimes, I let out a sigh of relief. "Time's up. Turn in your exam, complete or not. Ensure you have your name on it if you don't want a zero." I shut my laptop and stand by my desk watching as they trudge to the front, some happy and relieved, others like zombies, resigned to their fate.

"See you on Wednesday." It's my attempt at encouragement, letting them know tomorrow will come no matter their fate. Life is more than one exam on any given day.

After the last student turns in their paper, I head out, sloughing my unrest with each step that brings me closer to my car.

My errand is complete, quite successfully, I might add. My spirits are higher than they have been in a while, despite Susan James and the intolerable reminder that I'm failing as a professor. Not in quality of content, but in relational student-teacher interactions. My hard arse-demeanor has done nothing for the students who are there to get an education, nor has it protected me from unwanted advances.

I'm buggered, and yet my newly awakened spirit is oblivious. LaurenGate is to blame for the optimism, no doubt.

Inside the pub, I find Reese comfortably situated at our usual table, grasping a pint. He must have felt me coming as a second pint arrives as I hang my coat on the hook at the end of our booth. Perfect timing. I thank the waitress, smile, and shake Reese's hand. "Hey, mate, what's up?"

"It's been a crazy week, and it's only Monday."

Tell me about it. He has no idea.

He recounts the details of his day and this bird he fancies at work, which rarely turns out well. He's not the best at learning from his mistakes or thinking with the head on his shoulders instead of the little man between his thighs. And no, he wouldn't appreciate my *little man* reference. I'll keep that to myself, but my smirk is on full display.

Reese is a good-looking guy—muscular build, blond hair, blue eyes, silver-tongued devil—who does not have the best track record with women. He loves them. He just can't commit to one. He's twenty-eight, the same age as me. This really is the time to be wild and get it out of our system, right? At least for him, this works. I'm more of a one-woman kind of man, looking to find what my parents have and what my grandparents had. I desire quality over quantity.

I thought I'd found her a few years back. It ended up not to be the case, at least not for her.

I've essentially given up on women.

The vision from this morning pops into my head—Lauren—front and centre. Her warm smile and come-hither

25

eyes packaged in a body that was made for sin, but saints would worship.

"So, how'd it go with Simon? Did you like the place?" Reese draws my attention and saves me from a rock-hard cock while out with my mate—not ideal.

"It's great. Thanks for the introduction." Simon is an acquaintance of his who has space for lease in his new dojo. "It's perfect for my needs, top notch facility." I smile, thankful for the break. I've struggled to find good accommodations. I only hold a few sessions every couple of months, so it's difficult to find appropriate locations with space for evening classes.

"Glad to hear it. When does your next class start?"

"Next month." I've held off registration since the day and time couldn't be confirmed without a location. Now that I have it, I'm ready to go.

It'll be good to get another class started.

I need the distraction.

Chapter 2

FOR THE PAST WEEK, I'VE SCANNED every room, every street, every car. Crowded rooms fill me with hope. My usual coffee shop has me hard as soon as I open the door. Even the smell of the dark brew sets my cock twitching to attention. My surroundings have become a hunting ground, seeking out the one person I can't forget—I don't *want* to forget. A vision of golden hair and blue eyes that haunts me.

Lauren.

My attraction to her confounds me. It only took that one soul-penetrating, eye-locking moment to light a fire that I've been fighting to suppress ever since.

My recurring dreams are back full force nearly every night. The woman from the coffee shop is her. I know it's her. The woman from my dreams. My apparition. The lack of her presence in my life does not diminish its flame in the least.

I cannot explain it.

I cannot deny it.

And I absolutely cannot fathom the idea of never seeing her again.

"Jesus, man. Give it a rest." Reese shakes his head, scanning the bar, his hands splayed. "The chick is not here. Let it go already and move on to the next fantasy."

"I'll find her." I have to. I don't tell him she *is* a fantasy—a dream—come to life. Literally. He wouldn't believe me. I'm not sure *I* believe me.

To my right, Marcus chuckles, "Let him have this. It's been a long time since our boy's been interested in a woman." He takes a drink and shakes his head. "Long damn time," he whispers, piercing me with his stare.

He knows this is different. Marcus is an intuitive fuck. Sometimes I think he knows me better than I know myself. Where Reese is all fun and games, Marcus is deep, cavernous depths. He's all soul and heart, which fits since he's a professor and senior associate dean at SMU's

28

Meadows School of the Arts.

"Is that her?" Marcus nods over my shoulder. "In the back corner."

I've had my eye on the door watching every face that comes and goes. She's not here. Yet my gut tells me to take a better look.

My body follows my head as I turn, zooming in on the table with a brown-haired woman and two men, one dark and the other light-headed. The blond guy leans over, and that's when I see her, shining like the sky opened up, rays of light wrapping her in effervescence.

"Fuck me. That *is* her," I manage as all the air leaves my body.

She's here.

"What?" Reese's tone conveys his disbelief.

"Really?" Marcus' hopefulness speaks to the die-hard romantic he is. "I was kidding."

"That's her." I grip the bar. A flash of my dream, of that face, that smile, and those golden curls plays before my eyes. I didn't even remember I'd seen her face in my dream until now. I always remember it more of an essence of the woman and a feeling of complete joy and peace—the same feeling filling me now.

Goddamn, I'm rock hard at the sight of her, at the certainty that she is the woman from my dreams.

"What are you waiting for?" Reese nudges me forward.

Marcus grabs my arm. "Wait. Look. Are you sure she's not on a date?"

Leave it to Marcus to take the wind right out of my sails.

He's pragmatic—and correct. I need to scope out the scene to see what I'm stepping into.

We move to the end of the bar where she's in my sightline but I'm not directly in hers. As anxious as I am to be *seen* by her, I'm not prepared for the sight before me. She's even more exquisite than I remembered. A siren to my sealed-off heart that's found a reason to beat again, thumping in overtime, struggling to keep the blood pumping to my brain instead of my cock. If I thought our first encounter was a blow to my gut, this is a sucker punch to my bollocks. I fight to stay upright, hanging on to the bar, catching my breath, and ignoring my mates who, like me, wonder what the bloody hell is going on.

The blond guy sticks close, hovering, protective like a lover, or a man who wants to be—yearns to be.

I can relate.

"Definitely a date. See the way he's eyeing her?" Reese says between pouring beers from our pitcher.

"I don't think so. Or she's not that into him," Marcus postulates.

Her head falls back on a laugh I can't hear but imagine it's a joyous sound. But then her hand covers her mouth, stifling her reaction—censoring herself. She stiffens, averts her eyes before turning back to her friends with a smile that doesn't seem genuine.

Sad. She's sad.

Her friends are laughing, having a great time, and she's sitting there holding herself back, not fully engaged.

My gut clenches. *Why? My vision. Why?*

"Not a date," Marcus concludes.

The all-too-attentive Blond Guy notices her withdrawal. He studies her for a moment before leaning in—too close, too fucking close—and whispers in her ear while his hand tenderly caresses her back.

Fuck me if I don't want to pummel him for being in the same room with her, much less touching her.

She responds with a soft smile, small nod, and rises to her feet. Blond Guy stands, pulling her chair out.

"Motherfucker wants it to be a date." Reese laughs. "Guy's lovestruck."

Lauren says something to him and heads down a hall that leads to the loo.

Now's my chance.

"I'll be back." I hop off my stool, ignoring whoops from Reese and Marcus.

Arseholes.

I should have gone home instead of coming to happy hour with Tyler, Silvy, and Clint, the new guy. But I'm tired of saying *no*, of letting people down. Particularly Silvy and

Tyler. I can only turn them down so many times before they start to take it personally. It really isn't about them. They've been nothing but supportive, giving me space, letting me adjust, find my footing.

Washing my hands, I close my eyes and take a fortifying breath.

You can do this.

The reflection in the mirror is a woman I don't recognize most days.

Will I ever be me again?

If I linger much longer, someone will come looking for me. I step out, glancing left and right, then freeze. The hall narrows and stretches like a cartoon fun house, popping back into place with Mr. Dark and Dreamy standing there at the end. His broad shoulders and wide stance eat up the width of the corridor. There's no avoiding him, not that I want to.

He moves with the grace of panther, hands flexing at his sides, his dark gaze setting me aflame. He stops mere inches from me.

"You?" I breathe. His presence, sucking all the oxygen from the room, makes my head spin. I need to sit down.

"It's you." His deep rasp caresses the fantasies I haven't been able to pause in my head. "I've been looking for you."

God, that accent. I've forgotten how sexy it is—how sexy *he* is. "You have?" *I've been looking for you too.* Everywhere, insanely so.

He sticks his hand out. "I'm Theo."

"Theo." I try it on for size. It fits nicely. Too nicely. "I'm—"A zap shoots up my arm when his hand encompasses mine. Warm. Strong. Safe. Home. Those words dance in my head as I'm inundated with visions of being warm and safe, and loved—by him.

"Lauren." He smiles. "I couldn't forget you," he whispers in awe. His eyes slowly scan down my face to our joined hands and back up. "Did you feel—"

"Are you ready to go?" A normally welcomed face appears over Theo's shoulder, knocking me out of my haze. Tyler doesn't look too pleased to find me in the hallway with another man.

"I...this..." I squeeze Theo's hand as if communicating some secret, DNA-sequenced code that only we understand before releasing it reluctantly. "Yes." I don't know how to explain who Theo is.

He's everything. What? No.

Theo's furrowed brow and scrutinizing gaze turn ever so slowly from me to Tyler. His hand that held mine only seconds ago is offered to Tyler like a challenge. "Theo." His voice has an edge—a warning.

"Tyler." Tyler's response is curt, his voice huskier than normal.

Their eyes meet, hands flex. Theo's jaw clenches, and Tyler's eyes narrow. It's a standoff, contempt rolling off them, teasing the air with testosterone.

Tyler breaks the stalemate, placing his hand on my lower back. "We'd better go. We've got an early morning."

Theo steps back. A frown replaces the smile he wore

only moments ago. The heat in his eyes—gone.

He's given up so easily.

Or maybe I imagined the sparks between us.

"Okay." I barely make eye contact with either of them. "It was nice to see you again, Theo." I manage a small smile and glance at him one more time to see if he'll say something. Anything.

A nod and a side step are all the response I get.

I guess I read him wrong.

My heart plummets.

I don't look back as we return to the table to collect our things and head out.

I'm quiet on the ride home, wishing I'd driven myself, granting the solitude I desperately need right now.

It's better this way—my world staying small. I'm not in the market for making new friends.

And apparently Theo was only being polite, saying *hi*. If he'd truly been interested, he would've asked for my number or asked me to stay for a drink with him.

My heart flutters at the thought. Would I have stayed?

I guess I'll never know.

Chapter 3

AS IF SENSING MY SADNESS OVER the loss of Theo—not that I ever had him—Tyler has been more attentive than ever. He assumes my sadness is about Holly. Perhaps he's partially correct. I'm not the same person I once was. But truly, it's the loss of the idea of Theo. The possibility, the hope—the fact that I could be so wrong about his attraction to me—that has me down.

My need to withdraw, disconnect is stronger than ever.

I'm adrift with no tether to keep me grounded. Something drastic needs to be done, or I fear I will simply float away.

"Hey." Tyler's head pops into view before he steps through my office door. He's entirely too chipper for me today.

"Hey." I try to give him the genuine smile he deserves.

"I'm heading out for lunch." He motions to the door. "Do you want me to bring you something back? Or better yet, why don't you come with me?"

God, his panty-dropping grin should have me jumping up to accept his offer. I had a huge crush on him when he started working here. But when he became my boss, I worked doubly hard to see him as only my boss and not the red-blooded, Eddie Bauer model type he is. Most days I don't even see him in *that* way. But some days, like today, I wish I could fall in love with him. I know him. He knows me. He knows my past, well, most of it. I think I could make it work—if he was interested. He could make me happy. We don't have the live-wire connection I thought I had with Theo, but that turned out to be nothing. So maybe if I wasn't so sad, if I wasn't so broken, it could work.

But reality is a bitch, and my reality is that I *am* broken, and Tyler doesn't see me as girlfriend material.

They rarely do.

And I don't do flings. *I can't.*

"I appreciate it, but I think I'll pass. I've got a lot to get done before the end of the day." I can't work late. Not today. I need to get to bed early. I've got a big day tomorrow.

His smile falls, and his demeanor changes as if I've crushed his spirit. Not possible. I've got to get my head on straight. I'm seeing things that aren't there.

Change. I need a change. Tomorrow is a start, but it's not enough.

"Okay." He turns to go but stops at the door. "You know I'm here for you, right? If you need something, anything. I'm here."

"I know. I appreciate that." My hands fidget in my lap. "You're a great boss. Thank you."

"I'm your *friend* too." His voice is more censure than comfort.

"Of course." His eyes beseech me in a way I don't understand. Last week was the first time we'd seen each other outside of work in a long time. I'm not sure that truly constitutes friendship, considering it was all work people at the happy hour where we ran into Theo. Ah, he stressed "friend" for a reason. Not like he has to worry about me getting the wrong idea. "I just…"

He shakes me off, not letting me finish, though I'm not sure what I was going to say. "Text me if you change your mind about food. Good luck tomorrow." He doesn't give me a second look as he disappears out my door.

I feel like I broke something between us, something intangible I didn't even know was there. I push it to the back of my mind. If I dwell on it too much, I'll make it into more than it is. He feels protective of me. And that protectiveness comes from what happened last year, not from having romantic feelings for me. Tyler is a good guy. It's in his nature to protect. He'd be this way with any of his employees, I'm sure, friends too.

He clearly doesn't want me to get the wrong idea, mistaking niceness for romantic interest.

Before I can chicken out, I text Silvy.

Me: *If you still want to, sign us up for those classes.*

It takes mere seconds before the little dots start dancing.

Silvy: *OMG! Yes! Yes! I'm on it.*

Her exuberance makes me laugh. Even in texts she's a ball of energy.

Me: *Thank you. Send me the details.*

Silvy: *You won't regret this. It'll be great. You'll see.*

Me: *I hope you're right.*

Silvy: *I am. I so totally am!*

I'll have to take her word for it. Trust that this is the right thing to do—right for me—right for my future. A step in the right direction to keep me firmly planted.

The lake is serene as runners begin to trickle in, making their way to the sign-in tents, gearing up or stretching on the grass-covered shoreline. It's early, still an hour before the 10K begins. I've checked in, received my number, and stretched. There's not much to do besides people-watch and wait until it's time to line up for my event.

As much as I try not to, I can't help it. Everywhere I go, I look for her. I can't believe I let her slip through my fingers a second time, but she was there with someone. Still, she had to have felt that connection, the same connection I felt when we first met and only intensified when I took her hand.

Even if Tyler is her boyfriend, I still should have gotten her phone number, her email, her last name, anything to keep in touch. She's not meant to be with him. She's meant for me. I know it as I know the sun is shining and that each breath I take is another painful moment without her in my life.

After my fiancée left with her tosser of an ex-boyfriend, my father made me promise not to give up. He spoke like he knew my perfect someone was still out there. I didn't buy into the idea. I simply gave up hope. I moved to the States, got a job, found some friends with common interests, and reconnected with Reese, who had moved back to the States after graduation to start his own architectural firm.

I quench my thirst for a woman now and again. Never the same woman. Never someone I know — or who has a connection to me — and never in my home. My home is my sanctuary where I let my guard down and only friends and family are permitted. A one-night stand — a hard fuck — doesn't fit that bill.

Reese understands. He operates in much the same way, not because he's damaged from his past, but because he's a commitment-phobe with no desire to settle down. He's my wingman. Though, since meeting my dream in the flesh a few weeks ago, my body only craves her body — her touch — and not for one night, but for eternity.

It should freak me the hell out, but it doesn't. It's as if I was made for her, merely biding my time until the fates brought us together. And they have, only I've screwed up twice now in letting her slip away.

After having recurring dreams of her for as long as I can remember, I found her…and let her walk away.

Twice.

What is *wrong* with me?

The announcement for the next event garners my attention. The 15K runners line up, which means I have fifteen minutes before my race begins. I stretch one final time, check my laces, take a bottled water from a passing volunteer, and watch as the runners from this leg of the race pass by. As the pack thins, the opposite side of the course comes back into view.

And that's when I see her.

Hit square in the chest, I jerk back from the electrical strike. Literally struck, not a metaphorical strike of emotions, but a full-on physical attack that sends sparks coursing through my body and sucks the air out of my lungs. *Bloody fucking hell!*

I don't bother looking around to see if anyone else was hit. It's not a thunderstorm that narrowed its sights on me. It's *her. She's* the cause.

It's a sensation I'm weirdly becoming accustomed to. It hits me every time I see her—or touch her—though the other two times were not nearly as powerful. I catch my breath and eat up the ground between us. She hasn't seen me yet, but there's no chance in hell I'm missing this opportunity.

"Lauren," I growl. My need to claim her overpowers my desire to woo her.

"Theo?" Her brows shoot up in shock as she stumbles, turning towards me.

I catch her arm as she rights herself—skin to skin—and a blazing heat consumes me.

She gasps and glances at our connection before she locks on me.

"Tell me you feel that," I entreat. *Tell me you feel this thing between us too.*

"Yes." Her voice is a mere whisper. Perhaps she's in awe as much as I am.

Thank fuck.

I fight the urge to pull her into my arms. There's time

enough for that later. Now I need something else. "Tell me your last name." I search for my phone. Time is of the essence.

Fuck! I left it in the car.

"Frasier. Lauren Frasier. Why?"

"Why?" I nearly chuckle. "Because I'm not losing you again." I look around, trying to spot something to write with. "Do you have a pen?"

"No. Not on me." She's laughing. At. Me.

Of course not, we're getting ready to run a race. "Are you running?" I finally look at her, really look at her. She's dressed like me—shorts and t-shirt with a number on it. Fuck! No pockets. "Do you have your phone?"

"Yes, I'm running. And, no, I didn't think I'd need my phone."

"Don't move." I rush to the nearest volunteer, looking over my shoulder to be sure Lauren is still there. "Do you have a pen and paper?"

"Um…I should." The volunteer digs in her waist pack. "Just a sec."

I glance at Lauren, confirming she hasn't moved. *Come on, lady. I don't have all day.*

"Here! Here." She hands me a pencil and a piece of paper. "Will that do?"

It will have to. "Thank you," I reply over my shoulder as I head back to Lauren.

I rip the paper in two and hand one half to her. "Here. Write your name and number on it."

She glowers, pursing her lips. "But I thought you weren't interested."

Not interested? "I only have a few minutes before my race begins. Please, write down your information, and I'll do the same. Then we can talk about whatever you want." *Make it clear to you that I am most definitely* interested.

She smiles and bites her lip to tame it, unsuccessfully.

Bloody hell, I want to free that lip with my mouth.

"Okay." She acquiesces and motions for me to turn around. Her hand touches my back, and I can feel her writing on the paper.

"I can't believe I found you again." I glance over my shoulder.

"Be still," she chides, but I don't miss the glint in her eyes before I turn away.

"I'm done." She hands me the pencil and turns her back to me.

I set the paper on her back and start to write my name and cell number. "Can I write on your t-shirt?" *Your shorts, your shoes, your arm, your leg, and anywhere else I can write to ensure you have my information.*

"Sure, if you want to. Or you could have just written on my bib." She giggles.

"That would have made too much sense." Why didn't I think of that? I could have been writing on her chest, near those perfect, luscious breasts. I hand her my piece of paper. "Theo Wade."

She hands me hers. "Lauren Frasier."

"Lauren, I don't care if you have a boyfriend. Tell me

you'll go out with me one time. Give me a chance to win you over." *To steal you away.*

"I…boyfriend? I don't have a boyfriend."

"That guy. Tyler. He's not your boyfriend?"

"Tyler?" She laughs. "He's my boss."

"You're dating your boss?"

"No," she insists. "He's *only* my boss. I'm not dating him or anyone else, for that matter."

I'm not dating him or anyone else. That statement, right there, puts a cocky grin on my face. I stand a bit taller and my shoulders feel broader.

"He seemed rather territorial to just be your boss." *He was practically pissing on your leg.*

She blushes, shaking her head. "No. No. He's protective. He doesn't see me like that."

The hell he doesn't.

I'm not wasting another breath discussing this guy. She doesn't have a boyfriend. She's free…to be mine. "Listen, I'd like to skip this race." I scan the sky as if the solution will appear written in the clouds. "But I have supporters paying good money to see me finish. I…it's for charity, and I don't want to let them down."

"What charity?" She lights up, not at all hurt that I'm not canceling my plans for her.

"Raven's Hope. It's a children's charity."

Her ponytail bobs as she nods. "That's a good one."

I step closer. "Have dinner with me. Have coffee with me. Meet me at the finish line and have a gallon of water with me while we recover. Say yes."

"Yes." That blush is back, and I couldn't love it more.

"Yes?" I confirm.

"Yes. I'll meet you at the finish line." She taps my bib where it says which event I'm in. "But you'll beat me. I'm not running the 10K."

I inspect her bib, seeing the *5K* under her number. "I'll wait. I won't leave. I'll be there."

The announcement rings out for the 10K participants to line up.

"That's me." I regret our time has been cut short, again. "You'll meet me?"

"I'll be there," she confirms.

I grab her hand. The zing is still there, but calmer now. "Believe me when I say I've never meant anything more when I tell you—*I cannot wait.*"

The smile that lights up her face makes me feel like I could run my 10K in a minute flat. I kiss our joined hands and reluctantly let her go as I line up with the other runners.

Remaining behind the barrier, she keeps up with me. "Good luck."

"You too. You've got this." I don't know why I tell her that. I assume since she's doing the 5K, that she doesn't do this very often.

"I've got this," she whispers, confirming she needed to hear it.

The gun goes off. Runners all around me take off, and on reflex I start to jog. I look back in a moment of panic but ease when I see her running beside me with the barrier still between us, darting around spectators. "I'll meet you at the finish. I'll be there. I promise."

She nods and slows. I don't miss the worry on her face.

"I've got your number now. I'm not losing you. I'll be there."

She holds up her piece of paper with my name and number on it. "I'll see you there."

"I'll see you there," I repeat. Nothing could keep me away.

What am I doing? I shouldn't be here.

My nerves and pure adrenaline had me finishing my race in record time. Not that my time really matters. I ran to raise money for local women's shelters, not to qualify for additional events. This was a one-time deal. Probably. I could do it again for charity, but I don't see it going much further than that. Running doesn't do it for me. I've never hit that *runner's high* I keep hearing about. Perhaps I don't run long enough to reach that peak, or I'm just not built that way.

It's not the first time I've felt off-center — not normal.

Things affect me differently. Always have. I'm a bit broken. I think too much. I feel too much. I'm entirely too emotional, I've been told. I relate to everyone, yet fit in nowhere. My fantasy life is more active than my real life. And since last year, my disconnection has only grown. But I'm most disjointed when it comes to men. I fall hard. I fall fast—way too fast—and always for men who are unattainable.

Ms. Unrequited should be my name. It's all too fitting.

I stare at my reflection in the water, trying to tame my hair, but it's no use. Curls have broken free and swirl in wet ringlets around my face and neck.

God, what am I doing here?

One minute I'm thinking about Mr. Dark and Dreamy, fantasizing about how it could be between us. The next, I'm scolding myself for allowing such thoughts to take seed. Then I'm running into him at a happy hour, elated to see him again, only to have my hopes dashed by his indifference in the end. And today, he charged at me like I'm a prized possession he thought he lost and then happily found.

The last few weeks have been a rollercoaster for sure, and I'm teetering on the edge, unsure if I should get off or buckle up and hold on for dear life.

I suppose, as I scan the impressive crowd around the finish line, I'm leaning more toward buckling up and taking the ride for all it's worth. But the option to bail still weighs heavy on the scale.

Having not studied the routes of the other races, I didn't realize until I crossed the finish line that the 10K participants wouldn't cross until after most of the 5K runners. I figured since they started before we did and were likely in better shape, they would finish first. I was wrong.

As I sip my second bottled water, I watch the 10K racers come in. The crowd's cheers rise to near deafening proportions. I back up onto a hill to get a better sightline, my legs not thanking me one bit. I scan those coming in and those in the distance to see if I can spot Theo. My heart hammers against my chest with each passing moment and with each runner who crosses the finish. Slowly the number of runners dwindles to a trickle.

Where is he?

Besides the fact that I fear he may have changed his mind, I worry that something has happened. Even if he didn't want to meet me, he would still finish the race. Wouldn't he?

I sit on the hill. Waiting. As the mid-afternoon sun begins its decline, so does my faith that he's coming. There's still one more set of racers to come in, but the 10K leg is long over. It's time to go home. It's time to put these fantasies to bed and live in the real world, a world where men like Theo don't fall for women like me—women who are damaged with too many curves.

My sore body rebels as I stand and stretch. I make my way down the hill, weaving through the remaining crowd of spectators, runners, and news crews here to catch the last of the winners as they cross the finish.

"Hey!" I hear over my shoulder. I glance back, but it's not Theo or any voice I recognize.

"Hey! It's you!" A man points in my direction, his voice obnoxiously loud, drawing attention from those around him.

I look around, trying to determine who he's talking to. It can't be me. I don't know him.

"You're that woman from the news." He steps closer. "The one who was attacked. I saw you on TV."

"No." *Oh, God. No.* He continues moving in my direction. Faces around him begin bouncing between the two of us. One of the news cameramen takes notice.

I back up, looking for the quickest escape route.

Before I can gather my wits, his hand wraps around my wrist. "It's you. Isn't it?"

His hand burns my skin with tainted memories. My vision goes dark, and I suck in air, not able to get enough.

"Don't touch me!" I sound like a lunatic even to my ears as I twist out of his grasp.

He continues to advance. His lips are moving, but I don't hear him over the static in my ears and the fear racing through my bloodstream.

I turn and run. Run as fast as I can. Faster than I should be able to after running a 5K. His voice fades away the closer I get to my car. My escape.

I don't remember pulling the key fob out of the pocket in my bra, starting the car, or pulling onto the highway. I barely remember unlocking my apartment door, locking it behind me and setting the security alarm. It isn't until I sink into the hot bathtub to soak my weary body that I take my first full breath.

I focus on breathing—in and out—calming my body—in

49

and out—clearing my mind—in and out.

As the tension leaves, I sink lower, floating.

Floating weightless.

Floating untethered.

Floating away.

Away.

Away.

Chapter 4

FEBRUARY

I **FIND SILVY IN THE CAFETERIA** at our usual table.
"Hey, I thought I might find you in here." I set down
my lunch and take the seat beside her.

"Yeah, I'm avoiding my boss. He's got a stick up his ass

or something. I thought eating lunch in here was safer than at my desk."

"What's going on with Jason?" Her boss is usually a sweetheart.

She leans in. "Rumor has it his wife left him."

"Oh, no. No wonder he's messed up."

"I know. They were such a great couple." She shrugs. "Maybe it's not true."

"We can hope."

I unpack my lunch of uninspired leftovers. The food tastes like nothing and looks even less appealing. Not that there's anything wrong with the food; it's just that my appetite has been nonexistent since the race.

"Any progress on finding your mystery guy?" She's all too eagerly awaiting my response.

Sometimes I wish Silvy's zest for life would go take a flying leap. She makes me feel even more down in comparison to her never-ending stream of hope and positivity. She grabs life by the balls—without apology, without regret—and rides the hell out of it.

I want to be like her when I grow up. Though we're the same age, I aspire to find the well of light she has inside her.

"Progress? I'm not looking for him, Silvy. And he obviously decided I'm not worth the effort."

"Stop. That's not true," she chides.

Oh, but it is. If she only knew.

"You said yourself, maybe something happened. He didn't even cross the finish line. He could be injured, hobbling around right now, pining over why you didn't meet him. Maybe he thinks *you* stood *him* up."

"He has my number. He could have called."

"He could've lost your number like you lost his." She waves her hand in the air. "What idiots write their phone numbers on a piece of paper—in pencil, I might add—then go run miles and sweat all over said pieces of paper?" She waits like she really wants a response.

"Apparently, *we* do." I never did find my piece of paper with Theo's number on it. I assume I lost it in my haste to get to my car and escape the guy and the growing interest from the crowd as he continued to shout for all to hear. I never told Silvy about that little encounter.

"It wasn't meant to be." I take a bite of pasta, hoping she'll drop it.

"I don't believe that." Her face lights up. "Promise me this…*if* you run into him again, you won't run. You will stand there—put his name and number in your phone—and make plans to see each other again."

"What? No. I can't promise you that."

"Yes, you can. And you will." She sets down her sandwich. "Look. I know you're scared. And you have every right to be. But the universe is trying to tell you something. You've met the same guy three times now. I rarely run into anyone I know, much less the same stranger over and over again. It means something, Lauren. Mark my words—you will see him again."

I smile at her certainty and reverent tone. "Okay, I promise." It's not like it's going to happen.

"Good." A quick nod and she changes topics. "So, about tonight. Are you nervous?"

"Terrified." I've avoided thinking about it all day. I even allowed myself to think about Theo as a means to distract my worrying.

"Don't be. The guy who runs the class seems really nice."

"Yeah?"

"I bet he's hot too."

I laugh. "Silvy, you think every guy is hot." Not quite true, but she finds the good in everyone, and her tastes are wide-ranging.

"Not everyone. I don't think Jason is hot."

"He's your boss."

"I think *your* boss is hot."

That's because Tyler *is* hot. Crazy hot.

"And *you* think your boss is hot," she continues.

I do. "No, I don't." Tyler is in the unavailable, unattainable, off-limits category of hot. Like Theo.

"We're getting off point here. I think the instructor is hot. You might meet your *new* Mr. Dark and Dreamy and fall madly in love."

"When did you talk to him?" I'm curious since she hasn't mentioned him before.

"Talk? I haven't actually talked to him, but I can tell from his emails he's hot." She's entirely serious.

"You're certifiable. You're like a guy, thinking with the head between his legs instead of the one on his shoulders."

She chokes on her drink, covering her mouth as she cycles through laughing, choking, and coughing. After she's recovered, she simply beams at me. "My vajayjay has very good taste. I trust her implicitly."

"Yes, your vajayjay gets around," I tease.

"Hey, I can't help it if you're closed for shopping down there. I, on the other hand, am open for business." Her arms spread out wide, looking around the room as if to advertise her availability.

We laugh for what seems like hours. I relish the sweet release of tension, leaving me relaxed with my nerves reset.

"You never know, he may be the one." The awe in her voice gives me pause.

But I can't give in to her fantasies. I have enough of my own I'm trying to squash. "Yeah, I'm gonna meet the man of my dreams in a self-defense class, dealing with my worst nightmare. I don't think so. Besides, didn't you just ask me to be open to finding Theo again?"

"Yes, I did, but be open to this guy too. You never know," she urges.

"You never know," I agree. "I never dreamed I'd be the victim of an assault. I guess stranger things have happened than falling in love with the guy teaching me to kick ass."

I arrive early at Simon's dojo to set up and get the paperwork ready. The first class of a new session always takes longer before we get into the actual teaching because the students need to fill out forms and pay.

Simon still has one class in progress, but it will end before mine begins. Unless Simon adds an additional class to his already packed schedule, we will be alone here during my class time, 7:00 to 9:00 pm on Wednesdays and Fridays, for the next six weeks. It's perfect. It allows my students, who will most likely be beginners, to relax without being intimidated by experienced students. It's less pressure on them.

I have thirty minutes before class begins, though I'm sure a few students will arrive early, the eager ones. Brian, my second instructor, is arranging the rooms, getting things set up. He's a good guy, strong and agile as a cougar, likeable and easygoing. We've worked together for a few years now. We make a good team. He'll welcome the early arrivals while I focus on my mental preparation.

Silently, I walk through my opening remarks in the back room, getting my head in the right space. This is different than my teaching style at university. I need to be firm, confident, in control, yet open and engaging. These students need to feel safe and welcomed, not lectured to, and definitely not judged for whatever reason brings them to class today.

I try to keep my focus on the task at hand, but since

mucking up my third meeting with Lauren, she's never far from my mind. I don't know how I'll find her again. All I have is her name. Thus far, my internet searches have left me empty-handed. Not so much as a social media account, networking site, or even those sites that promise to provide people matching your search for a nominal fee. Everyone has some sort of digital footprint—except Lauren.

It's like she doesn't really exist.

I haven't been this preoccupied with a woman in a very long time, if ever. She is important. I know it to the core of my being.

I need to find her. As if on cue to taunt me, my right knee aches. The stitches from my tumble itch, ready to be removed. Only a few more days and all that will remain of my third missed opportunity with Lauren is a scar and the phantom pains of losing her—again.

The front door chimes, alerting me that students have probably started to arrive. I visit the loo before heading to the reception area to help Brian welcome our class.

As I make my way, I note five people already working on the paperwork and processing payments with Brian. There are three women and two guys. It's a good mix thus far.

The door chimes again. I turn to see a petite woman with brown hair holding the door open. I move closer, my hand outstretched, a smile on my face, and a *welcome* on the tip of my tongue. But as I open my mouth, my world freezes. My voice is lost. My breath halts. My step stutters to a stop. My brain jams into overdrive trying to comprehend what I see in front of me, rather, *who* I see standing behind the brown-haired bird.

With tremendous effort I croak the only word I can form, "Lauren."

How is this possible?

I latch on to Silvy's arm as she pulls me inside, my progress stilted at the sound of my name on *his* lips—in his deep, rich, British timbre.

"Theo," I manage around the tightness in my throat, my body so excited to see him—to be seen *by him*—that all cylinders stop churning.

"Theo?" Silvy stares at me, apparently as shocked as I am.

I can only nod.

"As in Theo, Theo?" she clarifies, as if I know other Theos.

My head bobs again.

"Holy shit." She looks between the two of us.

Yes, yes, holy shit. Still unable to form words, I stare at the beautiful man in front of me as he introduces himself to

Silvy, directs her to some guy behind the reception desk, and then takes my hand.

"Come with me," he rasps, pulling me along, glancing at me briefly—all too briefly—for me to surmise if he's happy or disappointed to see me again.

Maybe he's mad that he thinks I stood him up?

At the back of the gym, he opens a door, flicks on the light, and stands back, allowing me to enter before him.

I stop in the middle of what seems to be an employee lounge and storage room. The click of the door has me spinning around and coming face to face with the man I've thought about entirely too much, and yet not nearly enough.

He closes the distance between us in two strides, his hand capturing my cheek as his arm snakes around my waist. "Bloody hell, I'm happy to see you."

I gasp. My elation at his joy to see me breaks through my nerves and stupefied surprise. "You are?"

"Fuck, yes." His thumb caresses my bottom lip. "You have no idea." His warm, soulful eyes flit between mine and my lips.

Is he going to kiss me?

He wets his lips, leaning in. His breath sweeps across my mouth as he hovers. "I assume you're here for the class." His eyes close, and he presses his forehead to mine. "*Please* tell me you're here for my class."

His class? "Yes, I'm here for the self-defense class." I lean back. "Your class?"

His wolfish grin has my heart thumping harder. "Yes, my class."

"You're the self-defense instructor?" I clarify.

"Yes." His hand on my cheek skates feathery-soft along my arm and down to my hand, capturing it in his. "Is that a problem?"

"No...I'm...surprised. I didn't picture you as a self-defense instructor." I think of the first time I saw him in his suit and overcoat, looking every inch the professional I believed him to be.

"I wear many hats. At the moment, I'm your self-defense instructor. Later—" He squeezes my hand. "I hope to be something else entirely."

Holy moly, my thundering heart just dropped to the floor.

He steps impossibly closer. His lips graze my cheek on the way to my ear. "Tell me I can see you later, after class. We have much to discuss."

"Yes," I squeak and want to kick myself for sounding like such a mouse.

"Good." He steps back. "We need to get back out there. You've got paperwork to fill out, and I have a class to teach."

His in-charge demeanor is just plain hot. I don't know how I'll make it through this class. I doubt I'll be able to concentrate on much of anything besides what happens after class.

Chapter 5

I **FIND SILVY IN THE CAFETERIA** at our usual table.
"Hey, I thought I might find you in here." I set down
my lunch and take the seat beside her.

"Yeah, I'm avoiding my boss. He's got a stick up his ass
or something. I thought eating lunch in here was safer than
at my desk."

"What's going on with Jason?" Her boss is usually a
sweetheart.

She leans in. "Rumor has it his wife left him."

"Oh, no. No wonder he's messed up."

"I know. They were such a great couple." She shrugs. "Maybe it's not true."

"We can hope."

I unpack my lunch of uninspired leftovers. The food tastes like nothing and looks even less appealing. Not that there's anything wrong with the food; it's just that my appetite has been nonexistent since the race.

"Any progress on finding your mystery guy?" She's all too eagerly awaiting my response.

Sometimes I wish Silvy's zest for life would go take a flying leap. She makes me feel even more down in comparison to her never-ending stream of hope and positivity. She grabs life by the balls—without apology, without regret—and rides the hell out of it.

I want to be like her when I grow up. Though we're the same age, I aspire to find the well of light she has inside her.

"Progress? I'm not looking for him, Silvy. And he obviously decided I'm not worth the effort."

"Stop. That's not true," she chides.

Oh, but it is. If she only knew.

"You said yourself, maybe something happened. He didn't even cross the finish line. He could be injured, hobbling around right now, pining over why you didn't meet him. Maybe he thinks *you* stood *him* up."

"He has my number. He could have called."

"He could've lost your number like you lost his." She

waves her hand in the air. "What idiots write their phone numbers on a piece of paper—in pencil, I might add—then go run miles and sweat all over said pieces of paper?" She waits like she really wants a response.

"Apparently, *we* do." I never did find my piece of paper with Theo's number on it. I assume I lost it in my haste to get to my car and escape the guy and the growing interest from the crowd as he continued to shout for all to hear. I never told Silvy about that little encounter.

"It wasn't meant to be." I take a bite of pasta, hoping she'll drop it.

"I don't believe that." Her face lights up. "Promise me this…*if* you run into him again, you won't run. You will stand there—put his name and number in your phone—and make plans to see each other again."

"What? No. I can't promise you that."

"Yes, you can. And you will." She sets down her sandwich. "Look. I know you're scared. And you have every right to be. But the universe is trying to tell you something. You've met the same guy three times now. I rarely run into anyone I know, much less the same stranger over and over again. It means something, Lauren. Mark my words—you will see him again."

I smile at her certainty and reverent tone. "Okay, I promise." It's not like it's going to happen.

"Good." A quick nod and she changes topics. "So, about tonight. Are you nervous?"

"Terrified." I've avoided thinking about it all day. I even allowed myself to think about Theo as a means to distract my worrying.

"Don't be. The guy who runs the class seems really nice."

"Yeah?"

"I bet he's hot too."

I laugh. "Silvy, you think every guy is hot." Not quite true, but she finds the good in everyone, and her tastes are wide-ranging.

"Not everyone. I don't think Jason is hot."

"He's your boss."

"I think *your* boss is hot."

That's because Tyler *is* hot. Crazy hot.

"And *you* think your boss is hot," she continues.

I do. "No, I don't." Tyler is in the unavailable, unattainable, off-limits category of hot. Like Theo.

"We're getting off point here. I think the instructor is hot. You might meet your *new* Mr. Dark and Dreamy and fall madly in love."

"When did you talk to him?" I'm curious since she hasn't mentioned him before.

"Talk? I haven't actually talked to him, but I can tell from his emails he's hot." She's entirely serious.

"You're certifiable. You're like a guy, thinking with the head between his legs instead of the one on his shoulders."

She chokes on her drink, covering her mouth as she cycles through laughing, choking, and coughing. After she's recovered, she simply beams at me. "My vajayjay has very good taste. I trust her implicitly."

"Yes, your vajayjay gets around," I tease.

"Hey, I can't help it if you're closed for shopping down there. I, on the other hand, am open for business." Her arms spread out wide, looking around the room as if to advertise her availability.

We laugh for what seems like hours. I relish the sweet release of tension, leaving me relaxed with my nerves reset.

"You never know, he may be the one." The awe in her voice gives me pause.

But I can't give in to her fantasies. I have enough of my own I'm trying to squash. "Yeah, I'm gonna meet the man of my dreams in a self-defense class, dealing with my worst nightmare. I don't think so. Besides, didn't you just ask me to be open to finding Theo again?"

"Yes, I did, but be open to this guy too. You never know," she urges.

"You never know," I agree. "I never dreamed I'd be the victim of an assault. I guess stranger things have happened than falling in love with the guy teaching me to kick ass."

I arrive early at Simon's dojo to set up and get the paperwork ready. The first class of a new session always takes longer before we get into the actual teaching because the students need to fill out forms and pay.

Simon still has one class in progress, but it will end before mine begins. Unless Simon adds an additional class to his already packed schedule, we will be alone here during my class time, 7:00 to 9:00 pm on Wednesdays and Fridays, for the next six weeks. It's perfect. It allows my students, who will most likely be beginners, to relax without being intimidated by experienced students. It's less pressure on them.

I have thirty minutes before class begins, though I'm sure a few students will arrive early, the eager ones. Brian, my second instructor, is arranging the rooms, getting things set up. He's a good guy, strong and agile as a cougar, likeable and easygoing. We've worked together for a few years now. We make a good team. He'll welcome the early arrivals while I focus on my mental preparation.

Silently, I walk through my opening remarks in the back room, getting my head in the right space. This is different than my teaching style at university. I need to be firm, confident, in control, yet open and engaging. These students need to feel safe and welcomed, not lectured to, and definitely not judged for whatever reason brings them to class today.

I try to keep my focus on the task at hand, but since mucking up my third meeting with Lauren, she's never far from my mind. I don't know how I'll find her again. All I have is her name. Thus far, my internet searches have left me empty-handed. Not so much as a social media account, networking site, or even those sites that promise to provide people matching your search for a nominal fee. Everyone has some sort of digital footprint—except Lauren.

It's like she doesn't really exist.

I haven't been this preoccupied with a woman in a very long time, if ever. She is important. I know it to the core of my being.

I need to find her. As if on cue to taunt me, my right knee aches. The stitches from my tumble itch, ready to be removed. Only a few more days and all that will remain of my third missed opportunity with Lauren is a scar and the phantom pains of losing her—again.

The front door chimes, alerting me that students have probably started to arrive. I visit the loo before heading to the reception area to help Brian welcome our class.

As I make my way, I note five people already working on the paperwork and processing payments with Brian. There are three women and two guys. It's a good mix thus far.

The door chimes again. I turn to see a petite woman with brown hair holding the door open. I move closer, my hand outstretched, a smile on my face, and a *welcome* on the tip of my tongue. But as I open my mouth, my world freezes. My voice is lost. My breath halts. My step stutters to a stop. My brain jams into overdrive trying to comprehend what I see in front of me, rather, *who* I see standing behind the brown-haired bird.

With tremendous effort I croak the only word I can

form, "Lauren."

How is this possible?

I latch on to Silvy's arm as she pulls me inside, my progress stilted at the sound of my name on *his* lips — in his deep, rich, British timbre.

"Theo," I manage around the tightness in my throat, my body so excited to see him — to be seen *by him* — that all cylinders stop churning.

"Theo?" Silvy stares at me, apparently as shocked as I am.

I can only nod.

"As in Theo, Theo?" she clarifies, as if I know other Theos.

My head bobs again.

"Holy shit." She looks between the two of us.

Yes, yes, holy shit. Still unable to form words, I stare at the beautiful man in front of me as he introduces himself to Silvy, directs her to some guy behind the reception desk, and then takes my hand.

"Come with me," he rasps, pulling me along, glancing at

me briefly—all too briefly—for me to surmise if he's happy or disappointed to see me again.

Maybe he's mad that he thinks I stood him up?

At the back of the gym, he opens a door, flicks on the light, and stands back, allowing me to enter before him.

I stop in the middle of what seems to be an employee lounge and storage room. The click of the door has me spinning around and coming face to face with the man I've thought about entirely too much, and yet not nearly enough.

He closes the distance between us in two strides, his hand capturing my cheek as his arm snakes around my waist. "Bloody hell, I'm happy to see you."

I gasp. My elation at his joy to see me breaks through my nerves and stupefied surprise. "You are?"

"Fuck, yes." His thumb caresses my bottom lip. "You have no idea." His warm, soulful eyes flit between mine and my lips.

Is he going to kiss me?

He wets his lips, leaning in. His breath sweeps across my mouth as he hovers. "I assume you're here for the class." His eyes close, and he presses his forehead to mine. "*Please* tell me you're here for my class."

His class? "Yes, I'm here for the self-defense class." I lean back. "Your class?"

His wolfish grin has my heart thumping harder. "Yes, my class."

"You're the self-defense instructor?" I clarify.

"Yes." His hand on my cheek skates feathery-soft along my arm and down to my hand, capturing it in his. "Is that a

69

problem?"

"No...I'm...surprised. I didn't picture you as a self-defense instructor." I think of the first time I saw him in his suit and overcoat, looking every inch the professional I believed him to be.

"I wear many hats. At the moment, I'm your self-defense instructor. Later—" He squeezes my hand. "I hope to be something else entirely."

Holy moly, my thundering heart just dropped to the floor.

He steps impossibly closer. His lips graze my cheek on the way to my ear. "Tell me I can see you later, after class. We have much to discuss."

"Yes," I squeak and want to kick myself for sounding like such a mouse.

"Good." He steps back. "We need to get back out there. You've got paperwork to fill out, and I have a class to teach."

His in-charge demeanor is just plain hot. I don't know how I'll make it through this class. I doubt I'll be able to concentrate on much of anything besides what happens after class.

Chapter 6

MY HAND PRESSES TO THE SMALL of her back as we're shown to a secluded table in one of my favourite neighborhood bars. This place isn't big enough for live music, but there's a bloke rasping classic rock, plucking away at his guitar in a corner where the table has been pushed aside to make room for a stool, a mic, a small amp, and a tip jar that is painfully barren.

I take pity on him and relinquish my connection with

Lauren, if only for a moment. My hand feels the stark absence of her warmth as I drop a tenner in the jar.

When I reach our table, she's already sitting with her back to the wall, facing the room.

Scowling—not happy I didn't get to pull her chair out for her—I lay her coat and mine across the back of the other chairs and take the one to her right.

Her eyes scan the room as if she's looking for someone, but when her shoulders relax on an exhale, her eyes meet mine.

"Everything alright?" I try not to stiffen at the possibility that she looks for her attacker in the nameless faces of every room she enters. The need to protect her and make her feel safe hits me hard.

But she's not the one who needs saving.

I am.

She's like a life preserver to a drowning man. I need to grab her and hold on tight. I press my fists into my thighs, rerouting that energy, a necessary tactic to ensure I take this slow.

"Yes." Her response, while not clipped, is entirely too brief.

The waitress takes our drink orders, mentioning the specials, and flutters away.

"Tea?" I'm surprised Lauren ordered an iced tea to my dark ale.

A bashful flush warms her face. "Yeah, I don't drink." She lays her napkin across her lap, adjusting her silverware, ensuring proper placement.

She's nervous. I'd like to ease her nerves with my lips.

"No?" I cock a brow and tilt my head, drawing her gaze back to mine, silently urging her to elaborate.

"Well, sometimes. If there's an ocean involved."

An ocean? Her mischievous smile and bright eyes make me want to sweep her away to the nearest Caribbean island so that twinkle never fades.

I'd like to see the ocean try to compete with the blues in her eyes.

"I interpret that to mean a coconutty-strawberryish-frozen concoction of some sort?"

Her lips curve in a playful smile. "More than likely. Frozen concoctions go rather well with sun and sand, dontcha think?" She sweeps an errant curl from her eye—my fingers twitch to do it for her—as she takes a sip of water.

"Yes, I suppose they do."

She fidgets in her seat, and her swaying handbag reminds me... "May I have your phone?"

"My phone?" Her eyes search my body as if she's trying to find mine.

Her perusal has me stiffening, inconveniently. "Yes," I strain, my vocal cords as tight as my cock in my trousers.

Silently, she unlocks her phone and hands it over, watching my every move as I enter my information.

Leaning forward, she laughs. "Address too?"

"Yes." I save my contact information, just short of my complete life history and blood type, then send myself a text.

Once my phone chimes in my pocket, I hand hers back but don't release it until her eyes meet mine. "I've lost you three times. I will *not* lose you a fourth."

Her quick intake of air and the softening of her features make me want to draw her into my lap and tell her all the ways I intend to keep her. Instead, I hold her gaze until she finally nods in acceptance.

Taking up her phone, her thumbs type furiously, holding it close so I can't see what she's doing. Then she locks it and puts it away.

The chime from my pocket sets my heart pounding and my cock clamouring for attention. When I see what she sent, I'm floored. "You sent me your address."

"Yes."

"And your birth date."

Now she's full-on blushing. "Yes."

"Your work address."

"Yes."

"And work number."

"Yes. And email addresses—work and personal. Every conceivable way to find me, should you choose to do so."

Abso-bloody-lutely. It's like stalking—with permission. "I most definitely choose to do so."

When our drinks arrive, I talk her into trying one of the house specialties, Duck Fat Back Bacon Cheesy Fries.

"It sounds horrible for my figure." She giggles as she reads the ingredients from the menu.

My eyes peruse her this time. There's not a damn thing

wrong with her figure—curves in all the best places. "Worth every decadent bite." I make no attempt to hide the fire burning in my gut.

Red flares on her cheeks—again—but she ignores my double-entendre. "There's no way you eat like this on a regular basis and manage to look like that." Her hand sweeps up and down, indicating my body.

"No. I'll have to run a few extra miles tomorrow." Maybe for a few days.

"You mean the salads we ordered don't counteract the effects of all that fat?"

"Sadly, no." *But there are other ways we can work off those calories.*

"I guess I had better get up extra early tomorrow to pound it out on the treadmill."

Pound it out. Bloody fucking hell. She's either an angel or the devil. I'm not quite sure which.

I'd happily settle for either—or both.

"Oh. My. God." I think I just had an orgasm—a mouthgasm. Theo wasn't kidding, these duck fat French fries are to die for, and I imagine if you eat too many, you'd do just that.

His tight jaw and fiery stare mean I probably moaned entirely too loud for public consumption. He speaks around his bite. "Do that again, and I shan't be responsible for my actions." It's not a threat. It's a promise—one hell of a delicious promise.

"Actions?" I nearly chirp, my pulse speeding up at the idea of him not being able to control himself with me—*me*.

He loads up his fork, laboriously so, getting a chunk of the smoked BBQ back bacon, then a spiral or two of the gooey cheesy mac, and finishes it by stabbing a few duck fat-fried French fries. "Open." He dangles his fork in front of my mouth. "Make that sound again."

Holy hell. I open my mouth. His eyes narrow. I manage to wrap my lips around his offering—big as it is. He groans as he slowly slips the fork free.

I try, I swear I try to stifle it, but it's a duck-fat, cheese-laden, salty-pork, Theo hottie-induced moan that won't be denied. It vibrates in my chest, sending goosebumps rippling along my skin as it travels up my throat and around the most decadent thing I've ever had in my mouth.

"Bloody fucking hell." His molten gaze ignites a fire in me I've never felt before. His hand lands on mine, gripping it like a lifeline.

The zing that sizzles up my arm has me seeing white, my ears ringing, and my head thrown back in an instantaneous, total-body, muscle-thrashing orgasm.

Oh. My. God!

"Goddamn." His lips crash over mine. His mouth consumes my cries of ecstasy as he pulls me into his lap before hoisting me into his arms. "I don't know what the hell is happening, but your pleasure is only for my eyes." His growl is intimately close as his lips graze my neck. "Hang on." We're on the move, crashing through a back door as my mind reels and my body quivers with aftershocks.

Darkness. Everywhere. He carries me through the night, his lips pressed to my temple.

"Close your eyes," he says gently as light sweeps our surroundings. Then a chirp, a click, and I'm lying on something soft. His lips press to mine. "Don't move. I'll be back directly." He squeezes my hand before pulling away. "I'm going to pay our bill and get our belongings."

The moment his comforting touch is gone, I miss it. I miss him. Crazy as it sounds, it's like a part of me left me behind, and I physically ache for it like it's a phantom limb. I roll to my side, my eyes tightly shut, another tremor taking my breath away as I shudder, hugging myself for comfort.

It could be minutes, hours, or a lifetime, but the moment he's back in the car, my limb is back. I feel whole again. "Theo," I whisper from the backseat of his car.

He glances over his shoulder. "Relax, baby, I'll have you home in no time."

Baby? Home. He speaks to me as if we're already *something*.

Strong hands urge me to sit up. "Lauren, we're here."

I blink until his face comes into focus, and I right myself in the backseat. "Theo." My hands clasp his cheeks, not too gently by the surprise on his face. "Here?"

His hands cover mine. "At your apartment." He dangles my keys in front of me. "Which key?"

I blink and widen my eyes, pinpointing the one I need. I pinch it between my fingers and show it to him. "This one."

Why do I sound drunk? Why do I *feel* drunk?

No, not quite drunk. High, maybe?

"Alarm," I murmur.

He stops, studying me, then understanding sweeps across his face. "You have a security system?"

I nod and say *yes*, but it falls short of gaining any sound.

"Can you disarm it? Or tell me the code?"

"Text."

His thumb grazes my cheek, a wisp of a smile softening his chiseled face. "What the hell is this between us?" His warm brown eyes glisten with equal parts awe and desire.

He snaps his fingers. "Ah! The text you sent me earlier." His phone lights up the back seat as he searches, then scowls. "Don't ever send someone your alarm code."

I flinch from his reprimand and push around him, barely managing to climb out of his SUV and remain on my feet. I'm so frigging weak, my legs wobble, but I brush off his hand clasping my arm.

"I'm sorry." His arm bands my waist. "Let's get you inside. We can address this later."

As if he's done it hundreds of times, he unlocks the door, disarms the security system, and ushers me inside before the chill of the February night has me shivering.

The lock clicks behind me. Alarm is reset.

I slip off my shoes.

He picks them up, sets them by the dining room table.

I drop my coat.

He swoops down, catches it, drapes it on the back of a chair.

My keys hit the bar.

My purse lands next to them.

His coat and shoes mirror mine.

He guides me into the kitchen, backing me up against the counter, his hands landing on either side, caging me in. Pulse pounding in my ears, my breath hitches as he leans down, nuzzling my neck. "You alright?"

"Yeah." I clutch on to his forearms, wanting him closer. "You?"

His laugh brushes my neck with warmth, making me shiver. "You're cold." He captures me in his arms.

"No."

"You're shaking." His heated gaze caresses my face.

"You seem to have that effect on me."

"About that." He pulls away soberly. "We need to talk."

"I can't think straight if you keep doing that." She's the devil, most definitely the devil.

"Doing what?" She does it again.

"Grinding against my cock like a cat in heat."

I don't know how we even got in this position. Me on the couch. Her straddling my lap, and my hands squeezing her ass, urging her on.

"You pulled me into your lap after saying we needed to talk." It's an accusation, though it came out more like a pout.

Bloody hell, I'm so gone for this woman. And her warm heat rubbing me into oblivion is making it hard to remember that I want more than just a quick fuck. I don't know what this is between us, but I'm sure as hell staying around to find out.

"We're not having sex, Lauren." I squeeze her hips, and she whimpers her disapproval.

"No." She nods in agreement, then shakes her head, trying to clear the cobwebs, I imagine. "Why is that again?"

I cup her cheek, bringing her face closer. "Because you're drunk."

"But I haven't had anything to drink."

"I know. I can't explain it. But you're drunk all the same." I kiss her lips, relishing the way it makes my head spin. "I'm not doing much better. I think we're drunk on each other."

Maybe it's pheromones.

Maybe someone roofied us.

"Oh my god." As if a bucket of cold water has been dumped on her, she jumps off my lap and backs away, her head shaking as she increases the distance between us. She grips the back of the other couch so tightly her fingers turn white. "This..." She points to me and then to herself. "I..."

I'm on my feet, cautiously approaching her, my hand out. "Lauren."

"Stop." She moves to the other end of the couch. "Please. Just stop."

I freeze. I don't want to scare her.

"I can't..." She straightens her shoulders. The fog she's been in seems to dissipate. "I can't have sex with you."

"I know." I motion to the other end of the couch where she was straddling me mere moments ago, nearly grinding me to a happy ending. "I just said that."

"No. You don't understand. I don't only mean tonight."

"Alright." I venture a step closer. "I'm not rushing you." I can feel the panic radiating off her. She's like a feral cat getting ready to run.

"I don't do casual sex." The regret in her voice is

palpable.

Another step. I take deep breaths to calm my racing heart, hoping it will ease her anxiousness. "I never thought you did."

"No?" Surprise softens her features, her panic abating.

"No." I close the gap between us, cupping her cheek. "The woman I've run into over the last three weeks, and earlier this evening, wouldn't sleep with a bloke after only one date."

Her sad eyes peruse my face, leaning into my touch. "No, she wouldn't."

She takes a fortifying breath, closing her eyes momentarily, and then steps out of my grasp, but not out of reach. "She also doesn't plan on having sex again until she's married."

Again? Married?

She says it as if it's a deal breaker. It's not.

I step into her space, capture her chin, and kiss her softly. "I can work with that." I'll take whatever she's willing to give me. I need her in my life and not running away. "Can you tell me why?"

"Why?" She steps into me. Her lips may be saying no, but her body isn't quite on board.

"Why you're waiting for marriage." I'm not pressuring her. She doesn't plan on having sex *again*. I want to understand why she changed her mind. Was it bad? Was it the attack? What happened after she had relations to make her change her mind? I want to understand. And I need words between us to keep my hands to myself. Her pull, her need, her innocent passion is hard to resist, but she needs to know I'm not here to use her for physical release. No matter how good it sounds and might feel—I want more, more from the vulnerable woman in front of me whose words hold me at bay, but her eyes beg me to listen to our baser desires.

She's a contradiction, and she has no idea.

"Sex brings about a false sense of intimacy, heightened emotions—connection—that hasn't been earned. For some, it's no big deal. It's just sex. But for me, I can't keep my heart out of it." Her eyes, full of passion before, now plead with sadness and pain.

"I'll never hurt you."

"Maybe not intentionally." There's so much more she's not saying. She steps back and schools her face as her well-fortified walls fall into place.

She doesn't know you. Show her. "I'm not pressuring you for sex. I only wanted to understand."

She shrugs. "Now you do."

There's more she's not saying, but I don't think I'll get any more tonight.

I slip on my shoes. "Can I take you to dinner tomorrow?"

"I don't think that's a good idea." She crosses the room, closer to the door than to me. Her eyes study me as if she's cataloging every feature.

She's preparing for goodbye.

My gut clenches at that realization. Pulling on my coat,

I'm struck again by the sadness in her eyes. She doesn't want to do this, and yet she is, all because she thinks I don't want her for more than something quick and physical. "I'll call you."

"Don't." Her chin trembles.

"Fuck if I'm letting you go after finally finding you again." I step into her, tipping her face to mine. "You're scared. I'll never hurt you." I wipe a tear as it escapes. "You don't know that because you don't know me, and you never will if you don't give us a chance."

She presses a hand to her quivering lips. She's killing me here. I want to wrap her in my arms and make it all better. But she's not ready. She may want it—deep down—but she's not giving herself permission.

I capture her free hand, and I'm relieved when that buzz between us ignites, sizzling up my arm and through my body, making the hairs on my skin stand at attention. Her eyes widen and she frees her muzzled mouth on a whimper of pleasure.

"We've got an unworldly connection, Lauren. You feel it. I feel it. It means something. Whatever it is has proven it's not to be ignored. But I'll give you space—time—if that's what you need."

Reluctantly, I step back, and it's as if my skin is being torn from my body the farther I get.

She shudders on a gasp.

"You feel it too, don't you? It hurts like hell, but I'm doing it—for you."

Full-on sobs rack her body as I open the door and step into the cold night that feels like salve to my burning skin.

Every step I take is a study in determination and sacrifice. I'm ripping my heart out to give her what she thinks she needs. I'm leaving to prove I'll come back for her—that I'll always return to her.

But she has no idea.

Her sobs claw at me, and she offers no leniency by closing the door. No, she stays, gripping it like a lifeline out of cruelty or out of necessity to witness—take part in—this agonizing valediction.

When I drive away, I spare a glance over my shoulder and regret it immediately. I don't know what I thought I'd find. A closed, solid door between us? But what I see is pure torture.

My vision is on her knees, head towards the heavens as if she's praying to God himself. Her body rocks in sobs I can no longer hear but feel with traitorous clarity and devastating finality.

PART TWO:

After Effects

Chapter 7

TWO DAYS PASS. I CAN'T BRING myself to face him. I'm embarrassed. Ashamed. I rode him like a horny teenager who didn't know better or have a moral compass. Like I wasn't a woman who has been celibate for a reason. Like I was good with a wham-bam-thank-you-ma'am hook-up.

I. Am. Not. That. Girl.

Never have been. Never will be.

But I'm also afraid. Afraid of what our bizarre

connection means. Afraid of what will happen if I give in to it.

Afraid of what will happen if I don't.

If I give in to our connection, I'll lose myself.

If I don't give in, I'll lose him. Men like him wait for nobody, never mind someone as broken as me.

Yet, he said he'd wait...

Fear. Unrest. Doubt.

Feelings I know too well. Feelings that are at home in my body—in my mind—and take root far too easily, flourishing in detrimental ways, as evident by my waking in the throes of a nightmare for the past two nights. A nightmare I've had far too often. A nightmare that leaves me shaken and feeling even more alone and unworthy than ever.

Change is not easy. More days than not, it's two steps forward and six steps back. But I won't give up. As long as I'm still breathing and there's blood pumping in my body, I'll continue to fight.

However, since the incident with Theo, I've been in a six-steps-back kind of mode.

Doubt and fear are horrible companions. They cloud my vision, distance hope, and sequester truth. They lie to me so seamlessly it's hard to see reality.

I didn't tell Silvy what happened. I simply told her I couldn't make tonight's class and left it at that. She knows better than to press. Pushing me only pushes me further away.

Theo's been texting and calling. Even though I don't respond, he continues to reach out. There's not been a single harsh word, though I'm sure he's frustrated.

I finally replied yesterday, advising I needed a few days to get my head on straight.

I don't recognize the woman I was on Wednesday night. I don't like her. But the scary thing is, I don't entirely hate her either.

Is she the new me? A sexually forward new version of me?

What happened to the girl who promised to wait until marriage? Who thought of her virginity as a gift to her husband? She slept with the first boy who gave her the time of day—that's what happened. It wasn't love. It was lust. It was loneliness. A desire to feel loved, cherished. A chance to fulfill those fantasies in my head of what a man's touch would feel like. I traded a moment of pleasure, believing it was more than it was, only to discover I was blinded, unable to see it was just sex for him. It wasn't ground-shaking, life-changing. For him, it was a nice time but not a forever after.

I can't give in to it again. My heart simply can't take it.

And a man like Theo is not going to wait for a girl like me—broken, confused, and a bucket of tears always at the ready.

I hate myself sometimes—actually, most of the time for my sensitivity, for my inability to hold back my tears. I want to stand strong, impenetrable. But I fail miserably over and over again.

No man wants that.

Especially not a god like Theo who can have any woman he wants.

He wants you.

No, whatever this thing—this power—is between us is making him *think* he wants me. He doesn't. He can't. Men like Theo don't fall for girls like me.

It's better this way. As miserable as I am now, it'll be a thousand times worse if I let him in. If I believe it's true. If I fall further in love with him, and then he realizes I'm not enough and leaves me.

Distance is what we need and why I'm at dinner with Tyler. He may not be the one or even interested, but he's an amenable companion, and I'm trying not to be so antisocial.

It's not a date. We had a late meeting and stopped for dinner afterwards before heading back to the office. We're at an Indian place, the kind with the low tables with pillows strewn about for sitting and lounging.

"I'm stuffed." I lean back, thankful for the corner table and the wall to support my overindulgent body that can barely sit up and wants to slip on yoga pants and a tank top—bra-free—and lie dormant until digestion is well underway.

Tyler chuckles, leaning against the adjacent wall. He scans my plate and then me. "Don't take this the wrong way—"

"That's a horrible way to start a sentence. Nothing good can come after that."

His smile only grows, and my heart pangs for the man

who's not here and the sincerity in the eyes of the one who is.

"It's not bad. It's an observation, not a condemnation. I've never seen you eat so much." He full-out laughs. "God, that did sound horrible."

My aching soul laughs too. "It's alright. It's true." I've never felt a need to restrict myself around Tyler, but it seems since Theo's appearance, my need for food is overridden by my need for him. In the absence of Theo, my need for food is to fill that emptiness, to feed the sadness, and to stifle the tears by stuffing my face. Good times. My relationship with food has never been the greatest. It's better than it used to be, but it's easy to slip into old habits.

"It's good to see you eat, actually."

"Please, it's not like I'm going to waste away."

"Don't talk like that." The censure in his voice reminds me of Theo. He wouldn't let me get away with that self-deprecating remark either.

Why do these two remind me so much of each other?

Admittedly, I am drawn to Tyler. I always have been. But it's never gone beyond professional and occasional social events, a hanging-out type of friendship. He's never looked at me longingly. He's never made a move. He smiles at me the same as he does everyone else.

I'm nothing special, and Tyler knows that.

Theo doesn't.

And the crush I had for Tyler seem laughable in comparison to how Theo makes me feel.

"You've been so sad lately." Tyler's hand brushes mine.

"Do you want to talk about it?" His eyes caress my face, and I feel it as though it's the tips of his fingers. "Is it Holly?"

I shake my head. "No, it's not Holly. Though...she's never far from my mind." Or my broken soul. I play with the discarded cocktail straw from Tyler's drink, bending it into a joined triangle. "How are your parents?"

He huffs. "I guess that means you don't want to talk about it?"

"Not particularly." It's not a no. If he pushed, I might open up to him, but I hope he doesn't. It would feel like a betrayal to Theo and blur the lines with Tyler to talk about my love life—not that there is one—but, I suppose, that was my choice.

"My parents are good. Off on some cruise. My mom has been hounding my dad to slow down and enjoy life instead of trying to buy it."

His dad is some kind of investor, money guy. Tyler told me, but it kinda went in one ear and out the other.

"You should go with them sometime."

He frowns. "No thanks. The last thing I need is more time with my dad, giving him the opportunity to hound me about coming to work for him. We get along better the less we see each other."

"I thought you were close to your parents."

"I am, as long as we're not talking about my career."

"I'm sorry."

His hand squeezes mine. "Don't be. Other than that, we're good."

I let his hand linger longer than I should. The connection is nice, comforting, but there's no sizzle. Maybe a spark that could become a flame, but compared to Theo, it's nothing at all.

"Should we go?" Tyler lays cash on the table and offers me his hand as he stands.

"Thank you for dinner. It was nice." And it was. It's good to get out of my house and the memory of Theo there in my kitchen, on my couch, and the sight of him leaving after I pushed him away—giving me what I wanted. What I thought I needed.

Hindsight is a hideous gift, full of remorse and the reality of bad choices.

Tyler's hand grazes my back as we make our way to his car where he opens the door for me and holds my hand as I sit, scooping my skirt out of the way before he closes the door. Gentlemanly.

Another similarity between Theo and Tyler. Another reminder that falling for someone like Tyler could be easy, could be nice, could even feel good. But it's not game-changing, panty-melting passion where the world stops turning and my demons fall silent.

It could be nice, but it would never be otherworldly.

She missed three self-defense classes, left me hanging all weekend without a returned call or text. I haven't heard from her since her text last Thursday where she said she needed time. It's the following Friday. It's been nine bloody days since I've seen her, and I'm still as raw as I was when I left her place. It eviscerates me to think that I spent a month trying to find her, and when I finally did, I lost her in the same damn night.

This can't be all there is. The connection between us can't be for naught.

She visits me every night in my dreams—the same dream I've had most of my life. The dream I thought was only that until I met my apparition in the flesh. Now I know I was destined for her and she for me. She might not believe it, but she doesn't have the proof that I have. I know she feels our connection, but perhaps it's not nearly as strong for her as it is for me. If it were, I don't see how she could deny us our future.

It's taking everything I have physically—mentally—to not camp outside her door, ensuring she's safe, remind her of our bond, and beg her to give me a chance.

I don't beg. I don't stalk. I've never had to work for a woman's affections. Until now.

Lauren is different. I can see it in her eyes. I can smell in on her skin. And my soul recognized its other half as soon as it woke the fuck up in that coffee shop. All cards are on the table with this woman—and I'm going for broke.

Silvy made it to tonight's class—alone—as she has the other two nights. I sent her off with Brian, only exchanging pleasantries at the beginning of class. I recognize the pity in her eyes and the apology on her lips. It's not her fault. It's not even Lauren's.

The whiplash of our connection is scary as fuck, and with Lauren's past—which I don't even know but can sense—there's so much pain.

I'm a patient man despite the agonizing ache in me to get her as close as humanly possible. Perhaps, even un-humanly. Who the hell knows what our connection is and where it comes from? We were born continents apart and yet managed to find each other.

"Anything?" Brian joins me in the room after letting the last student out and locking the door.

"No."

"Fuck, man."

My sentiments exactly.

"She's into you. I know it. Silvy even said so."

"It's complicated."

"It doesn't have to be."

I stop cleaning and scowl at him, waiting.

"Look, you dig her. She digs you. You have an outie. She has an innie. BAM!" He slaps his palms together, his fingers interlocked. "Law of attraction. Enough said."

Idiot. But he makes me laugh. "It's not that simple. I wish it were."

"Then you need to talk to her, Theo. Tell her what's up. I've never seen you so torn up." He wipes off the last mat.

"Actually, I've never seen you give a shit about any girl. So, the fact that you've been a bigger grump than normal means something."

"Arse." I throw him his water bottle.

He catches it without even looking. "Takes one to know one." He smirks and throws the dirty towels at me. "Seriously. You leave a woman to stew too long, and the story she tells herself in her head gets all tangled up. You need to set the story straight. Be sure she knows where you stand. What you're offering. What you're not." He hits me on the shoulder as he passes. "She's not talking to Silvy. So, she's either talking to someone else, which Silvy doubts, or she's stewing. And a stewing woman is a dangerous woman." He winks as he exits the room. "Don't set her loose on the world. Go get your woman and save the rest of us mere mortals."

Mere mortals? God, did he have to use those particular words?

"Come have a beer and think about it," he calls from the front.

I could use a beer to unwind and figure out my next move. "Yeah, alright."

Chapter 8

THE KNOCK ON MY DOOR AT nearly ten at night has me jumping off the couch, clutching the phone, ready to call 9-1-1.

I scan the room, quietly listening, not moving toward the door.

My cell phone pings with a text.

Theo: *It's me. Please open the door so we can talk.*

The last time he said we needed to talk I ended up straddling his lap and grinding on him like I lap dance for a living.

Me: *I don't think that's a good idea.*

"I promise, I only want to talk." His voice filters through the door.

I move closer, hovering, calmed by the fact that it's *him* on the other side and not anyone else.

"Please, Lauren. Don't make me wait out here all night."

I disarm the security system, then unlock and open the door. His troubled brow is the first thing I notice before relief floods his face.

The knot in my stomach, the one I've carried around since I pushed him out, eases with one panty-dropping smile.

"Would you really stay out here all night?"

He closes the gap between us as if no time has passed. "You bet your beautiful, sexy arse I would."

I grip his jacket. "You haven't seen my *arse*," I tease.

His hands grip my hips. "Ah, but I've sure felt it, and I've a braw imagination." The gleam in his eye softens to worry. "May I come in?"

"Yes." I step out of his embrace, missing him more than I have these past nine days. I've been a stubborn fool. I regretted sending him way before he even drove off. But embarrassment over my behavior kept me from calling. And when that morphed into complete sadness and loss, I blamed myself for screwing it up. Pride and fear of rejection kept me silent.

Without my prompting, he locks and resets my alarm. Turning, he must catch my surprise. He motions over his shoulder, stepping toward me. "You wanted it armed, correct?"

I nod and move to the kitchen as he slips off his coat, setting it on a dining room chair.

"Drink?" I offer.

"Water, please."

I skitter around like a nervous cat, grabbing a glass, then heading to the fridge. "Ice?"

His eyes lock on me, smiling. "Yes."

He takes a long drink from my offering, scanning my face, settling on my captured bottom lip. He sets the glass aside, and his large hand wipes any remaining moisture from his mouth, casually running that hand down his jean-clad leg. He steps closer, reaching out to free my lip, but stops short of contact. His hand drops to his side. "I'm sorry for the other night."

My cheeks heat at the memory. "I'm the one who's sorry, and...embarrassed." Humiliated. Ashamed. The list is endless.

His groan is pure agony to the thundering pulse between my thighs.

He steps into my space, two fingers lifting my chin. "Embarrassed? Why?"

I cant my head, my eyes flickering toward the living room. "That...that woman was not me. I have never...would never be so forward."

He frowns, his eyebrows nearly meeting in the middle. He opens his mouth to speak, then stops. One brow quirks. "Never?"

I shake my head vehemently. "No. Never."

Never.

Never.

Never.

As I step around him to flee the kitchen, his hand captures mine, pulling me back. Anybody else would have my heart beating in fear, but this man has it beating fiercely for a whole other reason—which is just as scary.

His hands grasp my shoulders, his front presses to my back. He leans down. "I know things moved rather quickly. Got out of hand—scared you to the point where you felt you needed to push me away. *That* is what I'm apologizing for." One arm wraps around my waist. The other hand turns my chin to meet his heated gaze. "What I'm not apologizing for is seeing you orgasm at the touch of my hand, devouring your mouth, and watching you—feeling you—grinding against my cock."

A whimper escapes my lips, and I squeeze my eyes shut. His dirty words and the memory of the other night dance in my head.

"Bloody hell." His hand caresses my cheek. "Are you envisioning it now?"

Spinning me around, his lips capture mine. We crash against the entryway closet. I gasp for air as my hands find purchase on his heated, toned body. He clasps my thigh, bringing it up and over his. My hips grind, trying to make contact. He's too tall. I groan my frustration, our bruising kiss eating it up, his hardness crushed against my stomach.

Then—nothing.

His warmth—gone.

I'm bereft.

I clutch my chest, trying to catch my breath as he stands in the entry of my kitchen, hands braced between the wall and counter, panting.

"Fuck." His eyes roam my body. "I didn't mean for that to happen." His breaths deepen as he shakes his head. "I swear to you, Lauren. I did not come here for that." He swallows, his Adam's apple bobbing, making me want to suck on it.

I shake my head and wobble my way to the couch, plopping down rather ungracefully.

A moment later, he sits in the adjacent chair. "After class on Wednesday, I wanted to take you out to talk. I was— am—elated to have found you, and needed to explain why I didn't meet you after the marathon."

The sexual haze that seems to stifle my brain function when he's around lifts ever so slightly, enough for me to realize I never did hear why he stood me up. The fear of being recognized by that man and the reporters overshadowed my hurt of Theo not showing.

"But then…that…thing happened between us at the restaurant, and it all became a lust-induced encounter." He fingers his hair, confusion marring his handsome face. "I can't explain what's happening to us." He stands and paces in front of the fireplace. "I've never felt this kind of connection before." He eyes me speculatively. "I might not understand it, but I sure as hell don't want to give you up."

"You don't?" I know he's here. He was brave enough to reach out to me when I couldn't.

He rushes to sit on the coffee table in front of me, clasping my hands. "No, Lauren. I've tried giving you the space you need, but I don't believe that's what you need or really want. I think you're scared. I scared you." He motions between us. "This all-consuming energy between us scares you."

"I'm afraid to believe it's real—that you're really here wanting me."

He cups my neck, leaning till his forehead meets mine. "I've been miserable without you."

"Me too." When he's here in my presence, that admission seems so easy.

"Thank fuck," he all but growls. His relief makes me smile and sends my heart soaring.

He pulls back, his hand gliding down to hold mine. "We need to get a handle on it—"

"On what?"

He motions between us. "This attraction. It's nearly impossible to resist, but we must." A mischievous smirk tips his lips. "Well, perhaps not resist it entirely, but enough to be able to have a conversation and remain in each other's presence without mauling one another."

He sits beside me, turning my hand palm up on his thigh, and runs his fingers up and down the sensitive underside of my arm. I gasp at the shudder his touch produces. "Or be able to touch you without throwing you into an orgasm." His reverence conveys he's as surprised as I am that that's even possible.

Out of pure selfish preservation, I pull my arm back. "Why did you stand me up after the race?" If we're going to get back on track and talk, this is as good a place as any to start.

He nods, leaning back, allowing space to fill the void between us. It's a void I desperately want to broach in order to feel his touch—his body—again.

"When my race started, I watched you for as long as I could, looking back, seeing you standing there, growing smaller in the distance, until…you were gone. My mind wasn't in the race. It was at the finish line, waiting for you. I should have never run. I should have stayed, whisked you away, or run the 5K with you." He taps his right knee. "I was unfocused—a menace. I was on the ground in a three-person pile-up before I even realized what had happened. A bloke fell in front of me. I tripped over him, falling arse over tea kettle, and then the guy behind me fell on both of us."

"Oh, no." I feel bad for the doubt and negative thoughts I had about him standing me up. "I'm so sorry."

He squeezes my hand. "I'm the one who's sorry. I got off easy with a bump on the head and five stitches in my knee. Though the others were worse off, the medical team insisted we go to the hospital to get checked out. Particularly because of the blow to my head." He moves closer, tilting my chin to meet his eyes. "I swear, if I could have been there, I would have. It was after midnight before I got home. I couldn't call you because I lost your number. Somewhere between you giving it to me and my trip to the ER, I lost it."

It all makes sense. "I lost your number too. I guess we should have written it on our bibs as that did make it home with me."

Though tempted, I know I wouldn't have called him. *Would I?*

"I should have tattooed your number on my arm." The intensity of his stare makes me believe he's entirely serious. "I've found you now. I'm not letting you go."

We manage to make it through a movie without a single orgasm between us. Though a bit awkward at first, we slowly settled into the couch, close but not touching. As the evening progressed, getting up for drinks, snacks, or visits to the loo, we inched closer and closer. Now, Lauren is cuddled into my side, her head on my chest, her arm wrapped around my waist. Her warm body and tantalizing scent soothe me in ways I've failed to experience before.

The need to claim her—and be claimed *by her*— is sated by simply having her in my arms. The agony of her absence is all but forgotten.

As the fireplace burns, reflective light dances around the room. It's quiet and peaceful. Our breaths mingle. The beating of her heart is in sync with mine. The air is thick with reverence. It's as if the world stands still in recognition of our tangible connection, as if two souls meant for each other have finally found their mates—their home. And the universe sings a joyous song in silent benediction.

I can't explain it, but I sure as hell feel it.

The credits roll on the screen. I have no idea how the movie ended. My reverie breaks when Lauren sits up and stretches. A chill replaces the warmth from her body.

"It's late." I tease a curl and watch it bounce back into place.

She yawns. A sheepish smile follows. "Sorry."

"I should leave—" The last thing I want to do. "—and let you get to bed."

"Okay." Disappointment mars her face, but it thrills my soul that she doesn't want me to leave.

I lean in and kiss her warm lips, nuzzle her cheek with my nose, and whisper in her ear, "Believe me when I say, leaving is the last thing I want to do."

Her smile lights up her eyes. "Good."

I chuckle and stand. "But it's the right thing to do." I grab my coat, putting it on. "I have a faculty thing tomorrow. Would you come with me?"

"A *faculty* thing?"

Bloody hell. I've really mucked this thing up. "We've really gone about things in the wrong order, haven't we?" I pull her into my arms. "I'm a professor at SMU. I have a faculty party tomorrow. It's a yearly event, and it would be frowned upon if I missed it, but I really don't want to go this weekend without seeing you. Would you go with me?"

Her stunned look and silence have me on edge.

"Let's start over tomorrow. A proper date. A proper first kiss. We'll talk about what we do for a living, our families, our childhoods. Get to know each other in a way we've failed to do thus far."

Say yes.

She blinks a few times, crinkles her brow. "A professor?"

I laugh. "Yes."

"At SMU?"

"Yes."

"As in *Southern Methodist University*? *That* SMU?" Her eyes couldn't get any wider if she tried.

"The one and the same." I can't hide my amusement.

"A professor of what?"

"Philosophy."

"Wow." She swallows and steps back. "That's...that's impressive."

I step forward. "It's really not."

Her fingers toy with her hair.

What is she thinking?

"What kind of party? I mean, do spouses come? Is it

formal? I'm not sure—"

"I'm sure." I pull her close. "I'm very sure I want you with me. The party is plus-one, so spouses, significant others, boyfriends, girlfriends attend. You won't be out of place, if that is what you're worried about. It's a cocktail party, so a suit and a dress are appropriate."

Silence.

I could buy her a dress if she doesn't have one. Maybe that will prompt a *yes*.

"Okay," she answers.

"Okay?"

She nods.

I let out a punch of air. "Aces."

She said *yes!* I want to fist pump in celebration.

We discuss the particulars before I lead her to the door. "Lock up after me." I know she will, but I need to ensure she does.

I need her safe and secure. Not just for her sake but for mine.

"I will."

"I'll call you in the morning." I press my lips to hers one last time, needing the connection. Soft. Gentle. "Goodnight, baby."

She gives me a crooked smile, clearly amused at my term of endearment. "G'night, Theo."

Chapter 9

I'M HAVING A LAZY MORNING. **I** slept in and am lying in bed for a while after waking to a text from Silvy.

Silvy: *You alive? Theo wasn't happy you no-showed another class.*

Me: *I know. He showed up here last night.*

Silvy: *What? Calling. You'd better answer!*

I've barely read her text before my home phone starts to ring. I love that she knows I prefer to talk over my landline than my cell phone.

Answering, her squeal of excitement greets me. "Sweet baby Jesus. He really came over last night?"

"G'morning, Silvy," I singsong, knowing it'll drive her crazy.

"Don't 'good morning' me. It's girl-talk time. Spill. Did you know he was coming over?"

I laugh and roll sideways, stretching on a groan. "Nope. He just showed up."

"Wait. Is he still there?" She gasps. "Oh my god, is he lying next to you? Holy shit, tell me he's still there."

She's so darn hopeful. I hate to break it to her. "No. He left last night like a perfect gentleman."

"Darnit!"

"But…" I pause to ensure I have her attention.

"But? But what?" Her impatience brings a smile to my lips.

"We're…"

"What! What? Quit teasing me and spit it out already."

"…going out tonight. To a work thing."

The shriek that comes through the phone has me pulling it away from my ear until I'm sure my eardrums are safe. "Are you done?"

"A work thing? His, I assume, since we don't have a

work thing tonight."

"Yes, his. He's a Professor of Philosophy at SMU. It's a faculty thing."

Her reaction to Theo's job is identical to mine: shock and awe. I've never known a professor, and neither has she. It's right up there with being a doctor or a lawyer. And this professor teaches self-defense classes in his spare time. Seriously?

Once we're past the career revelation, we move on to a key detail of vast importance—what will I wear. The only thing I know for sure are my new glittery purple pumps with gold heels. They were an indulgence, and I haven't had an opportunity to wear them. I have a black dress with a shimmery purple skirt overlay that's cocktail-worthy. I think they're a match made in heaven.

Hours later, I've eaten, fussed over my outfit, and am currently knee-deep in my closet trying to find my little black clutch. Apparently, the less used it is, the more buried it becomes. I need a bigger closet.

My phone rings. In a mad dash to catch it before it goes to voicemail, I don't even bother check the caller ID. "Hello."

"Good morning, beautiful." The tantalizingly deep British-accented voice sets my heart racing.

"Hi." I totally fan-girl sigh. "Good

morning…handsome." I smirk. If he can call me beautiful, I can call him handsome.

His chuckle sets flutters dancing in my stomach. "You think I'm handsome?"

Gorgeous. Sexy as hell. Mr. Dark and Dreamy. "Yes, but don't let it go to your head. I'm sure you have enough women fawning all over you. You don't need my adoration too."

"What if I told you yours is the only one that matters?"

Then I wouldn't believe it. Plus, he didn't deny women flock to him like his own personal nor'easter swirling around him endlessly. "I would say you're crazy." *I'd also like to hear you say it again.*

"Hmm. You're not ready to hear it. Soon, Lauren, you will be."

He's so confident. He's the kind of person whom, when he walks into a room, everyone stops and notices. I can't imagine what it's like to be able to command attention simply by entering a room. And then have the confidence to take it in—accept it. I would shy away. I don't like being the center of attention, but that doesn't mean I'm not fascinated by it, or wonder what it would be like to be that self-assured, to wield that kind of power.

"How's your day going so far?" I spin on my heels to refill my water while moving on to safer topics than his confidence and my lack of it.

A beat or two passes. I fear he won't let me off the hook. Thankfully, he does. "It's good. I slept better than I have in a few nights…"

Does he have trouble sleeping too? Does he have nightmares? Does his unconscious plague him in the dark of night?

"...Lauren?"

"Yes?"

Silence magnifies the realization that I zoned out and missed what he was saying.

"I asked how you slept." His voice is lower, concerned.

"I slept great."

Lie.

Lie.

Lie.

"I told my mum about you." He says it on a breath of air like a confession.

"What? ...I mean, you did?" Who is this man? How can he so easily tell me he cares what I think of him and also tell his mother about me? He's obviously not like most men.

"We usually speak every Saturday. She could tell something was up."

"How?"

"She said I sounded happy."

Is he not usually happy? "How does that correlate to you telling her about me?" What did he tell her? That he met some crazy, sad girl in random places, and now she's in his self-defense class? Jeez, that makes me sound like a stalker.

"Lauren?"

"Theo?"

"What's going on in that head of yours? I feel like I'm

having half a conversation with you, and you're having the other half with yourself."

Busted.

On a sigh, my gaze lands on my bare feet. My back presses to the refrigerator.

Balance.

Strength.

Deep breath in—one, two, three—deep breath out—one, two, three.

"I'm nervous. I'm out of my comfort zone here. I don't know how to take the things you say." There. At least I'm being honest. Maybe that makes up for the lie about how well I didn't, in fact, sleep.

"Take them for what they are. The truth. I don't have a hidden agenda. I know we started a little nontraditionally. I want to rectify that by starting over tonight. There's something between us. I know you feel it. I'm willing to go as slow as you need, but I'm not willing to lie to you about where I stand or how I feel. You make me happy—a fact my rather intuitive mother picked up on—and in order to not lie to her, I told her about you. It's that simple."

It sounds simple, but it's not simple at all. And the notion that I make him happy isn't lost on me. I can almost hear the wall around my heart cracking open. I press my hand to my chest. "Despite my reservations, you make me happy too." The weight I've been carrying around—for what feels like my whole life—just lightened, a little.

"See? That wasn't horribly awful to admit, now was it?" I can hear the smirk in his voice.

"No, I suppose not. Hell didn't freeze over. At least, not yet."

"If it does, I'll be right there to keep you warm." The humor in his voice has morphed into a rich hue of desire that ignites a long-ignored yearning in me to be desired for who I am—right now—not who I wish I was. Not who I would be if I ate less and moved more, if I was bolder, prettier, sexier, funnier, taller.

But the me I am now.

Broken.

And less than he deserves.

I straighten my tie for the millionth time. *It can't get any straighter. Relax.* I take a deep breath, roll my shoulders, and say a silent prayer as I knock on her door and quickly shove the bouquet of roses behind my back.

With the click of the lock, my thudding pulse pounds even harder in my ears. Bloody hell, I feel fifteen again going out on my first date, praying her dad doesn't hate me at first glance.

When the door opens, the vision in front of me

simultaneously takes my breath away and eases my nerves—remarkably. Despite our lust-crazed encounters, the mere sight of her centres me as if I've stepped into the middle of a vortex, where the chaos going on all around calms and stills.

"Hi." Her voice is a little higher than normal, and she laughs, then quiets, as her eyes sweep me from head to toe. "Wow. You look really nice."

I'm struck speechless. She's stunning in a sultry black dress. Fabric covers her shoulders and wraps her breasts— like the gifts I'm sure they are—then flares in multiple iridescent layers of purple ending at her knees. I imagine if she twirled, the skirt would float and glide around her like a tornado—a billowy, shimmery tornado—of sheer purple and black fabric. "You look incredible." *Good enough to eat.*

My eyes land on her shoes. *Bloody fucking hell.* My cock twitches. Apparently, it likes shimmery purple shoes with a peek-a-boo toe. I have no hopes of keeping my hands off her tonight. "I'm fucking doomed."

She blushes on a giggle and ushers me in.

As I pass, I bend down and kiss her cheek. "You smell amazing." It takes everything I have not to pull her into my arms and show her how beautiful I think she is.

"These are for you." I present her with the flowers, feeling like I should bow. She looks elegant and regal. Though she radiates sexiness, her dress is actually conservative, showing her curves, but not baring them for all to see. I appreciate the allure and her demure nature. *Don't forget the sexy-as-fuck shoes.*

"They're beautiful. Thank you." Nearly burrowing her face in the flowers, she inhales deeply. "They smell so good. Are these Princess Diana Roses?"

I smile at the thought. Out of all the roses, I may have picked the ones named after a British Monarch. "I have no idea. I chose them because of their pink to peach hue and fragrance."

"They're exceptional." She pins me with her gaze. "Thank you. It means a lot—you buying me flowers."

Flares of pride heat my chest. "It's my pleasure."

She works through the two dozen roses, unwrapping and clipping the ends, carefully arranging them in a glass vase, commenting on every one being beautiful, perfect, and sweet-smelling. Her reverence has me wanting to go out and buy her dozens more.

She sets them on the bar overlooking the dining and living rooms, futzing a moment more. "There. Perfect." Her smile lands on me. "No one's ever bought me flowers before." Her eyes glisten as her hand grasps my shoulder. Bracing herself, she rises on her tiptoes to kiss my cheek. "Thank you," she whispers.

Leaving me speechless once again, she steps out of the room to collect her bag.

How can I be the first to buy her flowers?

On the way to the party, I ask her how that's even possible.

"I suppose that's not entirely true. I've gotten flowers when I've been in the hospital. But you're the first guy to buy me flowers that...well, weren't a get-well gesture."

Hospital? "The guys you've dated are idiots."

She laughs. "No argument there."

"So, you've been in the hospital then?" I glance over to gage her reaction.

Her eyes stay trained on the road, her posture rigid as if expecting a blow. "A few times."

The idea of her being sick—or hurt—guts me and feeds my need to protect her. "Maybe you could tell me more about it." I grab her hand and squeeze. "When you're ready."

Her shoulders relax on an exhale. She turns towards me, placing her other hand on my arm. "You said we should talk and get to know each other tonight. Maybe during the party, we could play twenty questions. Discreet, quick conversations about the questions, each of us having to answer the same question we ask the other."

"That sounds like a great idea." I pull my hand away to turn the wheel. "When do we start?"

"As soon as we enter the party."

Chapter 10

I **TOSS MY KEYS TO THE** valet in exchange for a ticket, pocketing it as I sweep around the car to Lauren. Once again, she didn't wait for me. "I was coming to open the door for you."

"Oh, well, now you don't have to." She fidgets with her coat.

"I don't do it because I *have to*. I do it because I *want to*," I chastise, taking her hand, leading her to the grand entrance. "Let me be the gentleman my parents raised me to be."

A quick tug on my arm pulls me to face her heart-melting eyes that inspect my furrowed brow. "I don't want to be any trouble. It's easier—faster—if I open my own door, pull out my own chair. It's not a reflection on you."

Moving into her space, ignoring the arrival of other guests, my hand skates across her warm cheek before sinking into her hair. "It *is* a reflection on me. In this day and age, a woman doesn't need a man to support her. She doesn't even need a man to have a baby. *You* don't *need* me to take care of you, but I *want* to. I want to open doors for you. I want to seat you. I want to hold your hand, touch the small of your back, run my fingers across your skin and kiss you lightly on the cheek. I want to do those things because I care for you. I honour you, not just as a woman, but as *my* woman."

She takes in a quick breath, her eyes glistening.

Christ, what daft pricks has she known in her life?

"Theo." It's only my name, but on *her* lips, it packs a wallop of meaning.

"Shh." I kiss her cheek. "None of that." I pull back, my chest tight with emotion and full of my need for her, for what she represents—a second chance. "Come on, no more dallying. Let's go inside so I can show you off."

With a nod, she turns to the door. "Whose house is this, anyway?"

"Dean Hightower's. Impressive, isn't it?"

"Yes, quite," she whispers, taking in the grandeur that is

status quo for this particular Highland Park neighbourhood. My house is in a quaint part of Highland Park that hasn't been overrun by mansions that span three to four lots each.

As we enter, our coats are checked, and we're directed to the opulent living room. A bit over the top for my tastes, but I'm not a dean, nor have I the need to impress anyone besides the beauty at my side. Before we reach the entryway, I lean down and kiss her temple, whispering into her golden mane, "In case I forget to tell you, I had a great time tonight."

She looks at me, eyes wide with surprise but quickly softening in understanding—I'll have a good time with her no matter what we're doing, no matter where we are, as long as she's with me.

"Don't be nervous. You look gorgeous. They're going to love you."

I'm going to love you.

Before she can respond, a familiar lanky form with strikingly white hair approaches, his dutiful wife at his side. "Dean Hightower." I shake his hand. "Mrs. Hightower." I kiss her cheek.

Stepping back, I press my hand to the curve of Lauren's back. "May I introduce you to Lauren Frasier. My girlfriend."

The Hightowers' brows raise in interest, looking between Lauren and me. I've always come stag to these functions. Never with a woman on my arm—or in my life, for that matter.

Lauren sends a questioning glance my way before laying her full, heartwarming smile on my boss and his wife. "It's a pleasure to meet you both."

"The pleasure is all ours, dear," Mrs. Hightower beams.

They shake hands, give kisses on cheeks, make small talk about what a lovely home they have. Blah, blah, blah. I already want to whisk her away for some *me* time. My need to explore the buzz that's been hammering between us since I entered her apartment has only grown with the demand to be friendly and social—my grumpy professor persona locked away. Granted, Lauren's magnetic pull eases when she is close, and calms when we touch, but it's a constant effort to remain composed and sufficiently dressed for a public outing.

The group around us grows exponentially. Apparently, news of me, the British Arsehole Professor, bringing a woman—much less my girlfriend—to a work function is of great interest. We're drawn into separate dialogues, but I keep a keen eye on her, ready to pounce if she needs saving.

As she converses seamlessly with my peers and co-workers, looking my direction occasionally—but not enough for my liking—my uneasiness grows. She seems unfazed by our distance. If she's feeling the same buzzing in her bones that I am, she is doing a better job of hiding it.

"You okay, man?" Marcus joins our little group.

"Aces."

He laughs, leaning in. "She's surviving without you." His eyes sweep over the group and then back to me. "Is that what's got your *knickers in a twist*?" His fake British accent is for shite.

I merely grunt in response.

"Are you going to introduce me, or will I have to do that myself?"

"Professor Wade." Dean Hightower interrupts my darkening thoughts, stepping between Marcus and me. "Excuse us, Marcus. There's someone I'd like Theo to meet."

"Of course." I glance at Lauren, getting her attention, mouthing *I'll be right back.*

Worry flits across her face before she schools it away and smiles, nodding her acceptance. She's really good at that. Hiding. My gut churns, remembering that stoic façade gliding across her face ten days ago, right before her walls slammed shut and she attempted to end our relationship.

"Keep an eye on my girl." I pat Marcus on the back and follow Terrance through the throngs of people. My hand presses to my chest, the ache growing with every step I take away from her.

Half-listening to the group of ladies I find myself in the middle of, my mind replays meeting Theo's boss, Terrance

Hightower, and his wife Minnie. They spoke highly of Theo, as if they really knew him beyond the normal boss-employee dynamic. Each person I was introduced to seemed as surprised as the last that I was connected to Theo in any way, shape, or form. He took it in stride, but I could sense his agitation growing.

Maybe he regrets bringing me.

We only just started seeing each other, and here he is having to put a title on our connection. Perhaps he's not ready to call me *girlfriend*. He certainly disappeared quick enough after.

One of the wives, whose name I can't remember for the life of me, nudges my shoulder. "How did you snag Professor Wade? He's the hottest bachelor on campus." She giggles. "Oh, and that accent. Oh my." She fans her face.

Seriously, lady, aren't you married? "I'm lucky, I guess." I smile through my nerves, feeling uncomfortable and judged by the wives.

I'm not worthy of him, and they know it.

"I'd say *he's* the lucky one." A purely male voice comes from behind before slipping into our group, standing at my side, offering his hand. "Marcus Henry, Associate Dean at Meadows School of the Arts at SMU." He kisses my proffered hand, a devilish smirk on his face. "And a good friend of Theo's." His voice is smooth, lyrical. He's tall with shiny black hair and green eyes that sparkle like emeralds. He's dashing in his well-tailored black suit, sophisticated— regal—someone well-bred, groomed for this type of social scene. I'm envious of the grace he emanates. I imagine he's rarely nervous or caught off-guard.

"Hello, Marcus. It is nice to meet you. I'm Lauren Frasier. You're quite the flirt, aren't you?" I like him already.

He leans in, whispering, "I only flirt with the prettiest woman in the room." His enjoyment increases as the blush rises on my cheeks.

"Marcus," another wife interrupts, "with Theo off the market—*for now*—you're the top bachelor among the faculty." She pats his chest, fanning her eyelashes, shamelessly flirting.

The thought of them ranking single men like meat rubs me the wrong way, and the fact that she thinks what Theo and I have is temporary—true or not—sends me into defensive mode. "I imagine Marcus has no need for such Paleolithic competitions. I doubt he or any of the other men on your list are hard up for company or appreciate being thought of in such a manner."

The women harrumph at my pointed remark.

Shit. I shouldn't have said that.

Marcus suppresses a laugh, squeezes my arm, and winks before addressing the ladies. "Actually, Theo passed the baton off to me the other day. Happy to relinquish the title. *Permanently.*"

Well, I guess *he* doesn't think Theo and I have an expiration date. I like him even more now.

"I'm sorry," I whisper while the women talk around me.

"Don't be. I rather like my honor being defended." He smiles like he has a secret. I want to know what it is, but I don't have the guts to ask.

Marcus and I talk quietly until the wives interrupt, insisting he join their conversation and not selfishly keep his attention solely on me. I am temporary, after all—not actually said but inferred.

After listening to their banter for a few minutes, I excuse myself, exiting the room in search of a restroom—any excuse to leave and regroup.

I wander, people-watching, avoiding eye contact or any interaction other than a passing smile or hello. This place is massive with halls leading to other halls and rooms. I feel like a mouse in a maze trying to avoid a trap, my unease growing with each passing turn.

I end up in another endless hall and freeze.

Theo steps into the hallway from the other end. His eyes land on me, and the smile that diminishes his chiseled scowl lights up the walls, awakens the butterflies in my stomach, and soothes my frayed nerves.

"There you are." His relief is apparent.

"Here I am." My feet are stuck, pinned by his hungry gaze. All I can do is wait for my gravitational pull to lure him closer.

Closer.

Stopping within inches, his hand captures mine. "I couldn't find you."

The emotions in his words reel me into the fantasy that he's been looking for me longer than just this evening—that he's been searching for me since we first met in that caffeine-laden cafe. Or maybe even his whole life.

"I haven't been hiding." I've been looking for him too—tonight and every day since our initial life-altering encounter. Though I've fought it, my heart still searched for him—longed for him.

His free hand cups my face, his thumb caressing my cheek. "Are you sure? It seems you're avoiding the party."

Truth. He sees right through me.

"I…yes, perhaps I am." I glance down the hall. "I'm trying to find a less crowded bathroom." It's true, only not the only reason.

"Come." He leads me down a long hall, stopping in front of a door, and knocks. With no response, he opens it, motioning me inside, and then closes it, remaining in the hall.

It's a small sitting room with a couch, a chair, and a mirror. The adjoining room is a bathroom. I might as well take advantage of the facilities while I'm here. I close and lock the door. After washing my hands, I quickly check my make-up—no adjustment required—and pop a tic-tac.

Theo is waiting for me in the hall, his eyes on the door, lighting up as soon as I appear. He kisses me on the cheek. "Wait here. I'll be only a moment."

When he reappears, I'm leaning against the wall, my hands flat on its cool surface, my eyes locked on his.

"Miss me?"

"Yes." The truth is easier than hiding behind a lie. I've ached for him since he left me in the living room among strangers eerily fascinated by his relationship status and my ability to ensnare him.

He smiles and nods. "Me too." Stalking closer, the flat of his hand presses into the wall above me, caging me in. "I'm sorry I left you alone. It won't happen again."

Pressing closer, his other hand caresses my neck, his thumb slowly tracing my chin and the underside of my bottom lip. My heart hammers to get to him. I'm not sure if it's treacherous or too intuitive for its own good.

"You seemed agitated when I first found you. Did something happen?" His gaze flicks to my mouth before returning to mine.

"I met Marcus."

He frowns. "He upset you?"

"No." A smile breaks free. "I quite like him, actually."

His face lights up. "I'm glad. He's a good bloke, one of my best mates."

"That's nice. I left him talking to a bunch of the wives. They were rather curious about you and me."

"Yes." His hand draws down my arm coming to rest on my waist. "What else?" His brow rises, punctuating his question.

"Imayhavesaidsomethingthatoffendedthem," I rush out.

His chuckle relaxes my shoulders and eases my worry. "I doubt that." His hand on the wall lowers to play with a curl at my nape. Leaning in, he presses it to his nose. "I love how you smell." His mouth, whisper-close to mine, has me swallowing a moan. "I can't imagine you offending anyone." He eases back. "What happened?"

I fill him in on the most-eligible-bachelor debacle. His

eyes glow with amusement the entire time. When I finish, he simply says, "Well done."

"You're not upset?"

"No, not in the least. It's a sexist discussion I've encountered since my arrival four years ago. I doubt they even realize how inappropriate it is."

"I'm quite sure they would have a thing or two to say about it if the men on the faculty were ranking the wives in such a manor," I huff.

"I couldn't agree more. I've endured it, not wanting to make waves."

"And here I am rocking the boat."

"A boat that needed to be rocked."

"Yeah?"

"Yes. What else?"

"Nothing else."

"There's more. You gave me a look when I introduced you to the dean and his wife."

"Oh...uh..." I glance down the hall, not really sure how to proceed.

"Hey." He squeezes my waist and tips my face to his. "Don't hide from me."

"I was surprised at how you introduced me, and then you seemed agitated when all your co-workers came up to greet us." I shrug, desperately wanting to look away, but I keep his gaze, his brown eyes so open and giving—not a wall in place. "I thought maybe you regretted what you said."

"You're talking around it. What did I say?"

"You know."

"I want to hear you say it."

"You called me your girlfriend." I bite my trembling lip, hating my damn sensitivity. Can't I have one serious conversation without it resulting in tears—and why always mine? Doesn't anyone else ever cry?

"Baby." His arms wrap me in a hug. "I should have asked you, I'm sorry. I didn't want to introduce you as a *friend* or only as *my date*. You mean more to me than what either of those two terms represent. I just got you back, but I want you to be my girlfriend. Exclusively. Only us."

I swallow around the lump in my throat. "Exclusive?" I tilt back to see his face. "You're giving up sex for me?" I cringe as the words leave my mouth. I should own them, but I feel guilty as hell asking him to give up something that I'm quite sure he's amazing at.

His forehead meets mine. "I'd be celibate for eternity if it means I'm celibate with you."

"Theo, I can't ask—"

"You can. I'm hoping celibacy isn't quite what you're asking for, but I'll take you any way I can get you. Just don't shut me out again."

The plea in his voice matches the ache in my chest. "I won't, and I'm not asking for celibacy. I mean…you know—"

"We've already broken that barrier," he offers.

"Yes, I'm okay with doing *stuff*. I only want to wait for—"

"Intercourse. Relations. Insertion. Shagging." His teasing smile is adorable and only grows with each word.

"Ugh, yes, all of those." I roll my eyes. "Until marriage."

"Deal." He holds out his hand to seal the deal. "On one condition."

My gaze flits between his hand and his glorious face that is lit up like a kid on Christmas morning. "And what's that?"

"Say yes to being my girlfriend."

"Didn't I already?"

"No."

"Oh. Well then, yes."

He leans in, his handshake forgotten. "Aces." His lips graze my cheek. "In the vein of this being our mulligan date, I'd like to jump ahead to our first kiss and seal the deal."

"Please."

My heart races in response, or maybe in anticipation. He kisses the nape of my neck, his lips moving tenderly up to my ear as his hard body reduces the air between us. His arousal, firm against my stomach, has me shuddering with need. I clasp his waist under his jacket, anchoring me to him—or him to me. Either way I'm not letting go.

His thumb swipes across my mouth—removing my lip gloss—his fingers tip my chin. "So beautiful," he whispers before his mouth captures my gasp in an all-consuming kiss that is gentle, yet demanding.

Our quickening breaths mingle as our arms pull each other impossibly close. Mouths, teeth, tongues nip, suck, and explore.

Slow and then fervent.

Tender and then hard.

Blissful and then urgent.

His hand moves down my back, squeezing my ass as my hand glides up his shoulder, sinking into his hair. A gentle tug has him moaning into my mouth, grinding his hips against me.

"Bloody fucking hell," he pants, pressing his forehead to mine. "Kisses to end all kisses."

"You can say that again."

"Bloody fucking hell, you kiss like a dream."

I stiffen at a voice down the hall, bringing me back to reality. "What if someone sees us?"

"Then they'll think I'm one lucky man." His voice crackles with desire. He's still holding me tightly. His breath sends chills along my body.

I slide away, releasing him reluctantly. His hands hold on until I'm out of reach. I give us both time to recover by slipping into the bathroom to fix my lips.

When I come out, he looks sheepish. "You alright?"

I touch his face, his barely-there whiskers tickling my palm. "I'm perfect."

He clasps my hand. "Yes, yes you are."

"Theo." I shake my head, feeling the heat crawl up my neck.

"Come. Let me feed you." Ignoring my blush, he leads us back to the party.

The haze of our kiss keeps my nerves at bay and the want strumming through my body.

Bloody fuckin hell is right. That was one hell of a kiss—mulligan or not.

Chapter 11

"FIRST KISS?" I WHISPER IN HER ear as we fill our plates from the buffet.

"What?" She giggles, her mood much improved, and pops a cherry tomato in her delectable mouth.

"Twenty questions," I remind her. "How old were you when you had your first kiss?"

She laughs again, her lightness of spirit warming my soul. "No *do you have siblings? Are your parents still married?*

What do you do for a living? You jump right into first kiss territory?" she teases.

I feed her a grape, leaning in. "I could have asked your favourite sexual position."

She coughs, nearly choking. "Shit." I pat her back. "Sorry." I guide her away from the crowd, abandoning our plates.

Her hand waves, brushing off my apology. "It's okay," she manages before taking a sip of water and clearing her throat. "You took me by surprise is all."

"So?" I prompt, wanting her reply now that she's recovered.

"What? First kiss or favourite sexual position?" She boldens and manages not to blush.

"Yes—either." I settle on, "Both."

She peruses the room as she leans into my side. "Mark. I was fourteen." Her voice quiets as if she's freeing a long-held secret. Her eyes touch on me briefly before looking away. "He was older."

My gut clenches, not liking the idea of another man touching her, even an innocent first kiss. I frown and narrow my eyes on her. *Is she teasing me?* "How much older?"

"Is that your next question?" The crook of her lips gives away her naughtiness as she moves past me.

I follow to refill our drinks, whispering to her back, "I think follow-up questions should be allowed."

"A gimme?" she casts over her shoulder, handing the bartender her glass. "Ice water, please."

"If that means a free question, then yes." I slide in next to her, setting my glass on the bar. "For me as well. Thank you."

With drinks in hand, I guide us through the main room, waiting patiently for a response.

"Seventeen," she breathes in my ear as a colleague approaches, shaking my hand and then hers. He fawns all over my girl as I contemplate how I feel about her first kiss being three years older than her, nearly an adult. A man.

I barely pay attention as the conversation wraps up and we're on the move again. I grip her waist, pulling her close, stopping our progress as my colleague steps away. "You're saying your first kiss—when you were fourteen—was from a man nearly eighteen years old?"

Sheepishly, she looks around the room, then slowly rises to her tiptoes, facing me. "I'm saying a seventeen-year-old man-child…" She's so close our lips nearly touch, and her breath teases me more than her words. "Kissed me on the lips." Her mouth presses to mine softly, scarcely moving. The hint of a moan escapes before she pulls back—a fraction. "A tender. Slow. Sensuous. Kiss." Her lips land on mine again. My arms pull her closer. The world around us fades away. Her tongue—dear God, that sweet, decadent tongue— brushes the underside of my top lip, and I go rock hard. "His lips to mine. No tongue. Just sweet tenderness. As if…" She lowers herself, feet firmly on the floor, and steps back.

I'm in a haze—one she masterfully produced with her slow cadence, breathy voice, and sweet, sweet lips. "As if?" She needs to finish that thought.

Her hand brushes mine as she moves away. "As if…"
She looks over her shoulder and shrugs. "He cared."

As if he cared.

As if. He. Cared.

Why do those four words bother me so much?
Capturing her hand in mine, we escape the main room and
drift down a corridor. "As if he cared?"

She shrugs again, her eyes on the artwork on the walls
instead of on me. "Your turn. First kiss."

I'm not ready to move beyond *her* first kiss. "Mary. I was
Six." My response is succinct.

I open my mouth to question her further when she halts,
her brows nearly disappearing in the mess of curls on her
forehead. "Six?" she exclaims.

I step into her space, my hand caressing the curve of her
neck, my thumb tracing the contour of her jaw. "It was
puppy love. Her name was Mary. I stole a kiss—or two—
before she tattled to her mum. Who, in turn, told my mum.
And that was the end of that. I pined over her for a few
weeks, but despite what my six-year-old heart felt, I did, in
fact, survive her rejection."

"Six is so young."

My lips whisper across hers. "I learned early."

"So early."

I lean back enough to take in her astonished expression.
Her bright eyes search mine with soul-wrenching intensity.
"What do you see when you look at me?" An indulgent
question to the woman who haunts my dreams, fills my

thoughts, and surges my body into mating mode.

"Everything." A mere whisper, like she didn't mean to give it voice.

The philosopher in me wants to read so much into that one word. I want to read *everything* into it. Because when I look at her, I see my future.

I see *everything*, too.

A quick kiss on the cheek breaks the moment as I guide us back to the party. Her sigh of relief, confirming I made the right choice to silently accept her word for what I want it to mean and not dwell on it. Yet.

I find Marcus in a window-laden room, lightly fingering the keys of a baby grand piano. Guests are milling around, visiting, deep in conversation, oblivious to his covetous lust for this beautiful, melodic creature under his hand. "Do you play?"

His green eyes jump to mine as a warm smile spreads across his face. "Lauren." He leans in, kissing my cheek as I move toward him. "Did Theo abandon you again?"

"No. Well...maybe." I laugh. "Another professor wanted to talk shop." Theo tried to get out of it, but in the end told me to find Marcus, and he'd come find me as soon as he was done.

"Come keep me company." He sits on the piano bench, patting the seat, smirking. "I won't bite, but I may make you sing."

"No," I chirp, sliding in beside him. "I don't sing."

"No?" He glances at me as his fingers move gracefully across the keys, strumming the melodic creature to life. "By the stricken look on your face, I'd say that's not entirely true." The nameless tune quickly morphs into a classical song I recognize but can't name. Mozart, maybe?

"You're good." My eyes follow his every movement. "Really good," I whisper, not wanting to interfere with his concentration. But as I look up, his eyes are on me—studying me—as if I'm as complicated as the piano concerto he's playing with such ease, like it's Chopsticks.

"I'm a classically trained pianist. I've been playing since I was two, but I found the voice to be the instrument I truly love." His eyes never break our connection. "You can sing. I hear the melody in your voice."

I pause, contemplating if he's serious. He is. "You're such a liar." I bump his shoulder. "You can't tell how a person sings from their speaking voice."

He nods on a smile. "Prove me wrong. Sing something with me."

"No." My face heats as fear rises up. I can't sing in front of these people.

His voice is soft in my ear. "They don't know you. Half

of these people wouldn't know a good voice if it bit them on the ass. Besides, they're not even paying attention. No one has even glanced our way since I started playing."

I'm not sure that's true. His playing is beautiful. How could they not take notice?

He bumps my shoulder. "I'll start. Join in when you want. If you don't know the words, I'll help. I won't leave you hanging. I promise."

The song morphs into a pop tune. Before I can even fathom an answer, he starts singing. His voice—a rich tenor—fills my ears and wraps me in goosebumps. His words of being *just a man* are familiar, and when he reaches the chorus, I join in without forethought—fear set aside—sucked into his safety bubble. We sing "Stay with Me" by Sam Smith. His smile grows with each word I sing, his head shaking in disbelief, making my confidence grow. Slightly. I only join in on the chorus, enjoying every nuance of his voice as he sings each verse.

"You have a beautiful vibrato. Your voice is rich like hot chocolate with heavy cream—not water," I share as he plays the last note and before he can say anything about my singing. I nearly close my eyes when I see his lips part to speak, fearful of what he'll say. He's a classically trained professor of music. What was I thinking?

"Not nearly as lush as yours." His arm bands my shoulders, sheltering me from the praise of those around us, who, evidently, *were* paying attention. He squeezes and kisses my temple. "Beautiful."

The reverence in his voice brings the sting of threatening

tears. He sees. Nods. And quickly moves on.

"So, do you know 'Beam Me Up' by Pink?" He searches on his phone, bringing up the lyrics, and places it on the music rack before looking at me expectantly.

"I...know the song relatively well—to sing along with Pink—not well enough to sing it on my own."

His smile is tender. "I'll sing with you. We're in this together."

He's sweet and gentle. He pushes, seeing my fear but not focusing on it. He simply starts to play and expects me to sing as if it's the most natural thing for me to do—as if I'm not terrified and shaking in my proverbial boots.

If I hadn't made it clear before, let me say it again: I really like Marcus. He's a great friend to Theo and now to me. I imagine he rocks as a music teacher, err...professor, as well.

We make it through the last verse, just beginning the chorus when the room begins to heat and my skin sizzles with recognition.

Theo.

Chapter 12

FINISHING MY CONVERSATION WITH PROFESSOR HOWELL, I set off in search of Lauren. As I leave the study and turn down another hall, Marcus' singing meets my grateful ears. She must be with him.

The instant a female voice fills the air, it's like a siren song calling to me. Pulling. Demanding my presence.

I step into the solarium and freeze. Behind the piano, Lauren sits next to Marcus. Bloody fucking hell, that voice—*her* voice. I should have known she would have the voice of an angel—one that calls to me, leading me home.

My fiery gaze meets hers.

Each stride brings me closer. The look of shock, perhaps fear, crossing her face has me clasping her shoulder, pivoting to stand directly behind her and pressing my lower body to her back in reassurance. I have no doubt she can feel the bulge in my slacks. *She* does that to me.

Her voice awakens my need to claim her—make her mine—in a way I haven't felt before. Libido aside, this is a need to not only claim her heart but to shout from the rooftop that. She. Is. Mine. The woman and the voice belong with me. Pride swells at the notion and recollection that she did, in fact, agree to be mine—only not publicly as my inner caveman apparently desires.

My hand remains fixed on her shoulder, caressing gentle circles as she continues to sing in perfect harmony with Marcus. Jealousy should be pounding down my calm façade, but the fact that her shoulders relaxed the moment I touched her tells me she's in tune with me, not Marcus. She may be singing with him, but her body is thrumming with want for *me*.

I feel her arousal as if *her* blood is pumping through my body.

The song ends. The growing crowd cheers their approval, but my girl stands on shaking legs and steps around the bench, backing into my embrace.

"I've got you," I breathe into her ear, my arms wrapped around her waist. She's shaking, maybe from the high of performing—even for this small audience—but my gut says it's more out of fear.

"Where are you going? We're just getting started." Marcus reaches to pull her back down beside him.

"I think she's had enough." My tone warns Marcus not to push.

He's not one to back down. He's heard her voice. She's fed his hunger for finding hidden talent. "Ah, maybe one more." He clasps her hand. "Theo will join us." He manages to get her to settle on the bench with that. "He's quite talented, you know. Wait until you hear him sing."

Arsehole.

Her wide eyes meet mine as I move to stand beside her. "You don't have to sing if you don't want to." Though, God, I *want* to hear her sing again. I can't deny that.

I'm torn. I want to get the hell out of here, take her away from whatever is making her uneasy, yet I want to stay right here and sing with her—for a year or two—until I feel I can breathe without her voice resonating in my ears.

Marcus pulls up another song on his phone, placing it on the piano.

"You don't have to," I reiterate. *She* needs to choose, for my choices are all selfish: hear her sing or sequester her alone. I win either way.

"What song?" She's speaking to Marcus, but her eyes stay locked with mine, pleading.

Guilt tugs at me. I should get her out of here. She *wants* me to rescue her. But I can't bring myself to move. One more song. *Then*, I'll save her.

"I was thinking we'd liven things up. How about 'Home' by Philip Philips?" Marcus suggests.

Her slow blink breaks our silent communication. "Home?" She turns to him, smiling. "I like that song."

But what I heard is *I can hide in that song*. She doesn't realize there's no hiding her gift. She can sing an upbeat, fast song, but her voice will still slay it and anyone within hearing distance.

The heat bouncing around Theo's car has nothing to do with the car's heater.

It's him. It's me. Together we're combustible—but something has changed.

"Tell me what scared you." His hand has barely left mine since I stood up from the piano bench to say our goodbyes.

I ignore his question—buying time—knowing full well he won't let it go. "What did Marcus mean, *you should bring me on Tuesday?"*

His hand tightens gently, but enough for me to meet his steely gaze. "He wants me to bring you to our music group next week."

"Music group?"

His eyes return to the road then flash to me. "Why were you scared?" His intensity is palpable.

I take a fortifying breath. "I don't like to be the center of attention. It unnerves me."

He nods once. "With a voice like yours it would be impossible to not draw attention."

Voice like mine? Ear-splittingly painful—make your eardrums bleed—or decent and okay to listen to? I have no idea what he thinks of my singing.

I pull away, shifting to look out the passenger window. "Did I embarrass you?"

"Is that what you think?" The bite of his incredulous tone makes me flinch.

"I don't want to cause trouble for you."

"Bloody hell, you do. You really think that." He mutters under his breath as he makes the turn into my apartment complex.

"That's not an answer," I challenge, opening my door before he even puts the car in park.

"Fuck." I hear before I shut the door, hurrying to my apartment.

I need to get inside. Tears threaten, and I refuse to cry in front of him.

"Wait!" More cursing as he rushes toward me, his feet

pounding the pavement. "Goddammit." His body encompasses mine from behind. "Whatever you're thinking, it's false."

"I need to get inside." My voice is shaking nearly as badly as my hands.

"Here." His hand wraps around the keys. "Let me." His soothing tone wafts across my ear, his body still blanketing mine.

He opens the door and guides me inside, tucked against his chest. His lips graze my hair as he locks up and sets the alarm. "Jesus, you're shaking."

"I'm fine." I pull away, but his strong arms limit my retreat.

"You're anything but fine." He pulls me square in his arms. "But you will be."

His chin rests on my head. The thud of his heart resonates in my ear, and the ease of his breathing invites calm. "I don't need coddling." I resist.

In the blink of an eye, he steps back, leaving me wretched. I hug myself, trying to lessen the loss of his touch.

His eyes scan my face as his warm hand cups my cheek and neck. "You need coddling more than anyone I've ever met."

"What? No," I protest, knowing full well I'd like nothing more than to be fussed over by *him*. "I'm not weak. I can take care of myself."

He pulls me farther into the apartment where he silently removes our coats, his suit jacket with his tie tucked into the pocket, and hangs them in the hall closet.

Does that mean he's not leaving as soon as he can? Maybe I didn't embarrass him.

Turning, he strides back to me. "Come 'ere." Sweeping me off my feet, he's undeterred by my half-hearted protests. "Shh." His arms grip me tightly. "I need to hold you." He settles on the couch with me on his lap. "As much as you need me to."

"I don't."

He chuckles. "Ah, my Lauren, you do." He peppers my face with slow kisses before landing on my mouth. His hands grip my thigh and the back of my head as his tender lips have me sinking into his embrace and gripping his shirt.

"Any anger you felt from me earlier was not directed at you." His lips graze my ear. "You are not a burden." He leans back, his piercing eyes tugging at my resolve. "You did not cause any trouble. You did not rock the boat—except where it needed to be rocked." His hands tighten their grip. "You. Did. Not. Embarrass. Me."

"Theo." Tears threaten to break free.

"I don't know what daft fucks you've known in your life, but the fact that they've made you feel *lesser than* pisses me the hell off."

A tear skates down my cheek, and before I can swipe it away, he pulls me into a hug, his head buried in my neck. "I'm going to coddle the fuck out of you," he rasps. "You need to get right with that. The way you feel about your place in the world is *not* okay with me."

Oh, my god. This man.

He's going to break me, then put the pieces back together again.

PART THREE:

Letting Go

Chapter 13

HER STOMACH RUMBLES FOR THE THIRD time. "You need to eat." We got completely sidetracked and only had a few bites of food at the party. Even if she did eat something while we were apart, she's obviously hungry.

"I'm fine."

I'm really starting to dislike that word—*fine*. "I can order food."

She starts to protest again, and I silence her with a kiss. I press my forehead to hers, breathing in her sweet scent. "I'm hungry. You're hungry. We need to eat."

"I can make something. Do you like eggs?"

The idea of her cooking for me sends blood surging south. "I love eggs. I'm not a picky eater. I love most everything."

She slides off my lap, fixing her hemline. "You'll have to tell me what you don't like so I can avoid making those foods."

I clasp her hand, keeping her close. "What if it's food you like?"

Her lips pucker. "I guess it depends on what it is you don't like. If it's a simple side dish, then it's no biggie, but if I cook steak, and you don't like steak, it would be better to know that upfront... Then I'll make you dry piece of boneless, skinless chicken while I have a big, juicy ribeye."

She's teasing me. I like it.

I stand, pressing my body against hers. "I like my steak just as big and juicy as any Texan." My hand travels down her back, over her plump arse, and I squeeze, pulling her closer.

With a gasp, her hands land on my chest, her lips part, but before I can devour them, her stomach growls again. A pink blush crawls up her skin. And when my stomach growls in response, we both start laughing.

Moment broken...for now.

"Food." I turn her towards her bedroom. "Go change. I'll grab my gym bag from my car to change as well."

"Okay." She points in the other direction. "The guest bath and bedroom are that way. Make yourself at home."

"See you in a minute." I grab her keys from the bar and glance back. She hasn't moved. Her eyes are glued to the keys in my hand. I hold them up. "To unlock the door when I come back."

"You'll only be gone a minute or two. You don't have to lock it." The words come out of her mouth with such hesitancy it's impossible to take them as genuine.

I step back to her and gently lift her face to mine. "It would make you feel safer if I lock the door while I'm gone." Not a question. It's written all over her demeanor.

She plants a smile on her face. "That would be silly." She swallows. "You're only going to your car." Her blue eyes glisten, betraying her forced bravado.

I press my forehead to hers, closing my eyes, trying to keep the rage at bay by not thinking about *why* she's so fearful. "Will it make you feel safe?" I push, needing her to be honest.

A single nod is her only response.

"Done." I pull her into a quick hug. "Now go change."

I wait while she retreats into her room, closing the door. The first click of her bedroom door lock is no surprise, but it's the second click—as she locks herself in the bathroom— that guts me.

There are three locks and an alarm system between her and the outside world. But truth be told, a man my size could easily kick through all of them in a matter of seconds.

That thought does nothing to ease the breaking of my heart.

I need to protect her.

But most importantly, I need to teach her to protect herself.

If I looked up *resilient* in the dictionary, it would have Lauren's name tied to it somehow, somewhere. She's bounced back to her shy yet confident, teasing self in the short time it took for us to change clothes and cook breakfast for dinner. *Binner* as she calls it. My girl's clever and a bit of a dork, and I love it.

I need to know about her attack. The result of it is ever-present, but if I'm to help her move past it—more than she already has—she needs to open up and offer those details. I could ask, and I may, if she doesn't open up and tell me soon.

I'm invested—I'm in deep—and I need her in the thick of it with me. It's her information to share, if she wants to, but she needs to know that there's nothing in her past that could make me look at her differently.

I may not know the details of her life. But I know *her*. I know the curve of her face, the smell of hair, the twinkle in her eyes when she's feeling mischievous or laughing, and the sadness in them when I say something that touches her deeply, in places left empty and bruised from her past. I know the kindness in her, the selflessness of her, the goodness of her. I know her soul. Her need to be seen, to be heard, to be loved and desired.

I know her, and I want to spend the rest of my life getting to know every detail.

"Everything okay?" Her soft voice pulls me from my thoughts.

She bites a piece of bacon while pushing scrambled egg around her plate.

"Yes, just thinking." I take another bite and compliment her on a wonderful meal.

"I'll have to make you my banana pancakes. Or waffles." She smiles on the last words.

"Are waffles your favourite?"

"I like pancakes, but it's something about the texture of waffles. The crunchy outside with the soft insides. But I don't like Belgian waffles. It's plain, standard waffles for me."

Her insistence makes me laugh. "Standard waffles. Got it."

I'd like to stay the night. Let her make me waffles for breakfast—the way she likes them. The idea of sleeping next to her, holding her all night, keeping her safe, has heat radiating in my chest. I check the clock. It's barely after ten. Maybe if I keep her talking, she'll be too tired to send me home and will invite me to stay.

Or you could ask.

"You relax. I'll clean up." Before she can protest, I stand with my plate in hand, kiss her on the head, and whisk our plates away.

I set the dishes in the sink, turning the hot water on. She enters behind me and refills our water glasses. "Thank you for cleaning."

"You're welcome." I thought for sure she'd fight me on it. "Thank you for cooking."

"My pleasure."

She grabs something from the freezer and steps into the living room with our drinks. Setting that something on the sofa, she pulls a blanket from the hall closet.

"How old are you, Theo?"

Twenty questions. Seeing her all cozy on the sofa quickens my pace. "I'm twenty-eight. And you're twenty-six."

"How'd…oh, the self-defense form?"

I nod, noting the wrinkle in her brow. "And your text."

"Did you read the *whole* form?"

"I did."

"Oh." Her face downcast, she fiddles with the blanket lying across her lap.

Oh? Is she truly surprised, or did she hope I hadn't read it? Which I have—quite thoroughly—a few times.

"I suppose you want to talk about it."

The resignation in her voice has me turning off the water and drying my hands. This last pan can soak. I slowly make my way to her side, not wanting to spook her. I slide my hand into hers. "Not if you're not ready."

"But you want to know…" She ventures a glance my way. "…the details?"

I pull her under my arm with her head resting on my chest and her hand warming my abdomen. The feel of her pressed against my body is still an unexpected comfort. I want to comfort her—give her peace—and here she is doing the same for me. "I won't lie. The self-defense instructor in me needs to know so I can help you move on with the skills you need—desire—to know. The protector in me wants to know so I can beat the shit out of those who hurt you, but mostly, to keep you safe from future threats. The man in me—your man—wants to know so I can hold you close, make you feel safe, and help you cope in ways I fear you haven't but need to."

She clutches my t-shirt—clearly uncomfortable with the idea.

I run my hand up her arm, kissing her forehead. "When you're ready, Lauren. No pressure."

"How about some easier topics first?" She smiles up at me, her wide eyes hopeful.

I nod, already planning my first question. "You first."

"Last girlfriend."

I'm surprised she went right there. I figured she'd wait for me to ask about her dating history. "I've seen women since moving here four years ago, but nothing serious. No girlfriends."

"And back home?"

"I was engaged."

"What?" She sits up, pulling away but then stops. "What happened?"

"She left me for her ex-boyfriend a week before our wedding."

"She what?" Her shock and indignation have me smiling. "Is she crazy?"

I laugh. "No, not crazy and apparently not the one."

"I can't say I'm sorry. Anyone who would cheat on you isn't worth your time or effort." She settles back into my arms. "Did you pine for her much?"

I like her word choices, a bit old-fashioned, talking beyond her years. "She did quite a number on me. Messed me up. It's the reason I moved. I couldn't stand to be close to her or chance meeting. I tried dating, but no one interested me. Eventually, I stopped looking, stopped trying, and only focused on work."

"Is that why you were so standoffish in the coffee shop to that girl trying to get your attention?"

"Yes." Guilty.

"Your alter ego was on full display."

"He didn't scare you off." I tip her chin to me.

"I wasn't looking for you." She wasn't looking for a connection, so my fuck-off demeanor didn't scare her. My girl is brave.

"And I wasn't looking for you, yet here we are. Quite soundly found." I press my lips to hers, no rush, no agenda, a simple kiss of thanks for seeing past my disguise and infusing life back into my soul, air into my lungs, and shattering the wall around my heart.

I break our kiss, not wanting to sidetrack our game. "My turn." I should ask about boyfriends, but I have a more pressing question. "What did you pull out of the freezer?"

"The ice for our drinks? Oh! You mean the icepack?"

It was large enough to be an icepack, but she tucked it under her arm so quickly, the thought never crossed my mind. "You're sitting on an icepack?" *That can't be comfortable.*

Her laugh fills the air and has me smiling. "No." She swats me. "It's on my back."

"Why?"

"I fell at work a few years ago. Injured my back. Ended up having surgery. But I have permanent damage, so I use ice to minimize the discomfort."

"What happened? What kind of surgery?" A hundred questions inundate my thoughts, but I manage to only spew two. I'm relieved it's not related to the attack, but wonder if it exacerbated her injury—serving as another reminder of what haunts her.

"It's a really drawn out ordeal, more than I'm sure you want to know."

She has no idea—I want to know it *all*.

"I'll just say this: I slipped on an uneven marble floor at work, landed on my butt, and slid across the floor, hitting a floor-to-ceiling window, shattering it. Thankfully, it was double-paned or I could have fallen approximately thirty feet to the ravine below."

"Bloody hell."

She smiles as I grab her hand and pull her back into my arms. "You could have died."

"No…well…maybe. I don't know." She's flustered by the thought but dismisses it quickly. "I didn't, and that's the important thing."

My hand continues to move up and down her arm, soothing her, but really trying to stop my growing unease, thinking of what could have happened, much less what actually did happen.

"…multiple doctors, years of therapy and treatments. In the end, surgery was my best option."

I pulled a Lauren and totally checked out, more in my head than in the conversation, and missed most of her explanation. "But you're better now?"

"Better is a relative term. I'm better than I was after the accident, but I'm not *better* as in *all healed*. I'll never be one hundred percent. I'll always have pain and discomfort." She shrugs as if it's no big deal. "It's my new normal."

Fuck. I hate that for her.

"Show me."

"Show you what?" She sits up. "My scar?" She scrunches her face like I'm crazy. So cute.

"Yes." I need to see it, touch it.

"Uh, no." She stands with such grace you'd never know she was in any discomfort.

I pull her between my legs, my hands resting on her hips, looking up into the eyes of a woman who is more resilient than I fathomed.

159

"Show me." My fingers graze up her sides, sliding under the hem of her black t-shirt, over the waist of her yoga pants to find her silky skin. She gasps at the contact.

I itch to explore every inch of her. "Show. Me." The gravel in my voice reflects my need.

"It's an ugly Frankenstein's monster kind of scar. You don't want to see it." Her protest is real. She's embarrassed by her scar—the scar that signifies she survived.

"The hell I don't." I pull her shirt up, revealing the strip of skin above her pants. I lay a kiss right in the centre.

She curls into me, her hands capturing my head. "Theo," she fucking groans my name, her need ever-present and equal to my own.

Let's get naked. The idea runs on repeat, short-circuiting my intent to only *see* her scar.

My hands run up her back, caressing strong muscles covered in the softest skin I've ever felt. "God, you feel good," I murmur against her abdomen, kissing from one side to the other. Running one hand up her back, over her bra—tempted to release her breasts from their confinement—I reach the back of her neck and squeeze gently, bringing her lips to mine in a slow, sultry kiss, parting her lips with my tongue, diving in. Tasting what's mine. Letting her moans ground me to the here and now where she is safe. Uninjured.

Fuck, not entirely uninjured.

I release her. "Did I hurt you?" What the hell was I thinking having her bend over like that to kiss me?

Her heavy-lidded eyes blink a few times. "No." Her shining innocence has me smiling and wicked thoughts tempting me beyond my control.

"Good." I turn her around. "Now. Show. Me," I command, sounding more like a dick than the throbbing one in my pants. I raise her t-shirt enough to land a single kiss on her back in restitution. "Please." My breath skates across her skin.

She growls her discontent but raises her shirt, holding it under her arms as she tentatively lowers her pants to reveal what is approximately an eight-inch scar running from her waist to just above her tantalizing bum.

I run a finger down the length of the scar, ignoring her arching back—not in pain—in pleasure. "It's not bad, especially not Frankenstein's monster-worthy."

She likens herself to a monster?

Leaning forward, I press kisses along her scar. Her body trembles, and I grip her hips, holding her steady. I lave the puckered part at the top with my tongue. She murmurs something about it not healing properly there. I do it again, deeper. Small hands land on mine, her head falling back as she gasps my name.

Her skin is cool and red from the icepack, but deliciously soft under my tongue and heats me to my core.

One more pass of my lips has me groaning into her skin as her legs start to quake, and when I dip my tongue into her warm crack that's teasing the edge of her pants, her legs give way.

"So beautiful." I catch her in my lap, turning her.

Pushing back into the sofa, our mouths collide.

This moment. My entire life has been building to this moment to capture the woman who has been my vision for as long as I can remember, at her most vulnerable, sharing her scars with me, both internal and external.

I was made for this moment—for this woman.

Chapter 14

HIS TONGUE DOES NOT ASK FOR admittance, and I don't even think of denying him entry. He holds me as if I'm a precious gift—a savored treat—he cannot wait to unwrap. His hands—his mouth—caress, entice, and implore, pulling at my resolve, my sanity, my very soul.

He is my undoing, my remaking, my freedom, my glory. He represents all that I have never known—desired—but feared to seek, to believe, to dare hope existed for me.

Me.

The broken.

Less than I was…

…and more than I should be.

The one who remains when the best was lost to this world.

Taken…

…leaving me behind.

"Hey," his sex-laden voice rasps in my ear. "What happened?" Warm succulent lips graze my jaw and press to my mouth. "You were with me, and then you weren't."

My eyes shut tight, I coax him back to me, my hands tangled in his hair and pulling on his shoulder. *Don't stop,* I silently beg, a heated mess of desire and desperation.

"Shh. Calm." His hand covers mine, still tugging on his shoulder. "I'm here. I'm not going anywhere."

A satiated breath quiets my ragged emotions. I press my lips to his, my body still encapsulated on his lap, in his arms. "Promise?" I whisper to him, to God, to the universe, and the demons I struggle to keep at bay.

He chuckles. "Yes, I promise." His eyes seek mine. "If you'll let me, I'll hold you all night, into the next day, and…" His lips press to mine. "Forever," he breathes against my mouth.

He'll stay. Forever? Shocked and speechless, I can only nod.

Setting me on my feet, he stands, kisses my cheek. "Get ready for bed. I'll join you in a moment."

My feet move of their own accord, but his hand stops me at my door. Pressing in, his hand sweeps my hair off my shoulder. "I don't want you to worry." His lips graze up my neck, sending new bolts of pleasure to my core. "I didn't forget. No sex. I remember."

Maybe I should rethink that stance.

I quicken my pace and slip into my bathroom, closing the door behind me. I hesitate for only a second before dropping my hand to my side, leaving the door unlocked.

A rushed shower, tank top and boy shorts donned, I stare in the mirror, toothbrush in hand, my eyes bright, my cheeks flushed. *Forever.* His words dance across my lips, keeping me company as I brush my teeth.

When I emerge from the bathroom, Theo stands in my bedroom, staring at my bed.

"It's daunting." His eyes never leave it, but he pulls me to his side.

I press two fingers to my lips to keep from laughing. The idea of a big guy like Theo being intimidated by my bed is humorous.

"Don't laugh." He glances at me, a smile tugging at the corner of his mouth. "Do you have to get a running jump?"

The laugh I've been holding back erupts. I know he means me and not him—he's plenty tall—but the visual of him running in from the other room and leaping into the air is too funny to ignore.

"I'm serious." His crossed arms and twisted lips nearly convince me, but the mischief in his eyes gives him away.

"I have a stool." I stifle my laughter and point to said

stool on my side of the bed.

He nods, uncrossing his arms, his hand running over the silky damask comforter in rich burgundy, plum, sage, cream, and gold hues. His eyes roam the three layers of pillows. "Have you ever gotten lost in all those pillows?"

"Don't make fun of my pillows." I reach for the first few decorative throw pillows and begin tossing them in the corner.

"Me?" He moves to the other side of the bed. "I would never." He grips one of the four massive bed posts as he rounds the corner, his strong hand and long fingers not able to surround its girth.

It's a big bed, I admit. But it's my pride and joy. An indulgence from its four-poster oversized footprint, to the ornate hand-carved mahogany headboard, footboard, frame, posts, and feet. The matching nightstands, dresser, chest, and armoire complete the regal set. "A bed like this deserves to be pampered with quality linens and seductive pillows."

He stops mid-throw in helping me remove the non-sleeping pillows, his head quirking to the side as his eyes land on me. "It's not the bed that deserves pampering but the woman who sleeps in it."

Not waiting on my reply, as if what he said doesn't rock my world—like most things that come out of his mouth—he continues removing the decorative pillows.

We slip under the covers. He on his back. Me on my side. With a single arm, he pulls me into his side, encouraging me to lie on his chest and cuddle close. Without prompting, he continues the twenty questions game.

"I've failed to inquire what you do for a living." His fingers toy with my curls. "I'm sorry about that."

"You don't need to apologize. I feel like we've covered that already, but I guess we haven't. I work for KassenAir. I'm the Layout Editor for their inflight magazine. I do a little content editing as well."

I can feel his smile against my forehead. "I bet you're exceptional at it, too."

"I don't know about exceptional, but Tyler and his bosses seem pleased with my work."

"No doubt." He stiffened when I said Tyler's name— probably best not to dwell on that aspect of my job.

"Next question?" I opt to let him go again over fielding pointless questions about Tyler.

"Siblings?" His lips press to my forehead. His hands slowly caress my back and side.

"Three. Oldest brother Bobby, middle sister Nicole, and my youngest brother Timothy. Bobby and I have the same parents. My dad had Nicole and Timothy when he remarried. But I don't consider them half-siblings. I love them the same."

He kisses my brow again, squeezing me tight. "Of course you do."

I ignore the warmth his words induce. "What about you? How many siblings?"

"Four. Two brothers and two sisters: Connor, Charlotte, Christian, and Claire. All four married with children, except for Claire. She's expecting her first in July."

"How did you escape the C-name train?"

He chuckles, hitching my leg up higher over his. I close my eyes and press into him. It's intimate, yet wholly comforting, like broken-in shoes that can only fit this well after years of contact, molding to my foot and only my foot. Theo is my broken-in shoes. Doesn't sound sexy at all, and still, here I am nearly panting and rubbing against him like a cat in heat.

His hands move, pulling at me, encouraging the contact, rolling to his side, pressing into my heat all while maintaining our conversation as if I'm not burning up in his arms. "I don't know. I've never asked. As the youngest—" His lips press to my neck. "I assumed they ran out of C names."

Gah, I can't think. Question. I need a question. Mentally, I palm my forehead. *Think.* Oh! "Birthday," I nearly screech.

"December sixteenth." His muffled reply tickles my ear as his lips kiss along my jaw. "You?" he prompts when I don't reply, too lost in his touch.

"Uh…December twenty-seventh." Wait. "We have December birthdays."

"Mm-hmm." He's not even sidetracked by this revelation.

"You knew?" I push on his shoulders, forcing him to look at me.

He blinks his half-mast eyes, his hair in tousled disarray. God, he looks like great sex and rumpled morning-afters. "Your form."

Of course. "I should have had *you* fill out a form. I feel like you know more about me than I do about you."

On a deep breath, he pulls back and settles on his elbow, hovering over me, his finger tracing the rim of my bottom lip. "What do you want to know, baby?"

I shake my head, not able to lock onto a single question. "I don't know…everything?"

He nods, pressing a soft kiss on my mouth. "I'll give you everything. You ask—" his tongue snakes across my lips before sucking on my lower lip, "I'll give."

Everything? His touch—his words—have me reeling, my breath hitching. "When you touch me. I can't think straight," I confess on a whisper.

His hand cups my cheek, and knowing chocolate eyes scan my face with tender reverence. "When you walk in a room, I forget to breathe."

It's dark, grimy. The maze of cars slow my steps. Round and round I run. I can hear her, but every time I get close, believing she's around the corner—she's not.

I can't find her.

I can't call to her, or they'll find *me*. And if they find me,

I can't help her.

Silently, I run up the ramps, trying to get to the third floor. The sound of my blood rushing in my ears, the pounding of my feet, and my ragged breaths keep me company, keep me going.

Another scream.

She's fighting, yelling.

"Holly," she cries.

Holly? Why is she calling her own name?

I have to get to her. I have to save her.

I finally make it to the third floor where our car is parked and run toward the screaming.

I can see her. I can see *him*.

But she's not moving. She's not the one screaming.

I catch my reflection in a car window.

It's me. I'm the one screaming, caught in the arms of the tall blond. Crazed. Fighting.

I punch him. Without hesitation, he punches me back. The shockwave rattles my brain, and I fall to my knees. Gasping for air, I open my eyes to find Holly lying on the floor—motionless—mere yards away with the dark-haired guy moving on top of her.

"No! Get off her!" I scream. "Fight, Holly, fight."

I struggle to my feet, shaking off the dizziness and the need to retch. "Holly," I cry, stepping closer. *Please fight.*

Strong arms grip me from behind. I thrash in his hold, my battle not done. Only this time the touch is familiar. Welcomed.

My name. I hear my name and search for its source. *That voice—I know that voice.*

"Lauren," he beckons me.

Theo.

My fight wanes.

"Lauren!" His voice, insistent.

I open my eyes, coming awake. My breathing is ragged. My heart pounds in my chest, and my eyes burn as I blink, trying to focus on Theo's face.

"There you are." His heavy breath mixes with my own. "You had a nightmare."

"Theo," I croak.

"You're alright." He wipes at my tears. My hand clasps his wrist, and he tenderly kisses my fingers. "I've got you."

I sink into his chest. "I couldn't save her." My tears turn into sobs.

"Shh." He envelopes me. "You're alright."

"I couldn't get to her. When I finally did, he attacked me. I was too late. I couldn't save her. She was already dead.

She was already dead."

Chapter 15

HER SHOULDERS WRENCH AS SHE CRIES. With each jerk, my heartache grows. Anger and remorse pump through my system like poison. My imagination's on overload envisioning the horrors she experienced at the hands of her attacker. I shake with need to keep her safe and annihilate those who hurt her. My hold is so tight, I fear I may crush her.

"You're safe. I won't let anything happen to you. You're

alright." I smooth her mess of curls, kissing her temple. "I'm here." *And I'm bloody well not going anywhere.*

She burrows in, nuzzling closer. Her breathing slows with each passing moment as her tears cease and her trembling wanes.

"I'm sorry." Her muffled words warm my chest.

Pulling back, I dry her tear-stained face. "You don't need to apologize." I press my mouth to her swollen ruby lips. "Never." She's been through hell, and she's apologizing to me? There are no words to express the depth of my sorrow. The world should be apologizing to *her*.

She caresses the side of my face, her eyes glistening in the moonlight seeping through the windows. "Can I tell you about it?"

A rush of air leaves my lungs. *Thank fuck.* But the fact that she's asking—like I haven't been waiting with bated breath for her story—guts me. Tight-jawed, I manage a "Please."

Rolling to my back, I tuck her into my side, tip her chin, and lay a soft kiss on her mouth, brushing wayward curls out of her eyes. "Take your time. There's no rush."

She graces me with the sweetest teary-eyed smile that has me holding her closer, saying a silent prayer, and envisioning a future where her pain is nonexistent and all her scarred, empty places are filled with my love, new memories, and nights where I hold her just like this, but for far different reasons.

"It was seven months ago, July eighteenth. My best friend, Holly, and I went to see a friend's band that was playing at the West End." She adjusts, laying her head on her pillow, facing me.

My arms are bereft without her. I hold her hand, needing the contact. She smiles and cuddles our joined hands against her chest.

"We had a great time. It was uneventful other than the fact that Pierce, the lead singer and the guy she'd been crushing on forever, finally made a move—got some balls— and asked her out...not as friends."

A lone tear slides down her cheek and is absorbed in the pillow.

I squeeze her hand and slide closer. "It's alright," I whisper encouragement.

She nods, swiping at her eyes. "It's just—" Her voice cracks.

I plant my lips on her forehead, wanting to imbue my strength.

"They'll never get their chance." Her voice is weighted by the loss.

"One of our friends pointed out two guys staring at Holly and me. They gave me the creeps. But in a blink of an eye, they were gone. I assumed they left.

"Around eleven we headed to our car, all concern for those guys lost in Holly's excitement over Pierce." Her blurry gaze focuses on me. "I was so happy for her. They'd spent years liking each other, but neither were willing to move beyond the friend zone. It was finally going to happen for them."

I swipe at the increasing stream of tears but remain silent, letting her work through the memory.

"When we stepped out of the elevator of the parking garage, I instantly felt something was wrong." Her eyes plead with me. Whether it's to take her pain away or to understand the depth of her remorse, I'm not sure. Possibly both.

I want both. I want to take her pain away with every passing breath, but I also want to understand her remorse — her shame — for what happened to her and Holly.

"We never should've been there." Her whispered regret tugs me to her like a lifeline.

I wrap her in my arms, unable to stand the distance between us and lacking the fortitude to continue witnessing her rawness. "Don't. Regret is a hungry beast. Don't feed it. You can't change the past. But more importantly, you don't need to justify your actions to me. I believe you did all you could to save Holly. Without even knowing all of the details — I know that."

"But—"

I crash my mouth to hers. I can't. I can't listen to her beat herself up. I silence her the only way I know how, with love. Thankfully, she sinks into my kiss, giving herself over to it — to me — otherwise, I'd be a complete arse kissing a girl while she's telling me about how she and her friend were attacked. It's a dick move. *Fuck.*

"I'm sorry." I pull back, scanning her face. "I couldn't let you castigate yourself anymore."

Her fingers take purchase in my hair, and her glistening

blue eyes transfix me. "You don't need to apologize for kissing me. Ever." The quirk of her brow emphasizes her point while her tone reminds me that she might be hurting, but she's no pushover.

A *yes ma'am* nearly escapes my lips before I replace it with an, "Understood."

Her finger traces down my cheek, landing on the cleft of my chin. "I like you being protective." Her eyes flash to mine. "A lot."

The desire on her face—in the mix of all this pain—has me kissing her again. Tenderly. Slow and easy.

She pulls back on a sigh. "Save that thought." Her fingers touch my lips. "I need to get this out."

She doesn't say the rest of what I hear: *If I don't tell you now, I may never get the courage to do it again.*

A simple nod is my only response. I don't want to hijack her moment more than I already have.

"As soon as we stepped off the elevator, an alarm went off in my head. Panicked, I turned to grab Holly's arm, to pull her back to the elevator, but he was already on her—dragging her away."

Her breathing increases, her eyes focused on a spot behind me. I caress the back of her neck to keep her grounded as she continues. "Holly was fighting, but she was so tiny, it didn't seem to make a difference. I lunged at him, but I was jerked back, grabbed from behind—"

Ah, fuck. There were two attackers? How the hell would two untrained women fight off two men? On autopilot, my body

176

cocoons hers, tensing and flexing around her with the need to protect.

Her words punch through the nightmare in my head. "I broke free, turning, my arms swinging, ready to hit whoever was behind me. I clocked him on the chin, and as he stumbled, I ran for Holly. The dark-haired guy had her pinned to the ground, her skirt up. She was screaming, trying to fend him off."

Lauren flinches and closes her eyes, the vision too much. "He hit her in the face so hard her head bounced off the pavement. She went limp." She flinches at the memory as a sob escapes.

I hold her impossibly tight. "You're not there. You're here with me. They can't hurt you."

She continues as if I hadn't spoken. "He didn't stop. Even though she was unconscious, he didn't stop. He went for his zipper. I rushed him—tackled him—knocking him to the ground and off of her. He was angry, cursing me, hitting me. I fought, but he was too strong."

Her cries, buried in my neck, test my willpower. I want to scream at her to stop. I can't take any more. But I know I must—for her.

And then she breaks me with her next words. "I felt helpless—like nothing I did made any difference."

I'm back to the first day of self-defense class hearing her words. Her desire to be able to *trust her body to defend herself* and her need to *feel confident and know that she can survive anything*.

She felt helpless, and those arseholes made her feel that

177

way.

Her words continue, but I can't hear them like I should. The two guys were on her, beating her up, trying to get her to submit, but she kept fighting. My girl kept fighting. One guy held her down while the other one raped her friend. And still, Lauren didn't stop, she didn't submit, she didn't cower.

My girl survived. Holly did not.

Lauren was knocked unconscious and woke up three days later in hospital.

"I only know what happened after that based on what the police told me. A husband and wife had come upon us and hit a panic button in the garage. The alarm scared off our attackers. The husband gave chase, but the guys were too fast. The wife covered me with her sweater, and the husband gave his shirt to cover Holly. The police said they stayed, holding our hands until the ambulances and police came." Her eyes lock on mine. "They saved my life."

No. You saved your own life. I don't want to argue the point. It's about perspective, and she's too close to see that her fighting spirit is what kept her alive.

She toys with her bottom lip, her eyes full of worry.

I bury my hand in her hair, bringing her eyes to me. "What are you afraid to tell me?"

"When the couple found us, I didn't have any clothes on." Her voice cracks, and she tries to avert my gaze.

"Look at me." My thumb caresses her cheek. "Do you think that matters to me? That I would want you any less?"

The stream of tears that drop free tell me she does.

I press my forehead to hers, our noses touching, our lips a mere breath away. "The idea of these guys hurting you kills me—angers me in ways that scare me. But what happened to you in no way makes me want you less. Hell, if I'm being honest, the fact that you've survived something so horrific and remained the person you are, makes me want you even more." I rub my nose along hers. "Not less. Do you hear me?"

She nods. "Yes." Her hand covers mine. "I don't have any memory of what happened after I was kicked in the head. But based on the evidence, the police, the doctors, don't think I was raped. I don't feel like I was, but I needed you to know—it's a possibility."

Relief floods me as I release a punch of air. "Then I'm sure you weren't. But hear me again when I say, it does *not* matter to me. I will love you no matter what. It only matters in what happened to you and how you feel about it."

Her gasp and the shock on her face has me backing up. "What?" *What did I say?*

"You"—She points at me—"said love." Her brows disappear behind her curls.

It seems wrong to feel such joy after she shared the details of her attack, but I can't help it. "Yes, I guess I did. Don't freak out." My smile nearly breaks my face. "I'm falling hard for you, Lauren Grace Frasier. And I'll tell you again when you're ready to hear it."

I don't miss her adorable blush as she buries her head in my shoulder.

My girl is a survivor. She's so ashamed, yet I'm so fucking proud of her.

And apparently, I let my love for her slip free.

She'll have to come to terms with that at her own pace, like she has with the events of her past—with heart-wrenching, soul-crushing excavation.

But this time, I'll be here to soften the blow, deflect the self-incrimination, and shine a light on the truth:

She's a survivor.

…and I love her.

Chapter 16

THE MORNING LIGHT CASCADING IN FROM
the window teases me from sleep. The large hand
squeezing my breast reminds me I'm not alone. I'd
nearly forgotten.

Theo kisses my neck, the hard length of his body
warming my backside. Without thinking, I stretch on a
groan, pressing my bottom into his crotch, not considering
the stiffy there to greet me.

With a moan, he presses back, running his thumb over

my nipple, and whispers in my ear, "Good morning."

I twitch in his embrace, my body not alert enough to know how to handle the stimuli induced by his arousal and his touch.

"Morning." I yawn, burying my face in his arm that I've been using as a pillow, and lace my fingers with his.

He closes his fingers around mine as his lips continue to explore my neck, shoulder, and arm left exposed in my tank top.

Goosebumps riddle my skin, and my hips move of their own accord, shaking off the cobwebs of my dormant desire, awakening me in ways I've never known. He whispers words across my skin, his body wrapping around mine from behind, his arms pulling me closer. His hand trails under my top, pushing it up, exposing my breasts to the morning light. I throw my head back as his arms cross my chest—a breast in each palm—plucking my nipples in a rhythm that is accompanied by his grinding pelvis. My hand tugs on his hair when his lips tease and nibble the curve of my neck, sucking and kissing his way up my jaw, to my ear.

A moan escapes my lips when I hear *I want to make you come*, and I swear it wasn't said out loud. *I need to touch you* precedes his left hand abandoning my breast to slip below the band of my boy shorts. His growl as he discovers how turned on I am has my clit throbbing and my core contracting in need—begging him to fill me.

As if he heard my body's plea, his fingers tease my opening, gliding to circle my clit before pressing a delicious path back down, sliding inside.

"Oh, God." My back arches, and my hand clasps his arm that controls those talented fingers.

His moan of encouragement vibrates in my ear as his entire body picks up the pace. His mouth devours my shoulder in open-mouthed kisses while his thick erection rubs against my rear, and his fingers pinch and pull at my nipples, sending my hunger for him soaring.

Any attempt to touch him, to give him relief, is thwarted by grunts of disapproval and an elbow pushing my hand away. "You," is the only response he gives. And when his fingers start to strum my g-spot like a master harpist, my legs start to shake, and my hips jerk in minuscule thrusts on reflex.

The tingling in my legs works its way up. My eyes slam shut, but all I see is white, and the only sounds I hear are my own rapid breaths mixed with gasps and moans in ever-increasing decibels. My heart pounds in my chest like it's trying to break free. I'm reaching—begging for release—but I fear it as much as I crave it.

It's too much.

"I've got you," he rasps in my ear. "Let go, baby."

And as if on demand that tingle explodes, ripping through my body in wave after wave. I thrash and convulse in his arms, his words of praise keeping me tethered—saving me from floating away.

He eases me back to him with tender kisses, fingers still deeply seated, moving at a leisurely pace. Not fully recovered but embarrassingly aware that I'm the only one who came, I roll over. Face to face, his state of arousal is still painfully obvious. The glistening head of his penis—having escaped the confines of his boxer briefs—calls me to action.

"You don't—" His protest is lost as I wrap my hand around his velvety steel shaft. "Bloody hell," he groans on the first pump, my thumb circling the head, spreading the moisture that slips free.

His arousal has me amping up like I didn't just blow a gasket less than a minute ago. My body clenches around his fingers that are still inside me.

"Ah, fuck me," he murmurs on a groan. "So fucking hot—you getting turned on as you get me off."

Of course, his words have me contracting again. With a growl, he rolls me to my back, and his eyes devour my breasts before he bends and sucks a nipple into his mouth. His resolve to abstain falls to the wayside, and I am lost to his touch once again.

In a mass of strokes, plunging fingers, sucking nipples— both his and mine—kissing necks and anywhere else we can reach, our breaths combine, our hips thrust, and our moans rise to the heavens as we make love to each other with our hands, mouths, and hearts.

"Come for me, and see what you do to me." His words skate across my breast before he bites my nipple and sucks it deep, throwing me off the edge and into the abyss of pleasure.

I explode around his fingers as his release detonates between us, covering my hand, my stomach, and places I'm sure to discover later—in total awkward embarrassment. Only, the moment I see the contentment and adoration in his eyes, I realize that what we just shared is not some base physical release, but a joining of two souls on a collision course with destiny.

He came into my life like an anomaly, neither of us open to being seen, our hearts locked down, and the keys long misplaced. But the moment our eyes caught, it was as if we had each other's master key. There was no choice, no decision, no fear greater than our pull to be joined, to be opened, to be made into more than we are as individuals.

The pull to be one with him in heart and body is still strong. His pulsing cock, still in my hand, his fingers, still buried inside me, connect us in a way that feeds that beast, but it's not enough.

I know that now.

I don't understand it, but I'm trying to accept it.

The beast will have to be fed, or my ability to breathe, to think, to simply function at the most basic of levels will be compromised.

Only, I'm not ready. I won't compromise on that. I can't.

The beast will have to learn to be patient.

"Where'd you go?" His voice brings me back, and his thumb grazing my clit keeps my focus on him.

I squeeze his cock, and his growl has me clenching around his fingers. "I'm coming to terms with the fact that this thing between us is inescapable. There's no stopping it, is there?"

My breath catches when he begins to circle my nub.

"No, Lauren, I don't believe we can stop the force that keeps bringing us together. We're inevitable."

He slowly moves his fingers in and out. His eyes catch the pebbling of my nipples before landing back on mine. "I, for one, don't intend to fight it. What about you?" His voice is calm, not reflecting the tensing of his body and the hardening of his cock in my hand.

"Tell me now," I sigh, my body already craving more—craving everything.

His eyes flicker between mine as he tries to make sense of my request. Recognition dawns, but before he answers, he flicks each nipple with his tongue, then sucks them until I'm tipping the edge, breathing heavy, and begging for release.

He pulls back, jaw clenched. His eyes burn with desire. His fingers strum my insides as he moves his hips, his cock pulsing in my hand. His breathing increased, he presses a tender kiss to my lips before whispering, "I love you."

Damn him. His words send me flying, my body unable to respond beyond panting moans and trembling limbs.

He comes in my hand, reigniting my orgasm, and I continue to quake in a second wave, struggling to respond but manage, "I love you too." My voice is buried in the sounds of our pleasure.

We fed the beast our hearts and part of our bodies.

Maybe that's enough.

For now.

Chapter 17

THE SMELL OF WAFFLES AND BACON fills the air, making my mouth water in anticipation. She moves around the kitchen as the waffle iron steams, placing drinks, cutlery, and the normal accoutrements for a sugary breakfast on the counter for me to place on the table.

I've showered and dressed in fresh clothes—thanks to a well-stocked gym bag—and still, I feel her wrapped tight around my fingers and in my arms as she came for me repeatedly. My cock pulses at the sense memory, blood starting to rush southward.

Mayday.

I promised myself there'd be no more sex play today. She needs to know I see her as more than a sexual object. I turn my mind to my lesson plan for the week, a guaranteed way to tame my desire. Though the idea of donning my professor façade after spending the weekend with my vision has me wanting to whisk her way to a deserted island instead of fortifying myself for Monday morning.

Returning to the kitchen, Lauren hands me two plates of food and then grabs the peanut butter on the counter.

"Peanut butter?" I've lived in Texas for years now and I've yet to see anyone put a jar of peanut butter on the table. My interest is piqued.

She smiles, her eyes meeting mine only momentarily— her shyness has been front and centre since this morning's arousing events. I need to address that before I leave. I won't leave her feeling uncomfortable or regretful. But for now, she needs to eat. Things always seem better on a full stomach.

"My dad"—she motions to the table—"put peanut butter on nearly everything."

We sit, me at the head of the table and her to my left. Not my choice. I would not presume to sit at the head of her table, though that is where I want to be. She sat me here last night, and I know this is my seat today because her insulated water mug was already set on the placemat where she now sits. It's a small detail, but I take pride in knowing she perceives me as the head of her table, whether she's cognizant of it or not.

I watch her butter her waffle, and I follow suit as she continues telling me about her father. "When I was a kid, he would carry peanut butter with him to restaurants so he could put it on his waffles or pancakes. He was particular about his brand, and not everyone stocked it."

She giggles and shakes her head, lost in memories as she slathers peanut butter on her waffle. "He'd put it on sliced apples and fix us peanut butter and banana sandwiches. We were never lacking for protein."

Syrup is next. I find it fascinating that she only puts it on a fourth of her waffle. When I ask her why, she shrugs. "I don't like it to get soggy, so I only put syrup on a section at a time."

"Makes perfect sense."

With a bite of waffle on her fork, her eyes meet mine and stay on me for the first time since we left the bedroom. "Will you try it?"

"I hoped you'd offer." I lean towards her, and she slips her fork into my mouth. As I chew, I taste the flavours in layers: first the warm, sweet syrup, then the creamy peanut butter mixed with the soft and crunchy waffle with hints of butter. It takes waffle eating to a whole new level. "Let me try another bite, to be sure."

She feeds me another, her eyes still pinned to mine, so hopeful. "I think even if I despised it, I'd tell you I liked it." My hand covers hers. It means a lot to her, this small piece of her father. Her eyes widen, her brows curve down, disappointment marring her beautiful face. "It's a good thing I love it." *But not as much as I love you.* I keep that last part to myself. I fear she's still trepidatious about our budding relationship. Better to ease her into it than to face-plant her with it. "Pass the peanut butter, please."

The resulting smile lights up her face. "That would make my dad very happy." She slides the jar of peanut butter to me. "Another convert," she whispers, a flash of sadness entering her eyes.

I prepare my waffle exactly as she did, only putting syrup on the section I plan to eat first. "Tell me about your parents."

"My mom, Carolyn Murray, lives here. She's an interior decorator. She remarried, but he passed a few years ago."

"I'm sorry," I offer my condolences.

She shrugs it off. "She's doing okay. She dates, but no one serious. I'm not sure she's open to falling in love again." She puts down her fork, pushing her plate aside.

I examine her half-eaten plate of food. "Are you done?"

She looks at her plate and then me. "Yeah, I've had enough."

Unsure how to address the need for her to eat more, I decide not to. "And your father?"

Leaning back in her chair, she takes a drink before answering. "William, my dad, moved back to California—where he's from—with his new family when I was sixteen and Bobby was eighteen. Nicole and Timothy, my half-sister and brother, were ten and eight, I think."

"Is that where they live now?"

"Timothy and Victoria, my step-mom, still live there. My sister is in school at the Cleveland Institute of Music." There's pride in that statement. She beams every time she talks about her siblings.

"And your dad?"

Her gaze moves to the kitchen before flitting over me to land in the distance, somewhere over my shoulder. "He died three years ago." Her remorse is palpable.

I squeeze her hand, getting her attention. "I'm really sorry, baby."

With a forced smile, she shrugs it off. "It's okay. We weren't that close." If I thought she was sad before, that statement right there sent her emotions plummeting.

Needing more details, I pry deeper. "Was it unexpected? Was he ill?"

"He had PKD."

I shake my head. "I have no idea what that is."

"Polycystic Kidney Disease. It's a genetic disease that's quite prevalent in our family. It causes cysts to form in the kidneys, and eventually they're so overrun with growths, they shut down."

"I've never heard of it." With my family's medical background, I'm surprised.

"Yeah, not many have, but surprisingly it's more common than Muscular Dystrophy, Cystic Fibrosis, Down Syndrome, Sickle Cell Anemia, and Hemophilia—combined. Yet, most people know nothing about it."

Does she have it? "When you say *prevalent in your family,*

what does that mean?"

"It's a genetic disease. You can't catch it. You're either born with it, or you're not. But if you have it, you have a fifty percent chance of passing that gene down to your children. And if you're born with the gene, you will get PKD. It's not a matter of *if* but *when*. For my family, my dad's mom and sister had it, and both passed away before he did. My grandmother lived on dialysis for a long time and was pretty old when she died somewhere in her eighties. My aunt, though, was only in her forties when she died. She never sought treatment.

"As for my dad, he was on dialysis for years before getting a kidney transplant. The surgery was a success, but he developed a blood clot in his leg. Three months later that clot traveled to his lungs. He died from a pulmonary embolism. He was only fifty-eight."

"I'm so sorry." I pull her into my lap, and she cuddles into me, fitting against my chest like it was made for her—like I was made for her.

"It's okay." Her soft reply lacks conviction.

I kiss her hair and cup her head, preparing for the worst. "Do you have it?" My heart races, and I hold my breath...waiting. *I'll love you no matter what.* I promise.

"No—"

My relief—a little too evident by the punch of air I release—stops her mid-response. "Sorry."

She smiles. "Don't be. It's nice that you worry about me."

God, this woman, so sweet and innocent despite the way life has treated her. My fingers delve into the back of her hair, holding her gaze. "It's my honour to worry about you." I press my head to hers. "I will love you through sickness and health."

Her hand grasps my wrist still holding her close. "You're gonna break me, Theo." Her voice is laced with saddened resolve.

Wrapping her in a hug, she buries her head in my neck. "No, Lauren. We're going to make you whole."

Her stuttered breath on a sob tears at my heart. "I'm going to love you so bloody hard, there won't be room for pain or sadness."

She chuckles through her tears. "That's not possible. You know that, right?"

I squeeze her, taking in her scent on a deep inhale and then letting it go. "Way to kill the romance," I deadpan. She laughs again, amazing me with how quickly she recovers. "Alright. I'll love you so bloody hard there will only be a miniscule amount of room for pain and sadness. Better?"

Her lips graze my neck, making me shudder. "Yes, better." She sits back, wiping her tear-stained, makeup-free face. "You're too good to me."

"No, baby, I'm exactly the right amount of good for you." The perfect amount.

We clean up breakfast and talk more about our families. She shares that both of her brothers have been diagnosed with PKD and that her sister, like her, doesn't have it. Her brothers' diagnoses is also why she doesn't drink.

Eventually, one or both will need a kidney transplant. She wants to be the first in line to donate, and not drinking and taking care of her body increases the chance she'll have a viable kidney to donate.

"The hard part is, I might not even be a match, but I could still donate a kidney and it would go to someone else on the transplant list, and then my brother would get a stranger's kidney. It's like the kidneys get thrown in the ring, and the best match wins. In the end, my donation will help, but it doesn't quite feel the same as it would if I was able to give the kidney directly to one of my brothers."

"I had no idea." It's impressive. She talks about the disease, the statistics, and transplants with true insight.

"Yeah, me neither. And who knows, when it happens, it might be a completely different process by then, or maybe I'll be a perfect match."

I pray, by some miracle, she doesn't have to donate. The idea of her voluntarily being cut nearly in half to get to her kidney is more than a little disconcerting.

"Okay, enough about me. Tell me about your parents, your brothers and sisters."

"My dad, Sawyer, is a philosophy professor as well. My mom, Janie, is a pediatrician. Connor, my oldest brother, is an orthopedic surgeon. Charlotte is the next oldest and she's a lady doctor—gynecology and obstetrics."

"Holy moly, you have three doctors and two professors in your family?"

I chuckle at her surprise. "And two more teachers.

Christian is a music teacher, and my sister Claire is a grade school teacher."

Lauren shifts in my arms to face me, her side resting on the back of the couch. "Don't balk when I say this." Her little pointer finger raises in emphasis, accompanying the arch of her brow. "It's impressive. Three doctors and four teachers *is* impressive. But besides the brains in your family genes and the dedication to schooling, what impresses me most is the heart that it takes to be a teacher or a doctor. Both, in their own ways, are service jobs meant to help people and for the betterment of society as a whole." She cuddles back under my arm, her hand landing on my thigh. "*That* is what I call impressive."

I rest my head on hers. "I love the way you see the world." She doesn't stick to superficial thoughts or expectations. She goes deeper, below the surface, to find the true meaning—purpose.

We sit in companionable silence for a moment, but we have a few things to discuss before I leave.

"Will you keep me company while I pack my bag?" I stand and pull her to the guest room, not giving her a choice.

"I guess that means you're leaving soon?" I don't miss the hint of sadness in her words.

Wrapping her in my arms, I gaze down at her, brushing her hair away from her face. "I don't want to, but I need to get home, do some laundry, grocery shop, and prepare for the week."

"I understand." The light behind her eyes fades as she pulls away emotionally, preparing to erect her protective walls.

I tug her closer. "Don't do that. Don't lock me out." Forehead to forehead, I breathe her in. "You shared a lot with me this weekend, and it means everything to me that you did." I run my lips across hers and groan when I pull away. "I like having you in my arms, asleep or awake."

"Me too," she whispers.

"I want to talk to you about tomorrow, but first I want to be sure we're alright." Her blue eyes search my face, and my skin heats under her attention. "I don't regret anything that happened this morning in bed. I don't want you to regret it either. I know sex is off the table, but I'd like to be able to make love to you like I did today." Her blush is irresistible. "Do you regret if? Is it too much? Despite how much I want you, I'll curtail our contact based on what's acceptable to you. Tell me what level of intimacy is alright with you."

"I don't regret it. I'm embarrassed, but I'm okay with what we did."

Thank fuck.

"Don't be embarrassed, and don't doubt that I want you every second of every day." Another kiss. "If I had my way, we'd never spend a night apart, and you'd get well acquainted with exactly how much I desire you on a daily basis."

She sighs, and her head falls to my chest. "The things you say."

"Truth. I only speak the truth." I rub her back, and she sinks into me. "As much as I want to stay, we've only just gotten back together after nine days of hell. I don't want to overwhelm you with how much I want you. I believe me going home is for the best." I need my girl to be sure about us when we're apart. It's easy to be lulled by the sexual haze that surrounds us. She needs to choose me with a clear head.

"I'll miss you." The vulnerability in her eyes has me wanting to give in but also hardens my resolve. She needs to be sure.

"I'll miss you too. I'd like to see you tomorrow. I'd like to start one-on-one self-defense training in addition to the classes, which"—I raise a brow and pin her with my best professor scowl—"you will begin attending, again. Correct?"

Her sheepish smile puts a stupid grin on my face. "Yes, I'll be there, and yes, I'd love any and all additional instruction you can spare."

Spare? "For you, all my time is yours." I'm a selfish prick like that.

In a matter of minutes my bag is packed, and she walks me to the door.

"I'll call you later, wish you sweet dreams."

Her lips crash to mine. She's as desperate as I am to delay my impending departure. I worship her with words of comfort between kisses, putting it all out there, sparing nothing.

It's everything or nothing with this woman.

And nothing is not in the realm of possibilities.

PART FOUR:

The Road to Redemption

Chapter 18

SHE'S HERE. **I SENSE HER PRESENCE** before I spot her in the distance, a meadow of wildflowers between us.

Lauren leans on a white picket fence, her face raised to the sun. "I miss you." Her voice trails to me on the wind.

"I miss you too. Don't leave," I whisper. She's too far away to hear, but miraculously, she does.

Her smile broadens, her face still soaking up the sun as

if it gives her life. "I didn't leave. You did."

I wish she'd open her eyes and let me see the blues I crave. "You needed time," I offer as explanation.

"I need convincing, reassurances, not distance." She lowers her face from the sun, her eyes glowing as she rakes my body with her gaze.

My steps still as I soak up the sight of her. The air is visible in thick waves of heat dancing between us. Her perfume tickles my nose and feeds the need to hold her close, burying my face in her neck. "Then come to me."

Her dress flows in the wind as she runs through the gate and across the meadow. Blonde curls bounce, cascading around her face and shoulders, lifting weightless in the air to fall again.

"Catch me." She leaps, her smile bright and her laughter joyous.

My arms wrap around her the moment her body melds with mine, her arms circling my neck, and her legs, my waist. "Always, my love."

When I wake, my dream floods my senses. My bed feels cavernous and empty, and the ache in my chest is nearly insurmountable.

Thank God it's lecture day. It keeps my mind focused, allowing the day to pass with little free time for wandering thoughts of Lauren and our weekend together. I'm even more spellbound than I was before—completely and utterly enraptured.

My day ends at half past two, allowing plenty of time to

arrive at Simon's, change clothes, and plan our first private lesson. I greet Simon and his wife before heading to the men's locker room to change into my workout gear. I grab a notepad and pen, water, and a towel before entering the training room we'll be using tonight.

As I finish up my notes, that familiar buzz of awareness has me glancing up to find Lauren standing in the doorway, her eyes already pinned on me. In a black skirt and a blouse the colour of her eyes, with her long hair cascading down her shoulders, she is beauty personified. Her smile has my heart leaping to attention before my body follows suit.

I float on air as I travel the distance between us. Clasping her hand, I kiss her cheek and relish the warmth on my lips. "Hullo, gorgeous. Been standing here long?"

"Long enough to enjoy the view." Her bashful blush contrasts with her bold words.

"Come with me." I lead her to the back room where we'll not be disturbed. Once inside, I slip her bag off her shoulder and set it down. With nothing but the air between us, I hold the side of her face, my lips hovering over hers in anticipation. Waiting.

Her lips part on a fortifying breath as if she forgot to breathe—as if she's anticipating our kiss as much as I am. She tips her chin, joining her mouth with mine, and I'm brought to my knees—hanging on by a thread—by the steam-train of lust coursing through me. If her nails biting into my skin and her body pulsing against mine are any indication, she's onboard the passion train, as well.

Swinging around, I pin her against the door with a not-so-gentle thud that has her gasping her surprise and her tongue joining mine. Our hands traverse the planes and curves of each other's bodies, tugging and pressing, demanding more…

"Bloody hell." I jerk back, both of us panting. Her hands grip the door as if it's the only thing holding her up. My hands tug at my hair to keep from grabbing her. "Damn, woman, it's good to see you."

Her slow smile breaks into a giggle and quickly rolls into a full body laugh. Her arms cross over her middle as she doubles over with laughter.

I shake my head, let out a punch of air, and adjust my hard-as-steel cock, but in my joggers it's of little use. "I'm glad you find this humourous."

That only seems to send her into another fit of giggles.

"Lauren," I chastise with little impact. I cross my arms and wait, fighting the smile that threatens to break free.

Slowly, her cackling stops. She stands, swiping at the corners of her eyes. "I'm sorry." She chuckles, apparently not fully recovered.

My hands fall to my sides, waiting her out, my brow pinched in my best professor glare, which apparently has the opposite effect on her as a cheeky grin creeps across her lovely, beet-red face. "Are you done?"

She nods and steps closer, her hands clasping the sides of my shirt, pulling it taut. Her devilishly teasing eyes flit over my face before she lays her head on the middle of my chest. "I'm happy to see you too."

My arms wrap around her of their own accord. "Yes, that's quite apparent by your laughter."

"Hey." She steps back. "I wasn't laughing when you kissed me."

"No, I suppose you weren't." I draw her back to me, pressing my head to hers. "I don't like sleeping without you." I can't dismiss the rightness of being wrapped around her in slumber.

"You missed me?"

Fuck, did I ever. I tossed and turned. The vision of her in my dreams was my only solace—a cheap substitute, to be sure. "Yes."

Her lips graze my cheek. "I missed you too."

My pounding heart begins to settle as her words remind me that I'm not in this alone. She feels it too. She's with me.

I hold her a moment more before she leaves to change. Remaining behind, I regain my composure then head to the room.

When she enters the training room, she's wearing black pants and t-shirt that fits her curves perfectly. She sets down her water bottle and towel, and joins me on the mat. "Ready?"

"Yes." I motion for her to sit next to me. "We'll begin with stretches, much like the *one* self-defense class you attended," I tease.

She rolls her eyes. "Okay, enough already. I had my reasons, but yes, I should have still attended class."

"Or at least told me you weren't coming," I mutter. I worried when she didn't show, and she didn't answer her phone or texts. She said she needed space, but she didn't say she would skip classes. I didn't like hearing it from Silvy.

Lauren's shoulder bump brings my focus back to her. "I'm sorry. I'll tell you next time," she promises.

"Or better yet, don't miss any more classes—group or otherwise."

Another eye roll from my blonde vision has me manning up. *Stop acting like a pansy who got his feelings hurt.*

My feelings were hurt, but I don't have to act like it. She's not my ex who continually disregarded my feelings. *Keep your baggage in check.*

We start with leg stretches. I move from one stretch to the next, and she follows me seamlessly.

"I want to increase your flexibility, and then we'll work on strength training." I see the question on her lips before she even asks. "Yes, we will work on defensive moves, but I want to take it slow today. Not overdo it."

She nods without complaint, so I continue to stretch our quads as we change positions. "When fending off an attacker, areas to focus on to cause the most damage are: the eyes, nose, ears, neck, groin, knee, and legs. Our training will focus on movements that inflict the most damage to these areas. Your movements must be quick, precise, and purposeful. *This* will be the focus in our sessions."

I stand, offering my hand, and pull her to her feet. "It's important that you listen, focus, and do as I say. Do you agree to this?" I'm all business—keeping my emotions at bay. I'll do more harm than good if I let my emotions get the better of me. I can't dwell on her attack—not now—not here, other than to consider what moves she could use to fend off multiple attackers. She needs me to be strong. I will be her rock.

"Yes." Her response is succinct and calm, the way I need her to be.

"Good," I respond with a nod.

We continue stretching our backs, arms, legs. I watch her every move. She's focused, determined, and...beautiful.

She smiles when she notices. "Do you like what you see?" she braves with a mischievous glint in her eyes.

"You know I do." *Very much so.*

We linger in the moment, silently acknowledging the electricity that's never far when we are near.

I clear my throat and attempt to stifle the attraction that is all too present in the room with us. "Right, let's move on to strength training. You need to keep your core tight." I stand behind her, my hand splayed over her stomach. The scent of her invades my nostrils, and I nearly growl my approval. My fingers flex, and her muscles contract below my touch. "I don't want to aggravate your back. Sore is acceptable, but pain—injury—is not."

Her desirous gaze meets mine over her shoulder, but the addition of gratitude solidifies my determination to teach her over my desire to lay her down on this rather convenient mat and make her moan my name.

"Thank you." Her reverent voice reinforces my decision.

"You're welcome." My lips still on her shoulder for a beat, my eyes closed.

One, two, three.

I open my eyes, disentangle myself from her body and pat her bum. "Lie on your back."

Once settled, I continue, "We'll start with bicycle crunches. I'm sure you've done them before, but I want to show you the proper technique for maximum results."

She only nods, her knees bent, her hands and feet flat on the mat. The perfect neutral position.

I demonstrate, alternating leg-elbow movement once, and then again before she joins me. We do a set of fifteen reps. Rest. Then, two more sets of fifteen.

When finished, I check how she's doing. "How was that? How's your back?"

"I'm good," she breezes. "I can do more."

"No." I want to take it slow with her back, see how much it can handle. "Let's move on. We can add more reps next time."

We go through all the exercises smoothly and quickly. She does them in silence, no complaining or requests to do less. She's a machine, a determined machine.

When we take a break, we're both drenched in sweat. I wonder if we should continue or end for the night. I don't want her to be too sore. "How are you feeling? Should we stop? I don't want to go too hard your first day."

"No, I'm fine." She swipes at the glistening sweat on her chest and neck. "I'd like to learn some self-defense moves."

"Your wish is my command." I lean in for a quick kiss. "Thirty minutes. No more. Alright?"

"Okay."

After a few more sips of water, we resume. I add on to the moves she's already learned—and those she missed from the group classes—only this time, I'm padded up, and she practices on me. Not full force, but enough to understand what it feels like to hit someone in the places she needs to, to accurately inflict the correct amount of pain and damage.

Thirty minutes come and go quickly. She's breathing hard, but beams with exhilaration. She is an excellent student.

As she enters the women's locker room to shower and change for dinner, I can't help but think of her naked, showering only a door away from me.

I shake my head to reset that train of thought, collect my stuff, and go shower.

I'm exhausted—in a good way—full of accomplishment. We're just beginning, but I feel like I've already learned so much more than I would in weeks of group classes.

I was worried how the one-on-one instruction would go, given our relationship. I didn't want to disappoint him or make a fool of myself. But after a few minutes it was clear it would be easy to follow his lead. It was the same as it was in the group class, but more personal—intimate.

He's strong, authoritative, in control, and...totally hot.

I shower and get dressed, fixing my hair and makeup. When I exit the bathroom, Theo is standing against the far wall talking to a guy in full gi.

Theo waves me over. "Simon, I'd like to introduce you to my girlfriend, Lauren Frasier. Lauren, this is Simon Lee, the owner."

I shake his hand. "Simon, it's nice to meet you. Thank you for allowing us to train here."

Theo smiles assuringly and puts his arm around my waist, pulling me to his side.

"You're more than welcome, Lauren. It's a pleasure to meet you." Simon turns his attention to Theo. "You must have done something right to deserve such a beautiful woman."

Heat creeps up my cheeks. Theo's eyes scan my face before he responds, "I don't know that I could do anything to deserve her, but I'm trying." He squeezes my waist, and I lean into him while his kind words wash over me.

They wrap up their conversation, and before I know it, we're on our way out.

Theo walks me to my car, pausing before opening my door. "I'd like to take your car home before we go out."

"Are you sure?" I don't want to inconvenience him.

"Positive. Besides, I'd like you to ride with me to dinner." He opens my door and waits for me to get in. Then he bends, giving me a soft kiss on the mouth. "I'll follow you."

My thoughts trail after him as he walks to his car. Handsome, kind, gentle, and thoughtful, what more could a girl ask for? This detour to drop my car off is his way of protecting me. He may want me in the car with him, but he also doesn't want me to drive alone late at night or traipse into my apartment alone, either.

As long as he's near, I'm safe. The problem is when he's not, hence the self-defense training. If all goes well, and I'm an apt pupil, he'll still be protecting me, even when he's not around, by the skills he's teaching me.

I lead the way to my apartment, feeling grateful.

Parking in my garage, I grab my bags and walk to Theo's car. "Do you mind if I put my bags inside? I'd rather not leave my laptop in my car."

"Of course. I'll come with you." Ever the gentleman, he takes my bags. His hand on my lower back, he gently guides me to my apartment. Once there, he uses my key to unlock the door, ushers me in, turns off the alarm, and closes the door behind us.

He then proceeds to set my bags on the dining room table and comes back to me. "You look beautiful. This blouse is the most amazing color of blue, like your eyes. I want to swim in that color with you." He kisses my forehead, his lips lingering, and then he pulls away. "Ready?"

I nod, feeling heady with him so close here in my apartment. He smiles as if he knows, takes my hand—intertwining our fingers—and leads me to his car (after arming my alarm and locking the door, of course).

I love that he's kind and generous, yet strong and confident in his role as a man. He leads, and I follow, not because I *need* him to lead me, but because I *want* to follow — him. I want *him* to be the lead. I don't want to be in control. I'm in control of everything. Always. It is nice to know that I can relax, be me, and not worry about taking care of him. He's the one taking care of me. It's comforting. I feel feminine and appreciated. Two things I'm not sure I've ever felt.

I squeeze his hand at the thought. He looks back, giving me his brilliant make-a-dentist-proud smile, and squeezes my hand in return. I could get lost in that smile, in his purely male handsomeness that screams *I am man, hear me roar*, but it's the softness in his eyes that does me in. It's not always there — except when he looks at me.

He pulls into the Houstons parking lot, my favorite restaurant. How did he know? "Have you been here before?"

"No, but a little bird told me this is one of your favorite places."

"It is. Would that little bird be named Silvy?" I try to hide the dopey smile his grin and teasing induce.

I would be happy eating anywhere with him, but the fact that he made the extra effort to find out my favorite place — that he planned ahead, thinking of what would make me happy — has those lonely dark places in me filling with light. His light.

Tears pricks behind my eyes. My emotional baggage is never far from the surface, threatening to darken even the lightest of moments.

"Yes, I believe it was." Looking satisfied, he takes my hand and leads me inside.

We settle into a booth in the back where it's secluded, minus the hustle and bustle near the bar area, and order drinks and the best artichoke spinach dip—ever.

His eyes bore into me like it's the first time he's seeing me—really seeing me. The world narrows and closes down around us. I don't flinch. I keep his stare, matching his intensity.

Moments pass, and I think for sure he's going to look away—realizing I'm nothing special to look at.

"You're fearless when you want to be." His baritone voice breaches the moment.

God, if he only knew how far from that mark I actually fall. "No." I break eye contact. "I'm not fearless." My hands flutter in my lap, smoothing my napkin. "I'm afraid of so much, it's sad really."

"Well, then it's bravery—facing your fear in spite of it. But the woman who just stared me down is fearless."

A smile ticks at my mouth. "I wish I was as you see me."

"You are. I need to help you see it." He places his hand on the table, palm up, eyes asking me to trust him.

With little reluctance, my hand finds sanctuary in his larger one. His fingers contract, his strength evident yet controlled.

"You did great tonight. I have no doubt you'll surpass

my expectations and blow yours out of the water."

Expectations are a dangerous thing. My world is soiled with shattered expectations, both mine and others'. I want to be the woman he sees—both brave and fearless. Maybe if he believes enough, and I believe in him, I will become that woman. Not a farce, but the true embodiment of the woman shining in his eyes, her reflection, a vague resemblance to me.

"Thank you. It was fun." I make light of his words, but his knowing gaze doesn't miss a thing.

Philosophy professor, remember? He's good at reading people—reading me. "I bet you're a really good teacher. I can imagine all of your students falling for you." His penetrating eyes, expressive brow, and pouty lips would have anyone swooning, but add in his stature, his accent, and his commanding presence—it's a full-on assault to the senses.

Indignation flashes across his face. He shifts in his seat, jaw clenched, clearing his throat. His hand, still holding mine, twitches like he wants to let me go, but he manages to hold tight. Clearly, I've ruffled his feathers.

"Did they ever catch the guys who attacked you and Holly?" His voice is harsh with a practiced indifference. I've done more than ruffle his feathers—perhaps I unintentionally plucked a few.

"No." It's all I can manage. Him bringing up my attack—here, in a public place—with such detachment cracks my fragile expectations. "I should know better," I mutter to myself, pulling my hand free. Without much thought, I grab my purse and stand. "Excuse me."

My feet move as tears threaten. I blink repeatedly, looking like an idiot, I'm sure, making my way through the throng of patrons and waiters. Almost to the restrooms, my pace slows at the sight of a rather amorous couple making out in the alcove between the men and women's entrances. His large frame engulfs hers, nearly sequestering her from prying eyes. The sound of their passion and the sway of their bodies has my distress morphing into something more pleasant.

Jeez, they're hot.

"Bloody hell." Theo steps in front of me, blocking my view.

I step to the side, ignoring him, and return my focus to the couple.

"Caveman," she moans.

Surely, she's not... They're not—

Theo's hand draws my eyes to his face. "Eyes on me," he commands.

"But—" I try to move away.

He stops me with a firm grip on my hip. "Can we go back to the table. *Please.*" He adds the last word to soften his demand, as it wasn't a question at all.

"I—"

"Please." His lips press to my forehead, stealing my protest.

"Professor Wade?"

"Bloody hell." Theo sighs against my skin. His shoulders straighten as he comes to his full height, releasing me and turning to face the couple who had been making out like horny teenagers. "Ms. Cavanaugh." His hand laces with mine, squeezing it tightly.

"I thought that was you." The stunningly beautiful woman beams up at the tower of a man standing next to her. Beyond her flushed appearance and his hungry eyes, there's little evidence of their make-out session. I wonder if this is a usual occurrence for them. "Joseph, this is Professor Wade, my philosophy professor."

The hunk of a man sticks out his oversized hand to Theo. "Joe. And it's McIntyre now. My wife." The pride in his words makes my heart flutter.

Theo takes Joe's hand, which surprisingly doesn't look all that big anymore. "Of course. You wed over the Christmas break. My apologies. Congratulations." Theo's smile seems genuine, and the angst he was emanating before seems to fall away. He releases my hand, putting his arm around my shoulder. "Lauren, this is Sam—one of my top-performing students—and her husband Joe McIntyre—of McIntyre Corporate Industries."

I don't miss Joe's brimming pride when Theo mentions Sam is one of his top students, or the shake of Sam's head as if she's dismissing the thought.

"It's a pleasure to meet you both." I shake their hands, stepping out of Theo's hold, only to be drawn back in once my hand is free. "Congratulations, by the way."

They both glow with wedded bliss as they thank me. Sam's eyes roam over us—not in a judging way, more like thoughtful interest as she's obviously madly in love with her husband. Her lips part to speak.

"Samantha," Joe pulls her attention, "we should let the good professor get back to his woman. I believe they were having a *moment*."

My skin warms that he even noticed after what I witnessed going on between the two of them. With a quick goodbye, he pulls her away, but their conversation trails back to us via the arched ceiling.

"A moment, huh? I seem to remember us having a moment too," she teases.

His hand slides down to her rear. "You can't blame a man for wanting to relive a fond memory in that alcove." He leans down, whispering in her ear. Her step falters, but he keeps her in pace with a firm grasp around her hip.

"I wonder what he whispered to her." My eyes follow them until they disappear around the corner.

Theo pulls me close, sinking into the darkness of said alcove, his lips dangerously close to mine, his body pressing me against the wall. "I imagine it was something like…" His lips graze my ear, and I shudder as goosebumps ripple down my arms. "The mere sight of you makes me hard as stone, and I'd give my left nut to sink balls deep in you right now."

A small moan escapes. *Did he mean me? Or was he speaking as Joe?*

He lips graze my jaw but stop short of my lips. His eyes lock on mine as if he heard my thoughts before he draws my hand along the hard length in his jeans. My fingers flex,

215

squeezing slightly.

"Bloodyfuckinghell," he groans, thrusting his hips, pressing my hand against him.

I guess he means me. *I* make him hard as stone.

Chapter 19

I **FIGHT THE URGE TO SIT** on her side of the booth, hold her in my lap, and make this right. But we're in public, and my cock is threatening to break free of my zipper; it's better that I'm across from her where I can plainly see desire, residual anger and hurt warring in her eyes.

"I'm sorry. For how I reacted to your innocent enough statement. For what I asked. My tone—my coolness." I clasp her hand that's resting on the table. I try to keep her gaze, but my next words are hard to admit. "I'm a bit of an arse at work."

"What? Why?" That was not what she expected.

"There's a girl—"

Lauren tries to pull her hand out from under mine.

"Please don't." I ensconce her hand in mine firmly. "Don't pull away from me."

She leans forward, her hand gripping mine back. "I'm sorry, it was a knee-jerk reaction."

I nod. "I understand. It's not what you think. I don't have feelings for her—at least not positive feelings. I feel plenty, mostly irritated indignation, to be honest."

Lauren's expression softens. There's no judgment. Her eyes search mine, waiting.

"Her name is Susan James. She's one of my students. Her infatuation is a nuisance. She thrives on disrupting the class, making a show of her...esteem." I huff out a relieved sigh to be sharing my dark secret and sit back. "When I decided I wanted to be a teacher at Uni, my dad warned me about such things. He spoke of his own experience—advised me to be prepared. But my coping mechanism is not the best."

"Which is?" she asks, her eyes glistening with curiosity, not recrimination. Thank God.

After a deep breath, I admit my faulty tactic, "I'm basically a curmudgeon, a right ole arsehole."

I've shocked her. Her wide eyes, her frown, pull at my scarred heart. "I know. It's not very nice. I figure if I'm an arse, it will keep the students at bay, and we can focus on learning instead of…other things."

"I'm surprised, but then I'm not. I witnessed your aloofness in the coffee shop that first day I met you."

"Ah, yes, the girl who was trying to get my attention."

She laughs. "I think she was trying to have your babies." Her eyes crinkle with humour.

I lean over the table, right in her face. "The only woman in danger of me impregnating her in that coffee shop—or anywhere else—is you."

"Oh." She quickly regains her composure. Her hands bracket my face. "Is that an offer?"

The corner of my mouth ticks to smile at her brashness. *There's that fire I love so much.* "It's a promise." I press my mouth to hers briefly before reclaiming my seat.

Her stunned expression is back. I relish that small victory of showing her how much she means to me. "I'm not playing around with you. This"—I motion between us—"is for keeps."

She simply nods, remaining silent as our waiter delivers our food, even though we haven't touched the appetizer.

Moments pass as we sample our meal. It's delicious, but we're both preoccupied. She's contemplative, based on the twist of her lip and the crease of her brow. When she looks up, she startles, finding me already watching her. Her broad smile is infectious. "Were you watching me?"

"Always." It's that simple. She's never far from my sight or my thoughts.

Her eyes narrow. "Hmm," is her only reply to that.

"Were you going to say something?"

"Oh, I was only thinking."

I prompt her to continue with a raised brow. It's beyond obvious that brain of hers has been working overtime since I silenced her with my comments of impregnation and playing for keeps.

For some, those revelations may have been over the top, but based on the depth of my feelings, it seems relatively prosaic compared to the inferno raging inside.

"Lauren," I manage without bite, but a command nonetheless.

Her mouth opens, closes, then opens again. "Okay." Her hands splay in the air. "I'm just going to put this out there. These are my initial thoughts." She pierces me with her eyes. "So, don't judge."

"Never." She doesn't know me well enough to know I'd never judge her. I want her every random musing. I don't want her to self-edit, only giving me some of her.

I. Want. It. All.

"First of all, I don't blame any of your students for crushing on you. Have you seen yourself?" She points at me. "I mean, you…" She looks around the room, her eyes landing on random blokes and then back to me. "You're not an average-looking guy. You're a thousand on a grading scale of one to a hundred."

I crack up, I can't help it. She's animated and clearly passionate about her opinion. "I'm honoured. But it's only a face."

"And a body." She leans closer, gesturing to me, nearly brushing her breast in her food in her exuberance. "You can't forget the body."

"Alright. It's only a face *and body*." I know my qualities are above average. I'm not daft—I own a mirror. "I'm more than the sum of my face and body."

She stills, her eyes warm with her smile. "Yes, you most definitely are. But unfortunately, we are judged by our outward appearance before we even open our mouths. And it's all uphill or downhill from there."

True.

"And you have the cards stacked in your favor. That's all I'm saying." She raises two fingers. "Second of all, if you were my professor, and not friendly, I'd see that as a challenge to win you over. I'd kill you with kindness, so to speak." Her finger taps against her lips. "I wonder if that's what this girl is doing." Her tapping finger now points at me. "She sees you as a challenge. She's trying to break through your steely façade." She shrugs. "The more aloof you are, the harder she tries."

"Huh, I hadn't thought of that."

"It's probably too late with her. If you start being nice now, she'll think you like her. But going forward, maybe being nice will actually reduce the flirting, if you don't show any signs of interest. I don't know. It's just a thought."

"Would you really do that? Try to win me over?"

"Yes, but not to date you. I'd never believe it was possible or think it was right. I'd want to win you over so you liked me, gave me a fair shake in the class. If that didn't work, I'd call you on your shitty attitude. Tell you to stop being so rude, thinking you're God's gift."

"I'd like to see you telling someone off." It makes me hot envisioning all that anger and passion being directed at me.

She laughs, shaking her head. "No, you wouldn't. I'm horrible at it. I get so worked up and then usually cry because I feel bad about getting upset. I hate conflict." Her gaze drifts down. "I try to avoid it when at all possible."

Is that why you run, to avoid conflict?

"You know, I never considered I'm making myself more of a target—a challenge—by being an arse over being myself. Thank you for that."

Her eyes return to mine. "You're welcome."

"I also agree that it's probably too late to change tactics with Miss James."

"If you need me to kick her ass, let me know."

"I may take you up on that." But maybe not in the way she imagines.

"Isn't it hard to be mean all day?"

"Yes, at first, but as time goes by, it's easier and easier to slip into that role, and harder and harder to slip out of it."

She reaches across the table and touches the furrow in my brow I didn't even know was there. "Don't stress. You'll figure it out."

Her touch, her confidence in me, and knowing I'm not in this alone, soothes my weary soul. "Then you show up at my coffee shop and brighten my darkened doorway, lighting me up in ways I've long ignored or had no idea were even possible." I pull her hand into mine, running my lips across the back of it, pressing it against my cheek. "I don't want to be that curmudgeon any longer. You make me want to do better—be better."

"Theo." Her voice, not even a whisper as if I heard it in my head, tugs at me, but it's the tears in her eyes that have me sliding into the booth next to her. "It's too much." A tear skates down her cheek before I can stop it.

Pulling her into my chest, I hold her soundly. "It's not too much. It's just right." My lips press to her hair, and the smell has me wanting to strip her down, discovering all her wonderful scents. "Someday it won't hurt. Kindness and words of love shouldn't hurt. It takes time for them to burrow their way through the scar tissue of your pain, filling the barren darkness left behind by those who hurt you."

She squeezes me tight, and I swear I'd take her inside myself—where she'd be safe and warm—if I could.

I will love her into healing and beat the shite out of anyone who dares to think otherwise, stand in my way, or think of doing her more harm.

She's had enough.

Her cup runneth over—and not in a good way.

She needs a champion.

And. I. Am. It.

Can you actually die from embarrassment? I would assume not. Otherwise, I would be dead instead of suffering in the passenger seat of Theo's Land Rover. He doesn't seem bothered by my emotional display. I, on the other hand, want to dig a hole and stick my head in it. No, it won't make it go away. And yes, I realized burying my head does not make the rest of me invisible. But it will spare me further embarrassment of *knowing* others can see me.

Unrealistic? Yes. But that's not a strong deterrent at this point in time.

I can barely function when he spews his soul-wrenching accolades like it's water when, in fact, it's liquid gold. He does more than fill my empty dark places with light. He breaches the barricade around my heart, mends the broken pieces of my spirit, and breathes life into my long dead dreams.

Hope is alive when he's around. He's like a Disney movie prince with sex appeal. And apparently, I'm the main character who has to experience death within the first fifteen minutes to give me grit and obstacles to overcome. I'm not sure I like their formula for success. I'd like to opt out. I'd like to know what I'd be like without that tragedy marring my character.

"Hey," my Prince Charming calls to me from his side of the carriage...er, car.

"Yeah?" Thankfully my musings have sidetracked my guilt and embarrassment, and when I look at Theo, I'm able to do so with dry eyes—free of tears.

"Would you go with me tomorrow night?"

"To your music thing?"

"Yes." His eyes spark with hope.

"Isn't it really a guys-only thing, getting together, playing music, drinking beer?" I don't want to be the girlfriend who tags along where I'm not welcome.

His smile is indulgent as if I'm being silly. "It's not like that. They'd love to meet you, and I'd like to share this part of my life with you."

How can I say no to that?

"Besides, Dan's wife, Nancy, will be there. It's at their house."

"Okay."

"You don't have to sing if you don't want to. I'll tell Marcus to back off."

"Okay." I will myself to not focus on the possibility of Marcus asking me to sing.

"You'll go?" The joy on his face today is worth any discomfort tomorrow.

"I'll go."

He pulls into my complex, parking in front of my building. "You won't regret it." He turns off the engine. "And if you do, you don't have to come again."

"You'll be there, so I know everything will be fine." He's

quickly becoming my sanctuary. I don't care how much that scares me, because the idea of him not being in my life scares me even more.

He beams as if I've made his day. "Everything will be perfect."

Chapter 20

THE RINGING OF MY HOME PHONE pulls me from sleep. I barely crack an eye before answering. "Hello." My drowsy voice reveals the fact that I was sound asleep a few seconds ago.

"Bollocks. I woke you." The sound of Theo's sensuous voice has both my eyes opening and my body thrumming in anticipation of seeing him tonight.

"It's okay. I had to get up to answer the phone anyway." It's an old joke, but hey, I just woke up.

"Hardy-har-har. You're a regular Groucho Marx."

"Groucho Maaaaaaarx?" I can't stifle the yawn that extends *Marx* ridiculously long. "Sorry." Another yawn. *Jeez, stop that.* "That's a rather dated American expression, isn't it?"

"Perhaps. But, well, it's early. My humor muscle hasn't quite woken up yet."

My laugh rings in my ears, louder than it should. "You're cute when you try to be funny."

"Cute? Ms. Frasier, I assure you there is nothing cute about me."

"And you're sexy when you go all British on me, Professor Wade."

"Sexy is acceptable."

"Hmm." I could get lost in this man's sex appeal. He oozes it like a pheromone. "Good morning, Theo." I try to get us back on track as my alarm goes off in four minutes.

"Good morning, My Vision." The warmth of his words enchants me through the phone line. "I am sorry I woke you. I wanted to hear your voice."

"I don't mind. In fact, I wouldn't mind waking up to your sexy voice every day." Truly. Every. Day.

"Don't tease. That could be arranged."

"How? By calling me every morning?" I am teasing him, of course, but I wouldn't mind him being my new wake up service. It would be better than an alarm clock.

"No." His voice crackles, deepening. "I would roll over and whisper in your ear."

My thighs clench, imaging his breath skirting my ear as his lips leave a trail of kisses down my neck.

"Though, most likely, I wouldn't have to roll over at all as you'd already be in my arms, our bodies wrapped around each other like we couldn't get close enough."

Holy shit.

"I want that, Lauren. I want to wake up to you in my arms…every day…for the rest of my life."

I can't breathe. That. Right there. I want that.

"Breathe, baby." His soothing voice coaxes air into my lungs.

I flop onto my back, breathing in and out.

"That's it. Better?"

"Yes."

"We'll table that for now." He's an intuitive sort. Seems to know when I need more time to process things than he does. "I want to firm up our plans for tonight. I'd like us to grab a quick bite beforehand. Can you be home by six?"

"Yes. Um, or I could cook?"

He chuckles. "You don't sound too sure."

"I'm sure. Something easy, like pasta."

"Sounds wonderful. Let me know what I can bring."

"I will."

We're both silent. I don't want to end our conversation. I like his voice in my ear. But I need to get to work early if I'm going to make it home in time to make dinner by six.

"Are you heading to work this early?" I didn't think he worked these kind of hours.

"I'm going for a run, actually. My first class isn't until nine."

"You're so industrious."

He chuckles again. "I have energy to burn. Someone has me all wound up these days."

"You need to tell that *someone* to get you unwound."

"I believe she would if she could." The levity from before is gone.

"I would." But I'm not ready—it's too soon.

"I know, Lauren." There's so much more he's not saying behind his calm, endearing acceptance. "I know."

"Dessert. I could make brownies to take tonight."

"The guys would love that. But you don't have to. You don't need sweets to win them over."

"But it wouldn't hurt."

"No, it wouldn't hurt."

"I've got to get ready." I don't want to hang up.

"Text me if you need me to pick up anything, and let me know when you're home as I'll probably come straight from campus."

"Okay."

"Lauren?"

"Yeah?"

"You don't need sweets or any other food to win me

over either. You've already got me."

Jesus. This man. "But it wouldn't hurt, right?"

"No, it wouldn't hurt at all."

I don't think we're talking about winning his heart anymore.

The sexual innuendo lingers as we say goodbye.

Flinging the covers off, I jump out of bed, hurrying to the kitchen, and pull out what I need to make spaghetti and meat sauce, noting I have everything except French bread.

Fast walking to the bathroom, I turn on the shower and text Theo to pick up bread if he wants some with dinner.

I quickly shower, dry my hair, and dress, running out of the door in less than forty-five minutes. That's a record for me.

The rush of thinking about dinner and getting to work early eased my nerves about meeting his friends. I pray my day is busy and passes quickly, eating up the time until I can see him again.

Gah, I sound desperate.

I am though. Desperate for his reassurance—confirmation—that it's *me* he's saying all those wonderful things to and not some other woman he's confused me with.

Stupid, yes, but my doubt has me fearing this is all a dream—a fantasy—I've conjured up in my head.

I'm going to wake up soon and realize it's not real.

He's not real.

And nobody will ever love me like he's promising to.

Jesus, I can't breathe.

My run is littered with thoughts of Lauren. Not surprising, really, she's rarely far from my mind. I've never brought a woman to meet my American friends. Only Reese met my ex, and that was in England. He never liked her. I should have given his opinion more weight—perhaps he could have saved me the heartache. Though, I'm fully aware had my ex not broken my heart, I wouldn't have found Lauren. And I most definitely would not be the man I am today, seasoned with a clearer vision of what's important—who's important.

Back then, my heart wasn't ready for Lauren. Now it is.

I turn up the music and pick up my pace. The air is crisp, and my heart pounds with each footfall as I find my rhythm, sliding into the slip-stream of a runner's high. My mind bounces between asking Lauren about the upcoming three-day weekend, shedding my arsehole persona to be the teacher my students deserve, convincing Lauren to introduce me to her mother this early in our relationship, and planning a Caribbean getaway for Spring Break.

I'm more excited than anxious for Lauren to meet my friends, but I am anxious to meet her mum. Once she agrees, perhaps I'll make a preemptive call to her mum beforehand to break the ice.

How will Lauren feel about me whisking her away to a surprise destination for Spring Break? Is she good with surprises? I have the feeling no one's gone that extra mile for her. I want to give her what she hasn't had before. And what she has experienced before, I want to do it better. I want her to know how much she means to me. I want to give her a break from being the one who has to plan, coordinate everything. Just because she can, doesn't mean she has to, or should.

I want to take care of her, be her rock. My chest swells with the idea of giving her everything she needs, being who she needs.

She's an enigma. Beautiful—yet she does not know it. Strong—yet she doesn't trust herself or believe in her strength. Shy, avoiding social situations—yet she's witty and personable. Chaste—yet seductive and sexual.

Desire, my constant companion, rages at the thought of touching her—being touched by her—devouring her sensuous mouth, sinking my fingers into her hair, and loving her into oblivion.

I sprint the last quarter mile home, trying to expel the sexual energy threatening to burst through my running pants.

As I undress, I turn off the music and check my phone, seeing a text from Lauren. I text her back and get in the shower, my arousal all too evident. The hot water beats against my ridged muscles, every drop slowly releasing the tension in them. All except one.

Almost reluctantly, I give in to my need, imagining it's her hand on my cock, getting me off as I finger her hungry pussy and suck her luscious nipples. My fantasy flips to her riding me, my cock buried deep inside the part of her she's not ready to give me. Her head thrown back, her tits bounce as she pounds me, crying out in ecstasy until she screams my name and comes on my cock.

That's all it takes. As I explode, my entire body is racked with an electrical surge that zings and stabs from my balls to my toes, to my hands, and out the top of my head. My hand on the shower wall keeps me from falling when my body arches on a feral moan that could wake the dead.

Bloodyfuckinghell.

Spent, I sink to the shower floor, releasing my cock, and wait until the twitching stops and I can take a full breath.

This wasn't like the times I've touched her and felt that livewire that connects us. This. This was far more intense and edged with a side of pain, almost like a shock collar, punishing me for seeking pleasure without her. An entirely crazy thought, but one I'm not sure is wrong.

My phone rings and vibrates on the bathroom counter, urging me to my feet. I dry my hands on my towel before wrapping it around my waist and step out of the shower.

"Lauren?" The timing can't be a coincidence. I answer on speaker as I run a towel over my hair.

"Theo."

I freeze. Her breath is ragged and her voice, shaky. "What's wrong?"

"I…uh…hold on." There's movement on the line, and then I hear a click like a door shutting.

"Where are you? Are you alright?" I take her off speaker as I pace my bedroom.

"I'm in my office, thankfully."

"Thankfully? What does that mean? What happened?" I start to throw on clothes in case I need to get to her.

"Theo." She starts to cry. "I think I'm going crazy."

Fuck. "Baby, you have to tell me what's going on." My voice is calm, soothing, a complete contrast to the uproar I'm feeling inside.

"I…it was like at the restaurant…when you touched me, and I—"

"Orgasmed?" *Bloodyfuckinghell.* "Are you telling me you just had an orgasm at work without stimulus?"

"Yes. I think I'm going crazy."

My lips tingle from shock. "Tell me what you felt, exactly."

"Pleasure. Pain. Shockwave." Her staccato speech punches me in the stomach with each word.

She felt what I did. What does this mean?

She had an orgasm at *work*. What if she hadn't been alone? Fuck, what if she had been driving at the time?

"Shit, I think I caused it. Are you okay? Do you need me to come get you?"

"No. I'm fine. I mean, I'm rattled, but I'm fine." She sniffles, her crying waning. "What do you mean you caused it?"

I'm not the blushing type, but I swear I can feel the heat creep up my neck. "I was a bit worked up this morning. My run didn't help. So…I…took matters into my own hands, so to speak."

"Oh, you…" God, I can feel her blush from here.

"Yeah, I bashed the bishop."

I'm not sure if her giggling is because of my choice of phrase, or if she's horrified by the act and cackling is her only way through it.

"I'm sorry," she mumbles and covers her mouth, or the phone, to stifle the sound of her laughter.

"No, I'm the one who's sorry." I truly am. A momentary weakness wreaked havoc on us, and it could have been worse if she'd had an audience.

"Did you enjoy it, at least?"

"It was a bit of a double-edged sword, to be honest."

"I'm sorry. Maybe you can explain that to me later." Her laughter has ceased.

"After I die from humiliation, I will."

"That might be a bit dramatic for spanking the bishop."

Her lightheartedness eases my discomfort. "It's *bashing* the bishop, not *spanking* him."

"Bash…spank…is there really a difference?"

"No, I suppose not." I exhale the stress of the last few minutes. "I really am sorry, Lauren."

"It's okay. It's a bit freaky, don't you think?"

"It seems par for the course with this thing between us. And weirdly, I'm not freaked out by the event itself, but the fact that it happened to you at work. You could have been anywhere, with anyone. I'm messed up over the idea of you being vulnerable like that, and me not being there—that I did this to you."

"You didn't know—we didn't know. How could we have expected *this?* You didn't do it on purpose."

I chuckle. "No. God, no. I didn't do it on purpose."

"Maybe next time you can give me a heads up."

Damn, she's being such a good sport about this. "There won't be a next time."

I'm met with silence.

Silence.

"You there?"

"Yeah, I'm trying to figure out why there won't be a next time."

"Because…I think I'm meant to save it all for you."

"Save what for me?" Her tone is wary, like I just said I'm going to save my cum in a jar for her.

"My pleasure, our pleasure. It's meant to be shared— together. Not wasted on self-gratification."

"Maybe we should test that theory when I'm not at work."

"No. I've learned my lesson." The memory of the pain edging out the ecstasy is enough for me to refrain.

I kiss her goodbye over the phone with the promise to discuss this further. But in my mind, whatever it is that connects us demands that we be together as much as possible, and there is no seeking pleasure apart.

Let it not be said that this old dog can't be taught new

tricks. This dog has learned not to howl at the moon—*alone*.

Chapter 21

WHEN LIGHTNING CRASHED INTO MY BODY, consuming me from the inside out, for a split second I thought I was dying. Fear of losing control and terror over what was happening had me gripping my chair, praying no one walked into my office. The razor's edge of pain mixed with the brilliant roll of pleasure consumed me, had me seeing white, and seizing in my chair like a fish out of water. Once my motor functions returned, I gripped my phone and called Theo. The moment I heard his voice, I broke down, unable to hold back the emotional onslaught over whatever the hell had just happened. Pleasure with the mix of pain was scary, but his voice released the fear and brought me calm. I don't know how he does it, but I'm thankful for it all the same.

Tyler and Silvy had only left my office a few moments earlier, stopping by for nothing more than their normal morning hellos. It's a conspiracy on their part—a pact formed after my attack—to check on me daily. Usually one, or both, will pop in on their way to their desks, or on the way to or from the kitchen for coffee. My priority falls somewhere between dumping their laptop bags off at their desk and the need for caffeine.

I don't mind. I actually look forward to it. I even bet on who it'll be each day. If I'm right, I get my Diet Coke an hour earlier than my standing noon minimum timeframe allowance—in my head, if I wait until noon to get my caffeine fix, then it's not really a habit, it's a drinking preference, a choice…not a habit…nope. If I'm wrong, then I push that little DC fix to one hour later. But, really, who's counting? The Caffeine Police have never shown up to slap my wrist if I fudge that one-hour delay. Besides, hello, coffee drinkers drink that sludge all day long. I wait until noon. It's a choice. Not a habit.

Today, I won the bet with myself. They both showed up. So, yay for the hour-early Diet Coke celebration. Except, the whole having a mind-blowing, slap-your-ass-until-you-scream orgasm kinda sidetracked me, along with the text I receive from Theo moments before his first class.

Theo: *I discovered I have a student conference with Susan James at 2pm. Any advice?*
Theo: *I want to apologize again for this morning. I'm all wonky because of it. I need to see you and make it right.*

My heart breaks a little. It's embarrassing to be sure, but besides the weirdness of it, really, it's a normal thing a guy would do, and most women. He shouldn't beat himself up about it.

Me: *Don't stress about this morning. It's hot. Weird because I felt it too, not because you did it. Okay? Regarding Ms. James... Honestly, I'm a bit jealous. I don't like the idea of you alone with a woman who wants you. But I know she's your student. You can't avoid her.*

His response is quick, and I feel possessed by his words.

Theo: *Jealous? You have nothing to be jealous of. I only have eyes for you. I only want you. I'll make up some excuse and cancel. Tell her to email me her concerns.*

Me: *No. Don't cancel. I'm only telling you how I feel. I'm not asking you to disrupt your life to accommodate my insecurities. Maybe I'll show up and show her that you're taken.*

Theo: *Show her how?*

Me: *I could throw you on your desk (hypothetically since you're entirely too large for me to man-handle) and rip your clothes off. Or perhaps a subtler approach – I strut into your office, sit on your lap, and rub all over you like a cat in heat.*

Me: *OR, I could simply call you at 2:05 p.m. You can answer if you want or let it roll to voicemail.*

Theo: *As much as I love the first two options, what we have is for our eyes only. I don't share, even to make a point. But feel free to do either of those things when we're alone. I look forward to your phone call.*

I add a reminder to my calendar, tell him I'll see him soon, and most importantly to not stress about this morning or his meeting with Susan James—the tramp.

Taking advantage of Tyler's flexibility in letting me work from home occasionally and a meeting-free afternoon, I leave at lunchtime to finish my day at home and start on dinner.

After setting up my laptop in my spare bedroom, I slip off my boots and don an apron to protect my black wrap dress from tomato stains. I'm tempted to change into something more comfortable, but I want to look nice when Theo comes, instead of wearing my lounging clothes he's seen me in so often.

The bolognese sauce simmers on the stove while I mix the brownies, then slip them in the oven and set the timer. I jump when the reminder sounds on my phone.

It's time to call Theo.

The phone rings only a few times before he answers. My pulse races like a giddy schoolgirl's.

"Lauren." His voice is low in that come hither *I want to sex you up* kinda way he has. *Lord, he's so hot, and I don't even think he's trying.*

"Jeez, you make my nipples hard."

"Bloody hell," he murmurs low enough that I doubt Ms. James could catch it. "Really?" His volume returns to normal, but the sexy rasp in his voice is stronger. "I'll have to check them out when I get home."

Home. I couldn't like the sound of that any more if I tried. "Yes, they most definitely need your attention."

"Vixen," his nearly imperceptible murmur is back. "Is there anything else that needs my attention?"

"My panties seem to have sprung a leak." My boldness over the phone knows no bounds apparently. I could never say such things in person.

His burst of laughter is surprising. I can imagine Ms. James is thinking how sexy he is when he lets loose and laughs with abandon. I'm sure she'll catch the twinkle in his chocolate eyes. She might even think it's for her.

"Then I would recommend you take them off. Let them breathe for a while. I look forward to investigating further — discovering the cause."

"Did you ever think I'd be so brave?" It's my turn to whisper, my emotions showing plainly for him to hear.

His laugh is replaced with tenderness. "I had no doubts. You make me proud."

"I'm home, by the way. Don't make me wait too long."

"I wouldn't dare. I'll be there shortly, as soon as my last class ends."

"Hey, Theo?"

"Yes, Dove?"

Dove? That's a new one. "You make me proud, too." My voice breaks, and my eyes water. I shake my head and blink them away. "How'd I get so lucky?"

"It's not luck, Lauren. It's fate, but if it were luck, I'd be the lucky one."

Look at us. Having a heart-to-heart with Susan James listening in. Take that, Ms. James. He's mine. You can't have him.

"You're mine." I'm not comfortable saying I love you with her in the room. I'm only willing to go so far. Besides, we haven't said it again since the first time.

"And you're mine." The possessiveness in his declaration has me forgetting all about little miss somebody or other sitting across from him.

I arrive at her apartment a little before four, three and a half hours before we're supposed to be at Dan's. I knock, feeling nervous all of a sudden, or maybe it's anticipation. The door opens, and I'm greeted with a shy smile and blue eyes that pierce through my nerves like a soothing balm. I'm amazed at how she does that—her presence, a glance, a simple touch, a reassuring word—I'm putty in her hands.

"Hi." She steps aside, waving me in.

"Hullo, Dove." I kiss her blushing cheek as I pass, liking my new pet name for her more and more, especially if it makes her blush.

She closes and locks the door behind me—always attentive to her safety, even with me here. Moving into the kitchen saying she *needs a sec*, she leaves the security alarm off. That's a first. Did she forget? Is she trying to make a statement?

The fact that I noticed leaves me with the need to arm it—so I do. Forgetful or not. Statement or not. It's done. Now, we can both breathe easier knowing that an additional barrier exists between her and the evil in the world that could harm her—even in the sanctity of her home.

At the cusp of the kitchen, I glance at her bare feet, and bare legs that end mid-calf where her black dress begins. My eyes continue their slow journey upwards. The dress hugs her curves, cinched at her narrow waist with a colourful sash of some sort. She turns and catches me staring, her eyes shining with mirth. Upon further inspection, I now see she's wearing an apron with vibrant purple flowers—so, not a sash at all.

She moves towards me, close but not close enough. "Is

that a loaf of bread, or are you happy to see me?"

"Yes," I reply to both, elated to see her boldness is not relegated solely to the phone.

She laughs and relieves me of the bread. "Thank you for getting this."

"My pleasure. May I be of assistance?" I note the two pots on the stove and a rectangular casserole dish of brownies on the counter. The mix of sweet and savoury smells are tantalizing.

She stirs the sauce, tapping the spoon on the edge of the pot before placing it on the spoon rest. "Everything's in a holding pattern until we're ready to eat." She salts a large pot of water, replacing the lid and adjusting the temperature. "Why don't you get comfortable." Her eyes hit mine over her shoulder. "Take your jacket off, your shoes, whatever you want."

"Whatever I want?" My mind fills with all kinds of dirty thoughts. It's only a dress, panties, and a bra between her and nakedness.

She blushes. "Yes?" Still so brave.

Moving to the dining room, I empty my pockets. "So, I can remove anything I want?" My jacket slung on a chair, I slip off my shoes, roll up my sleeves, and unbutton one button at my collar. I'm sans tie today.

She eyes me speculatively. "Within reason." Her bottom lip gets tangled between her teeth.

Joining her in the kitchen, I slip my arm around her waist, holding her cheek as my thumb runs across her bottom lip, releasing it from its prison. "That's mine." I kiss

245

that captive lip ever so gently, breathing her in. "So, I can take your dress off, then?"

Her doe eyes flit between my mouth and my eyes. "I meant on your body, but I could be persuaded. Perhaps." She looks up then, and I see desire in her bluer-than-blue eyes. "Are *you* going to undress?"

My wicked grin presses to her lips. "I could be persuaded."

On a cleansing breath, I step away, slowing things down. "It smells good in here. When do we eat?"

"It's up to you. I need, like, twenty minutes to finish it up."

"How about we eat around six?" That gives us approximately two hours to get in a world of trouble.

"Sounds good." She tilts her head. "Whatever shall we do to pass the time?"

Vixen. "Come with me." I lead her to the living room. "Turn around, please."

She presents her back, peeking over her shoulder as I untie her apron from around her waist. She pulls it over her head, and I set it on a chair. I press into her back, sweeping her hair off her shoulder as my lips connect with her neck. Her weight settles into me, my arm around her waist ensuring she stays there.

Her soft moan amps up my arousal, my cock stiffening in my trousers. "It's forecasted to snow this evening." I back off from our zero-to-one-hundred race to get naked. I want this to be a special night, not a sex-induced haze of regret if I move too fast.

"Maybe we'll get snowed in." She's teasing, but from the latest newscast, it's a real possibility.

"Here's hoping."

She turns in my arms, her eyes earnest and wanting. "If it's bad, will you stay?"

My resolve weakens with her desire to keep me close. All bets are off, at least for the next thirty seconds. One…my mouth joins hers. Two…it's a slow glide. A flick of a tongue—mine—then hers. Five…her lips part on a gasp, and I move in, paying homage to her dress, her scent, her soft curves against my hard edges. Fifteen…fuck. My hands slide down her back, over her arse and squeeze, holding her against me, my cock pressed to her stomach. Twenty…I grind. The swivel of my hips meets the swivel of hers. Twenty-five…horizontal. I need to get this woman on her back with me buried between her milky thighs. Thirty…*bloodyfuckinghell.*

Breathless, I break our kiss, and loosen my grip. "Snow or not, I'm staying."

Her giggle reverberates through my bollocks, causing my cock to twitch with hope.

Not now, arsehole.

I step back, taking her all in from the front, sans apron. Her dress has long sleeves and a deep neckline that comes to a point between her breasts, then wraps and ties at the side of her waist. Her cleavage is modest but highly effective.

"God, I missed you today." My breath is still laboured.

"So much so, you had to…you know." Her eyebrows

wiggle teasingly.

"Don't remind me of that debacle." I pull her to the couch, sitting side by side, her legs swung over mine. "I'm sorry about that." I smooth out the hem of her dress.

"Hey." Her fingers touch my chin. Our eyes lock. "I'm flattered." She shivers. "It was me you were thinking about, right? Did I get that wrong?"

"God, no. Yes. It was you I was shagging in my head." Crass but truthful. I can't leave her with any doubts.

"Shagging?" She smiles, not put off in the least.

I pounce, laying her on the couch, her legs still draped over mine. My lips tease hers as my hand parts the slit in her dress. "Yes, shagging. Having sex. Making love." I graze her clit over moist silk panties and then hold her pussy in my palm, moving slowly. Her whimper urges me forward. "In my mind I was here while I stroked my cock." My fingers breach the edge of her knickers. *Fuck, she's so wet. Her panties did spring a leak.* One finger slips inside, pressing slowly in and out. "Imagining I was buried deep inside you."

Her head falls back with a gasp. Her hips move, searching for purchase. On the next stroke I slip in two fingers. Unable to remain a spectator, my needy cock has my hips moving against her thigh in sync with my digits.

"Theo." She clutches my arm with the fingers inside her as her other hand squeezes my shoulder.

"Are you going to come for me, Dove?" My strokes quicken as I press against her bundle of nerves.

"Yeeesssss," she moans, nearly there, so ready, so

responsive.

I brush my lips over hers, sucking her bottom lip before whispering, "Come on my fingers as I envision it's my cock." I pinch her nipple, teasing it between my finger and thumb. "Come."

She blows, her hips grinding so fiercely against my hand, she swipes my cock with each gyration, and I nearly fucking join her. I hold off, watching her shatter in my arms. Glorifying her beautiful abandon, my shy, chaste girl, vulnerable and sensual as the vixen within comes on my fingers until she's spent and glowing like the sun.

Chapter 22

WILL THIS REVOLVING DOOR OF AROUSAL, coming, and then crashing embarrassment ever end? Will I forever want to slink away after letting loose and blowing a gasket like Old Faithful?

"You need to stop." His commanding voice is gentle yet firm.

I can't even look him in the eye. "You didn't even—"

"This isn't about me." He pulls me to his chest. "Well, maybe it is a bit about me, as I enjoyed it thoroughly."

Slipping his fingers from my body, I gasp in horror when puts them in his mouth, sucking them clean. I bury my face in his chest. "Did you have to do that?"

He chuckles. "Yes." He maneuvers to hover over me. "I need you to get over this embarrassment. You in the throes of ecstasy is the hottest thing I've ever experienced. Hands down, you are the sexiest woman I've ever seen, known, kissed, or touched. And I plan on giving you orgasms at every turn."

His mouth is on mine before I can avoid his me-flavored lips. I protest on a moan, but his persistent tongue wins when he squeezes my breast, his thumb skating across my beaded nipple. Pleasure surpasses the mortification of tasting myself on his mouth. "You taste better than I imagined. I can't wait to drink directly from its source."

I try to hide my embarrassment in his shoulder, but he pushes back when he sees my full-body blush.

Shock mars his handsome face. "Has nobody ever…" He sits up, pulling me with him. "Bloody hell, has no man ever kissed you there?"

I'm thankful he refrains from using a graphic description. I shake my head, unable to verbalize my shame that no one ever wanted to.

"Bloody hell." His jaw clenches, and his eyes narrow. He's stunned into silence, which stretches between us.

When I can't take it anymore, fearing the worst, I whisper, "I'm sorry," feeling like I've failed him.

251

He frowns. "Sorry? What in the world do you have to be sorry for?"

"For not—"

"No." He cuts me off. "Don't you dare feel bad about this." His hand caresses my cheek. "How many men have you slept with?"

I sink into the couch, pulling my legs under me, wrapping my arms around myself. "One."

The reality is harsh. I'm twenty-six years old, and I've only had one lover. I'm sure Theo will think it's because I'm selective, that I chose to only have one, and that my choice was worthy of my virginity. The truth is, he's the only one who tried. I'm not that sexy girl. Guys have never pursued me. They don't see me as a sexual creature but as a gal pal to hang out with.

"I know that look." He picks me up like I'm a bag of flour, settling me on his lap, my legs on either side of his. Firmly, he grips my sides, ensuring I remain anchored to him. "Don't shut down on me."

"You don't understand—"

His tender caress of my cheek increases the likelihood of tears. "You're right. I don't. I don't understand how you can look like this..." His eyes scan my body, my hair, my face before locking on mine. "And have such low self-esteem."

"I'm nothing special. Guys don't—"

"Stop." His palm comes up as if to block my words. His nose flares. His jaw tightens. "You need to stop. I won't allow such hateful things to be said about you—even if you're the one doing the talking."

I appreciate what he's trying to do. I'm even touched by it, but he needs to understand. I cross my arms, staring him down. "The fact that you don't want to hear it doesn't make it any less true."

"I—"

I squelch his protest with my hand over his mouth and fight the urge to laugh when his eyes widen, and then he scowls at me. "If you're seriously interested in a relationship with me, then you need to hear me. It's part of who I am. Just because you don't like it doesn't change my opinion of myself or make it go away." I remove my hand, waiting to see if he'll protest or let me continue.

"I'm listening." He's not happy, but he's quiet at least.

"Guys don't see me like you see me. I've never been *that girl*—the popular one, or the one who attracts men. You're an anomaly, Theo. You see things that aren't there, or you have some special vision that allows you to see what is, in fact, there, but invisible to others. I don't know which it is. But it scares me. One day you're going to break those special glasses of yours and realize I'm nothing special. And then where will I be? The fall from your love will do more than just break my heart. It'll shatter me."

"Dove." His tender reference breaks the dam of my tears. He catches the first few. "I'm not going anywhere."

"But you will," I manage through the flow of waterworks.

"No."

"Yes," I insist. I try to push off his lap, but his firm grip

253

keeps me seated. "Even my father…" *Shit. Don't go there.*

"What?" His fingers sink into my hair, his hand palming the back of my head, pulling my forehead to his. "Even your father…?"

"No." I close my eyes, shutting him out.

"Tell me." It's a whisper on a breath of frustration.

"No. It's prosaic." I push against his grip, meeting his glare. "I shouldn't have said anything."

"But you did." His hands bracket my face. "You said it yourself. I need to know these things if I plan on having a relationship with you." His eyes soften into tender brown orbs as he takes a moment. "I plan on having more than just a relationship with you. I'm staking my heart, my future, my everything on you—on us. Now, tell me what you don't want me to know."

I hesitate for only a moment, unwilling to hide my shame any longer. He needs to know. He needs to understand my brokenness, my unworthiness. "How can you possibly love me when my own father didn't love me enough to stick around?"

If he's surprised, he doesn't show it. His hands slide down my arms to capture my hands. "How old were you?"

"I was four when my parents divorced." He knows this. We touched on it briefly.

He nods, studying my hands in his. "How long before he remarried?"

"I was still four."

His eyes shoot up, his eyebrows question.

I shrug. "I guess he didn't like being alone. I remember living with him, my mom and brother. Then I remember staying a few times at his apartment. And then I was at his wedding reception—we weren't allowed at the wedding. I don't remember much in between. The next thing I know, he has kids, a boy and a girl—like my brother and me, but not us—newer and improved versions, I guess."

"You felt replaced?"

I shake my head. "I felt unlovable. Like there was something wrong with me."

He toys with a lock of my hair. "Because if he can't love you, no one else can?"

"I wasn't enough—I wasn't worthy—of his love, his time, his loyalty."

"Do you feel unworthy now?" He tips my chin, the pad of his thumb rubbing my bottom lip, his eyes on me.

A tear falls free on a single nod.

"You feel unworthy of *me*?" His voice cracks with emotion.

The brimming of his emotions is hard to witness. I'm used to the weight of my own anguish. It's difficult to take on his as well.

"Yes." He deserves my words, not a silent nod.

With a deep breath, he leans back. His head rests on the high back of the couch while his eyes hold me in place. "Do I look at you like you're unworthy?"

"No." I'm adamant.

"Do I treat you like you're unworthy?"

"God, no." My voice rises perhaps a little too loudly. I

won't have him thinking he's the cause of my insecurities.

The tips of his fingers caress my cheek as his eyes beseech me. "Do I touch you like you're unworthy?"

I lean into his touch, holding his hand to my cheek. "No. This isn't about you."

His brows arch. "But it is. Not because I make you feel unworthy, but because you doubt me. You doubt my fortitude, my commitment to you."

"I doubt my worthiness."

"Which makes you doubt *me*, *my* feelings, *my* ability to love you in spite of—or perhaps because of—your lack of confidence."

I shake my head, trying to wrap my mind around what he's saying. How did me feeling bad about myself turn into doubting him? "I didn't…I'm not…ugh. I don't know! I'd never thought of it like that. I believe your feelings are genuine. I don't think you're lying to me—if that's what you're thinking."

He nods, contemplative. "How about we eat and think on it?" He's so calm and patient. And I'm a brewing storm.

I stand and walk to the kitchen, my back to him as I stare at the pots on the stove, making no attempt to get dinner ready.

I feel his presence before he even touches me. He hugs me from behind, burying his face in my neck. I wrap my arms around his, leaning into him, letting him hold me.

"I don't want to leave it like this." The sour pit in my stomach ensures my discomfort is both physical and emotional.

"How do you want to leave it?" His lips graze my jaw before he presses a kiss near my ear.

"I feel disconnected. I'm sick to my stomach like I've ruined something between us."

I gasp as he spins me around, lifts me to the counter, and settles between my legs.

"There's nothing ruined between us. I learned a lot of things I didn't know before. I need time to process." My head tilted up to him, he barely touches his forehead and the bridge of his nose to mine. "But know this, I'm not that easily swayed, Lauren. I'm not going anywhere." He kisses me tenderly. "Take a breather. Let's eat. We can finish this discussion when we get back tonight, or we can skip the music thing entirely."

"I don't want to miss meeting your friends. Unless…you're having doubts."

He chuckles. "Dove, the only doubt I have is my ability to abstain from ravishing every inch of you. And now that I've tasted you, it's bloody near impossible."

"Tell me about Susan James. How was your conference

with her?"

She takes a bite of spaghetti, her eyes clear of the emotions that nearly had me pinning her to her bed and demonstrating exactly how much I'm *not* leaving her. She has no idea, but she will. Before this night is over, she will have no doubt about my feelings or my intentions.

And damn her father for every making her feel undeserving of love. Just thinking about the way he got inside her head and planted these seeds of insecurity make my hands shake with rage.

"She arrived right on time. Plopped herself down in the chair in front of my desk as if she owned the place. She was quite flirtatious. I was relieved when you called. We hadn't gotten too far in our discussion. I ignored the fact that she was even there. I'm pretty sure she got the idea I was talking to my girlfriend, but I emphasized the point after we hung up. She was surprised and didn't stay long after that. She couldn't leave fast enough, in fact." I pause, expelling a breath, letting go of the stress of Miss James. "Thank you for that. I hope she'll back off now."

"I'm glad it worked—at least for today. I might have to pay you a visit to make my presence more known." Her smile is devious, and I relish her claim over me.

"You definitely need to wear that dress when you come." I point to her boots in the corner. "And those, to be sure." I tip my head, watching her blush as I take a drink. "Maybe I'll be the one to lay you out on my desk and rip your clothes off. Fair's fair."

Her laugh is genuine and further eases the stress of the day. Though, I'm filled with questions from our earlier discussion.

After a few minutes of contemplative consumption of dinner, I give in to my most pressing question. "How is it that only one man has made love to you?"

She cringes and closes her eyes momentarily. "Don't say it like that. He was *not* a man." She points to me. "Not like you. He was a boy in comparison."

I'm proud she thinks me more of a man than her previous lover, but it pisses me off that he wasn't the kind of man who deserved her—or the gift of her virginity.

"...And he didn't *make love* to me." She shudders. "Ugh, it's unbearable to even say it." Her hands cover her face momentarily. "I'm ashamed I lost my virginity to him. I thought it was more than it was—I thought *he* was more than he was."

Her eyes flash to mine before returning to her plate. "You've shown me more kindness and respect than he ever did."

My anger flares. My need to claim her, to show her what making love to a real man feels like surges through me. I reach out, touching her face, turning her towards me. "You deserve better than that. I'm sorry."

She shakes her head. I can hear the argument on her lips before she even verbalizes it. "No. I deserve exactly what I got. It's not his fault. I'm the one who didn't stick to my plan to wait. It's my burden to bear, not his. My talking negatively about him is more about me and my shame, and not really about him. He was nice. He didn't hurt me or anything. He wasn't what I wanted, or needed, but I was lonely, and he noticed me when no one else did."

She's killing me.

Taking a deep breath, she squares her shoulders. Her eyes lock with mine. "It was my responsibility to be more—to be better—not his."

If I wasn't impressed with her warrior's heart before, I am now. This woman who has been through so much, more than her share, instead of coming out a victim, she owns it. She takes responsibility, not because it's her fault, but because she's a fighter, and fighters don't bow down. They stand tall and take the blows, reinforcing the barricade protecting their tender heart, waiting until it's time to fight back.

"It's honorable to take the blame. But you're too hard on yourself, and I'm still sorry this guy was your first experience." I stop her protest with a kiss on the lips, and then whisper, "Nothing you say will change my opinion on that."

We continue eating in silence. She twirls spaghetti on her fork, her brow furrowed, contemplative. As I eat, I'm enthralled by the thoughts that flit across her face. Some I can read. Others are a loss, but no less intriguing.

Her lips quirk as she slips a bite into her mouth. I need to know what brought about that whimsical smile.

Before I can ask, her gaze slides to me, her smile gone and her bright eyes shining with regret. "I wish it had been you."

She has no idea. "Me too, Dove. Me too." Lifting her hand, I press a kiss to her knuckles then to each fingertip. "From here forward, it's you and me. No more regrets."

On a shy smile, she blushes her agreement.

Full, she pushes her plate away. "I saw your email about the three-day weekend coming up. I sent a note to my boss and put it in as a vacation day. I don't think it will be a problem, but I'll let you know when I hear back. Probably tomorrow."

It's short notice. Hopefully her boss won't reject her request if he knows it's to spend time with me. She may not believe he sees her as more than an employee, but I know differently. I saw the look in his eyes, the tightness in his jaw, and the protective stance he took over my girl. He's no fool, and neither am I. "Does Tyler know we're together?"

Her brows disappear under her curly bangs. "No. Why?"

"I was wondering if he'll approve the request if he knows it's to spend time with me."

She laughs, taking her plate to the kitchen. "You almost sound jealous. Tyler and I don't talk about that kind of stuff. I don't know who he dates, and he has no idea if I date or not." Returning to the table, her hands resting on the back of her chair, she pins me with her soul-searching blue-eyed gaze. "He wouldn't care even if he knew."

"I wouldn't count on that." I stand and kiss her forehead as I pass, taking my plate to the kitchen.

My vision greatly underestimates the impact she has on

me. I have no doubt she's just as oblivious to the effect she has on Tyler and men in general. They may not be beating down her door, but make no mistake, she is not as invisible as she believes. I don't require special glasses to see the gift that she is.

Even a blind man could feel the heat radiating from her shining essence, and Tyler's eyes work perfectly fine.

Chapter 23

I RUN TO THE BATHROOM, FRESHEN my breath and reapply lip balm. Lipstick is a waste when Theo is around. He'll only wipe it off before he kisses me again and again.

When I come out, he has his coat on and mine in his hands, holding it up for me. I put my arms in, and he slips it over my shoulders, then untucks my hair, placing a kiss on the sensitive spot behind my ear.

"Ready?" His breath accompanies the goosebumps his

lips sent coursing across my skin.

"Yes." As I'll ever be.

We lock up and head to his car. I shiver from the chilly night air. The temperature has dropped significantly from when I left work this afternoon. "It definitely feels like snow is comin'."

He raises his ever-expressive eyebrows and smiles. "I'm staying either way, remember?"

God, how could I forget? "I remember."

Theo opens the passenger door, holding my hand, as I get in. I expect him to close my door, but instead he reaches over and buckles my seatbelt, his nose buried in my hair. "I may never leave." His gruff voice is so soft, I'm not sure he even meant for me to hear.

Closing my door, he rounds the car, placing the brownies in the backseat, gets in, and quickly starts the engine and turns up the heat.

We make it to Dan's a little after seven. It's a large house near the SMU campus with a circular drive long and wide enough for all the cars to park behind each other and still have room to pass. Which is good, considering the streets are narrow in this part of Highland Park and don't allow for curbside parking. Having a party here would be a nightmare. Not that I'm a party kinda girl, but it's a detail, and well, I love the details.

Theo turns the car off, taking my hand. "Nervous?"

Very. "Yes." I give him a bright smile, not wanting him to worry.

His lips press to our joined hands. "Don't be. They'll love you."

I pray the reception will be warmer than that of the faculty-wives-stick-up-their-asses club. Curious is fine, but downright cold and judgy I can do without.

Releasing me, he grabs the brownies and steps out on a, "Don't move."

He opens my door, offering his hand. Once outside, I tuck my collar up under my chin and eye the impressive home. This is the older part of Highland Park where the houses haven't been knocked down to build new lot-busting mansions that barely fit, like me when I try to squeeze into a pair of jeans two sizes too small—not that I do that anymore. But there was definitely a time when I did regularly.

"Would you mind holding these? I need to get my guitar out of the boot." He places the brownies in my proffered hands as I stifle my laugh, remembering the British term for trunk.

Opening the *boot*, he slings his guitar case over his shoulder and takes my hand. Before he knocks, he leans down and gives me a gentle kiss. "You look beautiful. Don't be nervous. You already know Marcus and heard a bit about Reese. The other guys will love you." Another Kiss. "Ready?"

I let out a breath. "I suppose it's now or never." I could go for *never* right about now.

He squeezes my hand as he knocks on the door. "Remember. No pressure to sing. I've already warned Marcus." The censure in his voice is clearly meant for

Marcus and not me.

I'm saved from the idea of singing in front of strangers when a tall, lanky guy answers the door. His short blond hair is styled in that *I just got out of bed* kinda way. His toothy grin and kind aqua eyes beam at me.

"You must be Lauren." He nearly throws the brownies I'm holding into Theo's hand, forcing Theo to relinquish his hold on me as Mr. Welcome Wagon wraps me in a bear hug. I gasp in surprise but relish his exuberance. He's obviously happy for his friend, which means he's heard about me, and it must not have been all bad.

"It's great to meet you. I've heard great things from Marcus." He releases me and steps back. "Please, come in."

He shakes Theo's hand with a brow wiggle and head tilt in my direction. "Nice, man." He pats Theo on the back as we step inside. "It's good to see you too, by the way."

Theo grins matches mine. "Lauren, this is Dan Gillard. This is his house. And I imagine his wife, Nancy, is here somewhere."

"It's great to meet you. You have a beautiful home."

"Thank you. Yes"—Dan motions to Theo and then to the back of the house—"Nancy's in the kitchen, more than likely. Come meet the guys."

With Theo's hand solidly attached to my lower back, we follow Dan through the entryway that opens into a grand room. And *grand* is quite apropos for the large room with a fire place in the middle of the back wall, seating around the hearth and all along the outskirts of the room. In the middle is a baby grand piano, a drum set, and multiple guitars. Instrument cases are strewn across the floor, some opened, some closed. The number of cases exceeds those in the room, leaving me to assume many of these guys play multiple instruments.

As we draw closer, all heads turn to greet us. I stutter a step, leaning back into Theo's strong hand as he urges me forward with a soft, "Breathe."

"Hey, everyone, this is Theo's Lauren," Dan introduces me around the room.

I shake hands with Chris Miller, who plays the electric guitar, and Mark Bryant, who plays the fiddle and various other instruments, according to Dan. Their welcomes vary from exuberant like Dan to shy, like me.

Theo gets *hellos* and pats on the back as we move down the row.

"And this guy here is Reese Pritchard. He's our bass guitarist." Dan motions to the nice-looking guy.

Two things hit me simultaneously. I recognize his name—he went to school with Theo in England, and I immediately peg him as Nicole's type. I smile as if I know him. "Reese, it's good to meet you."

"It's great to meet you, Lauren." Reese gives me a quick hug and a fist bump to Theo.

"And you already know Marcus," Dan concludes the introductions.

Marcus traverses the minefield of cases, giving me a kiss on the cheek and a hug. "It's good to see you again, Lauren."

"You too." I'm surprised by my relief in seeing him. I

was dreading it, afraid of what he'd ask me to do. But all I feel is welcomed by his warm embrace and the relief of knowing someone else besides Theo.

Marcus releases me, turning to Theo with a knowing smile and a handshake. "I'm glad you haven't scared her off."

"Never." Theo entwines our fingers.

"Make yourself at home. Put your purse and coat on the chairs over there if you like." Dan points to a sitting area on the far end of the room close to the entry we came through.

"Thank you. Oh, and we brought brownies in case anyone wants any." I offer the dish to Dan.

"Yeah, I'll take those." Marcus nabs them from me, beating Dan by half a second.

Theo guides me to the area with a chuckle. I drop my purse in a chair, and he helps me off with my coat. "See, they're all happy to meet you." His dancing eyes watch me as he takes his off. "It's not a boys-only kind of thing as you thought." He places his coat next to mine and captures my hand. "Let's go say hello to Nancy, Dan's wife."

We find Nancy in the kitchen talking to Marcus, who's eating a brownie. I smile at the sight.

Before Theo can say anything, Marcus points at us. "Theo brought his girl."

I blush, and Nancy exudes happiness. "It's so good to see you with someone." She kisses Theo on the cheek. His hand never leaves mine as he kisses her cheek in return.

"Nancy, this is Lauren, my girlfriend." He releases my

hand only to pull me into his side.

I get a cheek kiss too. "It's great to meet you, Lauren." Nancy is tall and thin like her husband. They look like they could breed a substantial basketball team.

"It's nice to meet you as well."

"I've never met anyone he's dated. You have no idea how happy I am to see him finally find someone." Her eyes dart between us.

The thought of Theo dating sends my stomach plummeting.

She gets distracted by Marcus taking another brownie. "Save some for everyone else."

Theo squeezes me, kissing my temple. "I didn't date," he whispers for my ears only. "No one's captured my heart like you."

I already knew he didn't date. He said so himself—he'd given up on love. But his comment and Nancy's only confirm that there were women. He didn't date them—he had sex with them. Probably lots and lots of sex. And here I am holding out on him.

I swallow my unease. This is neither the time nor the place to have these nagging, all too visual thoughts.

"Excuse us for a moment." Taking my hand, Theo retreats, pulling me down a hall and into a bedroom.

I circle on him as he closes the door. "You don't—"

He's on me in one stride. "I do." He eyes skate over my face. "I can see it written all over you." He presses his forehead to mine. "I wish I could say there was no one before you, but I can't, and that kills me." His grip on my waist tightens. "Because I know it's eating you up inside." He swallows, his emotions escalating with my own.

I whimper out a breath of air and close my eyes. *I can't hear this.*

"It was only sex. A release. A visceral need for female contact." His hands capture my face, spurring my eyes to open. "I'm no saint, Dove."

He presses a tender, needy kiss on my mouth. His lips suck on mine as if he can excavate the visual from my brain via my lips. "I wish I was. For you—God, I wish I was."

"I don't need a saint." I pull back, shaking my head, rattling the thoughts of him with other women free. "I don't want a saint."

He studies my lips, his thumb running over them. "No?"

"No." I urge him to look at me. "I want you."

He smiles on a sigh. "You have me." Kiss. "One hundred percent." Kiss. "I only want you, Dove." Kiss. "Forever—" Kiss. "Only—" Kiss. "You." His last kiss lasts longer than it should for being a guest in someone else's house, but not nearly long enough to satiate my need to claim him and be claimed by him.

We step into the kitchen right behind Reese. I listen to their boisterous comradery, giving each other shit the way only guys can. When Reese slings his arm over my shoulder, nodding to Theo, I know someone's feathers are about to get ruffled.

Theo straightens from leaning on the counter. "Reese."

It's one word, but I hear the threat.

Reese ignores him. "I could tell you stories about Theo and our college days."

My eyes flicker to Theo before looking up at Reese. He's tall but not quite as tall as my man. "I'm sure you could."

The group breaks out in laughter, and I smile, but sense Theo's unease. I slide out from under Reese's arm and into Theo's embrace.

Theo kisses my head and narrows his eyes at Reese. "Hands to yourself, Pritchard."

Reese laughs harder, looking at him in awe as if he's never seen *this* Theo. And maybe he hasn't. Theo said his love for his ex didn't compare to what he already feels for me. Perhaps Reese has never seen my Theo—the protective, loving curmudgeon who's opening up and living again.

He says I breathed life into his barren soul. Well, he's done the same. He's grounded me, yet given me wings. I may not be great at flying. I may not trust it all the time, but I'm working on it. I'm trying to believe—in him and me.

"You're afraid she'll like me more than you." Reese pokes the beast.

"That's not even in the realm of possibilities." Theo slugs him in the shoulder. "Now hand me a brownie before they're all gone."

Brownie devoured, Theo tightens his arm around my waist. "I need to set up my guitar." My serious professor kisses my cheek. "I'll be back."

I admire the view as he turns to leave. Reese follows to do the same, but not before surprising me with a kiss on my other cheek.

My gasp has Theo turning. "Hey. Hands and lips off my girl, Reese. That goes for you too, Marcus, in case you get any ideas. Nancy, I trust you to keep these horny buggers off my girl." He winks and gives me a wicked smile.

"That boy is smitten," Nancy says after Theo and Reese are well out of the kitchen.

"Yeah?" I don't know how else to respond without sounding cocky or insecure.

"No doubt," she replies.

"He's more than smitten," Marcus chimes in.

"It's more than mutual," I admit, looking through the kitchen arch into the grand room.

"I can see that. I'm happy for you both. You make a beautiful couple. I expect a wedding invitation," Nancy declares.

I laugh away my embarrassment. "Oh, it's too soon for that."

"I don't think so." Marcus' green eyes spout truth like he doesn't even need words. "I've never seen Theo like he is with you. He's a different person. He'd marry you tomorrow. Take my word for it." His sweet smile and gentle cant of his head make me think he knows something I don't.

"Okay, okay, y'all are too much." I plead for them to stop. It's nice to hear, but I don't want those ideas in my head. The idea of Theo loving me forever is hard to comprehend. I'm afraid to believe it, much less discuss it out loud with people I hardly know.

"Come on. Come sit with me." Marcus places his hand on my back, coaxing me forward.

As we step into the room, Theo's eyes shoot to mine. The static buzz that's my constant companion when he's around intensifies. His eyes flash, confirming he feels it too. His smirk grows into a knee-weakening smile that has me tripping over thin air and grasping for Marcus to keep me on my feet.

"Careful now. We can't have you breaking your neck just when things are getting good." Marcus' lyrical southern drawl seems thicker than usual.

"Getting good?" I flash back to Theo, who's scowling at Marcus' tight grip on my waist.

I want to tell Theo it's his fault for being so darn hot I can hardly think straight, much less walk. Theo narrows his eyes as if he heard my thoughts and motions for me to come join him.

"Yeah, you and Theo steaming up the room." Marcus looks at Theo over his shoulder. "She's mine. You can wait your turn."

I fight the urge to laugh at the way Marcus pushes Theo's buttons.

"Please, sit. Join me." From the piano bench, Marcus coaxes me next to him. "I printed off some lyrics in case you want to follow along or join in." He says it so smoothly, as if I won't notice his ploy to get me to sing.

I scan the songs, noting I'm familiar with most of them.

Marcus' fingers trail along the keys and begin to play as he takes in the state of the group's readiness. "Y'all ready to get started?"

The chaotic sounds of guitar chords, drumming, and a fiddle warming up cease as they focus on Marcus and agree they're ready.

"Warm-up song?" Marcus asks.

"'Some Kind of Wonderful,'" Dan offers.

"All right, Dan, lead the way," Marcus responds.

Dan counts down, banging his drumsticks together. On the count of four they all join in. I've never been this close to the action. It's pretty impressive to see how the timing all works. As Dan sings and the others join in at the chorus, I realize they all have microphones. This is more than the guys hanging out. They have a whole sound system. They're a well-oiled machine, not guys goofing off while drinking beer.

As Marcus reaches across me to the higher keys, I worry I'm in his way and scoot over, but he stops me, whispering, "Don't move."

"I'm in your way," I whisper back.

"You're not." He smiles as if having me sit next to him as he plays is no hardship.

I scoot back over, sitting shoulder to shoulder. He nods his approval. I look up and meet Theo's gaze. He was watching. He winks, continuing to play and sing. Once again, my heart skips a beat at this gorgeous man who says he belongs to me. How can someone as incredible as him be happy with someone as ordinary as me?

The guys transition from song to song with familiar ease. Marcus sways on the piano bench, forcing me to join him or look like a stiff fuddy-duddy. I slowly loosen up a little and enjoy myself. They're really good. Dan, Marcus, and Theo take turns singing lead vocals, and the rest sing back up.

"He can't take his eyes off you." Marcus nudges me.

"What?" I look at Marcus.

Marcus motions with his head toward Theo. "He hasn't taken his eyes off you since we sat down. He has it bad. You can't deny it."

I dare a look, Theo's magnetic stare holding me captive. "I have it bad too. He's a wonderful man. I'm blessed to have met him." I glance down, shyness taking root along with my rising emotions.

Marcus gets my attention with a nudge. His gentle smile has me nudging him back. "You should put those emotions to good use. Sing a song with me." Not really a question.

"I…if I put my emotions into a song, I'll cry. No one wants to see that."

"Not true." His eyes scan the group. "Look at these guys. They put their heart and soul into these songs. It's only us. There's no judgment here. When we take a break, maybe you could stay and sing with me—just you and me. Everyone else will head to the bathroom and kitchen." His raised brow reminds me of Theo. "Think about it."

"Okay, I'll think about it." My heart's racing at the

thought of singing in front of these seasoned musicians.

"I'll be back." I get up to find the bathroom down the hall. I do my business, wash my hands, check my makeup, and take a few deep breaths to calm my nerves.

When I open the door, Theo's standing there, leaning against the wall. A smile spreads across his face. "You alright?"

I move closer. "Yes. Why?"

One arm snags me around the back, pulling me flush, as the other slowly brushes the hair away from my eyes. "I saw you and Marcus talking. You looked serious and then got up all of a sudden. I wanted to be sure you weren't upset."

"No, I'm fine. He asked me to sing with him." I toy with the collar of his shirt.

"And that upset you?"

"I thought my heart was gonna beat out of my chest."

He smiles, running his hand down my neck, pressing it over my heart. "It's still here." His eyes flit to mine. "Don't feel pressure. You don't have to if you don't want to."

"That's the thing, I actually do want to."

His brow quirks.

"Y'all were having such a good time," I offer as explanation. "But the idea is terrifying. He said maybe we could do it when you take a break."

"Break is now." His hand slides to the back of my neck. His lips descend on mine. His mouth glides with gentle pressure, and my heart skips a beat for a whole other reason than nerves. I moan and suck his bottom lip.

He pulls away on a chuckle. "My girl likes her kisses."

Yes. Yes, she does.

A quick press of his lips to mine before he steps back. "Come on, we only have ten minutes or so."

We enter the big room to find Marcus looking through sheets of music. Everyone else is gone. As we approach, he looks up and smiles. "I see you found our songbird."

"My songbird," Theo clarifies with authority.

Marcus simply chuckles and pats the seat next to him. "As you wish."

Theo's mouth possesses mine in a passionate kiss that ends with tug on my bottom lip. "I'll be in the kitchen enjoying your brownies."

I sigh and blink, trying to regain my composure.

He glares at Marcus. "Don't pressure her."

Marcus raises his hands in surrender. "I wouldn't dare."

I laugh at that. He would dare. He'll just gentle me through it.

Taking a seat, Marcus gets right to it. "What about 'Stay' by Rihanna? It's a duet and would suit your voice beautifully."

"Don't expect too much, Marcus." I glance to the kitchen. No one is paying us any mind. "I'll try."

"Excellent. Do you know the song well?"

"I'm familiar with it, but I can't say I remember all of the words or the melody."

"Not a problem. I haven't sung it either. We'll work our way through it. Together." He starts to play. "Why don't you take the first verse? I'll help with the melody if you get stuck."

"Oh, Lord." I sigh. "You're killing me."

His fingers continue to play. "I know you're scared, but I also know you can do it. There's no failure here, sweetheart. No right or wrong. Just a chance to use that God-given voice of yours."

He's gentling me through it, and it makes me want to cry. "Okay."

Without delay, he starts the intro and prompts me when to come in.

I sing the first few lines, managing to make it through without any major trip-ups. But I'm thankful when it's his turn to sing, and I get to listen. His voice is soulful, with rich warm tones and his perfect vibrato.

He nods, and we both sing the rest of the song together, with effortless harmony like we've sung together for years. With each passing note, my nerves lessen, the safety of the Marcus-bubble strong.

When we finish, I look up. Theo, Nancy, and the guys are standing around the kitchen door smiling and start to clap and cheer. I hide my face in Marcus' shoulder, knowing I'm blushing from head to toe.

Marcus wraps his arm around me. "I knew you could do it. You're amazing. We'll have to do that one again, next time with the guys."

He looks up at Theo. "Are you ready?"

Chapter 24

"**I**'ll BE READY AS SOON AS you release my girl." Theo offers me his hand.

I take it without hesitation, slipping out of Marcus' comforting hug and into Theo's side-embrace.

"Give us a moment." Theo nods to the guys and pulls me down the hall.

His stride is long and determined. I increase my pace to keep up. I can't get a read on him. I don't know why he'd be upset. "Are you mad?"

He grunts, continuing down the hall, opening a door to the bedroom we were in earlier and tugging me inside. He spins me around, pressing me against the closed door.

"Dove," he breathes, his forehead against mine. "I'm so fucking proud of you." He dots kisses across my face.

"So, not mad then?" My arms rest on his shoulders, one hand cupping his face, the other, the back of his neck.

His hands grip my sides. "No. I'm not crazy about you seeking comfort in Marcus' arms, but I understand he was your security blanket at that moment. I don't begrudge you that. I do, however, have to stake my claim, even with Marcus, whom I know enjoys provoking me entirely too much."

I bite my lip to stop my grin. "He does love giving you shit."

"Yes, he does." He traces his fingers along my throat reverently. "I could listen to you sing all day."

The edge in his voice has my insides clenching, my clit throbbing.

"I'm torn up inside. I want to praise you, fawn all over you and your voice. But at the same time, I want to ravish every inch of your body. Your voice does things to me — things not meant for public consumption." His lips press to mine as I moan over his words, his touch, his adamancy. "I want to be the one you sing with."

"I want that." My voice is more breath than sound, my body trembling with need.

His hands press my hips and secure me to him. "I've got

this thing I set up with Marcus, but after that…" He tilts my face to his. "I'm taking you home and making love to you." He stifles my reply with his lips. "In our way, Dove. In our way."

"Ms. Frasier, please take a seat." Theo motions to the stool that now sits beside his. He doesn't release my hand until I'm settled. I look over my shoulder to Marcus, wondering what's going on. He only smiles and winks, being no help at all, obviously enjoying the spectacle.

Theo picks up his guitar and takes the seat facing me. He adjusts the mic and wipes his palms on his pants as a nervous smile pricks his lips. "This is for you, Dove."

He starts playing the guitar—solo.

Within a few bars, I recognize his selection: "Thinking Out Loud" by Ed Sheeran.

"You're gonna make me cry."

He smiles and shakes his head no as if willing me not to. But truly, how could I not? This song, or any other—he planned this, wanting to sing to me with all of his friends around, witnessing this moment. No doubt it'll be my undoing.

I take a deep breath as he does the same, readying for the first verse. His beautiful mouth starts to sing, his voice filling the air that sizzles around us.

I'm mesmerized by the rich edge of his voice, the deep

resonance of his vibrato that echoes in my pulse. The tender glow in his brown eyes keeps me captive, only seeing him and the gift that he is—that he's offering.

When he reaches the chorus, telling me we've found love right where we are, I'm done. Waterworks ensue. As the guys join in, I blink away the tears so I can see my beautiful man's face and the pure adoration of his gaze—for me.

When the song ends, he sets down his guitar, stands, lifts me off my stool and into his arms. Tears stream down my face as he whispers into my hair, "I love you, Lauren. Truly, madly, deeply."

A sob is my only response. His arms tighten. He kisses my face, wiping away my tears. "Don't cry, Dove."

Seriously? How can I not? "I...I love you too, Professor," I choke out.

His lips find mine. His kiss is soft, deep, and passionate.

I hear bustling around us, whistles and cat-calls, but I don't care who sees us kissing. After a few minutes, we come up for air, thoroughly out of breath.

Wiping my eyes, I look around and laugh. "We sure know how to clear a room."

He chuckles and wipes the last of my tears away, kissing me once more. "I love you."

"I love you." I lay my head on his chest and give him a squeeze. "Thank you. It couldn't have been more perfect."

"You're welcome." His lips find mine again. "I don't mean to be a buzzkill, but we should head out soon. It's sleeting."

He packs up his guitar, and we say our goodbyes as others begin to do the same. I thank them all for making me feel so welcome.

I give Marcus a big hug and a kiss on the cheek. "Thank you." It's a thank you full of gratitude for taking me by his side, making me feel a part of their group, not pressuring me to sing, but easing me into it with only the two of us.

"My pleasure." He squeezes my hand. "Promise you'll come next time." He glances at Theo. "Besides, I don't think the big Brit would come without you."

I promise, and I mean it. It's a wonderful group of people who obviously care deeply for Theo. I want to be a part of it, not keep him from it.

We bundle up, collect our belongings and make a run for the car as we're pelted by frozen rain.

We throw ourselves in my car, shivering. We're laughing as Lauren sweeps the sleet out of my hair and hers. I turn the car on and crank up the heat, waiting long enough for the car to warm up and melt the thin layer of ice that's formed on the windshield.

It's only 9:00 p.m., but the streets are deserted. Driving is slow due to the reduced visibility and slippery slush on the roads. Thankfully, Lauren lives fairly close, and it only takes thirty minutes or so to make it to her place.

She makes her way into her apartment, walking cautiously on the slippery sidewalks. I grab my guitar, laptop, and gym bag with extra clothes.

Closing the apartment door behind me, I wipe off my shoes on the doormat, lock the door and arm it, and leave my wet bags in the entryway. I remove my coat and gloves, finding Lauren still in hers, kneeling at the hearth of the fireplace.

She looks up and smiles. "Did you get everything? Do you need help?"

Shouldn't I be asking her that? I motion to the fireplace. "Do *you* need help?"

"No, I've got it."

Of course she does. "Do you mind if I grab a towel to dry my bags?"

"Sure. Grab a few beach towels from the guest bath closet. They're bigger." With the fire lit, she adjusts the gas so the flames flicker above the fake logs.

I've never been a fan of fake fireplaces, but I can see the benefit of not having to keep real wood, particularly in an apartment, where personal outdoor space is limited. Plus, the idea of Lauren having to acquire and lug around enough wood for the winter doesn't sit well.

Using two large towels, I dry off my guitar case, moving

it off the wet tile and onto the carpet, then wipe off my laptop case and gym bag. Lauren starts to pick them up, but I stop her with a firm but gentle, "I've got it, Dove."

I place my bags in the guest room, coming back to find her on her hands and knees, wiping up the wet tiles. "You shouldn't be doing that with your back. Let me."

She sits back, her big eyes flashing to mine. "It's done, but I'll leave a towel here for our shoes."

She's an independent woman, used to doing it all. I understand it, but I still want her to let me help, especially when I'm right here, able and willing.

I offer my hand, helping her up, and take her coat before she can protest, placing it on the back of the dining room chair—right next to mine, where it should be, always—to dry.

"I'm taking off your boots," I warn so she doesn't try to do it while I slip off my shoes and place them on the towel in the entry.

I kneel at her feet, on my haunches.

"You don't have to—"

"I want to." I run my hand up her inner thigh, above her knee hidden under her dress. My caress is feather-soft, only a hint of what's to come. Her shiver and gasps have me gazing into wanton eyes reflecting my own desires.

Slowly, I unzip her boot as my other hand draws lazy circles on the back of her thigh. I lift her foot and pull the boot at the heel, while trailing my fingers down the length of her leg as the boot slips off, followed by her sock.

Goosebumps ripple across her silky skin, and her hand

rakes my hair. I lean into her touch, fighting for control, loving how she responds to the smallest of touches. Lightly, I kiss her inner thigh. Warmth radiates from under her dress.

It. Is. Intoxicating. I close my eyes, breathing in, letting her scent wash over me.

I set her now naked foot on the floor, placing her boot on the towel next to my shoes. Then, as if in slow motion, I move to her other leg. The dance is the same, but her responsiveness is heightened with anticipation—hers and mine.

Once she's free of the other boot and sock, I rise to my knees and pull her to me, wrapping my arms around her legs, under her dress, resting my head against her abdomen. I move my hands up the back of her bare legs, my fingers curved to the inside of her thighs, moving slowly, stopping short of touching her intimately as my thumbs graze the edge of her panties cupping her bum. I squeeze gently, nuzzling her stomach and the underside of her luscious breasts with my face.

Her hands sink into my hair as a moan breaks free, and I pull back to see her eyes closed, her head tilted back, her lips parted, and her breasts rising and falling with each breath.

"Christ, Dove, you're beautiful."

She looks down with a tender smile, her lids heavy with want, and touches my face. "This coming from Adonis himself."

"No. This coming from the man who's fallen hopelessly in love with you."

She tumbles into my grasp as if I've knocked her off her feet. Arms wrap tightly around my shoulders, and she buries her face in my neck.

"The things you say." Her muffled voice is thick with emotion, and her heart thumps solidly against my chest.

"Aren't nearly enough to convey what you've done to me." I can't get her snug enough. Resting on my heels, I urge her legs to wrap around me. I massage her back, pressing her into me, absorbing her warmth as she squeezes me with her entire body. "There, I think we've melded together."

Her whole body shakes with a laugh. "You feel it too? I can't get you close enough. It's like I need you inside me, or I'll cease to exist."

My fingers sink into the hair at her nape, tugging slightly so I can relish her bluest blues. My arms, still tightly banded around her back, ensure there's not a breath between our bodies. "I feel it. I don't believe this magical pull will be sated until I'm fully seated inside you, Dove. But we're going at your pace—your timing. I'm not pressuring you. I'm just trying to explain why I believe we both feel so desperate to get closer, as if we need to be one in order to catch our next breath."

"Yes, that's exactly it." She trembles, causing her heat to rub against my cock that's snuggly buried between us and hard as steel, only separated by her panties and my clothes. Her wrap dress is of no consequence, having ridden up her thighs in our intimate embrace.

"Do that again, and you'll blow my plans." I cup her bum over her panties, squeezing as I flex my hips into her.

She gasps and grinds against me—on purpose, this time. "I kinda like our plans, right here."

My vixen has awakened. "Then kiss me, Dove, and show me what you need."

Chapter 25

WHEN DID I BECOME SO BRAZEN? Oh, that's right. When a man hotter than the sun looks at me like I could melt the clothes clean off his perfectly sculpted body, brazenness is duly warranted.

My hands sink into his hair, tugging slightly, changing the angle of his face to match the alignment of my lips. A tsunami crashing against the shore barely touches the force with which I want to devour this man's mouth, lips, and tongue. If he's bothered by my clawing to get him closer or the vacuum I have on his tongue—he's good at hiding it.

My hips move forward and back as if we're on a tandem swing, though I'm not a hundred percent positive that he's not the swing in this scenario. His hardness, blazing a heated trail against my core, only feeds the fire.

Clothes. We have too many on.

I pull back, releasing his mouth with a *pop*. "Shirt." I tug at his buttons with an urgency that should mortify me, but the need buzzing in my body, boiling in my blood, and throbbing in my clit supersedes such a wasteful emotion.

"Here." His capable hands take over, and in seconds he's pulling his shirt over his head, leaving him naked from the waist up.

I fumble with the tie of my dress, groaning in frustration.

My calm professor chuckles, deftly loosening the knot, ridding me of my dress in one fell swoop. His hands bely his demeanor as he eagerly traverses my newly exposed skin, kissing, licking and sucking my breasts through my bra.

"Off," he barks, and I stifle a giggle, elated his control is unraveling. I don't want to be the only one undone by this *thing* between us.

His roar of appreciation when he peels my bra off my shoulders, revealing my proffered breasts and eager nipples, has my panties soaked with arousal.

I reach behind me to remove it completely and unpin my arms from the bra's confining grip. I'd burn every one if I wasn't against my breasts seeking lower ground.

Theo slings it away as if he's all in on the bra-burning bandwagon.

"Beautiful. Absolutely beautiful." His hands encapsulate each breast, squeezing and kneading, watching as his thumbs tease my nipples to hard peaks.

When his mouth returns to my now naked breasts, my hips shoot forward, my eyes slam shut, and my arms band his head, ensuring contact is not lost as I ride him like a bull.

"Bloody hell," he groans. His hand squeezes my rear, increasing the power of each thrust. "Just like that." He kisses his way to my other needy nipple.

His arousal, his encouragement, causes my insides to flutter and clench around nothing. He moans as if he felt it, slipping his hand underneath my panties, over my *arse* and into my wet folds. Thank God for long arms, big hands, and deliciously probing fingers.

Nearly rocking myself off his lap when one slips inside, I grab his shoulders to right myself as he pops off my breast. "Hold on, Dove."

I steal his mouth, cheating my breasts, for the need to suck his tongue while he makes love to me with his fingers and mouth. His hunger not to be outshined by mine, his hips rock into me, meeting my thrusts, driving our rhythm—the rhythm he's set with his penetrating fingers—claiming me in our way. Over and over again.

"You're close." His breath cascades over my mouth. "Take me with you when you fly."

His kiss is brutally sensual. Each skillful maneuver with his mouth matches that of his fingers. Taking me. Taking me. Taking me. Tipping me over the edge until I can see the horizon of tomorrow dawning through the shattering of yesterday and the pulsing of forever.

"Dove," he groans as I come around his fingers, grinding my clit against his hard-throbbing cock still stifled in his pants. His smooth thrusts hitch into a jerking motion as he falls apart for me—as I did for him.

Our movements gentle, our mouths panting more than kissing, but his fierce embrace ensures I remain right where I am—straddling his lap, at his mercy and beyond sated.

"Take a bath with me." His voice is lower, courser, replete with satisfaction.

I snuggle into his neck, thinking of how to gracefully turn down his offer and come up empty. "I can't be naked with you like that."

He chuckles. "I hate to break it to you, but we're on the floor between your entryway and your kitchen, lights on, my hand between your arse cheeks—lovely arse, I might add—my fingers buried inside you, your beautiful breasts in my face, and you're naked except for the scrap of panties between your cum and mine." He urges my head back and kisses my nose. "I've seen enough to know I can't wait to see it all." He presses his lips to mine. "Now, come bathe with me."

When I want something, I usually get it. And getting Lauren naked is top on my list of wants. Though, getting and taking are two completely different things, and I will never *take* anything from her. I want her to give me all her gifts freely, without reservations, without fear.

We're not there, obviously, based on her reaction to my request to bathe with me. When my vixen is out to play, she's all in. The moment the passion dies, her self-doubt comes crashing in, drowning any confidence she has—otherworldly connection or not.

I guide her into the tub under the cloak of darkness, the only sliver of light coming from the cracked door between the bathroom and her bedroom where the far nightstand lamp is on. The rest of the apartment is dark.

She doesn't seem to mind my hands feeling her nakedness, as if I'm not fully capable of piecing together a glorious image from each caress of her silky curves.

With her intimately settled between my bent legs—her back to my chest, my cock to her arse, my hands on her belly and breast, and her hands resting on my thighs—it's time to address the naked demon in the room.

"What do you sleep in when I'm not here?" Maybe I can play this off as a twenty-questions game.

She twists her head, glancing at me. "The same as I do

when you're here. A bed."

"Har har." I squeeze her breast, feeling her nipple pushing against my palm. I ignore it. Nearly. I squeeze again and *then* ignore it. "Very funny. What do you *wear* when you sleep in that lovely pillow-laden bed of yours?"

"Nothing."

Nothing—she says like it's *nothing*. "Absolutely nothing?" My mind races with visions of her curled up next to me in bare-naked nothing.

"Naked as a jaybird." I can hear the smirk in her voice.

"That's quite a thought. You cuddle all up to your king pillow between your legs—naked?"

"Yep. All of me, buck naked."

She's far too cavalier about this.

"Every time I think of you sleeping in your oversized bed, I'm going to picture you naked now, too." I'm envious of her pillows and sheets—the damn air that gets to kiss her naked skin.

"So, you're saying you didn't think of me naked before?" she teases.

"You have a point. I did, yes. But now that I've seen you sleep, that vision is more vivid."

I grab the bar of soap, urging her to sit up, and start washing her back. I need to think of something else besides her nakedness in front of me.

"Will you sleep naked with me tonight?" Yeah, I'm not winning the don't-think-of-her-naked war going on in my head.

She's quiet. Her arms are wrapped around her bent legs. Her cheek rests on her knee as she glances at me over her shoulder. My hands slip down her back, below the water, gripping her hips, massaging her lower back with my thumbs.

She moans her approval, and I have to remind myself again to *not* think of her naked.

"That wouldn't seem quite fair, now would it? No sex, but I'm going to sleep naked in your arms." She shudders, and I chase the goosebumps popping up on her arms with my warm, soapy hands. I guess she's having a hard time not thinking about being naked with me too.

"Is this a trick question? No sex, and I can either sleep with you clothed or sleep with you naked?" I chuckle, rinsing her off with a washcloth.

When she doesn't respond, I answer for her. "Naked, of course."

I pull her down so she's resting on my chest and begin soaping up her front. "What about when it's cold? Or you're not at home?"

"Naked. No matter when, no matter where. Except…that time of month."

"Do you walk around naked?"

"Of course."

"But not with me?"

"Not with anyone."

"No one?"

"Nope. Never."

It's a shame. She sounds so certain that she never will.

"You're going to walk around naked with me."

Her laugh is cut short as my fingers caress her folds, washing all of her.

"Don't hold your breath." Her response lacks the commitment mine holds.

"Maybe not today. Maybe not tomorrow. But soon you'll be walking around naked and not even realize it."

"If you say so."

She's easing into it already.

"I'm going to love you into confidence, Dove." My fingers continue their own form of loving her.

"Mmm," is her only response as her hips take up the rhythm I've started.

"Will you let me love you the way you need to be loved?" My voice is shallow in her ear, having given up the battle of not thinking of her naked.

For fuck's sake, she *is* naked—in my mind, in my bed, and in my arms.

Her smallest of nods is all the confirmation I need.

She may not realize I'm talking about more than loving her body—right here, right now. I'm referring to loving her into healing, filling all those dark, empty spaces, mending the broken pieces with the salve of my love—as she's doing for me.

PART FIVE:

Hibernation

Chapter 26

I **BLINK AWAKE TO A SOFT** caress on my cheek. Once I'm able to focus, it's Theo's handsome and entirely too-awake face I see.

"Morning." I stretch and yawn, covering my gaping mouth with the back of my hand.

He smiles warmly, his hand lightly caressing my waist. "Good morning, Dove. Breakfast is ready."

"You made breakfast?" A man has never made me

breakfast before. I stifle another yawn and sit up, clenching the sheet to my chest, nearly forgetting we went to bed naked.

Naked—with him.

"I did." His perusing eyes and all-too-satisfied gleam tell me he didn't forget.

"Have you been up long?"

"Not long." His hand slides from my waist to my stomach, rubbing back and forth. "When I awoke, your stomach was growling for food."

"What—" My blushing indignation is superseded by a traitorous growl from my mid-section.

He chuckles. "Yes, like that." He stands, cups the back of my head, and presses his warm lips to my forehead. "Get dressed." He turns to leave. "Don't take too long. Food is getting cold," he says from the doorway, not looking back but not closing the door either.

I leap out of bed and rush to the bathroom before he can turn and witness my graceless streaking. As I close the door, I hear him chuckling again. Apparently he knows exactly what I'm doing.

Teeth brushed, panties and a tank top donned, and robe fastened, I step up to the table just as Theo comes out of the kitchen with our plates. Perfect timing, though he probably heard the bathroom door open.

"You're smirking." I take a seat, laying the napkin in my lap, and eye the plate of bacon and eggs he's set before me.

"I'm amused how quickly you disappeared into the bathroom the moment I turned my back."

"You didn't see anything, did you?" I almost whisper, wishing I was bold enough not to care if he did. I salt and pepper my eggs, avoiding the pity I'll see in his eyes.

His hand on my cheek stills my movement. "Dove." His love name for me is so soft and tender on his lips. I close my eyes, stilling the rising tide of emotions.

He clasps my chin, tilting my face to his. "Open," he commands, gentle but sure.

When I open my eyes, it's not pity I see in his chocolate almond-shaped eyes but acceptance.

"Don't shut me out." His thumb caresses my cheek. "I won't ever look to see what you're not ready to show me."

A lone tear skates down my cheek. He swipes it away. "Eat. Your eggs are going to be cold." His gaze darts to my stomach, an amused smile brightening his face. "Your stomach is growling mad you're making it wait."

I groan with embarrassment. *Shush, stupid stomach!*

"It looks wonderful. Thank you." I cut up my eggs and dig in.

"I hope you like it."

He made it. How could I not? "I'll love it. How'd you sleep?" I ask, taking a bite of yummy fried egg.

"Very well. And you?"

"I always sleep well when you're here."

He nods, his brow furrowing as he butters his toast and then swaps it for mine to begin buttering again. "You had a nightmare the last time I was here."

"But that's not because you were here."

"Do you have them often?"

I shrug, not really sure how to answer. "Often enough, but not every night." I'm not even sure I remember all of them. "When you're here, I sleep more soundly."

I feel safe, like I can truly let go and give in to sleep.

"I don't like the idea of you waking up alone after having a nightmare." He's seriously drilling deeper into my heart with each word he speaks.

"Then I guess you can never leave."

"Be careful what you wish for, Dove." His warning doesn't scare me. Him leaving scares me.

He eats a few bites of eggs and then continues to dress our toast, offering me grape jelly. But with my mouth full, I simply motion to the jar of apple butter in the mix of jelly jars he arranged on the table. His brows quirk. He reads the label and glances at the jar in contemplation as he smears it on my toast.

"Try it," I urge him to sample my toast.

He tentatively takes a bite. Chews. And then takes another bite. "It's good. Not as sweet and has fewer calories and sugar." He approvingly sets my toast on his plate then proceeds to smear more on his toast and give it to me.

I guess he likes it.

"Have you looked outside? I wonder how bad it is out there." I'm glad we both checked our emails last night before bed. His campus is closed with a high likelihood of Thursday's classes being cancelled too, and he doesn't have classes on Fridays. Tyler's email advised the office is closed and to work on critical items from home. I'll probably check in with him later to be sure there aren't any fires I need to be aware of. We're just beginning to work on our next publication, so missing a few days shouldn't be too difficult to make up, and my piece doesn't really come until the end with editing and layout.

"It's all white and frozen. It was snowing when last I looked."

"Really?" I stand. "I have to see." I open the blinds to the patio. "Wow, it's beautiful, like a winter wonderland. Everything is white, shiny, and wet-looking, which means it's mostly ice." I squint from the reflection, making the light seem so much brighter. "Have you ever seen it like this? We rarely get weather like this here in Dallas. Now, Lubbock—the panhandle—they get weather like this all the time."

"No." His voice in my ear makes me jump seconds before his arms wrap around me from behind.

"Shit. You scared me."

He squeezes me tighter. "I'm sorry. I wasn't thinking."

"No." I pat his arm. "I don't mean like that."

He lets out a bunch of air. "No?"

I lean into his embrace, wrapping my arms around his. "No. You make me feel safe, Theo. Not scared." At least not physically scared. I'm still scared shitless he's gonna wake up one day and see me for who I really am.

"And who's that?"

Shit. I said that out loud.

"I see you, Dove." His lips brush my ear, sending my heart pounding all over again. "I'm glad I make you feel safe." He gives me another squeeze. "Let's finish breakfast."

"Have you talked to Simon? I assume tonight's class is cancelled."

"Yes. I called first thing, then emailed the class."

She pushes her plate way, finished with her half-eaten breakfast. I want to point out that she needs to finish it—it was only two eggs, two pieces of bacon, and two pieces of toast—but think better of it.

"What do you want to do today? I mean, we're basically housebound, unless you're feeling particularly daring. Do you need to do some work? Watch TV? Go to the gym?"

I perk up. "You have a gym?"

"The complex has a gym. It's nothing special, but it does the job."

"I need to check my email, but I don't really have any work I need to do, maybe tomorrow if we're still snowed— iced—in. I wouldn't mind watching a movie. But I'd really like to go to the gym if you'll come with me." I take my last bite of toast, deciding I'm done as well.

"Sure, I'll go. I have my treadmill here, but the gym offers more options."

"Sounds good."

We agree to wait, letting our food settle before we go. As we clean up breakfast, I sense her reticence to go out in the weather, but she doesn't give any hints as to why. Obviously, it's cold, but I sense there is more to it than that.

Lauren touches my arm as we set up our laptops in her spare bedroom. "Thank you for breakfast. It's a nice treat to have someone cook for me."

I kiss the tip of her nose. "Then I shall do it more often."

She laughs, pushing the office chair towards me, taking a dining room chair for herself. "That wasn't a hint."

"I didn't take it as such."

With our laptops set up side by side on her desk, I catch her looking at me. "Something on your mind?"

She focuses on her screen. "I like having you here—like this. It's nice."

I lift her chin, attaining her attention. I don't like it when she hides from me. "It is nice. I like waking up with you in my arms."

Her blush has her squirming in her seat.

I lean in, laying a kiss on her apple butter-flavoured lips. "I like it a lot."

Outside of seeing my family, I never understood what coming home feels like. Now, I know that it's Lauren.

She's my home.

And I dearly love coming home to her.

"I won't let you fall," I promise, now understanding her reticence from earlier. She's nervous about her back, understandably afraid of falling on the slippery ice. I don't blame her. If I'd sustained the type of injury she has, I'm not sure I would even tempt fate.

But in this case, I believe fate has brought us together, and one of my jobs is to keep her safe—and unharmed. That includes keeping her on her feet or providing a safe place to land in the event of a fall.

"I'll walk on the grass. It'll provide more cushion if I do fall." Her eyes scan the winter wonderland we find ourselves in the middle of.

I had no idea Texas gets weather like this. According to the news stations, the roads are treacherous, and the city has already run out of sand for the main roads and the de-icing mix used on the overpasses. Apparently, salt isn't used here. Her apartment maintenance guys are out spreading cat litter on the walkways so people don't fall and break their necks. But Lauren has me.

"I *will not* let you fall," I forcibly reiterate.

Her eyes widen as she looks at me. "Okay." Her cheeks and nose are already rosy from the cold. Her hair is secured under her coat's fur-lined hood. There are snow boots on her feet, gloves on her hands, and a bag on her arm carrying her tennis shoes, water, and towels. She looks ready to embark on an Alaskan adventure rather than a quick jaunt to her apartment's gym.

"I won't let you fall," I soften my edict.

Her wide eyes crinkle at the corners as she smiles. "I heard you the first two times, Professor. I just…" She steps out from under the covered pathway and into the falling snow. "I don't want to be a burden."

Bloody hell, this woman.

"You are not a burden." I catch up to her, pulling the bag from her shoulder and slinging it over mine. I link our arms, with mine below hers and gripping her hand. She's not going down without me cushioning the blow.

As she does with most things that make her uncomfortable, she ignores my comment but does let me guide the way, leaning into me the few times she slips.

"They say once you fall, you're more prone to fall again." She stops, taking a deep breath and letting it out. Her shoulders lower an inch or two. "I did, you know. I fell again, at work, outside in the rain, right there in the parking lot. My heel slipped out from under me. I landed on my butt, in the same damn spot as before." She looks up at me, blinking away the snow that lands on her lashes. "It hurts like a bitch." She motions with her head to continue. "I think my fear of falling again makes me less surefooted."

"Was your second fall before your surgery?"

"Yes."

Thank God for that.

We stop at the gate surrounding the pool area. She points to the building on the far side of the two pools, a hot tub, and a gazebo. "The last door is the gym." Her gaze meets mine. "If we fall would you rather land in the pool or the cobblestone deck?"

"Woman, for the last time, I will not let you fall." I capture her protest with my mouth. Her cold lips contrast with the warmth of her mouth as she succumbs to my demanding kiss. I wrap her in my arms. Her hood and my hat protect us from the falling snow as she clutches my jacket, keeping me close—as if I'm going anywhere.

Breathless and overheated from the inside out, I break our kiss. "Step confidently, knowing I will keep you safe."

Her eyes scan mine, and I press my forehead to hers, waiting until we catch our breath. "Ready?"

"Yes."

The minefield of peril avoided, she quickly keys in the door code, unlocking the gym door, and steps inside. I follow, closing it behind me. She's already taking off her coat and hanging it on a hook on the wall. I join her and do the same, putting our gloves in our coat pockets.

She moves to a bench to swap her boots for her sneakers.

"Thank you." She smiles up at me, and I'm caught off guard by her radiant beauty of mussed hair, rosy cheeks and nose, and eyes alight with accomplishment.

I capture her chin with my fingers and thumb to keep her eyes on me a moment longer. Such a normal, simple task of walking to her complex's gym turned into a trial of trust and determination.

"You're welcome." I brush my lips across hers, wanting more, but settling for a taste.

Stepping away while she ties her shoes, I look around the smallish room packed with two stationary bikes, two treadmills, an elliptical machine, free weight station with a bench, and two different nautilus weight machines to work out multiple parts of the body. It's not a bad set up, really.

"I'm starting on the treadmill to warm up." Lauren steps on the nearest treadmill.

"I'll join you." I grab our waters and towels from her bag, handing one of each to her before mounting the treadmill next to her.

"Thanks. How long do you normally work out? You're probably really hardcore, huh?" Her sour-puss face at the idea of me being a workout fanatic is priceless.

"I wouldn't say I'm hardcore, but I do work out usually five days a week, sometimes more. It's a good way to work off steam. On average, I'd say I go about an hour or two. It depends on the activity and how much time I have." I set my water bottle in the cup holder and sling my towel over the top. "We can go as long or as short as you like."

She motions to the TVs mounted on the wall. "TV or music?"

"I'm all yours. Show me your routine."

She connects her phone to the treadmill's Bluetooth, accesses her playlist and hits play.

I match her starting speed as we warm up. "How long do you usually walk on the treadmill?"

"If it's all I'm doing, I'll go for an hour, alternating between walking fast and running. The songs start off slow, gradually get faster, then slow and fast again. I adjust as I go. The timing—the beat of the songs—keeps me motivated." She increases her speed. I match it. "If I'm only warming up on the treadmill before moving on to weights or something else, then I only go for twenty to thirty minutes."

She adjusts the music's volume with the pounding of our feet. "Is this okay?"

"It's perfect." She's perfect. There's no one word answers from her—rarely, if ever. She's detailed-oriented. I appreciate that trait thoroughly.

We start out slowly, but within a few minutes she's walking fast, swinging her arms, focusing ahead, lost in thought. She walks faster as each song's beat increases. Before I know it, we're running. She keeps it up for two songs, and then the next song slows down to a fast walk. Then back to running. We cycle through the fast then slower songs a few times. She rebounds each time, going faster than before.

I'm breathing hard and soaked in sweat. She's as sweaty but not as out of breath. My Dove is in great shape to be able to keep this pace for an hour. The last five minutes we slow down to cool off.

At the end of the hour, she stops her treadmill, steps off, and starts to stretch. I do the same, copying her. She's far more limber than I am, but then I knew that from the group and individual self-defense classes.

"How many times a week do you do this?" I ask, still working to catch my breath.

"Four times, sometimes more and sometimes less. I try to keep it at four times, as it doesn't take long to lose the stamina to keep it up. It took me a long time to build up to an hour. The alternating walking and running really made a difference, plus the music."

Before hitting the weight machines, we rehydrate and swab off our sweat. Hopping on a machine, she starts with her arms and switches to legs. She continues to alternate, doing three sets each time.

I work my way through the other machine, and then we switch. She's precise and focused, keeping tension in and out of each rep, never letting the weight slam down or fully resting between reps. I never thought working out with my girlfriend would be so arousing, particularly when she does the chest fly, watching her breasts rise and fall with each rep. I shake my lusty thoughts out of my head and focus on my own workout—what's left of it.

When done with the weight machines, she stretches again, then lies on the floor on her back.

I move on to the free weights and catch her in the mirror watching me. "Enjoying the view?"

"Immensely." She beams, dabbing at the sweat on her chest and neck.

"I suppose that's only fair, considering I've been watching your every move since we walked in here." She always has my attention.

"Really?"

"Really." Someday, she won't be shocked to know she's all I see. Perhaps right after she unconsciously strides around naked in front of me.

She smiles, bending her knees with her hands flat on the mat at her sides, and closes her eyes. I continue with the free weights, watching her chest rise and fall as she relaxes and cools down.

When I finish, I quietly stretch out beside her, close but not so close that our bodies touch. She doesn't move. Based on her breathing, I believe she may be asleep. She's beautiful even post-workout. Her nipples push against her sports bra, visible under her white tee. I lightly run my finger over one and still when her breath catches. I touch the other until she arches but doesn't open her eyes.

Eliminating the gap between us, I palm her breast and kiss her lightly on the mouth. She makes a quiet noise. I rake my thumb across her nipple, prompting her to kiss me back. I tug gently on her bottom lip before sinking in.

She opens her eyes and graces me with a crooked smile. "Careful. My boyfriend is rather protective."

"He is, is he?"

She scans the room, arching her back, pressing her breast into me when she looks over her head. "He was here a minute ago, but I guess he's gone."

Pushing on my shoulder, I let her roll me to my back. Her lips press to mine as she straddles my hard-on, never breaking our kiss. Her soft moan penetrates our liplock as she flexes her hips. "Someone's happy to see me."

"Always." I clasp her bum, holding her tight as I grind my cock against her core. Her moan spurs me on, deepening our kiss and repeating the motion.

She pulls away, panting. "Maybe we should continue this elsewhere, given that we're not really alone." She looks over my shoulder through the glass-paned door that stands between us and the clubhouse and office beyond.

"I suppose you're right." I help her to her feet as I stand, adjusting myself as I go.

Once we're out of view from the glass door, I pin her against the wall, kissing her with the passion raging through my body. She gives it back to me in equal measure.

Stopping eventually, I scan her face. "Let's go home."

I help her out of her shoes and into her boots only to end up in another make-out session that ends in heavy breathing and both of us ready to fall over the edge.

We eventually make it out of the gym, all bundled up in our winter gear, and head back to her apartment. No discussion of her trusting me to keep her on her feet—she just does.

Inside, the sexual tension is palpable as we shed our outerwear. Once done, I pull her close. "Come shower with me."

Not saying a word, she takes my hand and leads me to her bathroom.

Chapter 27

AFTER OUR SHOWER—AN AMAZING SHOWER, even better than our bath the night before—I started making chicken soup for lunch while Theo checked in on his family. As timing had it, my sister called to see if I was surviving the ice-in and advise she's coming to visit for her spring break instead of going on a trip with her friends as she had originally informed me.

"I need to meet this man who has you all atwitter," she says quite commandingly, not even asking if she can come.

Not like I don't want her to, but it's nice to be asked.

"I'm not all *atwitter*." I. Don't. Get. Excited. "It's all fresh and new. I don't want to think it's more than it is."

"It's definitely more than *you* think it is. I haven't even met the man, and I know that for fact."

"How?"

"Seriously? He took you to a work event. He introduced you to his music group friends. He's spent the night. You haven't had anyone stay over since...well, you know since when..."

I do know. Since the attack. I don't talk to my sister about the attack. I want to shelter her from those details. But most everything else in my life is a free-for-all, open to her inspection whether I like it or not. You'd think she was the older sister the way she tries to rule my life. I may not have had a great relationship with my dad, but what I have with my sister is worthy every painful dad-memory.

"...he told you he loves you, did he not?" she continues her sales pitch.

"He did."

"And you said it back."

"I did," I answer, though she wasn't asking.

"It's more. Get all atwitter. Get all hot and bothered, for that matter. This is big—huge. And I'm coming to be sure he's good enough for you."

She has no idea how hot and bothered I get or how out of my league he is. I acquiesced as if I had a choice in the matter. She's coming. End of discussion. Literally.

I just finish putting the last of the vegetables in the pot when Theo charges out of the guest room. "I have a few things I want to talk to you about," he says in a rush, as if he'll burst if he doesn't get this conversation over with.

"Okay." I wipe off my hands and give him my full attention.

"Firstly, I'd like to meet your mother." He nervously shoves his hands in his jean pockets.

"Okay."

"Soon. I'd like to meet her soon."

I plant my hand on his chest. The pounding of his heart thumps against my palm. "I'll call her while I make lunch. Maybe she's available this weekend. Is that soon enough?"

He lets out a punch of air. "Yes, that would do fine." His smile shows relief. "I'd like to meet your brother too."

"I'll see what I can do. This weekend might be too soon—"

"That's fine. Your mother first, then your brother." His hands link behind my back, holding me close.

"You'll get to meet my sister, Nicole, when she comes to visit at the end of next month. She'll be on spring break from college and wants to come see me—us."

"When? Exactly?" His urgency is back, perplexingly curious about her dates.

I show him the note I jotted down with her travel information.

His shoulders loosen as his smile widens. "That's perfect." He relaxes into our embrace only to pull back with an arched brow. "Oh, and you'll also get to meet my oldest brother, Connor, a few weeks before your sister when he's here for a medical conference next month."

"Wow, sounds like March is going to be a busy month."

"Speaking of spring break, I'd like to take you somewhere on my break, which is also next month." He eyes the piece of paper still in my hand. "We'd leave after my brother's visit and get back the week before your sister's."

"You want to take me on a vacation?"

His fingers delve into my hair at the back of my neck as he leans down until we're face to face. "Yes. Would you be interested in that?"

I move into his embrace, hugging him—hard. "I'd love that."

He chuckles in my hear. "I'm glad to hear it. Our destination is a surprise, so no digging for information. I'll let you know what to pack as we get closer."

After a sound kiss and checking my work calendar for availability, I submit my vacation request, and Theo disappears into the guest room to make arrangements.

I lean on the counter and sigh. That was quite a whirlwind conversation. I'm exhausted thinking of what all next month brings. But then a stupid grin takes over my face. *He wants to take me on a trip.*

I'm all atwitter.

My sister would be proud.

Stealthily, I ease into the kitchen behind Lauren, millimetres from touching her.

"Is that my favourite professor?"

I sigh in disappointment. I swear she has some kind of Spidey sense. "Do you know other professors?" I press against her backside, clasping her waist.

"No. Unless you count Marcus and all those other professors I met at your faculty get-together." She chuckles, apparently amused with herself, continuing to mix up some sort of batter and completely ignoring the hardening of my lower region pushing against her.

"I don't count them." I nuzzle into her hair, smelling her shampoo laced with— "You smell like lunch."

"I hope that's a good thing." She brushes her head against mine.

Stepping back, I pat her bum. "It's a very good thing." I lean against the far counter, crossing my arms and legs. "What are you making now?"

"Cornbread." She glances over her shoulder before pouring the batter into a cast-iron skillet sitting on the cooktop. "Do you like cornbread?"

"Love it." I take the empty bowl and set it in the sink,

filling it with soapy water.

She hip-checks me. "I'll do this if you'll put the skillet in the oven and set the timer for twenty-five minutes."

I do as she asks. "Is that how long we have before lunch?" I could start a bit of trouble in that time.

"Give or take." She places the bowl and whisk on the drying rack, turns the water off and dries her hands, turning to face me. "Did you finish what you needed to get done?"

"Yes. I booked our trip for spring break and answered a few work emails." I step into her space, settling my hands on her hips.

She tosses the towel on the counter, placing her hands on my chest. "I know you invited me, but I don't expect you to pay my way. Let me know how much, and I can write you a check or send an electronic transfer—"

"Nothing. I invited you with the intention of covering all expenses." I press a finger to her lips when she starts to balk. "This is my gift to you as much as to myself. Let me do this."

"Okay."

I relish her acquiescence with minimal fight. She's letting me in, trusting me more and more, and I'm eating it up like the love-starved man I am.

"Thank you for not fighting me." I kiss her—one soft press of my mouth to hers. "As a reward, I will offer this: we're going to the beach, and we depart the Friday Connor leaves and return the following Saturday." I run my lips across hers. "No more details until it's time to pack."

"Thank—"

I don't let her finish that thought. By my calculations I've got twenty-two minutes and I plan to use every one to whet my appetite for chicken soup, cornbread, and Lauren, the latter being my favourite main dish.

Chapter 28

WITH BOTH OF OUR JOBS CLOSED, the next two days pass deliciously slowly. We spend all of Thursday inside, only going to the gym to work out. The rest of the time, we spend cooking, eating, and enjoying each other's company—and bodies.

Today, we braved the roads and ventured out to the grocery store without incident. There's significant ice and snow everywhere, though it's supposed to warm up enough later to melt what's on the roads at least. The dojo is still closed, so no self-defense class either.

The city has basically shut down. The DFW Metroplex simply isn't prepared for this type of weather, especially when it lasts more than a day and given that we rarely get this type of weather.

Saturday, tomorrow, we're meeting my mom for lunch. I'm nervous but looking forward to it, having no doubt they'll hit it off.

Now, we're in the kitchen making turkey chili for dinner. Let me clarify: I'm making chili. Theo is distracting me—rubbing his hard body against mine, his hands looking for hidden treasure, and his lips seeking sustenance anywhere they can make purchase.

"Professor, if you keep this up, we won't be eating anytime soon." I wiggle my behind, half-heartedly trying to dislodge him.

"And if you keep rubbing that delectable arse against me—" He presses his impressive hardness into me. "I shan't be responsible for my actions, Dove."

Chills course to my sensitized core. I can't hide the effect his words have on me. "Five minutes. Give me five minutes, and then I'm all yours."

With a peck on the cheek, he peels himself off me and leaves the kitchen.

I take a cleansing breath, shaking out my body, and focus on the task at hand. Finishing putting everything in the pot, I set the timer for a mid-cook stir and search for Theo.

He's not in the living room, so I check the guest room. Not there. I head to my room. Nope. Not there either.

Where could he be? My place isn't that big. Guest bathroom, maybe?

I turn and nearly jump out of my skin with a yelp.

"Looking for me?" His satisfied smirk only irritates me.

I swat at him with one hand as the other clutches my chest. "You scared me half to death! Where were you?"

"Right here."

"No. No, you weren't." I glare at him before turning on my heels.

I hate being scared. I always have. Kids think it's so funny to jump out at you around corners or closets. There's nothing funny about it, especially when it's at my expense. Not funny.

I barely making it a step before his arms wrap around me. "Where are you going, Dove?" I struggle to get free, but his grip only tightens. "Your five minutes are up. You're all mine now."

"No. I'm not." Anger getting the best of me I consider trying a self-defense move to get free.

But then his lips press to my neck, and I still.

"Don't be mad. I'm only having a bit of fun." His voice is gruffer. "Stop fighting me and be mine."

His words hit me right in the heart and between my thighs. I lean into his embrace and lay my head on his chest. "I've been lost to you since the first time I saw you."

"Not lost, Lauren. Found." He sweeps me into his arms

and carries me to the fire where he's made a bed of blankets and pillows. He sets me on my feet and kneels, pulling me to my knees in front of him. "I'm sorry I scared you. That was not my intent." He tenderly caresses my cheek, his thumb rubbing my lips as his eyes scan my face. "So beautiful."

"I'm not—"

"Don't finish that thought," he growls. His brow and glare are fierce and determined. "Beauty is in the eye of the beholder." His lips brush my neck, moving up to my ear. "I'll have to show you."

My heart catches, and I grip his sides. "Theo." I close my eyes to shut out the storm raging inside.

Hot and cold, that's what I am. So afraid to give in, to believe he truly loves me for who I am. That I am enough. Trust doesn't come easily, and vulnerability even less so, and yet, here I am at his mercy. He could end me with a word. Thrash my delicate spirit that wants to believe what he says is true. That he's fated to be mine and me, his. That he sees me without blinders or filters. That he's not fooled, or under some spell—for I am about to leap and pray he'll catch me.

"Shh, I've got you." He kisses my cheeks, my mouth delving in and taking no prisoners. Pulling me closer, he palms my breasts, teasing my nipples to hard peaks, subduing my emotions, harnessing my fear, and stoking the flames of desire.

I pull him down to the blanket, wrapping around him, my hands lost in his hair and digging into his taut muscles, kissing him back, feasting on his hunger, quenching my thirst for more. For him. For everything.

I claw at his shirt. "I want to feel you."

Our breaths waft around us, swirling with heated desire as he reaches behind his neck and pulls his shirt off over his head in that purely masculine kind of way, his lips barely leaving me as they ravage my skin with groans of approval.

I delight in the golden flesh before me, kissing his chest and nipples, teasing them with my lips, my tongue, and my teeth. My hands knead along his sides, his back, and down to the most succulent ass ever created.

He pulls at my shirt. "My turn."

I lift my arms, and he dispenses with my shirt, bra, and yoga pants as if he's done it a million times.

He probably has. I cringe at the thought of how I compare to all the others.

He bites my breast and growls, "Out of your head and here with me." His brown eyes pierce mine as he hovers over me. "Stay with me."

The vulnerability in his voice, the tenderness in his eyes reminds me that I'm not the only one who's a little broken.

I palm his cheeks, holding his gaze. "I'm here. Promise."

Sitting back, he pulls me into his lap, my legs wrapping around him.

"You won't leave me."

"No," I answer, though he wasn't really asking.

"I won't let you." With one arm around my back, he pushes my shoulder until I lean back enough for my breasts to rise to meet his mouth. "I was made for you." He flicks his tongue across my nipples. "And you for me."

Each exquisite lash of his tongue draws a moan from my lips and has me grinding my panty-clad clit against his fully-clothed erection.

He cups my rear, slowly gyrating his hips. "I want you to come for me, Dove."

A sound that I can only describe as a coo leaves my lips as he sucks a nipple into his mouth and his hand slides under my panties, sinking two fingers inside me.

I grab on to his shoulders, needing to meld with him, pulling him closer. We move in sync, gyrating with precision, maximizing clit to cock contact as his mouth ravages my breasts and his fingers take me over the edge. It's a choreographed dance we've never learned yet instinctively know.

His muttered curses as I contract around his fingers—knowing he's close to coming—only fuels my release, taking me higher, wave after wave crashing me against his hardened shore, breaking apart—shattering—as he erupts.

Laid out and decimated, he cocoons me with his body. His soft lips and gentle caresses piece me back together in front of the fire that burns nearly as bright as our passion.

Our hunger satiated, my eyelids draw heavy, but my mind drifts. No longer impeded with voracious want, the doubt seeps in.

Shattered.

Decimated.

That's what I'll be when he realizes I'm nothing. Unworthy of his time.

His touch.

His love.

He'll leave like the others when the spell that binds us is broken.

The timer sounds, jerking me awake. I disentangle from the sleeping vision beside me to check on the chili. It looks delicious and smells even better. My girl can cook. It's been too many years since a woman has cooked for me. My ex rarely did, and my relationships since never involved food, only sex. In and out. Quick. No entanglements and most definitely no shared meals.

A noise from the living room has me looking past the kitchen bar to see Lauren stretching, her eyes fluttering, breasts barely concealed with the blanket edging its way south. A little further and I'll feast my eyes and mouth on something other than chili.

I put the lid back on the pot and pick up my discarded t-shirt. "Here, slip this on." I help her sit up and then pull the shirt over her head, holding the bottom while she slips her arms in. She's sexy as fuck in my shirt.

I offer my hand. "I believe the chili's done, but you should confirm."

She takes my hand and stands, tugging at my t-shirt, which falls right below her plump bum. I growl and turn her towards the kitchen. "Go before I strip it off you."

Her giggle has my head shaking in disbelief. This thing between us feels right...and easy. So, fucking easy. Like memory foam—we fit.

I follow her to the kitchen and watch her stir the chili, my eyes doing the wandering my hands would like to do.

"It's done." She smirks over her shoulder, catching me ogling her most wonderous assets. Her blush doesn't deter her from checking me out in my boxer briefs, the fresh pair I put on before falling asleep.

"Don't look at me like that, or I'll be coming in this pair too."

Her laugh is contagious, and I begrudgingly laugh at my reverting teenage self who comes in his pants while dry-humping his girlfriend. But if it keeps my cock out of her pussy in support of her desire to abstain from sex, then I'm all in. I'll buy more undergarments—hers and mine—in support of our sexual escapades.

"Ready to eat?"

I nearly choke on my tongue, her innocence not letting on that she *might* mean me eating her. *I wish.* "Yes."

Sadly, she pulls two bowls from the cabinet, and I know she truly did mean eat *chili*—and not *her.* Sad truth.

We settle against the hearth, our backs to the fire, bowls propped in our hands. She blows on her spoonful before taking a tentative bite.

"Ah, yep, that's hot." She sets down her bowl and takes a drink of water. She watches as I take my first bite, having let my spoonful cool off longer. "Remind me to take some chili and soup to my mom tomorrow."

I nod as I savour my bite. "Bloody hell, woman, is there anything you can't cook?"

She thinks I'm kidding, but everything she cooks is perfection. I've never had better.

Expectantly, she brushes off my compliment and goes for self-deprecation. "Yes, plenty. I'm horrible at fruit pies. I can never get them right, or if I do, I can't replicate the results. They're too runny. And…I don't know how to fry anything." She says the last like it could actually be a deal breaker, like I care if she can fry food.

"You're from the South and don't know how to fry? Isn't that sacrilege?"

"Actually, Texas isn't really part of the *South*. I believe it's because Texas originated from Mexico, and the Southerners never accepted Texas as one of *them*."

My girl, always giving me more than I ask for. No one-word answers from her.

"I don't care if you can't fry or bake pies. What you can do is plenty enough for me." I scoop another bite. "You keep cooking like this, and I'll be a happy, fat professor in no time."

She looks horrified. Should I tell her I gained forty pounds after my ex dumped me? Probably not. I don't want to ruin the look in her eyes when she sees me near naked.

After a few more bites, she sets her bowl on the hearth and lies down on an exhale.

"Are you done? You didn't eat much." I've yet to see her finish a meal.

"Yep."

"I wish you'd eat more. I don't think you've eaten enough today."

She yawns, turning on her side. "I'm fine. Believe me, I'm not going to waste away."

I let it go, not wanting to push, but not agreeing with her either.

"Do you want to go back to England?"

Her question—out of the blue—surprises me. "Do you mean to live or visit?"

"Both, I guess."

"I go home every summer." I place my bowl aside and lie down next to her, propping up on my arm, toying with one of her curls. "I'd hoped you'd come home with me this summer. Meet my family."

Worried blue eyes meet mine, and the uncertainty there tugs at me. "You want me to meet your family?"

"Yes, but mostly I don't want to leave you for the summer. Come with me."

"I'd love to, but I can't go for the whole summer. I can't leave my job for that long. Plus, I don't have that much vacation time."

"Quit. Move in with me. Marry me. Let me take care of you."

"What?" She sits up faster than I can catch her, my flippant reply sending her reeling.

I put my hand up to still her fearful reply. "Come home with me for however long you can." The rest will take care of itself.

Once her head hits the pillow, I position myself between her thighs. I'm not letting her scurry away. "Come with me. We'll go for a week…two…as long as you can." I brush her lips with mine. "Say you'll come."

"I'll come."

I press my forehead to hers. "Thank you." I roll to my back, holding her hand. "As for living in England, when I came to the States, I didn't envision going back permanently. I saw myself staying here." I look to the side, meeting her stare. "But now that I've met you, I think of going back. I'd like to show you where I grew up. How I grew up." I shrug. "I'd live anywhere with you."

A smile tugs at her lips. She rolls towards me. "I think I'd live anywhere with you, too." She lays her head on my chest. "But I'm a modern girl. I grew up in America. I like modern conveniences. And I don't mean indoor plumbing. I like hot showers and large refrigerators, modern appliances, a toilet and toilet paper that doesn't feel like sandpaper. Hair dryers and washing machines…dryers. I'm not a roughing it kind of girl. I love the ocean and the beach, but I want to come home to a clean, hot shower to wash the sand away. I'd live anywhere with you, but if you want to camp out in a poverty-stricken country, I'm not that girl."

I smile at that and kiss her head. "Understood."

We're quiet a moment, my hand alternating between playing with her hair and rubbing her arm. "If money was no object, what would you do for a living?" Might as well get in more twenty questions.

"A singer, a doctor, and a novelist. Not necessarily in that order," she spouts, not even having to think about it.

Interesting. "Why didn't you pursue singing? You have the voice."

"Too shy. Too insecure."

"And doctor?"

"Honestly, I never thought of it when I was younger. It wasn't until I was older that I realized how fascinated I am by medicine and the human body. So, it's a…hobby."

That's quite a hobby. Even more interesting. "And novelist?"

"That's the one I think I could still do with what I have now. I have to take the time to do it. What about you?"

"We have writing in common. I need the time. Next would be a venture capitalist. I think I'd like to start my own VC firm, but I'd like a partner. Someone who has as much to gain or lose as me. Total dream would be an astronaut."

She looks up. "VC firm?"

"Venture capital company. Basically, provide seed money for startups. Consult with their vision, direction, investments. Whatever's needed."

"Wow. That's impressive."

I chuckle. "Not impressive. I'd give them money and help point them in the right direction. They'd have to do all the work, and I'd sit back and reap the rewards."

"If they're successful."

"Yes. *If* they succeed. Which is why I'd want a partner to share the burden of finding sound investments."

"Maybe we should quit our jobs. Find a little beach house—with indoor plumbing—and write. Make love, eat, sleep, write, repeat," she says dreamily.

"I vote for that." I roll her to her back, hovering over her. "You think I'm joking, but I'm not. We'll talk about that idea again."

"How many kids do you want?" She thinks she's changing the subject, but her words only feed the beast in me who wants to whisk her way to an ocean-front property and plant my seed deep inside her, and watch her body bloom with our children as we write side by side for the rest of our days.

"Is that an offer?"

"No. It's a question." Her brow quirks. She bites her lip, trying to stay her smile.

"Hmm, it sounded like a heavenly offer to me."

"Heavenly?" She still doubts my intentions.

I kiss her nose. "Heavenly." I plop on my back, watching the firelight reflect on the ceiling. "Two to six."

"Kids?!"

I catch her gaze as her incredulous look softens.

"Too many?" I could go with less. Figured I'd reach high and settle for middle ground.

"Not as long as your wife agrees."

"Well, does she?" I'm not letting her brush it off as if I'm talking about having children with someone other than her.

"Maybe you could carry them, and I'll breastfeed."

She didn't say no. "Maybe you could carry them, and I'll carry you *while* you breastfeed." I prop up on my arm. "I'd massage your feet, rub lotion on your pregnant belly, feed you all your cravings, and keep you satiated in every way possible."

"You'd be a good dad." She's softening to the idea.

"You'd be an amazing mum."

"Mum?" Her eyes shine. "Would they look like you? Be handsome and strong, protective and caring?"

"Yes, *mum*. Unless you're opposed to the name."

"Not opposed, it didn't occur to me that I wouldn't be *mommy* but *mum*."

"I like *mommy*, too." My little blonde-haired, blue-eyed children running around calling after their mommy— looking like her—loving like her. "They'd be beautiful like their mommy, thoughtful and kind, generous and selfless."

"Brown curly hair and chocolate almond eyes with expressive brows and cherub-red lips," she insists.

I pull her into my arms, a chuckle on my lips, a fullness in my heart, and a cock ready to make these idyllic children come to life. "Maybe a mix of both."

"Mayb—"

I steal the words straight from her lips. Enough dreaming, enough teasing about our future, enough of using our mouths for things other than pleasuring our bodies. I whip off my briefs and her t-shirt and settle between her legs on a gasp and a groan—hers and mine. I'm taking our dry-humping to another level. Only one of us will be clothed, and since her panties are silky—she wins.

Chapter 29

"**M**Y MUM IS ECSTATIC TO MEET** you this summer. I told her we still have to work out the particulars, but she was happy with any length of time you could come visit. Though, I didn't mention my stay would only last as long as yours." He smirks. "She'll have to get used to my change of priorities."

Priorities? I'm his priority?

"Yes," he answers my silent question.

"Wha—"

He chuckles and skims a kiss across my cheek. "The disbelief is written all over your face. You'd make a horrible poker player." He pushes through my stupor. "You're top of my list, Dove. Get used to it."

My head spins with how fast he moves and how easily he speaks about his feelings. What guy does that? None I've ever known. I've always heard the British are closed-off about their feelings, keeping their emotions close to the vest. But this Brit is the complete opposite. At least with me.

"...she agrees with me. You're beautiful."

Shit. I checked out again. "What?"

He smiles instead of being exasperated at having to repeat himself. "I sent Mum a picture of us from the night of the faculty party. She says you're even more beautiful than I described. She said our babies will be more beautiful than words."

I pull back in horror. "No she didn't. She hasn't even met me...she can't...babies?"

"Bloody hell, you're easily ruffled. Yes, she talked about us making beautiful babies. *Heavenly blessed, angelic little cherubs too beautiful for words* I believe were her exact words."

My face heats as the blush creeps upwards from my neck. "Well, that's embarrassing."

He quirks a brow. "Embarrassing?"

"Yes, your mother even thinking about us *making* babies—is embarrassing."

He laughs as he pulls me to his side of the couch. "No,

that's bloody hot is what that is."

I know he talking about us actually making babies and not about his mother *thinking* about it. But still…

"Tell me about your brother…the conference." I jump to a more comfortable topic.

Theo smiles, his knowing eyes not letting me go, though he does let the topic go.

"It's a medical conference. He'll be here Saturday through the following Friday. You'll like him. He's a great guy, and I know he'll adore you."

"He's your brother. I'm sure I'll love him."

"He's also the perfect doctor for your back issues—an orthopedic surgeon. He'll probably have some thoughts on how to make it better and maybe help with your pain."

I cringe at the thought. "I'm sure the last thing he wants to do is give free advice. That has to be a huge pet peeve for doctors, always getting asked medical questions."

"Not for family. He won't mind, trust me. Plus, I already mentioned your surgery to him."

"But I'm not family."

"Yet. You're not family, *yet*. You will be, and in my heart you already are. So, he'll see you as that as well. Besides, he was interested in your case and offered to talk to you about it. I didn't ask."

He's trying to convince me, but I'm not sold. I don't want to inconvenience Connor. He's here for a conference, not to give away free medical advice. "Is he staying with you or a hotel?"

"He's staying at the Anatole where the conference is

being held. So, not too far from us."

"Maybe I could cook dinner the Saturday he arrives or Sunday."

His perfect-teeth smile conveys his agreement before he even speaks. "He'd love that—I'd love that." He plants a kiss on my head, and I settle into his embrace a little deeper.

I'm going to miss this when we have to go back to work and reality next week, but for now, I'm going to eat this up and enjoy our little bubble of solitude where only he and I exist.

We talk about mundane things, neither of us really watching the TV. It's only background noise and something to look at.

"Tell me about your sister." He lies down, pulling me with him, situating us on our sides, my back to his front.

"Nicole is a sophomore at The Cleveland Institute of Music. She's six years younger than me. She plays the harp and piano, incredibly talented. She's outgoing, way more comfortable in social situations. She's been performing since she was three, so she's used to being the center of attention. She is funny and loving. And nowhere as sensitive as I am— or she's better at hiding it. Very pretty with great hair— brown and really thick. Her eyes are a different blue than mine. Bobby and I have the same blue, and she and Tim have a lighter shade. She's the only one of the four kids with lily-white skin—the kind you see in soap commercials. She's my best friend."

"I can't wait to meet her." His hand, resting on my hip,

flexes as he kisses my neck. "She sounds wonderful."

"She is."

Please, don't love her more than me.

"Can I ask you about your religious beliefs? You obviously believe in God since you pray before your meals. What denomination are you?"

She noticeably stiffens, but her words don't suggest any discomfort. "I am a believer. I'm just Christian, non-denominational. I grew up in a Bible Church. So, not Catholic, Baptist, Methodist, or any other category you can think of. What about you?"

"I believe. I grew up Catholic, but I'm not practicing." I haven't been to church since leaving England. "I like the idea of defining myself as just Christian. Do you go to church regularly?"

The stiffening is back, accompanied by her fingers clutching the couch cushion until they turn white.

I place my hand over hers, pulling her fingers loose. "It's alright, we don't have to talk about this now." I've obviously touched a nerve.

"It's okay. It's a fair question." She swallows, trying to

suppress her emotions. "I used to go regularly with Holly and her family. But…"

I wrap her in my arms and whisper, "It's alright," in her ear and press my lips to her neck.

Her nod is the only acknowledgement. "After the attack, I couldn't bring myself to face them, the stares, the questions, the sadness of what had happened to Holly. They were devastated, understandably. I only served as a reminder of their loss and their questions of why her and not me." She rolls over, her eyes locking on mine. "It was too much."

I wipe away a lone tear, cradling her cheek, keeping her locked to me, to the present.

She takes a deep breath, steadying herself. "I'm too shy to try a new church alone. So, I…don't go. It's not a good excuse, but it's the truth." She offers me a small smile with a shrug.

"Has her family reached out to you since the attack?"

"No."

That one word pisses me off. I know they lost their daughter, but her best friend survived and could have used their support. It could've been healing for both sides.

"Not at all? Nothing?"

"I heard they came to see me when I was in the hospital, still unconscious. By the time I woke up—three days later— they had already pronounced Holly brain dead and had removed her from life support. They asked that I not attend the funeral." She lays her head on my chest. Her words are muffled as she continues, "I didn't even get to say goodbye to her properly. Though, I really was in no shape to go anywhere, much less a funeral where I would have scared everyone with how bad I looked and only served as a visual reminder of what happened—and attracted media attention, as well as public gawkers."

A sob escapes, and I fear I will crush her as I tighten my embrace.

"It was for the best, but it still hurts."

She lost more than Holly that day. My anger grows towards her attackers and Holly's family.

After a few staggered breaths, she continues, "The day I got out of the hospital, I visited her grave. Charlie took me. It's not the same, but it was something."

"Charlie?" My hackles rise. Who the hell is Charlie?

She swipes at her tears. "He's the lead detective on my case."

My hackles smooth out. "I'm glad he was able to give you some closure."

Her silent shrug tells me she doesn't see it as closure at all but a reminder that she wasn't welcome because she had the gall to survive what Holly couldn't.

They deemed her unworthy. Now I'm pissed off all over again. "It's not your fault."

She contemplates for a second before replying, "Fault or not, it is what it is. Can we talk about something else?"

I should have known she wouldn't want to dwell on the attack or the impact Holly's family's actions have had on her. We don't have to tackle it all today. I'm thankful she at least let me in, shared the details that obviously still plague her. "Of course, Dove." *Anything you wish is my desire to give.* I kiss her softly before sinking into the couch, holding her head to my racing heart.

We simply breathe until we both feel calmer—until the attack has sunken into the background where I wish it would stay, but I know it can't until fully dealt with.

I'm in the kitchen getting drinks when I hear music. I glance into the living room and do a double-take when I spot Theo on the couch with his guitar, forearms bare and corded with muscles. His deft fingers strum the guitar with the ease of a seasoned musician. His head is bowed as he hums in contemplative thought.

Lord, this man put S-E-X in the word *SEXY*. He's hot without a guitar, but add a guitar, and he's defcon delicious.

As I sit, he starts a new song. It's familiar, but I can't identify it until the first words come out of his mouth. "Make You Feel My Love."

I doubt I'll make it through this without crying. His eyes stay locked on mine as he sings of all the ways—of all the things he'd do—to make me feel his love.

My heart aches, and the tears start to flow. But I don't take my eyes off him.

When he gets to the line about *never seen anything like him before*, I couldn't agree more. I definitely have not seen anything like him. His heart is so big and open to me. It's an amazing feeling that I never thought I'd find, not in my real life—in my fantasy life, yes—but he's here, in front of me, and I'm overwhelmed.

I can feel his love.

He finishes the song, lays down his guitar, and scoops me into his lap so that I'm sitting astride his legs. He pulls me close, and I wrap my arms around him, laying my head on his shoulder. "There's nothing I wouldn't do to make you feel my love."

I break down in his arms. I've come undone. It's not the first time, and it most definitely won't be the last, but it feels significant. Like there is more going on than it appears to be on the surface. Something clicks inside me, like a joint falling into place, a puzzle piece locking with its adjoining mates. It takes the breath out of me, and I suck in air as I tremble in his embrace.

"You're my world, Dove." His voice cracks, and his hold on me tightens as if I can stay off his emotions when mine are pouring out of me.

I nearly laugh at that thought of being his dam to hold back the flood of his emotions.

Not likely.

Not a chance in hell.

"And you're mine." It's not a confession, it's the truth.

When I wake on a scream in the middle of the night, tight in Theo's embrace, it's no surprise. We'd been digging in places better left buried.

"I've got you." His warm tone and heated breath skate along my skin.

"I'm sorry," I whisper, pressing into him as if his body could absorb the memories in my nightmare—some false and others all too true.

"No apologies." His lips graze my skin.

"Make me forget." My shaky hands skirt along his hard planes—solid and strong—seeking redemption. Asylum. I was foolish to think finding love would heal my past. It only seems to have aggravated it.

My world is breaking apart, and I'm left standing on two broken pieces that are slowly drifting apart. I'll have to choose or jump ship all together. And though I'm a good swimmer, I'd rather choose the piece where Theo resides. It shouldn't even be a choice—a hardship—and yet, it feels like the hardest choice of all.

My future or my past.

Jump or swim.

Drown or prevail.

"Dove." His raspy voice pins me to the present as he settles over me between my legs, his hands sliding into mine, bracing himself. Our lips meet, his legs widen mine, and his body rolls into me like a slow wave that promises to be a tsunami. Turbulent, devastating, and cleansing.

Maybe, just maybe, if I hold him tight enough, he'll be my life preserver and I won't have to choose.

PART SIX:
The Light
Returns

Chapter 30

S ATURDAY COMES QUICKLY—TOO QUICKLY. I wake up earlier than I care to, considering the late-night disturbance of yet another unwanted nightmare. Though, who would *want* a nightmare? Perhaps, *unwanted* is not the correct term, but the dazed, hungover sluggishness keeps my brain from finding a better word to describe how much I dislike having nightmares.

Again…who likes them? *Ugh, enough. Get out of bed already!*

I did sleep amazingly well post-nightmare in Theo's

arms. He gives me such peace, but sadly, it's not the shield I'd like it to be against my mind's nightmarish escapades. *Wasn't I getting out of bed? Enough of the damn musings.*

I glance over my shoulder after slipping out of bed. He's sound asleep. His broody brow is calm and scowl-free, his lips full and begging for a kiss. His hair, in bed-head disarray of the sexist kind, calls to me to smooth its curls or sink into them as his lips work their magic on my breasts.

Yeah, I need a shower...a cold one.

No sex stuff this morning. We've things to do and people to see. Namely, my mother. I'll shower, get ready, *then* wake him up.

I let the shower warm up as I collect my towel, throwing it over the shower rod and brushing my own tangled mane of curls into submission. The scent of Theo wafts off me, and my heart skips a beat as I consider not washing him off, but my hair is now a frizzy mess. There's no coming back from that. I have to wash it and start over with fresh curls. I make a mental note to cover myself in his scent as soon as humanly possible.

It's only eight when I step out of the shower. I've got plenty of time. We don't meet my mom until eleven-thirty. I wonder if Theo needs to stop by his place for clean clothes. I should have considered that last night and done a load of laundry. I'll have to ask when he wakes up.

I dry my hair, put on makeup, and dress. I opt for jeans and boots rather than a skirt, due to the cold and remnants of ice that cling to every surface not being driven on. Taking one last look in the mirror, I'm happy with my reflection, and spray on my namesake perfume, the same perfume I've worn since I was sixteen. The same perfume my mother named me after. Image that, being named after a perfume. How many people can say that?

I turn off the light and quietly step into the bedroom, leaving Theo asleep as I close the bedroom door behind me. I grab some water and head to my laptop in the guest room to check my email and pay some bills.

But first, I call my mom to confirm we're still on for lunch.

I can tell she's been awake for hours by how chipper her voice is when she answers. "Hello."

"'Mornin', Mom."

"Good morning. How are you?"

"I'm good. Are we still on for lunch?"

"Yes, yes, I can't wait. I'm looking forward to meeting this man who stole my baby's heart." My mom is not one to beat around the bush.

"Be nice. And no embarrassing stories, please." It's of no use, but I at least try to quell her desire to see me blush. Though she'll never admit it, she enjoys watching me squirm in embarrassment. She thinks eventually I'll grow out of my shyness—my fear of being the center of attention. To her, her stories are simply a bootcamp, forcing me to face my fear. For me, it's something I endure because I love her and know she means well. Plus, she loves garnering attention—she can't fathom why I wouldn't want the same.

"I'm always nice, but I can't make any promises about

stories. You know when I feel moved, I have to share."

Lord, don't I know it. This coming from the woman who called all her friends the moment she found out I got my period for the first time, saying *my baby is a woman now.*

I cringe and want to climb under the table to hide from that memory alone.

"Oh, before I forget. I made chicken soup and chili over the last few days. Can I bring you some to eat or freeze?"

"I'd love that. Are you sure you don't want to freeze it for yourself, honey?"

"I'm sure I have plenty to give to you and Theo, and still have leftovers. I have spaghetti also but assume you don't want any of that." Mom has never been a big spaghetti fan— not a fan of tomatoes altogether.

"No, but I will take the soup and chili."

"Okay. I'll see you in a bit. Love you."

"Love you too. Bye, honey."

"Bye, Mom."

I finish paying bills, forgoing email as it can be a bottomless pit dragging me into tangents I don't have time for. After packing up food for my mom in a small cooler, I decide I should probably wake up Theo. Give him the option to run home for clothes before lunch.

I turn on some music and quietly open the bedroom door to find my professor still sleeping so peacefully, I hate to wake him up.

I softly sit on the edge of the bed, reaching out to stroke the side of his beautiful face. He's handsome, but beautiful too—not feminine beauty, but how a work of art is beautiful, or the breathtaking beauty of a flower, or a mountain, or the ocean's rolling waves crashing on the beach. He *is* beautiful, and I can't believe this beautiful creature is asleep in my bed, much less in love with me.

He doesn't move, so I brush his lips with my thumb. "Theo, it's time to wake up."

He moves on a groan and opens his eyes. "Hullo." He blinks likes he's trying to bring me into focus. "What time is it?" He sits up. "Why are you dressed?"

"It's ten. We need to leave in an hour unless you want to run by your place for clothes."

Stretching on a yawn, he keeps one eye on me as the other closes. "It'd be great to stop off at my place beforehand." He scratches his head, surveying the room before his gaze settles on me once again. The tips of his fingers touch my hair. "You look beautiful, Dove."

"Thanks."

"How long have you been up?" His fingers move lower, tracing the edge of my blouse, stopping at the minuscule amount of visible cleavage.

I *try* to ignore his touch. "Um, a while, I guess. I showered, dressed, talked to my mom, paid bills, and packed food for my mom."

"You've been productive, and all I've done is sleep."

"You needed it. You missed out on your beauty sleep as someone woke you up last night."

He studies me, his hand clasping mine. "You alright?" I know he's asking about my state of mind after my nightmare last night.

I nod, laying my other hand on top of his. "I'm good."

"Glad to hear it. I don't know about needing beauty sleep, as you got less than me, and I'm looking at beauty personified." He kisses the corner of my mouth.

Ignoring my blush, he moves to get up. "Give me fifteen minutes." He stops, his feet dangling over the side of the bed, the sheet covering his lap. "It appears we have a dilemma." His eyebrow rises, and his eyes gleam with mischief.

"We do?"

"We do." He brushes the hair off my shoulder, his thumb caressing the soft spot below my ear. "I am, as God intended, naked under these covers. You'll get an eyeful if you so desire, or you can close your eyes."

He waits for my reaction; I try not to smile. I've seen him...mostly...in minimum light, not in the full brightness of day. Not entirely naked and not from a distance—the distance it will take him to walk from my bed to the bathroom. Naked.

"Are you thinking? Or have you decided to gaze upon me with your brazen self?"

Brazen? Hardly. My smile breaks free, spreading across my face. I attempt to rein it in and fail miserably. "Do you, Professor, have a preference? It's your body, after all—you control whether I see it or not."

A thoughtful smile dons his lips as his eyes shine with love, all joking aside. "Quite the contrary, Dove. As is my heart, my body is all yours."

My heart leaps, and my breath catches on a desperately needed breath of air. What this man does to me with a turn of phrase. "You are, as ever, the silver-tongued devil. I should look away, but I seem to be lacking the fortitude at the moment."

I kiss his cheek, lingering, not wanting to move away. My smile, gone. Lightness of mood, gone. I'm in awe of him and his ability to lay it all out there and tell me he's mine, fully, in all ways. The magnitude of his words touches my heart, and tears well up.

He tips my chin so our eyes meet. I'm as naked to him emotionally as he is to me physically. I cannot hide from him—as much as I try—he sees right through me.

"Dove," he whispers, his voice is raspy, full of emotions, wrapping around mine like a glove.

On the next breath, I'm in his arms, his lips pressing to mine, tender yet determined to put into action what he's feeling inside.

Tears run down my cheeks, and he swipes them away with tender kisses. "My girl, overflowing with emotions. I love you so." His hands palm my face; his thumbs dry my tears. "I want to stay here like this—with you—but I have to shower so I can meet your mother and tell *her* how much I love you." He leans in. "Close your eyes."

I do as his lips meet mine, capturing my bottom lip, tugging gently, before sweeping in for a more thorough taste. He pulls away as I sink into him. "I'm going to get up now. Keep your eyes closed." His lips linger on mine for a final kiss. Then he slowly pulls away and slips into the bathroom.

I don't open my eyes until I hear the click of the bathroom door.

I sit motionless, raw, and turned on, staring at the closed door hoping he'll come back—naked or not—and finish what he started.

The words that come out of that man's mouth couldn't cause more churning inside me if he tried. They elate and sadden me at the same time.

Maybe it's all the sadness—all the hurt—oozing out as he fills me up with his love.

Maybe one day, I'll be so full of his love, my heart near bursting, that I'll no longer cry when he says nice things to me.

Maybe one day, loving affirmations won't seem like a foreign language.

I can only hope.

I slide off the bed and make my way to the guest bath to fix my makeup. I turn up the music on my way in an effort to lighten my mood.

Fifteen minutes on the nose later, I step out of the bathroom in search of Lauren. I find her in the guest room on the phone, looking beautiful as usual. She smiles when she spots me, and I'm relieved to see no sign of her previously teary state.

"I have to go. We're meeting Mom for lunch, but I'll talk to him and let you know." She pauses, listening to the person on the other line.

"Sounds good. Love you too."

Insecurity stirs. Who's she giving her love to?

"Hey." She stands, hanging up the phone, and steps into my arms.

I hug her back, despite my irritation. "Who was that?"

"My brother Bobby." She pulls back, worry in her eyes. "You sound upset, jealous even." Disbelief is written all over her face, oblivious to how desirable she is.

"I was, until you told me it was your brother." *You're not the only one with insecurities.*

She cocks a brow, momentarily studying me before pushing on. "We should go." She steps around me.

I follow, the imprint of jealousy still marring my psyche.

She powers off the music and collects her purse, the food for her mom, and her coat. Then she turns, catching my frown, and dumps it all on the counter. "I love you, you know."

"I know." I link my hands behind her back, relishing the feel of her body pressed against mine. If only we had thirty minutes to spare—and if we weren't meeting her mother.

"You have no reason to be jealous—over me, especially."

Now I'm angry. Forget jealous. "Don't. Don't knock yourself down to make me feel better."

She sighs and pushes off my chest, forcing me to release my hold on her. "Let's not do this. It was a misunderstanding. There's no reason for you to feel threatened. So please, don't turn this into a *make Lauren feel good about herself* moment."

The bite of her response takes me back. A beat or two pass as I compose my thoughts and reel in my distaste for her self-deprecation. "Alright."

I pick up her coat before she does and hold it out for to slip on. She turns, and I pull it on over her shoulders. She leans back, and I kiss her neck, lingering, making peace. "I love you," I gruffly whisper.

"I know."

Does she, really? I don't think she can fathom the depth of my love for her. Not yet.

I pull my coat on, grab the food for her mom, and see her out the door.

I'll have to work on that.

My thoughts linger on my reaction. I've never been the jealous type, but I suppose I've never felt quite like this. My ex would be disappointed to know she wasn't the love of my life as I had led her to believe.

Who knew?

I surely didn't, or I never would have proposed to her in the first place.

Apparently, she did, or I simply wasn't the love of her life.

Tomato tomahto. It doesn't matter. Not anymore. I've lost enough time—self-respect—over my ex and her choices making me second guess my every move. I thought I was in love, but her cheating right under my nose was a swift kick to my ego. I haven't let another woman close enough to care about fidelity or to even doubt her word. Lauren is a gamechanger. Apparently, my old wounds are not as healed as I thought.

Lauren has shown me that every misstep brought me closer to finding her. And I no longer regret any of those faulty steps. Except, perhaps, the four years it took me to finally run into my vision that morning, months ago, where I was merely seeking caffeine and found my destiny instead.

Chapter 31

THEO DOESN'T LIVE FAR FROM ME, surprisingly close, actually. He pulls into the driveway with plenty of time to spare before we have to meet my mom. Opening my car door and taking my hand, he leads me to the front of the house. It's a small Tudor-style home, fitting for him, and makes me smile.

"What?" He watches me closely.

"The style…it's so you."

He chuckles. "Yes, I guess it is. A piece of home, I suppose."

"It's a beauty."

"Don't make hasty judgments. You haven't seen the inside yet. It needs a lot of work." He kisses my cheek. "And a woman's touch."

My heart pitter patters at the thought of making his home mine. *Hopefully, he means me and not just any woman.*

He unlocks the front door and holds it open. "After you, Ms. Frasier."

"Why thank you, Professor Wade." I step inside, boldly grazing my hand across his maleness, thinking of this morning. But as soon as I pass the threshold, I stop. "Theo…it's beautiful…truly." I'm in awe.

"Thank you." He urges me forward so he can close the door behind us.

It's like a cottage but larger than I anticipated. We're in his living room with a stone fireplace with a white wood mantle on one wall, flanked by white bookshelves. In front of the fireplace are two wingback chairs on either side, with an area rug and side tables. Quite cozy.

The other half of the room holds two long, brown leather couches in an L shape, and a large flat screen TV on the wall, and a square coffee table and matching end tables. Beyond this room, the dining room is on the left and on the right, a formal living room, or what looks to be his study, with a rolling chair and a large mahogany desk looking rather lived in. It makes me smile, thinking of him sitting there, grading papers, coming up with lesson plans and lectures.

On the far wall, past the dining/study room is a wide arched doorway that leads to the kitchen. Dark hardwood floors run throughout, joining one room to the next in an open floor plan with expansive beams overhead, giving the house structure but character as well.

"I'm in love." I turn, surprised to see his eyes already on me.

He intertwines his fingers with mine. "I should have brought you here sooner."

I wondered what his home looked like. "It's okay."

"No, it's not. It wasn't intentional." His eyes flit across my face as his fingers skim my hair. "I think subconsciously, I believed you'd feel...safer in your surroundings."

Safer? I suppose he's right. I'm a creature of habit. My home. My stuff. My locks. My alarm system. But... "I feel safe with you."

His smile brightens up the room. "I'm glad to hear it." He motions to the kitchen. "Let me show you the rest."

He leads me to the large eat-in kitchen that spans the width of this part of the house. To my immediate right is a table large enough to seat six. The oven and cooktop are to the right next to the refrigerator, framed with white cabinets. The back wall holds the farmhouse sink, dishwasher, cabinets, a marble counter top, and a large window overlooking the backyard. The left corner has a back door, and the left wall is a mass of upper and lower cabinets and more counter space. The cabinets may have been refinished, but the appliances are definitely new stainless steel.

"It's a dream kitchen."

His eyes sparkle as they catch mine. "Come on."

He leads me back though the living area to a hallway. Turning left, there's a nice-size bedroom with a queen bed, night stand, a chair and two dressers, starkly decorated. The bathroom, right off the hall, is a typical three piece: bathtub-shower combination, a sink, and a toilet. Small and efficient.

Returning down the hall the other way, is the laundry room that leads to the garage, a linen closet, and then at the end is the master bedroom. His room.

It's big, larger than the other bedroom, with a king-size bed, two nightstands, another wingback chair, a tall dresser, a long dresser with a flat-screen TV mounted above it directly across from the bed, and two more built-in bookshelves flanking the bed.

There are two other doors on the same wall as the bedroom door. Theo steps into the middle door, flicking on a light.

I move closer to watch him collect clothes to wear from the long walk-in closet. He smiles when he catches me.

Shyly, I step back, my heart fluttering, feeling at odds being here in his place, in his bedroom. It's overwhelmingly intimate.

He motions to the third door. "That's the bathroom if you want to look."

His bathroom is double the length of his closet. On the right is a long counter with two sinks and a mirror running the length of the counter. On the left is a door with a toilet, and there's a large glassed-in shower, large enough for two with a bench seat.

I blush at the thought.

At the end, on the far wall, is an oversized tub. I move closer and see it's twice the size of my tub, more than large enough for two. It's Theo-sized for sure. My mind jumps to the baths we've taken at my place and how much easier it would be to fit in his tub. My nipples harden, and I squeeze my legs together.

"Penny for your thoughts."

I jump and scream, turning around and swatting at him. "Theo!"

He's all smiles and laughter. He's changed into a deep blue button-down shirt, dark jeans, brown belt and shoes.

"How can I be mad when you look so handsome?"

He tugs me closer. "You can't." His brow rises suggestively. "What were you thinking so intently about that I could sneak up on you?"

"Us in here. Together."

His satisfied smile widens. "It's hot, right? Welcome to my world. When I'm at your place, among your things, the places where you sleep, shower, bathe, where you are naked, it's intimate," he presses his forehead against mine, "...and arousing."

Gah, this man reads me too well.

His kisses my forehead. "Come on, we'll be late if we linger much longer." He takes my hand and leads me back to the front door.

Before he can open it, I stop, pulling free. He turns,

questioning.

"Can we come back here?" I'm tentative, afraid he'll say no.

He closes the gap between us, his lips crashing over mine as his arms crush me to him. He kisses those tentative thoughts away. "Yes, bloody hell, yes."

She's been antsy the entire ride here. Fidgeting. Distracted. I park at the steakhouse—her mom's favourite place—but instead of going in, I take Lauren's hand, study it for a minute. It's small and delicate compared to mine, but by no means weak. Her nails are natural and grow millimetres past the tips of her fingers, the whites nearly glowing from the sun gleaming through the windows. I massage her hand in both of mine, turning it over, pressing along her flat palm, over her fingers and down, linking my hand with hers. It fits perfectly in mine—her yin to my yang.

I press our joined hands to my lips, my eyes on her as I kiss her delicate, fair skin. She takes a cleansing breath as if my touch was all she needed to calm her nerves.

"Are you nervous about me meeting your mum?" I switch hands to caress her cheek as she contemplates her response. Thoughtful, as always.

"Not in the way you're thinking. She'll love you, I've no doubt. I just…" Releasing her seatbelt, she turns to face me. "I don't do this." She points to me. "Bring guys to meet my mom."

Extremely happy to hear that, I don't even try to hide the smile that breaks free.

"What?" She swats at me, overly fond of that defensive move, but I catch her hand and kiss it again.

"I'm honoured." I lean over the console, pulling her to me, hovering over her pouty lips before pressing forward.

She stutters a breath and then sighs, "Can we go home now?"

Home? Hers or mine? I chuckle, eating up the affect I have on her. "No, Dove. Meet mum first, then home—my home." *Soon to be your home.*

"You'll be the first to meet my family." That's the admission that's making her so nervous.

"You've *never* brought home a boyfriend?"

She shakes her head.

My cock hardens. *Maybe we could go home. Reschedule.*

"Come on, let's get this over with." She slips out of my hold and out the door before I can redirect my thoughts.

Bloody hell.

"The sooner we get in there, the sooner we'll get home." She shuts the car door.

I like her calling my place home—or anyplace we're going together as *home*—not *her* home or *my* home. Just *home*.

Adjusting my jeans, I meet her at the front of the car, clasping hands. "You should have let me open your door."

Her bright eyes meet mine. She smiles and shakes her head on a shrug. "Sorry."

She's not in the least. But she didn't argue about me wanting to open her door for her—I consider that progress.

"Let's go meet the woman who raised an amazing daughter like you."

As we approach the entrance, a woman's voice rings out, "Lauren!"

We stop and turn.

"Hi, Mom." Lauren squeezes my hand and glances my direction before releasing me to hug her mum.

She's a tall, slender woman with a warm smile. Pretty, but they look nothing alike. She has black hair, olive skin, and small hazel eyes. I was not prepared for that. And it dawns on me that Lauren doesn't have a single family picture in her home. Her walls are decorated with artwork. She has knickknacks strewn about, but no personal photos. I'm not sure what that means, but it's something of significance.

Releasing her daughter, she turns to me and sticks out her hand. "Hi, Theo, I'm Carolyn Frasier Murray, Lauren's mom, but I guess you figured that out." She laughs, a laugh completely unlike her daughter's.

I take her proffered hand and kiss her cheek. "It's an honour to meet you, Mrs. Murray. I'm Theodore Thomas Kellen Wade, but please call me Theo."

"Call me Carol." She gives me a knowing smile.

365

Pointing to the front door, I place my hand on the small of Lauren's back. "Shall we?"

We're seated by the hostess at a cozy booth on the outskirts of the restaurant, followed by our waiter, who takes our drink orders. It's immediately apparent he's enamoured with Lauren. He hardly takes his eyes off her. Carol and I get brief glances as we order our drinks. Lauren doesn't seem to notice.

Sitting across from Carol, I settle my left hand on Lauren's thigh, claiming her. Even though he can't see it, I feel better for the contact. Her lips quirk, and she places her hand over mine. Oblivious to our connection, the waiter scurries away to fill our drink order. I hope he'll be a while; otherwise, this could be a long lunch, or possibly rather short if I have to stake my claim more aggressively.

It's now or never. "Lauren, I have a confession to make."

Her eyes widen, looking at me and then her mom, obviously wondering why I would choose to make a confession right here, right now. "O…okay," she stammers.

I squeeze her leg and take a fortifying breath. "Today's not really the first time I've met your mother."

"What—"

"It's the first time in person, but we actually met on Thursday when I called her. I was anxious to break the ice and state my intentions. I thought it might make today less stressful." I pause, waiting for Lauren's reaction.

She blinks, darting her gaze between Carol and me. "Wow." She frowns. "Neither of you thought to tell me?

Ease *my* nerves?"

God, she's right. I should have told her. "I'm sorry. Honestly, I wasn't thinking about you being nervous, only that I was. I wanted to make today more comfortable and not put your mum on the spot." Though, I suppose I did put her on the spot when I called. Still, over the phone seems kinder than expecting a congenial response in person.

Carol smiles as if she can read my mind. "I was glad he called me. It did make getting to today less stressful—for me, too."

Lauren nods, contemplating.

The waiter returns with our drinks. We're silent as he sets them on the table, ensuring Lauren's makes it in front of her, but Carol's and mine are switched. As he stares at Lauren, he doesn't even notice when Carol and I swap glasses.

I arch a brow at Carol, silently asking if she sees what I see. She glances at the waiter before winking at me, and then gets his attention by asking for lemons—the lemons he forgot to bring for the iced tea.

As he walks away, her warm smile hits me, and I'm struck, for the first time, by the resemblance between mother and daughter. They have the same smile that lights up their eyes and transforms their face into something warm and inviting.

"Are there any details you both care to share, or any outcome of the discussion I can be privy to?" She's not angry, but maybe a tad miffed.

Carol pours sweetener into her tea as she speaks, "I was

impressed that Theo called at all. I don't know too many men who would do that nowadays. It's endearing." A smile tugs at her lips as her eyes sweep from me and land on Lauren. "He was really quite complimentary toward you. He wanted me to know he not only cares for you but respects you, and he intends to marry you."

My heart hammers in my chest hearing her mum repeat my words, and my smile slides to Lauren.

"Wow," Lauren whispers on a blush, her teary eyes meeting mine.

I pull her into my side, kissing the top of her head. "It's true. All of it."

Carol continues, her eyes darting between the two of us. "It made me proud. You've always been an old soul." She points to Lauren's head. "You were born with the grey streak to prove you've got wisdom in your bones. You're an old-fashioned romantic. It's fitting, really."

"Grey streak?" I nudge Lauren, curled up to my side. "Where?"

Her smile is sheepish when she pulls away, pointing at the left side of her head, which is facing away from me. "I'll show you later. It's hard to see with my hair down. It's underneath, an inch or so behind my left ear."

"Plus, it's harder to see now with your hair lighter," Carol offers.

"Lighter?" Is blonde not her natural colour? And how did I not see a grey streak? It's an unusual feature for someone so young. I should have noticed. Perhaps I'm not as attentive as I pride myself in being.

"She was born with black hair, tons of it, sticking out every which way and a grey streak in the back like a skunk," Carol answers before Lauren can.

"Black hair?" I'm stunned and repeating words now.

"Anyway…" Carol continues, ignoring me.

"Later," Lauren whispers.

"…I thought it was quite sweet and traditional. Fitting for my sweet Lauren." Carol turns to me. "It really was touching. Thank you. She deserves to have someone who believes in her and treats her with respect and love. She has so much to give. You couldn't find anyone more loving." Her smile returns to her daughter, full of adoration.

"Stop. You're going to make me cry," Lauren beseeches.

"No surprise there," Carol teases, but I feel Lauren stiffen at my side.

Is this why Lauren doesn't like to cry in front of people? Always apologizing for being so emotional? Did her family make her feel ashamed of her tears—her sensitivity?

"You're right, Carol. I've never met anyone like Lauren. She is quite special, and I plan on spending the rest of my life loving her the way she deserves." I squeeze Lauren's shoulder, my need to protect her surging through my blood.

We peruse the menu, falling quiet as we decide what to order.

"Thank you," my vision whispers in my ear.

I steal a precious kiss, locking eyes. "Always."

Chapter 32

THE WAITER RETURNS, LOOKING AT LAUREN, asking if *she's* ready to order.

Bloody hell. "Yes, *we* are, in fact, ready," I correct his statement.

The boy nods, not even having the good sense to be embarrassed.

As we order, his eyes remain on Lauren, only occasionally making eye contact with Carol or me. It's disturbing yet humourous because Lauren has no idea.

Carol is eyeing him. When he leaves, Carol gives me a *can you believe that asshole?* look, and we bust out laughing.

"What? What's so funny?" Lauren laughs with the two of us. She can't help it, even though she doesn't know why.

"Since we walked in, our waiter can't keep his eyes off you. It's as if your mum and I aren't even here."

Her mouth falls open, and her eyes widen in shock. "No." She shakes her head. "No, he's only being nice—attentive."

My sweet girl. "Dove, even your mum noticed."

"He's right, honey. From the moment we sat down, he hasn't stopped looking at you," Carol confirms.

"No." Lauren frowns at me. "Why would you say that?"

Sighing, my eyes meet Carol's. "She has no idea how beautiful she is."

Carol nods. "I know, and she won't listen."

"Y'all are crazy," Lauren insists. "Plain crazy." I can hear her internal voice telling her *she's nothing special.*

"Crazy for you." I capture her fidgeting hand and kiss her cheek. "Crazy for you, Dove. Only you."

Her head hits my shoulder on an exhale. She may not accept that others find her attractive, but she at least accepts I do, and *that* is all that matters.

Lauren mentions her brother Bobby wants to have us all over for dinner to meet me. We agree to check our calendars and determine a date that works in the near future.

That settled, Lauren moves on to my brother's visit, which then morphs into talking about my family.

Apparently, she's had enough talking about her.

"How much older is Connor?" Carol asks.

"Ten years. He's married with two kids."

"Mom, he's an orthopedic surgeon."

Carol seems impressed, but Lauren steams forward, not giving her a chance to respond. "They're all highly educated. Between the two parents and five kids, there are three doctors, two professors, and two teachers. Impressive, huh?"

"Yes, it is."

"It's not." I don't want to focus on that. I'm lucky. I was born into a well-off family where education was paramount and feasible.

"I'm highly undereducated," Lauren throws out dismissively. "The amount of brain power at one of your family dinners *is* impressive," she adds fuel to the fire.

I squeeze her leg, hoping her gushing over my family will cease. "No more than your family. Education does not equate to a high IQ."

"Says the professor," Lauren teases, but I can hear the meaning behind her words.

I won't have her feeling inferior to me—to my family. But I don't want to discuss it in front of her mum. I squeeze Lauren's hand this time, capturing her gaze, trying to convey my feelings.

When I'm sure my message is received, I change the subject. "Does your mum know about Nicole coming to visit?"

That does the trick. The two of them set off on that

tangent. Carol seems happy to hear about Nicole. I find it fascinating. Carol seems to really care for Nicole, despite the fact she's her ex-husband's child from his second marriage. I'm sure Lauren's love for Nicole has a lot to do with it.

As our food comes and goes, the conversation flows easily. Wanting to know more about my love, I take the opportunity to delve further. "Carol, what was Lauren like as a child?"

An adoring smile takes over Carol's face as she looks at Lauren and answers me. "She hated to sleep from the get go, fought it tooth and nail." She shakes her head in exasperation at the memory.

"Now, Bobby, was a different story. As young as two, if he was tired, he put himself to bed, but not this one." She points at Lauren. "She never liked to sleep, at least until she hit puberty. Then I couldn't drag her out of bed."

"I was afraid everyone would be gone when I woke up." Lauren shrugs as if she didn't just drop a bomb. "I don't know why. I always remember feeling that way."

"I don't know why either, honey. We were always there when you did."

Lauren's eyes flit to me before looking away. I've had inklings before, but now it's solidified. Lauren's afraid of being left behind. She has abandonment issues that stem from childhood, if not infancy. I'm not sure if it was her father leaving when she was four or some earlier trauma that's triggered that fear. Whichever it was is deep-seated and has been with her for a long time.

Carol continues as my mind works to absorb this new

detail. "She was very shy, painfully so. She would hide behind my legs and not talk to anyone. Though, in school, she would go around and help the other kids finish their work after hers was complete. She was always a little mother, wanting to take care of everyone. She was—is—a very sensitive old soul. She has the grey streak to prove it." She waves her hand dismissively, a move I've seen quite often from her daughter. "I've already mentioned that. But what I didn't mention was that by the time she was a year old, her hair was blonde, having gradually changed colour."

My eyes capture Lauren's. "Most definitely a sensitive old soul."

We finish our meal and say our goodbyes outside with promises to see her mum soon. Before we leave, Carol pulls me into another hug, whispering, "Love my daughter like she deserves to be loved. Make her happy, and you'll know true happiness."

Those are words to live by. "Like my life depends on it," I promise.

The roads are clear of ice, and the sun, bright in the sky,

will have the rest melted off the ground by midafternoon. I take a deep breath and let it out. I feel lighter. The weight of my boyfriend meeting my mother no longer weighs on my shoulders.

"It went well," I murmur, more to myself.

"I believe so."

"Thank you." I glance at Theo in time to catch him watching me.

His eyes warm with heat as he takes my hand. "No need to thank me. Your mum is nice. I enjoyed meeting her." He chuckles as he focuses on the road. "I was shocked, though. You don't look like her. I was expecting her to be blonde and fair-skinned, but she's the complete opposite."

"I look like my dad. Although, he had dark hair too, so I don't really know where my hair came from." I can't tell where we're heading since both our places are in the same direction from the restaurant. "Are we going back to your place?"

"Home. We're going home." He moves his hand to my knee, caressing it lightly.

I rest my head against the seat and watch the world pass outside my window. *Home.* At this point, wherever he is feels like home, so I guess it doesn't really matter if it's my place or his, but it's interesting he didn't specify. I suppose he's trying to make a point. Though, I hope it's his place.

I'm giddy when he pulls into his garage. He notices and smirks when he opens my door, offering his hand.

Standing in the living room, I'm not sure what to do with myself as Theo drops his keys and empties his pockets on his desk. My purse is set beside his belongings. I wrap my arms around myself and take in my surroundings. It's peaceful, quiet. Barely any sound creeps in from the outside world.

Warm hands slide around my waist, his body blanketing my back. "My home looks good on you." He nuzzles my hair before sweeping it off my shoulder.

You look good on me. I sigh as his lips caress the tender spot below my ear.

"You smell good too."

I shiver as he draws my earlobe into his mouth, sucking and nipping tenderly.

"Take a bath with me," he whispers against my lips as he cups my cheek, turning me toward him.

My response is lost in his mouth as he consumes every gasp and whimper while we devour each other for mere seconds before he releases me.

"Bloody hell, Dove." He shakes his head as if he's lost his bearings. His hand drops from my face and clasps mine.

In his bedroom, he stops by his bed, releasing me. "Have a seat if you like." He motions to the bed or the chair beside it before continuing to the bathroom.

I sit on the side of the bed, facing the open bathroom door, watching. He turns on the tub faucet, pouring something into the stream of water. Bubble bath or bath oils, I assume. The smell of vanilla hits me and eases my nerves.

I'm in awe of his body, so strong and masculine. Muscles flex below his clothes with each movement. I can't imagine being that fit, that in command of my body. He's a sight to behold. I called him beautiful before, but he's magnificent—a god among men.

He turns, catching me gawking. I lick my lips as he stalks closer. My nipples hurt, they're so hard. Warmth creeps up my neck, knowing he's well aware of what he does to me.

He tips my chin so our eyes meet, his thumb brushing my lip as his heated gaze rakes my face. "Dove, you're killing me with that look."

"What look?" I fall back to the bed as he comes over me, his hand behind my head ensuring a slow descent.

"Like you need me to devour you."

"Yes." *God, yes.*

His lips sweep across mine, sucking on my bottom lip before pressing forward. His tongue dances with mine, twirling and gliding, tasting, commanding. His hands travel up my sides, lifting my shirt as he goes. My legs twine around the back of his, pulling him where I need his touch.

He breaks our kiss, but his lips never leave my skin as they travel down my body while he pulls my shirt over my head. My arms fall free, and I sink my fingers into his hair. He groans and grips my breasts over my bra, his lips trailing kisses over the plumped-up mounds. His teeth graze my satin-covered nipples before he tugs them free, tucking the cups under each exposed breast.

I arch into him as he sucks a nipple into his mouth. "Oh, God." My breathing is harsh as I grind against him, pulling him closer with desperate hands and needy words.

His hand slips between us, pressing against my jeans right on my clit. He releases one breast to suck on the other. Circling, circling my nipple and clit, a beautiful synchronized dance that has me trembling with need, crying out for more, and arching for release.

As I get closer, he's more demanding. His breath is jagged, and his moans nearly surpass my own as he answers each one, his touch determined. He's so turned on as a result of my arousal, and that—right there—flips the switch.

Clinging to him like a spider monkey, I convulse in his arms, under his body.

My head thrown back.

My eyes seeing stars.

My mouth screaming my release.

A small moan accompanies each exhale, trying to calm my racing heart.

His touch gentles.

His lips ease.

"Holy hell," I huff on an extended puff of air.

He chuckles somewhere near my chest. "Devour, Dove. Devour." He kisses my lips, and then he's gone, and I feel cold from the absence.

I blink my eyes open. He stands next to the bed, his eyes dark with need. The bulge in his pants is undeniable.

But I'm a mass of useless limbs.

"Don't move." Then he's gone.

"Move? Who could move after that?" I mumble.

He chuckles from the hallway. Apparently, he can.

Cold air brushes my damp nipples, making me painfully aware of my state of undress. With a groan, I lift my two-ton arms and pop my boobs back into my bra. Satisfied I'm decently covered, I let my arms fall to the mattress however they may.

Theo's moving around the house, opening and closing doors and drawers, then heads back to his room with towels and a candle in his arms. I manage to roll to my side so I can see what he's doing. He places the towels on the corner of the tub and lights the candle on the counter, then tests the water and adjusts the temperature.

When he turns, his eyes catch mine—again, his knowing smirk ever-present. Making his way back to the bed, he leans over me, brushing my hair from my face. His eyes shine with love, and a gentle smile now coats his lips. "You alright, Dove?"

I nod and manage a, "Yeah."

"Up you go then." He pulls me into a sitting position with my legs dangling over the sides. His bed is high, not nearly as high as mine, but my feet are still inches from the floor.

His lips move across mine in a kiss that ends with his tongue flitting along the underside of my top lip, quick but highly effective, as he kneels. His hands move down my thighs to my boots, unzipping, and slowly slips one off and then the other, followed by my socks.

He pulls me to my feet and into his arms. His kiss is soft and coaxing. Each time he stops, I chase his lips, wanting more, and more, and more. By the time he steps back with a hand on my hip to stop me from falling into him, I'm weak-kneed and heavy-lidded.

After removing his shoes and socks, he takes my hand and leads me to the bathroom, stopping at the tub to turn off the water. When he stands, I reach for his belt, unbuckle it, and tug his shirt free.

He caresses my face, his forehead pressed to mine, his fingers grazing my hair. Our breaths mingle as I unbutton his shirt, exposing the hard lines of his chest and abdomen. *God, I could lick every nook and cranny and be here for days.*

"Do you have a clip or something for your hair?" His eyes scan my head.

"Yeah, in my purse." I reluctantly extricate myself from his grasp, grab my clip, and
secure my hair as I step back into the bathroom.

His eyes sweep down my face and neck, landing on my breasts. I lower my arms as he steps into me and runs a finger down the curve of my neck, sending chills down my spine. My eyes close when his lips press to my skin, and he sucks gently on my pulse point.

No longer feeling his touch, I sigh and open my eyes to find Theo looking in the mirror, his hands at his sides and his eyes focused on my reflection. His belt hangs loose. His arms flex as he reaches out to me, gripping my hips. His chest rises and falls, the etched lines of his ribs and muscles on tantalizing display.

My gaze returns to the man—not the reflection. "You're beautiful." My voice is in awe of the man who's captured my heart.

A smile flashes, amused by me calling him *beautiful*, before his brow falls, and his lips fall into line. "No, Dove." He pivots so I'm facing the mirror with him standing behind me. "You're the one who's beautiful."

My head shakes in denial, my eyes locked on his in the mirror.

"Will you not look at yourself?" His voice is soft as his hand gently runs down my side.

I close my eyes under his touch, turning and wrapping myself in his arms. "I'd rather look at you."

He smiles down at me, but before he can say something else I'll find embarrassing, I kiss him, hard and unrelenting. He groans at my attack. His hands try to still mine as I go for his jeans. He succeeds when he pins me to the counter with his body, my hands behind me.

His breath glides across my skin as we stare at each other, panting. "Patience, my love." His grip gentles. His brow rises as he waits for my acquiescence.

"Okay."

He releases me and steps to the door, gripping it with his back to me. His breathing is rough, and when I glance in the mirror, I can see his eyes are closed.

Perhaps his plea for patience was as much for him as for me. That never-ending pull between us is strung tight, nearly impossible to resist. But somehow, he manages. I, on the other hand, feel more like a pawn to my desires. I need to work on my discipline to be half as controlled as he is.

The click of the door brings my eyes back to him. For a

second, I feared he left me alone behind this closed door. He turns off the light, plunging us into near darkness except for the lone candle, flickering on the counter.

Silently, he undoes my jeans and kneels to slip them off. Once my legs are free, he wraps his arms around my waist, and his lips traverse my stomach from one side to the other as he caresses up my back, unhooking my bra and slipping it off my shoulders.

I clutch his hair, and his head tilts up. His eyes meet mine before his hands bracket my breasts, and his thumbs sweep my hardening nipples. My insides clench with the need to be filled, and my head falls back on a moan.

"So beautiful." His words skate across my chest before he latches on to my breast, squeezing and plumping it up for his barrage. One and then the other.

To hell with patience. I glide my nails across his waist as I make my way to the front of his jeans. His growl around my breast and his muscles contracting under my touch only spur me on. I flick the button and unzip him, the sound filling the room, emphasized by my gasp as Theo teethes a nipple before sucking it deep.

I slip my hands inside his jeans, over his firm ass, and squeeze before pulling them down, granting me better access. When my hand makes contact with his velvety steel cock, he releases me with a pop and rises to his full height. His eyes glide down my body and land on my hand stroking his shaft and teasing the tip with my thumb. I lick my lips, wanting to know what he tastes like, but I've never done that, and I'm not about to embarrass myself now.

"Dove," he warns and steps back. Sitting on the edge of the tub, he motions for me to get in. He looks away, closes his eyes, and holds out his hand.

I slip off my panties and take his hand. Stepping over, I can barely get in without straddling the edge of the tub. I use his shoulder for support and graze my breast across him in the effort. Not very graceful. Thankfully, his eyes are closed.

Once in, I move to the far end of the tub and let him know he can open his eyes.

His fiery gaze burns a hole through the water and straight to my clit. Leaning over the tub, he sucks my bottom lip and pulls back. "Don't look away."

When he stands, his cock teases me from the top of his underwear. I start to avert my eyes, but I remember his words. He wants me to see.

He hooks his jeans and boxer briefs under his thumbs and pushes them down and off in one steady motion. My breath catches when he stands and his impressive erection bobs against his abdomen. He's huge. I've felt him, and I've seen a little, but not like this. Not fully naked and aroused for my perusal.

"You're beautiful," I whisper, repeating my words from before. My awe, no less. My arousal, so much more.

His jaw clenches, and he palms his shaft, stroking it a few times. "Beautiful?"

My eyes lock on his. "Yes." It's more of a groan than a word as I get to my knees, forgetting my own nakedness is on full display, and reach out to replace his hand with mine.

"So fucking beautiful."

"Lauren." He thrusts his hips into my grip and closes his eyes on a growl. "That feels so bloody good." My hand is wet, and his cock moves easily through my fingers. I add my other hand, and when he feels the additional grip and wet heat, his eyes fly open. "You're going to make me come."

"Yes." I close my eyes as the desire to see him undone bursts through me. One flick on my clit, and I know I'd join him.

With ninja precision, I'm lifted from the tub as Theo steps in and settles me on his lap, straddling his legs. I don't even have time to yelp my surprise before his lips crash over mine. His hunger is fierce and domineering, and I take it. I take his fingers as his hand slips below the water and push into me. I take his groan and replace it with my gasp as he presses my clit against his shaft and starts to move me against him. I take his nips and his bites, and his soul-sucking kisses. I take his growl of pleasure when I slip my hand around his cock and stroke him in time with his fingers as they delve deep, sending my hips thrashing into him over and over again. I take his shudders and trembling muscles as he finds his release, and give him my own on a shattered cry of empowerment.

I take it all.

And he gives it back tenfold.

Chapter 33

I AWAKE TO FIND MYSELF ALONE in Theo's bed. I glance to the dark, empty bathroom and then to the rest of the room. It's empty too. I run my hand under the sheets to Theo's side to find it no longer warm from his body. He's been gone a while. Disappointment pings inside me. The bedroom door is closed. I cock my head, listening for him, anything, to tell me he's near. I'm met with silence.

Bathroom first, then Theo. I start to slip out of bed and pause. *Shit, I'm naked.* I look around for my clothes and spot a t-shirt folded on the end of the bed. I hop up and grab it, pulling it over my head before he walks in and sees me naked in the light of day—gravity in full effect. A piece of paper drifts to the floor. Picking it up, I read it as I stand.

Dove,

You feed my soul.

I've run to the store so I can feed your body.

Make yourself at home. I'll be back soon.

Love, Theo

My heart flutters at the sentiment. He's thoughtful, informative, and romantic—all in one little note. I set it on the nightstand and see by the alarm clock it's nearly 4:00 pm. I guess I slept a couple hours. I don't know when he left but decide to take a quick shower to wash the smell of sex off me before getting dressed.

The hot shower is dreamy on my skin. I contemplate dipping my head under; to be surrounded by the heat would feel even better. Tantalizingly close to giving in, even though I washed my hair this morning, it's the thought that I don't have any of my hair stuff to fix it afterwards that stops me.

Begrudgingly, I resist and quickly wash off.

Dressed in my jeans and Theo's t-shirt, I make my way to the living room, looking around, confirming he's not home. In the kitchen, I search for a glass, finding them in the third cabinet I open. I get ice and water from the refrigerator dispenser, drinking it down in two gulps, and refill it.

With my glass in hand, I take a better look at Theo's home. Out the kitchen window is a nice-sized backyard with two large trees—that should provide nice shade from the Texas heat during the warmer months—a stone patio with a grill and deck chairs, and a new-ish wood fence framing it all in. Having grown up in an apartment—still living in one, too, a backyard is appealing, but the idea of yardwork, not so much. I wouldn't have the first clue how to mow a lawn, much less trim hedges. Though, I suppose that's what a gardener is for, or a man like Theo. The idea of him working shirtless in the yard, a glistening sweaty mess, has me sighing as I turn away from the window.

I wander to the fireplace and eye the bookshelves that flank it. The shelves contain a mix of books, pictures, and keepsakes. Most of the pictures include Theo with other people. Looking closer, I assume it's his family. One picture has Theo with an older man and woman, and two boys and two girls. They all have the same dark brown hair with a touch of curl. I can't make out their eye color, but the resemblance is uncanny. Theo looks like his dad, the same lips, bone structure, and coloring. One brother and sister look like their dad too. The other siblings take after their mom. In all, they're a handsome bunch, and really smart—

quite the combination. With my blonde hair and light skin, I would definitely be the odd man out.

Their pictures remind me of those Kennedy family albums I remember seeing as a kid: a beautiful, successful family living in a world completely different from my own.

They are other pictures with his siblings, minus Theo, and who I assume are their spouses and kids. I like that he has pictures of his family. I don't know too many single men who decorate with, much less have, pictures of their families on display in their home. I'm more like those single men who don't have personal photos canvassing their homes, though not for the same reason, I'm sure.

I grab a book off a shelf and plop down in one of the wingback chairs in front of the fireplace. Settling in sideways, I swing my legs over the arm. The fireplace wasn't lit when we arrived. Theo must have started it before he left. My considerate man, taking care of me even when he's not here. Maybe he did it more practically for the warmth, as it's still quite cold outside.

I open the book, read through the dedication, and flip pages to the first chapter. But my mind's not in it. It's too busy multi-tasking, thinking about other things; the words are not sticking.

Thinking of our vacation, I make a mental list of things to pack and buy for the trip based on the fact it's a beach destination. I should confirm it's a *warm* destination, as there are plenty of beaches that will still be cold in March.

A twinge of sadness hits me when I realize we only have

two more days together, Sunday and Monday, before our bubble bursts and we return to the real world. I try not to dwell on it. Instead, I ponder what we could do with our remaining days, knowing full well that what we've been doing since lunch is probably exactly what we really want to do. But getting out of the house would be good for us. I don't need outside entertainment to enjoy my time with Theo. Having a simple conversation with him is enough for me. But he's an athletic kind of a guy and would probably enjoy doing something physical—beyond *sex-stuff* physical.

An idea hits me, and I grab my phone, calling my brother Bobby for his assistance. A few minutes later, a plan is hatched. He'll make a few phone calls and text back with the details.

I'm excited. I hope it pans out.

I place my phone back on the end table and open the book, trying to concentrate on the words this time.

Rustling has my eyes flying open. *Shit, I fell asleep.*

Theo smirks at me as he passes through the room to the kitchen with grocery bags in his hands. "Hullo, beautiful. I'm sorry I woke you." I move to get up, but he stops me.

"No. Don't get up. You look too comfortable."

"Are you sure I can't help? I don't mind."

He shakes his head. "I've got it. Relax."

He sets the groceries on the counter, sluffs his jacket, placing it on the back of his office chair. His long legs eat up the distance between us. He's wearing black jeans and a black t-shirt, and some sort of black workman-style boots. He'd be sinister with his scowling brow and chiseled jaw if it weren't for the heat in his eyes and the warmth of his smile. He takes my breath away.

He kneels in front of me, and I run my fingers through his hair. "Hi."

"Hi, Dove." His eyes roam my body as he leans in, brushing his lips across mine in a tender kiss. "What are you reading?" He lifts the book I'm clutching in my lap and reads the title, "*The Last Lecture.* That's a good one. Have you read it before?" He sets it on the end table, his hand drawing up my leg to rest on my thigh.

Warmth floods my body. "Years ago. I remember it was quite inspiring." I motion to the fireplace. "The fire lulled me to sleep. Thanks for that, by the way."

"I thought you might enjoy it, so I started it before I left."

"I do. Have you been gone long?"

"Not long. I wanted to stay…" Another kiss. "And sleep with you, but I needed groceries. I bought Diet Coke. Would you like one?"

He bought me Diet Coke? The thought nearly has me in

tears. "Yes," I manage around the tightness in my chest. "Is that part of *feeding my body?*" I reference his note teasingly, but I know he can see my emotions as if they're lit up like a neon sign.

"Dove." He presses his forehead to mine. His eyes close as he cups the side of my face. "Everything I do is to feed your soul." His voice is whisper-soft, a reverent revelation.

I clasp his wrist and tilt my head, blending my mouth with his, feeding on his goodness, his light, his belief that I am worthy of him.

His arms encase me, pulling me upright so he can settle between my legs. He takes over the kiss, commanding my surrender. But it's not my body he's after. It's my pain. He wants to devour it—free me from its grasp—breaking the chains that bind me.

I pull back on a shuddered breath, cupping his face, my eyes all but bleeding my love for him. "I'm not sure a Diet Coke feeds my soul, but I'll take it."

He laughs and wraps me in a hug. "It does, and you know it."

It does, because it's not about the Diet Coke at all. It's about him going out of his way to do something nice for me. Like starting a fire for my enjoyment and buying me my indulgent drink that is no good for me but makes me happy.

He's cherishing me, and my heart is near to bursting with love.

With a quick kiss to the cheek, he stands, holding his hand out. "Come join me in the kitchen."

Standing, he pulls me into his embrace. His hands move

up and down my back while his eyes roam my face as if he hasn't seen me in ages. "You alright?"

"I'm perfect."

"You are." His hand shifts, moving to cup my breast. His eyes light up as he confirms I'm sans bra. "Fucking perfect." His thumb grazes my nipple seconds before he lifts my shirt, bends me back—I yelp—and sucks my nipple deep into his mouth. One, then the other.

"Theo." My fingers sink into his hair, holding on, keeping him close, struggling to keep my balance.

"I won't let you fall," he chastises, kissing up my chest, then up my neck as he pulls my shirt down and rights me in his arms. "And if you do, I'll catch you."

My hand lands on his racing heart, beating with a rhythm that matches my own. It does something to me, knowing he's as affected as I am. "You're too good to me, Professor."

He pulls me toward the kitchen. "No, Dove. I'm exactly the right amount of good for you."

I pray he never stops thinking that.

He halts and turns, grabbing my shoulders to stop me from bumping into him. "I nearly forgot." He reaches into his pocket, producing my keys. "I picked up a few things from your apartment I thought you might need. I hope you don't mind."

"Seriously?" Why would I mind? I can't believe he did that.

"Seriously." He kisses my forehead. "Be right back."

He disappears down the hall and out the garage door, returning with one of my overnight bags.

"I hope I packed everything you need." His smile is surprisingly sheepish. Not like him at all.

"I'm sure whatever you brought will be perfect. It's more than I had before you left, right?"

The corners of his eyes crinkle as his smile widens at that. "Yes, I suppose it is."

Instead of giving me my bag, he pulls me to his room, setting the bag on the bed. "You can put your stuff anywhere. I meant it when I said *make yourself at home*. My home is your home, alright?"

"Thank you. Truly."

"Welcome." He kisses my temple. "Come join me when you're done."

"I'll only be a minute."

"Take your time." And with that, he's gone.

I delve into the overnight bag, not believing my eyes. He packed my toothbrush and toothpaste, brushes, hairdryer with the diffuser and the concentrator, shampoo and conditioner, mousse, deodorant, facial soap, bras, panties, yoga pants, a couple of shirts, socks and tennis shoes.

Jeez, I can move in, except I can't wear this stuff to work. I love how thoughtful and thorough he is.

Love is in the details. And right now, I'm feeling his love—hard.

I put all my toiletries in the shower and on the bathroom counter, hoping he won't feel invaded. I leave everything else in the bag, setting it on the chair by the bed.

In the kitchen, Theo hands me a Diet Coke with a wink. He knows he did good—crazy good.

"Thank you for my clothes and everything."

"I was happy to do it." He kisses the tip of my nose on the way to the stove. "I rather enjoyed it. It was hot going through your bras and panties." He raises his eyebrows and gives me that mischievous smile of his. "Though, I'd be happy if you didn't wear any of them." His gaze meets my chest before he turns back, stirring the veggies in the pan.

"I'm not wearing my bra or panties, so I guess you got your wish." I back away slowly. Baiting him will have consequences. Delicious consequences.

The gas pops off, and the pan is moved to the back burner. The devilish twinkle in his brown eyes greets me before he's fully turned.

"You're not wearing panties either?" His eyes lower to my crotch, making me squirm and fight the need to cover myself as if he can see right through my jeans.

"No." I take another step toward the kitchen archway.

"You're commando?" He stalks closer, each step matching one of mine.

"I didn't say that."

His head tilts, assessing my words. "Are you teasing me?" There's an edge to his voice that wasn't there before.

I shake my head, passing the arch and stepping closer to his desk. "I'm trying to entice you."

"Dove, one look at you is all the enticement I need." His response—too quick to be anything but sincere—has me

394

stilling for a second too long, and he nearly reaches me in one stride.

I jump to the side and continue my backsteps toward the hall.

He smiles, shaking his head, and licks his lips. "You're not wearing panties and you're not naked under your jeans. So, what do you have on under there?"

Wouldn't he like to know?

I hold up my hand, and he stops, sinking his hands into his pockets, his brow questioning. His eyes still scan me as if he has x-ray vision.

I rock on my feet, biting my lip. "I kinda went through your underwear drawer too."

"You what? Why?" He's amused, not irritated. Thankfully.

"I…uh, showered and didn't have anything clean to wear. So…" I hedge a second before turning and darting around the corner, yelling out in a rush, "Iborrowedapairofyours."

He's on my tail milliseconds from reaching me. I can feel it but don't dare look for fear of smashing into the wall. He might catch me if I fall, but he can't stop me from face-planting into a wall if he's behind me.

I squeak when he grabs me around the waist, lifting me off my feet as I enter his room. I'm laughing so hard, winded and trying to catch my breath, that I can't even fight him as he swings me around. One arm bands my waist, the other around my chest, his hand firmly planted over my breast.

"I've got you now." He breathes onto my neck, laughter

rumbling in his chest and teasing my ear.

I shiver and wrap my arms around his, leaning into his chest, my back to his front. Lowering me, he holds on, turning me once he's sure I'm steady on my feet.

He cradles my cheek, tilting my head toward his. "Show me." He's grinning, and his eyes are bright with excitement.

"Not yet," I pant.

He runs a finger along the waistband of my jeans. I suck in a breath as he bends, stopping when his lips are whisper-close to mine. "Show me."

"No." I grab his seductive hand and try not to squirm, smile, or laugh. Serious, I'm going for serious here. "Maybe if you're a good boy, you'll get to see them later." I close the distance and peck his lips. "Now feed me. Please."

Narrowing his eyes, he rises to his impressive height of 6'3". He considers me for a second before a smile breaks free. "Come on."

He lifts me effortlessly. My legs wrap around his waist and my arms around his neck while his hands grip my back and rear, holding me as he turns and heads back to the kitchen. "Good boy or no, I'm seeing them later."

I can't wait.

Chapter 34

I **POP THE BREAD IN THE** oven and finish up the pasta with chicken and vegetables while Lauren makes the salad. Her phone whistles from the other room, and she jumps to answer it.

I try not to think about who she's texting. Yes, I've learned the sounds her phone makes, and *that* is definitely a text. That jealous beast in me raises its ugly head.

Her bare feet pad back to the kitchen. I glance over my shoulder and see her eyeing her phone. "Theo, do you have plans for tomorrow?"

I cover the pasta to keep it warm, then turn the oven off and pivot, crossing my arms over my chest. "Other than ravishing your body?" I feign disinterest. "No. Why?"

"Well, that's a given." Her smile is disarming. Her cocksureness, adorable. "But other than that..." Her façade falls, and pure vulnerability covers her like a blanket. "Would you be interested in doing something?"

Anything. But why's she nervous to ask? "Sure. Do you have something in mind?"

"I do." She places her phone in her pocket and fidgets with the end of her t-shirt—*my* t-shirt.

Damn, I love seeing her in my clothes. The idea of my boxer briefs cupping her intimately nearly has me begging her to slip off her jeans right here in the middle of my kitchen.

"...It could be a surprise, or I can tell you." Her words draw my eyes back to hers.

I'm not sure what I missed, but I'll give her this. "Surprise," I respond, wanting to ease her nerves while she chatters on.

"...outside activity, and my brother and a few of his friends will be there."

"I'm in." All in. From day one. Whatever she wants— I'm in.

She laughs. "Okay. Let me call him. I'll be right back."

I set the table and pause when I hear the bedroom door open.

Lauren is beaming when she reappears in the kitchen.

It's good to see her so happy. Not that she wasn't happy before, but this is a child-like lightness I haven't seen before. "You look mighty happy."

"I am. It'll be fun. I think. I hope."

I grab her hand. "Whatever it is, as long as I'm with you, it'll be aces."

She lets out a punch of air, her smile grateful. "We leave at nine tomorrow morning."

"Sounds good." I hand her the salad, and she places it on the table and then gets us drinks.

When everything is on the table, I pull out her chair. "We're ready to eat."

As she sits, it hits me. She's the first woman in my house besides my family. I like having her here. I like being at her apartment too, but it's different here, among my things, sharing my life with her.

I've been thinking about us having to go back to work on Tuesday. I don't want to say goodbye to her on Monday. I like going to sleep with her in my arms and waking up to her. It's not only the physical aspect either. I, of course, love touching her, but it's also the fact that I like being with her whether it's at her place or mine. I enjoy her company and want to share my life with her.

I don't want to wait until we're married to live together.

I want to share the big and small things with her. I don't want to *tell* her about my day. I want to experience my day *with her*.

"You're deep in thought. Anything you want to share?" She brushes her fingers over my brow, softening my frown.

"Not yet. I'm still mulling it over. Alright?" I don't want to hurt her feelings.

"Sure." She shrugs and stabs a bite of salad. "I'm not going anywhere, at least not tonight." She smiles, but it's not genuine.

I did hurt her feelings. I should tell her.

But she jumps into discussing clothes for tomorrow and maybe watching a movie later. *My girl loves her movies.* I enjoy talking to her. She has an easy way about her. I'll never understand why she's uncomfortable in social situations. She's smart, witty, and kind. Anyone would enjoy her company. I relish the fact that she's given this rare gift—of herself—to me.

As we finish up, I decide to share what I've been mulling over all day. "Lauren, I've been thinking about us going back to work and to our own places on Monday."

"Don't remind me." She groans as she sets her fork down, leaning forward, her elbows on the table. Her chin rests on her shoulder as she looks at me. "It makes me sad to even think about it."

"Me too. That's my point." I take her hand and squeeze. "I have a proposal."

"Okay." She lights up.

"What if I stayed with you during the week?"

"What?" She sits back, her hands dropping to her lap, eyes wide and mouth agape.

I barrel through. "I could bring what I need for the week. Then, if you like, we could come back here for the weekend," I offer, hoping she doesn't feel I'm going too fast.

"Really?" Her brows disappear under her bangs.

"Really."

"You won't get sick of me, seeing me every day?"

Is she serious? Her doubt pisses me off sometimes. "I wouldn't suggest it if I didn't *want* to see you every day. That's the point of my proposal." To. See. You. Every. Bloody. Fucking. Day.

"And if you have plans with your friends?" she asks softly, so uncertain.

Then you come with me, I want to say, but decide to not push my luck. She may faint if I push too much togetherness. "If we have plans with other people, we'll still come home to each other at the end of the day. What do you think?"

She gets up, surprising me by plopping herself in my lap. "Seriously?"

Laughing, I grip her hip. "Seriously." Though I'm laughing, I've never been more serious. I'm not spending days, weeks, months apart from her until she's ready to say *I do.*

I brush her hair off her shoulder, cup her cheek and kiss her beating pulse on the opposite side. Making my way up to her lips that are waiting, parted and panting, I pull my eyes off her mouth to meet her dazzled gaze. "I love you, Lauren. I don't want to be away from you all week, living only for the weekends. I want to go to sleep with you in my arms and wake up with you still in them. I want to kiss you goodbye in the mornings and kiss you hullo in the evenings...for as long as we both shall live."

"Theo." She buries her head in my neck, her arms tight around my shoulders. A whole-body tremor has me squeezing her tighter, holding her closer.

"I've got you, Dove."

"You have no idea how happy you make me."

"I do know, because you make me just as happy." I grip the back of her neck, urging her to look at me.

She does, and the tears streaming down her cheeks nearly knock me over.

"I was actually sad today, thinking about having to leave you in two days. I enjoy being with you so much. It means everything that you want to be with me too, and miss me when we're apart."

I kiss her tears. "I always miss you." *I've told her that, right?*

"Are you sure you want to spend the week at my house? Wouldn't you rather be here?"

"I *like* my house, but I *love* you."

She presses a chaste kiss to my lips. "I love your house," she whispers.

That makes me chuckle. I know she's not saying she loves my house more than me. She only wants me to know how much she likes it. "I'm glad." I shrug. "I figure, as a guy, it's easier for me to get ready wherever I am. It's not an issue for me to get ready for work at your place."

"And we come here for the weekends?"

"If you want to."

"I want to."

"It's no pressure. We can try it this week and see how it goes. And if you have plans with other people, I'll see you when you get home."

Home. God, I love the idea of making a home with her. A future with her.

"You'll need a key to my place." She couldn't seem happier about that.

"And you need a key to mine and a garage door opener." I kiss her then, pulling her close. "I love you, Dove. Thank you being open to this. I don't think I could bear to be away from you all week." Is it wrong to be excited about seeing her car parked right beside mine in my garage?

"Promise you'll say something if you need a break?" She needs my confirmation.

"Never going to happen. You too?"

"Yes, but I'm a woman. You realize that, don't you?"

I squeeze her arse. "Believe me, I'm well aware."

She's the best kind of woman. *My* woman.

We seal the deal with a kiss.

"Now, about my boxer briefs, Ms. Frasier." I kiss her

nose, patting her jean-clad leg. "It's time these come off."

I set her on her feet and stand, glancing at the table. I'll clean up later once she's fallen asleep.

"What about the dishes?" She reads my thoughts, always so in sync.

"Later." I've been a patient man—a good boy—it's time for my reward.

Once we're in the bedroom, I pull off my shirt, leaving me in only my jeans and my own boxer briefs, having discarded my shoes and socks hours ago. Like Lauren, I prefer bare feet when I'm at home.

I step into her personal space, as if there's such a thing between the two of us. Her hands trace the lines of muscles on my abdomen—her eyes following, coming to rest on my chest, drawn like magnets. Her eyes continue their journey until they lock on mine. A shy smile graces her lips as if I caught her doing something wrong. On the contrary, her hands and eyes on me is exactly what I want. The fact that she enjoys it this much and is still shy of it makes it even hotter.

My head tilts down, hers up, and somewhere in the middle our lips meet. The first touch is tender, reverent even. It only takes the flick of her tongue, her desire for a taste to send me into overdrive. I fist her shirt—my shirt—around her back, pressing her to me as my lips seek entrance to the sanctuary of her mouth. With a moaning sigh she grants me admittance. Her hands grip my shoulder and hair as I take refuge in the depths of the mouth I love, kneading her back and arse, drawing her closer and closer until I'm convinced we will meld together by our sheer will of wishing it so.

She whimpers against my lips, but instead of taking it further, I break our kiss and kneel before her. Some men would never, but they obviously haven't met their queen. I kneel to her in reverence, in worship, in awe of the goddess she is. That doesn't make me less of a man, it makes me *her* man, and that's all I care about.

I clasp her hips, looking up into shimmering blue eyes. "I love you, Dove."

Her hand glides to my cheek. "I love you, Theo."

Her legs bend as if she's going to join me on the floor, but I hold her steady, firming my grip. "Let me."

I've been thinking of ripping her jeans off since I found out she's wearing my underwear. I don't, though. Instead, I pull them down slowly, kissing her tummy as I slip them off over her hips, down her legs, and pull them off as she holds on to my shoulders. Tossing them to the chair, I sit on my haunches, starting at my love—in my t-shirt that's way too big and my boxer briefs that I can barely see under the edge of the shirt. I need to rectify that.

Leaning forward, I lift her shirt and kiss across her stomach as her skin is revealed. I slowly stand, my kisses trailing up and up until I reach her glorious breasts with sweet, succulent nipples. I groan when she shivers under my gaze and flick my tongue across each tempting peak as I free her from my t-shirt—at last. I pull her closer, my hands on her arse, squeezing, lifting her to her tip-toes as my lips find hers and suck her bottom lip before drawing her tongue into my mouth.

Skin to skin, her moans, sighs, and quickening breath all drive me crazy, sending more blood to my already rigid cock.

Slow. Down, my blood-starved brain screams.

Releasing my grip, I stand back, holding her hands as our bodies separate. My eyes traverse the sight before me. Her breasts are large, round, and beautiful with pink nipples that beckon me to kiss them — suck them — worship them.

I love the *all access, no bra when we're at home* rule. Well, not really a rule. She hates bras and prefers to not wear one when it's only us at home. I very much appreciate and support that stance on the matter.

My eyes move lower to her tapered waist and round hips. And there sits my underwear. A pair of black boxer briefs, hugging her curves, touching her everywhere below the waist — intimately. I'm jealous of them.

I need a closer inspection. Back on my knees, I grip her thighs and kiss along the waistband. Her hands, lost in my hair, massage and tug as she trembles under my touch. Of their own volition, my kisses move lower — her scent intoxicating as I breathe her in — until my mouth hovers over her clit. One good tug and my mouth would be on her, my tongue piercing her heat and sucking her clit until she comes undone.

"Theo." She tips my head with a small tug of my hair.

My heavy-lidded eyes meet hers. I'm shaking with need,

holding back, reining it in. "I want to taste you."

She gasps.

"I want to sink my tongue deep inside you."

"Oh, God." She releases my hair.

"I want to kiss you in the most intimate way possible and feel your juices drip down my chin."

"No." But I know she wants to say *yes*. Her nipples are hard, and I can smell her arousal. She means *yes*. She can't say it. She can't admit it.

"I want to finger you, lick and suck your clit until you clamp down on my fingers, sucking me back in with each thrust, over and over until you come so hard you can't stop screaming my name, and it takes minutes before the stars in your eyes dissipate. And then I want to do it again. And again, and again..."

Her hands fly to her face, and I know she wants to disappear. She wants to run from the raw desire in me and the equally raw desire burning her up from the inside out.

Standing, I pull her hands away from her face. Her gaze is not one of fear but pure unadulterated lust.

Bloody hell, this woman. Her want could burn the flesh from my bones.

I place her hands on my chest and cradle her face. "I want to make you come until you beg me to stop. Until you know you are mine. That I am yours. And that there are no boundaries to our love. There are no walls that can contain us. There are no taboos between us. We are the alpha and the omega—our love begins and ends right here."

I swear the room is brighter, yet I can see nothing but

her—shimmering and pulsing before me—as if she is my heartbeat, my very life force, my eternity, tied to hers.

Removing my jeans, I slip my hand in hers. "I want to show you something." I lead her to the bathroom, turning on the light as I cross the threshold.

Her hand rips from mine, and I turn to see her stopped dead at the doorway. Her hands cover her breasts—hiding from me.

That won't do.

"Do you trust me, Dove?" Please, say *yes*.

"Yes."

Thank fuck.

"Do you think I would do anything to be mean to you, or make you feel bad about yourself?" Say *no*.

"Not *intentionally*. But this—" she lifts one finger from her covered breast to point to the bathroom, "—is too much." She backs away with tears brimming.

I didn't miss how she stressed the word *intentionally*. It's a warning that even my good intentions may not sit well with her. I could hurt her, or I could make things better. It's a chance I have to take.

I capture her cheek. "I wish you wouldn't cry, but I know that's who you are. You feel things deeply, irrevocably. I'm not asking you to change. I'm only asking you to give me a chance to show you what I see. Then maybe you won't feel so self-conscious with me." I kiss her cheek and whisper, "It's important you trust me. I would never harm you."

I step back and hold out my hand. "Have faith in me."

Tears stream down her face, her internal battle evident on her face. She loves me. She trusts me. But is that love and trust stronger than her fear?

All I want to do is envelop her in my arms and make everything better. But I've come this far. It might do more damage if I don't follow through.

I wait patiently with my hand extended. I can't take this leap for her. If I could, I would have already.

On a staggered breath, she closes her eyes and shakes her head as if to squelch the thoughts that plague her. Her eyes open, and she releases her breasts to wipe her tears away.

I hold my breath.

It's a millisecond, but it feels like an eternity before she places her hand in mine.

My eyes close on a silent prayer of thanks. The warmth of her touch reaffirms her gift of trust, and I let out a relieved breath.

"Thank you." I pull her into my arms and kiss her tenderly before backing us into the bathroom.

I maneuver so we're standing side by side, facing the mirror. I take her hand in mine, clasping it firmly between us.

Her eyes are locked to mine in the mirror. I smile in reassurance. She squeezes my hand, but her smile in return barely touches her lips. Then complete sadness takes over her face—some errant thought has taken over—and her eyes lower.

I squeeze her hand, drawing her gaze back to me. "What just happened? What are you thinking?"

She shakes her head. Her bottom lip trembles. "I'm completely inadequate standing here next to you." Tears stream down her cheeks and drop down her breasts to the floor, but her eyes never leave me.

I fight my instinct to protect her, hide her away—even from herself. "Why?" I don't understand her reasoning, and I need to.

"Seriously?" She scoffs. "Have you seen you? You're the perfect male specimen. Every inch of you is toned and muscular. There's not an ounce of fat to be found."

I thought this would be hard for her, but it's turning out to be a test for me too. Every fiber of my being wants to collect her in my arms and do everything possible to end her pain by giving her pleasure. But I know this is more than a quick fix. She needs to face this demon, the one that makes her feel lesser than and unequal to me. And I need to stand here and let her.

"Despite what you see, I'm not perfect, Lauren. I have insecurities about my body too. It's not about perfection. It's about being the best you can be and accepting what you can't change. Do you want me to tell you what bothers me about my body?"

She shakes her head. "No. You're perfect to me." Her love shines through her smile, and I see a glimmer of hope.

"Exactly. That's what I'm trying to show you. *You* are perfect to me. Regardless of what you think about your body, you are perfect to me—as you are right now."

I move behind her and slip my arms around her chest, hugging her possessively. She wraps her arms over mine and hugs me back.

"Look at us in the mirror."

Her eyes leave mine and slowly rest on our reflection. She's wrapped in our arms, her breasts still hidden.

"The woman in my arms is the one I love. *You*. I love you more than I ever thought possible." I kiss her shoulder and loosen my grip so only my hands cover her breasts.

Her eyes stay locked on us.

"I don't love you because of your body, but the fact that I love your body is a bonus." I smile, and this time she smiles back.

"Do you think I want someone who's all muscle?"

She doesn't answer.

I continue, "I want your curves and your softness, your full breasts." I move my hands on her breasts, squeezing and kneading them.

She leans into me as her nipples harden in my palms, and my arousal is awakened. I slowly reveal her breasts, continuing to tease her nipples, relishing the flush of her skin and the sigh on her breath.

"You have the most beautiful breasts. If I were you, I'd show them to everyone. But you're you, and you don't flaunt them. I love that they're all mine, and you don't share them with revealing clothes."

I grind my hips, pressing my erection against her. "Feel what you do to me." I pull her hand between us, placing it on my cock. "This is for you, Dove. Only you."

She closes her eyes, grips my shaft, and strokes me over the fabric of my briefs.

My hips jerk, wanting more. But I still her hand. "Not yet."

Still behind her, I move my hands to her stomach and waist. "You're fit and toned, but still all woman." I squeeze her waist. "I love your curves." She smiles, and I kiss her shoulder, running my hand across her abdomen, and I feel her suck in a breath. "I don't want a ripped six-pack. That's not attractive to me. It may be impressive, but it's not what I want pressed against me. It's not what I want to make love to. And it's not what I want in my arms at night."

Her hand squeezes mine, and I feel her gratitude for my words. I hope they sink in, and she doesn't think I'm only being nice, blowing hot air up her arse.

I grip her hips and grind against her. She gasps her shock. She'd really be shocked if she knew what I'd really like to do to her—bend her over the counter, eat her out, and then plunge in balls deep, pounding her until her doubt of my attraction for her shatters into a million pieces.

Instead, I stick with words. "These are hips I want to make love to, that I want to bear my children."

A warm, teasing smile snakes across her face. She loves it when I talk of getting her pregnant. *Me too, Dove, me too.*

"And this glorious arse..." I cup it with both hands and squeeze, "...is exactly what I want sitting on my lap and under my palms when you grind your clit against my cock."

I nuzzle into her neck. "And someday I'll be holding it tight when we make love, and I'm lost inside your glorious pussy."

She shudders, looking at me with such love and tenderness.

I motion to the mirror, wanting her to look at herself. And this time she does it without hesitation. I slip one hand around her waist and the other one into the front fold of my boxer briefs she's wearing.

Her hands rest on my arms as she leans back, giving herself to me.

Beautifully. Unconditionally. Brazenly.

My fingers slip into her wetness, and I nearly growl. "Always so ready for me."

She breaths in deeply.

When I graze her swollen clit, her grip tightens, her nipples pucker, and she closes her eyes on a moan, tilting her head back, giving herself to me completely.

I'm undone by her trust, my eyes locked on her reflection, unable or unwilling to look away. I latch on to her neck, slipping two fingers inside her. Her hips jerk, her legs tremble, and her needful sigh has my cock twitching in response as if answering her call.

"This." I move inside her. "*This* always surprises me— how amazing you feel. I'll never get enough of you."

"Theo," she moans my name in reverence, as a plea, as a call from her soul to mine.

"I know, Dove."

And I do. I know her.

I know she wants me as much as I want her.

I know we will never tire of this otherworldly connection that draws us together—body and soul.

I know I will spend the rest of my life loving her.

Showing her how beautiful she is and how much I love her.

Just. The. Way. She. Is.

The End

Theo and Lauren's journey continues in
The Price of Atonement.

THE ROAD
TO
Redemption

A FINDING GRACE Novel

Book 1

D.M. DAVIS

Did You Enjoy This Novel?

This is a dream for me to be able to share my love of writing with you. If you liked my story, please consider leaving a review on the retailer's site where you purchased this book (and/or on Goodreads).

Personal recommendations to your friends and loved ones are a great compliment too. Please share, follow, join my newsletter, and help spread the word—let everyone know how much you loved Theo and Lauren's story.

About the Author

D.M. Davis is a Contemporary and New Adult Romance Author.

She is a Texas native, wife, and mother. Her background is Project Management, technical writing, and application development. D.M. has been a lifelong reader, and wrote poetry in her early life, but has found her true passion in writing about love and the intricate relationships between men and women.

She writes of broken hearts and second chances, of dreamers looking for more than they have and daring to reach for it.

D.M. believes it is never too late to make a change in your own life, to become the person you always wanted to be, but were afraid you were not worth the effort.

You are worth it. Take a chance on you. You never know what's possible if you don't try. Believe in yourself as you believe in others, and see what life has to offer.

She is currently working on two series of romance novels: UNTIL YOU and FINDING GRACE.

Please visit WWW.DMCKDAVIS.COM for more details, and keep in touch by signing up for her Newsletter.

Acknowledgments

I'm not sure any words could accurately express how much Lauren's story means to me. Yes, it's Theo's journey too, but Lauren's struggle with worthiness is closer to that of my own, and therefore, near and dear to my heart.

I want to thank my husband who stuck out the four year wait for me to finish what I started with GRACE. That's what we call **The Road to Redemption** in my house as it's the first in the FINDING GRACE series, and the first book I ever wrote. It's been a long journey of starts and stops, but we finally birthed our baby. Hallelujah!

To my children, thank you for your endless support and for loving that your mommy is an author. I do this as much for you as for myself to show us both what it looks like to work for your dreams.

Thank you to the rest of my family for your unwavering support. I'm able to do this because you believe I can. And…I'm still amazed you don't laugh at me for pursuing my dreams instead of getting a 'real' job. Not their words, mine. Remember, I'm still working on the whole *worthiness* thing.

To my fellow writerly peeps, thank you for your endless support on social media with post shares, comments, and love. To my MP group, your support and early critiques are priceless. A never-ending stream of thanks to Teddy for keeping me grounded, keeping me going, and giving me a soft place to land when I freak out.

To my editor, Tamara, for sticking it out through three Until You books and now GRACE. I'm thankful to have you on this journey. I live for your praise like the needy author I am.

And lastly, to the readers and bloggers, thank you for your kind words and support. For sending me notes, sharing my posts, and asking when my next book will be published. I do this because like you I love books and love to read. So, the fact that you like to read *my* books blows me away. Thank you, thank you, thank you.

Until next time, I will continue to write…

"What only the heart hears…"

Additional Novels

BY D.M. DAVIS

UNTIL YOU SERIES
Book 1 - Until You Set Me Free
Book 2 - Until You Are Mine
Book 3 - Until You Say I Do

FINDING GRACE SERIES
Book 1 - The Road to Redemption
Book 2 - The Price of Atonement
Book 3 - A New Beginning
Book 4 - Finding Where I Belong

STANDALONES
Warm Me Softly

Stalk Me!

Visit WWW.DMCKDAVIS.COM for more details, and keep in touch by signing up for my NEWSLETTER.

CONNECT ON SOCIAL MEDIA:

Facebook: http://facebook.com/dmckdavis/

Instagram: http://www.instagram.com/dmckdavisauthor/

Twitter: http://twitter.com/dmckdavis

FOLLOW MY AUTHOR PAGES:

Goodreads: https://www.goodreads.com/dmckdavis

Amazon: http://www.amazon.com/author/dmdavis

BookBub: https://www.bookbub.com/authors/d-m-davis

What only the heart hears...

dm DAVIS

CONTEMPORARY & NEW ADULT ROMANCE AUTHOR

WWW.DMCKDAVIS.COM

Printed in Great Britain
by Amazon

32577896R00243